INTIMATE

DON'T MISS THE NOVELLA

Tangled

BY KATE DOUGLAS IN THE ANTHOLOGY

Hot Alphas

AVAILABLE FROM ST. MARTIN'S PRESS

INTIMATE

KATE DOUGLAS

St. Martin's Paperbacks

This is a work of fiction. All of the characters, organizations, and events portrayed in this novel are either products of the author's imagination or are used fictitiously.

INTIMATE

Copyright © 2015 by Kate Douglas.
Excerpt from *Redemption* Copyright © 2016 by Kate Douglas.

All rights reserved.

For information address St. Martin's Press, 175 Fifth Avenue, New York, NY 10010.

ISBN: 978-1-250-06476-9

Printed in the United States of America

St. Martin's Paperbacks edition / December 2015

St. Martin's Paperbacks are published by St. Martin's Press, 175 Fifth Avenue, New York, NY 10010.

10 9 8 7 6 5 4 3 2 1

This book is dedicated to three truly wonderful authors—talented ladies all, who have encouraged and inspired me for much of my career: Stella Cameron, Robyn Carr, and Jayne Ann Krentz. You each know exactly what to say when I need to hear it, and I appreciate you more than I can express.

Also, to my agent Jessica Faust—you say what I need to hear as well, Jessica, though not nearly as diplomatically. For that I owe you my thanks and my career.

ACKNOWLEDGMENTS

An author isn't the sole creator of a book—it really does take a village, and I have a wonderful village of supporters who work very hard to make my stories better. My thanks and appreciation to my beta readers Rose Toubbeh, Lynne Thomas, Kerry Parker, Jay Takane, Ann Jacobs, and Karen Woods, who so willingly take time out of their very busy schedules to read my final draft before it goes to my editor.

Because of their efforts, my editor, Eileen Rothschild, has no idea just how bad I can be, but she gets more than her share of credit as well. I promise, Eileen . . . no more meltdowns. Really. Thank you for your patience, your persistence, and your knowledge of what it takes to make a story even better. I am really enjoying working with you.

CHAPTER 1

Jake paused outside the fourth modeling agency he'd been to this morning—not counting the easy dozen he'd checked on after more than a week of searching. He still wasn't any closer to finding anyone remotely suited for the job, and the manager of this agency had been flat-out rude when he'd told him what he wanted.

Was it too much to ask for someone unique, an attractive young woman with a sexy, dark, and edgy look—and piercings? Nothing grotesque—ears, nose, eyebrow, the popular spots.

You'd think he was searching for a freak-show contestant.

He was running out of agencies, which meant he was running out of options. Marcus Reed, the one who'd hired him for the ad campaign, had specifically wanted a model from the San Francisco area for a potential long-term commitment. L.A. was out.

Sitting in his car in the parking garage a few minutes later, he sent a text to Marc. *Struck out again. One more on my list before I start dragging strangers in off the street.*

Slipping his phone into his pocket, he paused when a tone alerted him to a new message.

Marc must be bored this morning. Chuckling, expecting

a snarky reply, he checked the text. It wasn't from Marc. Stunned, Jake stared at the message on the screen, one that said *number blocked* instead of a name.

He scanned the text and his stomach clenched. *Hey, RJ . . .*

He hadn't been RJ for almost twenty years.

The rest of the message was simple, appeared harmless. *Saw you over on Battery. It's been a long time, bud.*

A tight knot coiled in his gut. He couldn't take his eyes off the text. No one called him RJ anymore. As far as he was concerned, RJ Cameron was dead and gone. Except someone had found him—someone who could connect him to the Olympic wonder kid he'd once been. The same stupid kid who'd spent time locked up for manslaughter after a drunk-driving accident that took two innocent lives.

He sucked in a couple of deep breaths. He had a job to get done. There was no time for crap like this. With a tap of his finger, Jake deleted the message.

Kaz Kazanov looped her tote bag over her shoulder and shoved open the heavy door into the office of Top End. Her roommate Lola was at her usual station at the front desk. She glanced up when Kaz stalked into the office, nodded at the door behind her desk, and shrugged.

Kaz glanced at the closed door to the general's office and whispered to Lola. "You don't know what he wants?"

Lola shook her head. "No idea. He just told me to get you here stat."

"That doesn't sound good, especially after the way my morning went."

"What happened?" Whispering, Lola leaned across her desk.

Kaz waved her off. "Nothing good. I'll fill you in later. Mind if I leave this here?" She dumped the heavy bag on the floor beside the desk.

"Go ahead, but you better hurry. He was blowing steam out both ears." The phone buzzed, and with an exaggerated eye roll, Lola turned to answer it.

Kaz headed toward the door. She rapped twice, heard the familiar bark, and walked into the office.

"Close the damned door." The pudgy little man behind the desk glared at her, lurched to his feet, and leaned forward, both hands planted firmly on the scarred oak surface.

Taking a deep breath, Kaz shut the door, folded her arms across her chest, and stared right back at him. He was such a weasel. She'd had her fill of him long ago, but she liked the steady income and loved the other people she worked with. He'd been more of an irritant than a real issue.

"The Smithum account is no longer ours, Ms. Kazanov. Do you want to know why?"

Oh, crap. She'd shown up on time and done everything they'd asked, but the vibe had not been good. "Not particularly," she said, except she really did want to know.

"Well, I'm telling you anyway. They not only dropped you, they dropped the whole fucking agency because the model we sent them, the one they spent a week preparing for, the one who required specially ordered size-twelve shoes, had a fucking tattoo on her goddamned belly."

Oh, this was just wrong. It took her a bit to find her voice—but she found it just fine. "My torso wasn't even in the shoot. This was a shoe ad, for crying out loud. Feet. They wanted feet." She lifted one of the feet in question and then stomped it hard on the tile floor. "I've got two of them. Pedicure's perfect, tan's perfect, and maybe they're big, but so am I. You put little feet on a six-foot-two-inch woman, she's gonna fall over." She let out a frustrated huff. "Why should they care about my tattoo?"

He really did get spit in the corners of his mouth when

he was pissed. Yuck. Kaz blinked, then focused on the wall behind him.

"They are a deeply conservative company. They do not approve of tattoos. Neither does this agency. Your contract with Top End specifically spells out that there will not be any body art, tattoos, or piercings of any kind beyond simple earrings." He glared at her, and she watched, fascinated, as his eyes narrowed and he focused on her face. "When did you add that disgusting stud in your nose?"

Kaz clenched her hands into fists to keep from touching the offending stud. *Damn it all!* She knew better than to wear it when coming anywhere near this guy, because he was always looking for something to bitch about. It didn't seem to matter right now anyway. The general had already worked himself into a self-righteous froth.

"Today, Ms. Kazanov, you really fucked up. I can't believe you showed up for the shoot in a pair of shorts and a cropped top with your midsection on full display, flaunting . . ."—he paused, obviously for the dramatic effect—"a large tattoo."

She took a deep breath and let it out. Carefully enunciating each word, she said, "For your information, I showed up in the jeans and T-shirt I'm wearing now, completely covered, as you can tell, and was changing into shorts for the shoot when the owner's son decided to invite himself into my dressing room. I was not flaunting anything—I was being spied on by a pervert."

Before he could respond, she added, "And furthermore, the contract I signed says nothing about body art or piercings. I have never signed an amendment that says anything different."

"The contract you signed has been updated. You are well aware of the rules and policies of this company."

She planted her hands on her hips and glared right back

at him. "They may be your rules, Mr. MacArthur, but they are not in my contract. Not even mentioned in mine. I have never been offered another version, nor have I read one. Believe me, *sir*," she said, emphasizing the title, "I read the small print."

"Well, Ms. Kazanov, it really doesn't matter. You're still fired."

"What?" Good God, the man was practically spitting, he was so pissed, his face purple, his body leaning forward as if he were ready to attack, shaking his fat little finger in her face.

"You heard me, Kazanov. Fired. Clear out your locker and leave the premises. Your check for this morning's fiasco, minus costs for failure to perform, will be mailed by the fifteenth."

He stood straighter and still had to look up to her. Then, as if he realized the height disadvantage hadn't improved, he quickly sat in his big leather chair.

Not that it changed anything. "I said get out, Ms. Kazanov. You don't work here anymore, which means you're trespassing in my office. Now go. I have work to do."

She stood there a moment longer, staring at the stupid little man and wishing she could think of something particularly pithy to say, something that would make her feel better as she slowly turned and headed for the door, except all she could think of was how expensive the rent was and how little money she had in her bank account.

Kaz opened the door, but she took satisfaction in slamming it as she finally found her backbone and stalked out of the office.

Jake glanced at the door of the final agency on his list. Top End. Sort of off the beaten track, but the place looked better once he stepped through the door. An attractive receptionist was just answering the phone, but she faced away from the entrance, her attention apparently focused on the office door behind her.

He took a moment to check out the pictures of all the beautiful people along the wall. They were almost interchangeable from agency to agency. This wasn't looking too promising, but he stopped in front of the receptionist's desk and waited for her to finish her call.

She set the phone down, but continued staring at the door behind her. Finally, he said, "Excuse me?"

She spun in her chair and blushed, looking up, and up even more. His height had that effect on people sometimes, but at six-and-a-half-feet tall, he was hard to ignore.

Her fair skin blushed a deep rose as she apologized. "I'm sorry. Busy day. How can Top End Modeling help you?"

"Jacob Lowell, R. Jacob Lowell Photography." He shot a quick glance at the wall of photos. "I'm looking for a model with a particular quality. I've been to a few other agencies, but had no luck. I'm not sure if you can help me or not."

She smiled broadly and spread her hands. "I won't know until you tell me exactly what you're looking for. Man? Woman? Hands, feet, face, whole body, or other body part? Particular style? What do you need?"

He let out a frustrated breath. He'd been describing the look he wanted for over a week now, and it hadn't gotten him anywhere. He gave it another shot.

"Not the traditional look," he said. "I've got a client who wants edgy, someone sort of dark and mysterious. Female, not necessarily traditionally beautiful, but someone unique, eye catching. Piercings are important. Ears, nostril maybe, or cheek. Eyebrow." He shrugged. "The usual spots for those who do piercings. I want, you know, a sense of danger. I . . ." He shook his head. At least this receptionist wasn't laughing at him. "It's hard to explain. I'll know her when I see her."

The office door behind the receptionist opened. Then it shut loudly as a tall, absolutely stunning young woman slammed it behind her.

The receptionist spun around in her chair. "Kaz? Are you okay? What happened?" She glanced at Jake and then focused on the woman.

He couldn't take his eyes off the model, because that's what she had to be. No woman this tall, this beautiful could be anything but a high-end model.

"The son of a bitch fired me," Kaz said, ignoring Jake standing there, staring at her. "He's got a major issue with tattoos." Her laugh was harsh and angry. "To make matters worse, I forgot to take the fucking stud out of my nose. The general was not pleased, to put it mildly." Then she sighed, leaned over, and grabbed her tote bag. "The Smithum people dropped me and the agency because of my tat. A tat on my belly they wouldn't even have seen if not for a pervert employee checking me out in the dressing room. They're doing a freaking shoe ad! My belly's not even in the shoot."

She stopped, finally noticed Jake standing there. "I'm sorry. Bad day." She gave him an apologetic smile, then focused on the receptionist. Her shoulders slumped.

"My locker's already empty." She held up the bag. "Guess it's a good thing I'd already planned to clean it out today. I'll see you back at the house, okay?"

"Oh, Kaz. I'm sorry, hon. There are other agencies, and they don't have Top End's stupid rules. As popular as you are . . ." She glanced at Jake again, but he was more interested in the model than anything Lola had been saying. "I'll come home as soon as I can."

Kaz merely nodded, but she flashed another quick smile

at Jake and said, "I really am sorry. That was totally un-professional of me." Slinging her bag over her shoulder, she added, "It's been one of those days," and headed for the door without waiting for an answer.

Jake stared at the slowly closing door, fully aware he was actually aroused. The thrill of the hunt? Hell, he didn't know, but she was beautiful, she was edgy, and she was exactly who he was looking for. He turned to the recep-tionist. "Tat? What kind of tat's she got?"

Blinking, the woman straightened in her chair and gave him her professional smile. "A butterfly," she said. "A beautiful monarch butterfly that runs across her hip and her stomach and up her rib cage. She got it to honor her sister." She glanced once again at the door. Then she smiled softly. "Last year, before I knew Kaz, her little sister was killed. Some guy ran a stop sign, a stupid kid out joyriding."

Jake's simmering arousal disappeared in a heartbeat, buried in a kaleidoscope of images that flashed through his mind—darkness and a rain-slicked road, faces locked for-ever in terror, the sounds . . .

He shook it off and focused on the young woman, on what she was saying. Consciously pushed the memories away. That was another time, another place.

He'd been a totally different person.

For all intents and purposes, RJ Cameron died almost twenty years ago, and Jake had no interest in resurrecting the body, though that text he'd deleted a while ago was a reminder that even the best-kept secrets had a way of get-ting loose. What the hell was that all about?

The receptionist was still speaking. He focused on her red lips, forced himself to pay attention.

"They released monarchs at her funeral," she said. "Kaz got the tattoo in memory of Jilly. It was tough."

Jake sucked in a deep breath. "A monarch butterfly across her torso?"

"Yes. It's absolutely beautiful." She shuffled some papers on her desk and smiled at him. "Now, Mr. Lowell, back to business. I need specifics, exactly what you're looking for." She reached for an album on the shelf behind her and pulled it out, set it on her desk.

Jake watched the receptionist, really looked at her, at the coal-black hair slicked back from her pale face, darkly drawn eyes, and blood-red lips. Upscale Goth? No matter—she was as sleek, as beautiful, and perfectly professional as a young woman could be. Then he glanced over his shoulder, at the door the tall, dark-eyed beauty had just exited.

He'd never felt such an instant attraction toward a woman—something he definitely didn't need. But she had piercings, and the tattoo was an omen. It had to be. Except . . .

Damn it all. She might be perfect for the job, but not for him. Not a woman he felt this kind of visceral attraction for. She could ruin everything he'd gained over the past ten years—his reputation, his career, his new life.

His anonymity.

He had too many secrets hiding in his own personal closet, secrets that were just fine when he left them alone. This morning's text was a reminder of how easily his hard-won sense of security could be shaken. There was no way in hell he could work with a woman he was attracted to—not if he wanted to keep the truth hidden. Hiring her would be the biggest mistake of his life.

No, he'd already made the biggest one—that long-ago night on a rain-slicked road—and two innocent people had died because of it. But damn it! She was perfect for Marc's ad campaign. And he owed Marc. Owed him more than he'd ever be able to repay.

"Her," he said, still staring at the door. "She's what I'm looking for. I want her."

"Kaz? But the general . . . uh, Mr. MacArthur, just fired her. I can't send her out on assignment if she doesn't work for the agency."

He turned on the charm. "She's your roommate, right? I heard her say she'd see you at home later. Call her. Ask her if she's willing to meet me. I've got a hot assignment, one that could be a terrific career opportunity for her." Not to mention what it could do for his professional reputation. "I don't care if I hire through an agency or independently, but I definitely want . . ." He paused. "Her name's Kaz, right? She's the one I want. She's perfect for this job."

He yanked his wallet out of his back pocket and dug through it until he found one of his cards. The corners were bent a little, but he quickly straightened it out and handed it to the receptionist. "My Web site's on there, and all my professional info is on the site. Check me out. I'm legit, San Francisco born and bred. Well, Marin, but close. There's a portfolio of my work, my Facebook, Pinterest, and Twitter accounts and a list of the magazines I've done shoots for."

He watched her as she studied his card, thankful that none of those social media sites mentioned the stupid kid he'd once been. R. Jacob Lowell was a successful photographer with an excellent reputation and a long list of professional credits. There was no mention of RJ Cameron on any of his sites. That kid belonged to his past.

But the model? He wasn't sure why, but he had a feeling she was going to be all over his future.

Whether that was a good thing or bad, he'd just have to find out.

Jake glanced at the door again. Maybe he could just chase her down. The sidewalk was filled with pedestrians headed in all directions, but she was tall and gorgeous. She'd stand out. Except he didn't have a clue which way she'd gone.

He doubted the suspicious receptionist would give him a lead.

"I don't know . . ."

"Please?" He tried the sad puppy-dog eyes. The look always worked with women, but this gal wasn't buying. He said it again, desperate now. Terrified he'd lose her. "She's the one I've been hunting for almost two weeks now. That honey tone to her skin, the cut and color of her hair, and those beautiful dark eyes. Right down to the stud in her nose. And the tattoo. Especially the tattoo."

The receptionist didn't even blink.

"I'm serious. The art's like an omen—the company is new, their logo is a monarch butterfly. It doesn't get any better."

The receptionist took a deep breath. Shook her head. Jake's gut clenched.

"I just don't know . . ."

That was better than a flat-out no, but not much.

He was clenching and unclenching his fingers. Not good. He shoved his hands in his back pockets. "This job is important to me and to my client. He's a successful guy with deep pockets, starting up another new business. The model who gets this job will be the focal point of an international media blitz on a big budget, but we're on a tight deadline. I need a commitment right away."

He didn't tell her it was more than just a job—that this was the biggest job Marc had ever offered him. He already owed the success of R. Jacob Lowell Photography to Marcus Reed, but this would take him to an entirely new level.

A level that much farther away from RJ Cameron.

He didn't just owe his success to Marc; Jake owed him his life.

He ran his hand up the back of his head and stared at the door. Then he realized he'd just made a mess of his hair, which probably made him look disreputable as hell, so he tried to shove it back down, which only messed it up worse. He took a deep breath, fully aware he was acting way out of character. Not his usual manner at all.

"You've got my cell phone number. Tell her that if she's at all interested in the job, she has to call today."

"Look." The woman studied him like he was a bug on the wall. "I can't give you Kaz's personal number. I'll give her your card, have her call you, but you'd better be who you say you are."

Score! "Who else would I be?" He chuckled and glanced toward the closed office door behind her desk. "I'm no general, that's for sure."

She laughed, then glanced at the door. "Thank God," she said.

The phone rang. Jake didn't hesitate. As she reached for it, he was flying out the door, searching for Kaz. Even as tall as he was, tall enough to see over just about everyone, it was the lunch hour, and the sidewalk was packed. He had no idea where to look, which way she'd gone.

With those long, long legs she could be blocks away by now.

"Crap." Still watching for the model, Jake headed toward the next block where he'd parked. He'd take a run down Nineteenth, see if he could spot her. If he didn't, he'd have to hope like hell she called him.

Tires squealed. Jake spun to look, but the unmistakable scream of tires on asphalt had him leaping out of the path of a sliding car. The older sedan rammed a parked car just ahead of him. A policeman giving someone a ticket at the stoplight raced across the street, halted traffic with one arm raised, then reached for the car door where a guy was slumped over the steering wheel.

Jake kept walking, but his head was once again filled

with images from long ago. The rain falling, his brother's face, the horror of death. The guilt. No matter how far or fast he walked, the reboot of bad memories stayed with him.

CHAPTER 2

Kaz had just parked her butt at the kitchen table with a peanut butter and jelly sandwich and the end of a bottle of really cheap red wine when Lola called. "Slow down, Lola. Who?"

"The man who was standing at my desk when you stomped out. Do you remember him?"

"Yeah, I got a good look at him. Very tall, very hot-looking guy, needs a haircut. Why? He looked sort of familiar. Has he hired from Top End before?" Kaz poured a little more wine into her glass and took a swallow, wishing she had something stronger. Better.

Who needed to worry about weight or red eyes? Models did, but she'd obviously screwed that gig. "He what? Wants to hire me? For what?"

She set the glass down. Listened to Lola, and jotted down the Web site and phone number.

Twenty minutes later, she felt like she knew the guy inside and out. R. Jacob Lowell, age thirty-five, single, successful—if she could believe all the credits on his Web site and his social networking pages—and well educated. Computer science, business and accounting, film studies. Was there anything the guy hadn't gotten a degree in?

She stared at the photo on his Facebook page and

laughed. He was wearing the same shirt in the profile shot that he'd had on today, a San Francisco Giants shirt, black with orange logo. Then she checked out the pages he'd "liked" and decided the guy was a geek at heart. A geek who liked baseball.

Sort of like her.

She took another swallow of wine and picked up her phone. Thought about the rent, about the odds of landing a decent job—without references—with a different agency, and tapped in his number. Calling him was a no-brainer. It wasn't like she had all that many modeling options out there, and the thought of actually using her business degree gave her the cold shivers. Working in an office wasn't at all what she wanted out of life.

At least she could ask R. Jacob Lowell what he wanted.

Jake ordered a cup of black coffee and found a seat near the front window where he could watch people while he waited for Kaz. She'd called a few minutes ago and said she'd meet him here at this funky little coffee shop across from the modeling agency, but he was a few minutes early.

He checked his phone. No more texts. That message he'd gotten earlier really bugged him. Who the hell could it have been? And why were they contacting him now? RJ had been gone for almost twenty years, though Jake was pretty certain a good scandal never died.

He'd check into it later. The coffee shop was almost empty. A couple of women sat near the door, an older dark-haired guy had just come in, ordered, and then sat at a table across the room from Jake, staring at his iPad. Other than that, there was no one but the cute little barista manning the counter.

No one paid any attention to Jake. He loved the anonymity of this older self, but today it felt as if the Fates had conspired to drag him back to that period when everything had gone so wrong. During the Olympics and then through the ensuing media frenzy after the wreck, the trial and sentencing, he'd been hounded by the press. As a public figure, there'd been no chance of keeping his name out of the papers. The paparazzi loved his looks, and his face had been splashed on the cover of every cheap tabloid around.

He'd been RJ Cameron then, thanks to dear old Mom, who'd thought RJ had a better ring than Richie. Cameron was her maiden name, and while she was all about making at least one of her sons famous, she had no problem inserting a little bit more of herself into the equation. She thought the name was classy, he'd thought it was stupid, but as an adult he'd learned to appreciate the anonymity of having screwed up so badly under a fake name.

Until today, no one had made the connection between R. Jacob Lowell and RJ Cameron.

Who the hell sent the text? How could anyone see the man he was today and recognize the stupid kid he'd been almost twenty years ago? He might have been almost as tall as he was now, but he'd been a lot thinner, his body lean and muscular from hours of training, his hair short, spiky, and blond—bleached by both the sun and his mother in her ultimate quest to make him a star.

She'd sold him like a damned product.

She'd only cared that he look good. Winning was expected, but her goal was Hollywood. She figured he had a better chance getting in as a sports star—win big at the Olympics, then the studios would come calling.

And, suck-up little jerk that he was, he'd gone along with everything she wanted, and he'd been good enough to make it work.

Up until he blew it.

Thank goodness his hair was naturally dark brown. Now, with it loose and curling around his face, he looked nothing like that manufactured image his mother had nurtured.

Who had found him? Who remembered RJ? He drummed his fingers on the table, pissed off and frustrated.

A shift in the flow of people on the sidewalk caught his eye, and Kaz was there, impossible to miss as she drew closer. He pushed the damned text message out of his mind and watched her. She was a good head taller than the pedestrians around her, and she moved with an easy stride, like a woman perfectly at ease in her own skin. He liked that, the sense of purpose as she got closer to the coffee shop.

His heart rate picked up when she stepped through the door and headed straight to the counter. The barista, a tiny blonde, met her with a hug and proceeded to build some sort of coffee with froth and stuff all over it without Kaz even ordering.

The two women talked nonstop, quietly enough that he couldn't make out what was said. Still, it was fun to watch the various expressions crossing Kaz's face. Damn, she was really something.

Absolutely unique. He'd never seen anyone like her.

It wasn't until she took her cup and paid the bill that she turned and, without having to hunt for him, headed directly to his table.

"Hey," she said, sliding into the seat across from him before he had time to stand. She held her hand out. "Kaz Kazanov."

He shook her hand. "Jake Lowell. Thank you for agreeing to meet." He didn't want to let go. Her hand was as beautiful as the rest of her, the fingers long and slim, nails trimmed short with clear polish.

Glancing up, he met eyes like dark chocolate, a wide smile in an angular face that was far from traditionally beautiful, but one he had trouble looking away from. High cheekbones, a long, sharply bridged nose, full lips, and a firm chin. Her hair was a short, dark brown cap, cut in a jagged, off-balance style that merely accentuated the angles and shadows of her face, her long, slim neck, the deep hollows at her collarbones.

She wore an oversized white cotton man's shirt over a pale blue tank top. He'd noticed when she walked in that her belly was covered. Damn. He'd really wanted a look at the tattoo.

She had turquoise studs in both ears and a tiny matching stud in her left nostril.

This was looking better and better.

"Seen enough?" She tilted her head and smiled at him, but there was a bite to her words.

"Actually, no, but I must admit I like what I see. What nationality are you?"

"Does it matter?"

Yeah. She was definitely pissed, but why? He shrugged. "Only because I want to know if your skin color is all over or if you've got tan lines we'd need to cover."

"Oh, crap." She slapped a hand to her forehead and just left it there, covering her eyes as she laughed. Jake grinned as a dark burnt umber flush spread across those outstanding cheekbones. After a minute, she peeked through her fingers. "I am so sorry. I was treating you like a bad date getting a bit too personal." Then she snorted rather inelegantly, which had him biting back a grin. "I totally gapped out this was a job interview. My apologies. Obviously you're aware this has not been one of my better days."

He was still smiling when he answered her. "I know. I heard what happened, and then I wasn't sure if the receptionist would give you my number. She's very protective of you."

"Lola's one of my roommates. She's a really good friend. She was there for me through some very dark times.

She's just watching out for me." Kaz shrugged and glanced away. The emptiness in her eyes sent a chill through him. He thought back to what Lola said to him and he knew Kaz was thinking of her little sister—knew it as clearly as if she'd told him—but then she sort of shook herself and smiled at him again.

It felt like a punch to the heart.

"I don't know what I am," she said. How was it she could so easily rock his world and yet remain totally unaffected? She was chatting away as if nothing had happened.

"Dad's fairly dark," she said. "Hispanic maybe, or Middle Eastern. He was adopted at birth, an abandoned baby, so he has no idea what his genetic background is. My mother was mostly white, almost as tall as me, but with some Native American in her background. It shows more in me than it did in her. She was a natural blonde. I get my hair color from my father."

"Past tense? Your mother?"

Kaz sipped her latte, glanced away and said, "She's dead. A long time ago."

"That's pretty tough, losing someone you love."

She cocked her head to one side and stared at him. "You say that as if you know."

He merely nodded, repeated her comment. "A long time ago."

She watched him a moment longer and then lowered eye lashes much too thick and long to be real—except he knew they were.

"So, you thought I was a bad date, eh?" He chuckled, changing the subject, and laughed when she gave him a snarky look out of the corner of her eye—and then blushed again. She was absolutely intriguing, exotic rather than beautiful, and her appearance changed with each movement, every smile, every glance. He couldn't wait to photograph her, to see what he might discover with his lens that was hidden within her rapidly changing expressions. After only a few minutes in her presence, he saw endless possibilities for the ad campaign—and more. Beyond her amazing looks, everything else about her was just as appealing—the low, husky voice, the broad smile, the easy laughter.

"I hate to admit it," he said, "but I wish this wasn't strictly business. I haven't had time for too much play lately."

"Tell me about it." This time she merely smiled, but it was another expression that changed her entire look.

He took another mental snapshot, framing her in one more perfect shot. "Yeah," he said. "Relationships are totally out, and dating isn't penciled in on my schedule for, oh, about the next ten years or so, but this is actually a job that could be a lot of fun as well as good for both our careers. The shoot is for a new line of jewelry, called Intimate. Very expensive, unique designs, many for intimate piercings, hence the name, though they've got more traditional designs as well. You have exactly the look I've been searching for the past couple of weeks. I was just about ready to give up before I saw you. I noticed you've got ear and nostril piercings. Are there any others we could use to display some truly beautiful pieces?"

She blushed again, and he wished he had his camera with him, but he'd dropped the equipment off at his apartment. He wondered if the camera on his phone could catch that beautiful burnt umber shade, but then she was laughing, her color was back to its perfect warm honey, and the moment passed.

"Why the blush?" He took a sip of his coffee and watched her eyes.

"I've done a few nude shoots, but very few." She grimaced, but her eyes twinkled. "I'm not real comfortable posing nude, if that's what you're looking for, but beyond my ears and nose, both of my nipples are pierced, my navel, and the hood of my clit." She laughed. "I'm not sure I know you well enough to model all the available options."

He had to consciously will himself away from thinking about those piercings if he was going to function at all as a professional. "I'm guessing you're okay with the nose and navel piercings. Maybe the nipples, once you get to know me, feel more comfortable?"

Before she answered him, he added, "I'm especially interested in seeing your butterfly tattoo. The company logo is a monarch butterfly. The receptionist at the agency told me that's what your tattoo is. A monarch."

Her lips parted and he could have sworn there were tears in her eyes when she nodded. "I would love to show you the tat, though this probably isn't the best place." She glanced over her shoulder at the line of people at the counter and then unexpectedly laughed out loud. "I might shock poor Mandy—she's the barista—right out of her Tevas."

Resting his elbows on the table with his chin propped on his folded knuckles, Jake studied her, the curve of her lips, the shimmer in those dark eyes. Why did he feel such a strong connection to this woman? There was such a comfortable sense about her. So often the models he'd met and worked with had been more like mannequins without an ounce of personality, so caught up in their looks they had nothing else to offer. Kaz wasn't like that at all.

She absolutely sparkled, and that sparkle was contagious. Was it all Kaz, or was it his perception of her? He didn't know why, but something was happening.

Something well beyond the photo shoot.

Whatever it was, if he could capture it, he'd be shooting gold.

He fought a strong desire to grab on to her hand, as if

holding her in place would make her decide to take the job. Instead, he wrapped his hands around his cup. His coffee had grown cold, but the heavy pottery mug anchored him.

"Here's the deal. I honestly think you've got the perfect look for the ad campaign. It's a new company, but with deep pockets. They're willing to spend money to make money. The theme behind the ad campaign is the link between jewelry and fine wine. Glitz with an edge for the younger moneyed crowd. I realize you don't know me and have no reason to trust me, but this is an important job, and you really are the perfect model."

He was scheduled to be at the vineyard Thursday and Friday, but it was only Tuesday. Enough time for her to talk herself out of it, to change her mind? Before he really thought it through, Jake looked her in the eye and lied. Very convincingly. "I really want you for this job, Kaz, but we'll need to leave tonight."

"Leave tonight? To go where?" She sat back in her chair and stared at him.

"Sonoma County wine country. If we can get close to the site this evening, we can start first thing in the morning. The owner of Intimate has a vineyard north of Santa Rosa, in a beautiful area called Dry Creek Valley. The plan is to do a series of shots in among the vines, maybe some in a renovated barn on the property. Mostly in the vineyard, though. Bud break was a couple of weeks ago, so the vines are just leafing out, and the leaves are a perfect shade of pale green with a lot of the woody part of the vine still showing. Beautiful texture for photography. Picture this— it's still green between the rows with lots of wildflowers. With your skin tone, the morning light, and some sparkling diamonds, I think we can get some killer shots."

Resting his elbows on the table, his chin on his clasped hands, he studied her for a moment. "My original schedule had me doing the shots this coming weekend—arriving

Thursday and working through the weekend, but now it looks like there's a chance of rain, which is why I want to go tonight. I'm under a real time crunch to get this series of photos done—I honestly didn't expect it to take me so long to find a model who was right for the campaign. I booked rooms for Thursday and Friday night, hoping I'd have someone by then, but with the weather in question I can't risk waiting."

He shrugged. "If you agree to do the shoot, we'll need to find rooms for tonight and tomorrow night, but that shouldn't be a problem. Not midweek. I've got the jewelry and the cameras, and if you're willing, I've got the perfect model. What'd'ya say?"

She was frowning, obviously unsure, and why shouldn't she be? Strange guy walks in off the street and . . . Damn, he didn't want to lose her. "It pays really well." He named the full sum he'd been given to work with, including his cut. If she didn't go for it, if she wanted more, he'd have to dig into his own stash, but he could afford it. He'd discovered a real talent for photography and he'd grown surprisingly successful in a relatively short time. He really didn't want to lose her.

When her eyes went wide, he figured he had her. He knew for sure when she said, "Do you have a contract I can look over?"

"I do." He reached into his briefcase and pulled out the papers. Two copies, standard contract, one she shouldn't have a problem with, but he gave her time to read it. And, amazingly, she did. All four pages. He watched the way her eyes tracked, the businesslike manner when she pulled a notepad and pen out of her shoulder bag and jotted down some numbers.

"Do you have any questions?"

Smiling, still concentrating on the contract, she shook her head. "My major was business, emphasis on law. Even though I don't ever see myself working in a fully business environment, I'm still taking post-grad classes when I can fit them in. Dad always told me it was never a good idea to depend on looks and good luck. He wanted me to be able to get, as he puts it, 'a real job' in case the modeling gig didn't pan out." She laughed, and this time she raised her head and gazed at him directly.

He felt her look, a tactile stroke over nerves already sparking. "I fully expect it to pan out," she said. "Which makes it even more important that I understand contracts."

"Smart man, your father."

"I know. I was thinking that today when I got fired." Shaking her head, she added, "Your timing couldn't have been better."

Did she have any idea the effect her smiles had on him? Would she even care? If she did, he'd be sunk—even deeper than he already was. "I'd love to say it was brilliant planning on my part," he said, "but this time I think it was pure luck." He held out a pen.

She took it, and he was much too aware of the soft brush of her fingers across his palm, the way her shaggy brown hair fell so artfully across one cheek.

Pausing, she held the pen just above the contract. "Do I need to bring any particular clothes or props? Is there a style you're looking for?"

"Dark and dangerous, but classy. Think edgy sophistication. If you've got anything you think will work, bring it along. I've got a small budget for clothing, but your own might be more comfortable for you."

"Black leather skinny jeans with a really low rise. They show most of the tattoo and my navel really well. And I wax, so the low rise isn't an issue." She laughed, the sound deep and throaty and so contagious he laughed along with her. "And, for your information, that's professional info. I'm no longer thinking of this as a date."

They both laughed, but Jake couldn't help imagining how much fun she would be on a date. He hadn't laughed like this or enjoyed a woman's company this much in way too long.

"Black heels," she said. "Very high." She sort of squinted at him and laughed again. "Like I'm not tall enough already. But ya know, I think I could wear them around you and you'd still be taller. Oh, and some blood-red accessories. What about hats?"

"Throw in anything you can think of. I've got an Escalade. Too big for San Francisco, but perfect for hauling all the stuff I need for jobs. There's room for whatever you want to bring, along with my gear. As far as physical props, we'll mostly work with what's available at the vineyard. There's an old barn that's been upgraded, but it's got a bunch of antique stuff in it. I'm a very minor investor in the winery, so I've got keys for everything." He glanced at his watch.

"It's almost two. If I can pick you up by five, we should be able to make it to the inn by seven unless the traffic is really awful, but there's a good restaurant just down the street and we can get a late dinner there. I expect we'll need at least two days, maybe three, to get enough photos. Is that okay with you?"

"Not like I have anyplace else to be." She signed both copies of the contract, then handed them to him as she pushed back her chair.

Glancing at the signature, he read, "Marielle Leigh Kazanov?" He laughed. "Kaz fits you better." He quickly signed the contracts.

She almost giggled, but it came out as more of an inelegant snort that made him like her even more. "That's why no one knows my real name. You call me Marielle, the deal's off." Playfully, she reached for both contracts. He gave one to her, but held his copy over his head.

She huffed out a deep breath, gave him directions to her house, and said she'd meet him out front at five. "I need to let Mandy know."

"The barista?"

"She and Lola, the receptionist at Top End, are my roommates. They're sisters."

"That explains it. I thought it was really weird that the little blond barista reminded me of a receptionist working the Goth look."

Laughing, Kaz leaned over, grabbed her bag, and shoved her copy of the contract into the side pocket. She raised her head and smiled at him. "Just in case you're wondering, their dog's name is Rico. Mandy and Lola's mom is a huge Barry Manilow fan."

"Crap. 'Copacabana.' Now I'm going to have that song running through my head all night. I can never remember all the words. It'll drive me batshit crazy."

"I can help. With the words, not driving you crazy, though I'm sure I'll do that as well." She winked at him. "I know all the words to 'Copacabana,' 'Mandy,' 'I Write the Songs'—you name it, I know it." She slung the strap to her handbag over her shoulder. "And I can sing it, though not nearly as well as Barry. See you at five."

He wanted to cheer, but all he said was, "I'll be there."

She stopped and turned around, and every move she made was like watching a ballet. Tall and lean and so perfectly put together, he wanted to reach for the camera he'd left at home, which made him glad he hadn't brought it because he'd be making a damned fool of himself. He'd never seen anyone like her. Ever. But he'd have plenty of time for pictures.

"Kaz. I'm really looking forward to working with you."

"Thank you. Me, too. You." Her gaze was pure, sensual intensity. He'd felt it since the moment he first saw her at the agency. The feeling had intensified when she'd walked into the café, but now it was directed solely at him.

The strength of it almost knocked him back in his chair. Good Lord, if he could capture that in his pictures . . .

"I have a feeling I can trust you, Jake." She laughed softly, sort of a gravelly, husky laugh that clenched the muscles across his abdomen and sent shivers trailing down his arms. "See you at five."

And then she was gone.

It felt as if she took all the air with her.

CHAPTER 3

About forty miles from their destination, Jake pulled the Escalade over for gas and called ahead to make sure they could get a couple of rooms. After a short conversation, he raised his head and grimaced. "Okay. The place where I have reservations for Thursday is booked solid tonight and tomorrow night. Guess I should have called before we left, but I never imagined there'd be a problem on a Tuesday night. There's some kind of wine-tasting event going on, as well as a bike race. We might have trouble finding a place."

He stared at his iPhone and shook his head. Then he handed the phone to Kaz. "Do you mind seeing if your luck's any better? The vineyard is at the northern end of Dry Creek Valley, so rooms in either Healdsburg or Geyserville would work. Santa Rosa's too far to be practical. Don't worry about the cost. I'm good for it. See if you can find us someplace to stay while I fill up the tank."

She looked at the phone in her hand and sighed. She hoped he knew what he was saying when he told her not to worry about the cost. Any room in wine country was bound to be expensive. Then she went online, made a list of hotels and motels in the area, and started calling. And calling.

She ended another call, another no vacancy response, and crossed that one off her list. Stretching her arms overhead and arching the kinks out of her back, Kaz glanced to her left. A man stood on the other side of the next bank of pumps, staring at her. He reminded her of the guy she'd noticed in the coffee shop when she'd met Jake. After a moment, he stepped to one side to remove the gas nozzle from his car and disappeared behind the pump.

That was creepy. She went back to dialing hotel numbers, watching while Jake filled the tank and washed the windshield of the big SUV. It didn't take long for her focus to shift to the smooth line of his broad shoulders and the way the T-shirt hugged his perfect body. As he stretched to wash the windshield, she could make out the sharp definition of what had to be six-pack abs. The orange Giants logo on his black shirt—a little different from the one he'd worn earlier—stretched tightly across the muscular breadth of his chest.

Definite eye candy. She was still ogling, though a bit more subtly, by the time he was back behind the wheel, pulling onto the highway. It was another twenty miles farther down the road before she finally found what sounded like the last available room in the whole area.

"Found one. It's expensive, in Healdsburg, but they just had a cancellation. There's only one room. It does, however, have two beds."

He shot her a quick glance, but she couldn't read anything in his sharp gaze before he quickly turned his attention back to the busy freeway. Staring straight ahead, he shrugged his shoulders and she heard his sigh. "It's up to you. I can bunk in the car if you're uncomfortable sharing a room. I'm really sorry, Kaz. I didn't think everything would be full midweek. Did you try Santa Rosa?"

"You said earlier that's too far from the site where we're doing the pictures." She studied his profile a moment, imagined it framed by a soft pillow. What would it be like to wake up beside a guy as gorgeous as Jake Lowell? "I'm okay sharing a room," she said. Her gut said he was a good guy. Her hormones thought he was fantastic. She definitely liked what she knew so far.

He shifted in his seat and snagged his wallet out of his back pocket, flipped it open and slid out a credit card. "Use this to hold the room. Let them know we're less than half an hour away."

She glanced at the name on the card. R. Jacob Lowell. It was on the doors of the Escalade, too—one of those fancy decals that said R. Jacob Lowell Photography along with his phone number and Website. Probably what the weird dude at the gas station was staring at. Not at her. She wondered what the *R* stood for.

Then she glanced at Jake, at his beautiful profile. The way light and shadows from the setting sun played across the stark planes of his face caught hold of her, until Kaz had to consciously force herself to concentrate on the phone in her hand. She redialed the hotel, gave the desk clerk the credit card number, and reserved the room.

She yawned as she ended the call. "Got it."

The cell phone vibrated in her hand. "You've got a text." She held the phone up so he could see what it said. He glanced at the text on the screen and took the phone when she handed it to him.

"Business," he said. "It can wait." He closed the screen and stuck the phone in his back pocket. Then he turned his eyes back to the road.

Kaz stretched again. Damn, it had been a long day. She'd arrived for the Smithum photo shoot before seven. What was it about these frickin' photographers and their morning light?

She leaned back in her seat and closed her eyes. It was quiet, other than the steady hum of the engine. The Barry

Manilow CD he'd stuck into the player had ended a few minutes ago, but he'd proved to her that he knew all the words to "Copacabana."

He was smart and fun, with a quick wit and a great laugh. Plus, he was a good driver, even in this horrible bumper-to-bumper traffic. She liked watching the way he handled the car.

Liked him.

How would she respond if Jake came on to her? She watched him as he easily handled the traffic, which had grown even heavier as they passed through Santa Rosa, heading north. He was definitely hot. A big guy, but not bulky. Lean and muscular with a sharply chiseled face that could keep him steadily employed as a model, and yet he was on the other side of the lens.

What made him turn to photography? Why was it so important that she find out?

The moment she actually formed that subtle question in her mind, Kaz realized that, over the course of the last ninety or so minutes of driving, she had started to see Jacob Lowell as more than a job.

What was it Lola had said? The minute you started wondering about a guy, it meant you were interested in him.

She had way too many questions for a disinterested woman.

When she glanced at Jake again, she felt that shivery sense of need, the kind that seemed to connect all those tiny bars and studs she wore. No wonder they were popular for erogenous zones. Her clit and nipples—even her belly button—seemed to tingle in response to Jake's nearness, and she realized her thinking had done a full one-eighty, not so much about possibilities, but about down and dirty sex. Of getting naked with a man merely because she liked him, liked his laugh and the way he made her laugh, and it didn't hurt one bit that he was damned hot to look at.

And the setting was looking better all the time.

Even a nerd like her couldn't screw up with so much material to work with. An elegant hotel room with two beds in the wine country was a good start. She almost laughed, imagining how other women would work something like this.

Seduction might not be her strong suit, but Jake? Wow . . . he made it worth at least trying.

She was still thinking of the evening's potential when they pulled into the off-street parking area behind the hotel. The sun had set behind the western hills, but it was still bright out and the streets were filled with people enjoying the small town and central plaza.

Jake didn't want to leave his camera gear in the car, so Kaz helped him carry the extra bags inside the hotel. She waited while he registered, standing off to one side, admiring the way he seemed to take control of the counter, and she was almost laughing at the flirtatious looks the young clerk gave him.

Looks he either ignored or just didn't see. For some reason, she had a feeling it was the latter. She loved the way he occasionally glanced in her direction and smiled.

Once he'd registered, they turned everything over to the bellboy before following him to the elevator and up to their room on the second floor.

Kaz stood there staring at the gorgeous room with her mouth hanging open while Jake tipped the bellboy. When he closed the door, she turned to him and raised an eyebrow. "This is nice."

Nice didn't even come close.

Jake merely smiled.

That smile was deadly. She shivered, imagining the potential in this room.

He set his bags on the floor beside the bed closest to the door. "Any preference which bed you want?"

She wished she had the nerve to say, "Whichever one you're in," but there was no way she'd get that out without cracking up.

Her arousal had been growing with each mile they traveled, until now she wanted him with an almost visceral need. Wanted to run her hands over those broad shoulders, dig her fingers into his dark, silky hair. She wished she had the courage to say what she was thinking and then casually saunter across the room and pop the button on his jeans, slip her fingers into the waistband, and tug that black denim down to his ankles. Yeah. That would work. Or not.

As relaxed and easygoing as he'd been on the drive up, that would be crossing a line he might not like at all.

This was still a job. One she needed badly, but a girl could dream, right?

Damn, she was so aware of him. So confused. Kaz shivered, physically shaking off the need to touch him. "This one," she said, and carted her bags across the room to take the bed near the door to the balcony.

Jake put his bags on the other bed and headed to the bathroom for a quick shower.

Kaz had showered before Jake picked her up, so she took the time while he was out of the main part of the room to change into a pair of skinny jeans, platform sandals, a tight crop top camisole, and a shaggy sweater that covered her belly—and her tat.

She knew she'd have to show it to him eventually, but not yet. That was something she was going to have to work up to, because Jake already wasn't just anybody. It was going to be really personal, showing it to him.

She hadn't had it all that long and had never had to expose it for a modeling gig. It wasn't something she comfortably flashed around, at least not when someone just wanted to see it. This morning she hadn't planned to show it off, but she certainly hadn't expected that jerk to poke his head into her dressing room without knocking to "see if she was ready." Yeah, right. She'd complained to the client—maybe that's why he'd made such an issue about her tattoo, because he knew she had a valid complaint against the employee who was also his son.

She hadn't expected to lose her job because of it.

On the other hand, it had led to her meeting Jake. She glanced toward the bathroom door, imagined him in there, naked under the spray in that shower.

She had a feeling the reality would be even better.

Then she looked at the bed next to hers and shivered. God, she was lame, standing here imagining how he was going to act when he saw her tattoo, practically plotting the poor guy's seduction. He'd only see the ink and the art of it. He wouldn't know what it meant to her. Not really. She'd shown it to very few men. Even Jerry hadn't seen it, since they'd broken up right before Jilly died, before Kaz had the tat done.

Kaz stared at the bed where Jake had left his gear. He'd told her they had to be on-site by six in order to catch first light, but there were a lot of hours between now and dawn. A lot of hours and two queen-sized beds.

The room was beautiful, very upscale with all the right touches, but all she saw were the beds. Jake, of course, had been a perfect gentleman. She was the one with her mind in the gutter.

The bathroom door opened with a soft cloud of steam. "Hey, Kaz? Did I leave my overnight kit on the bed?"

She glanced at the bag in question. "You did. Want it?"

"Yeah. I need my razor and shaving cream."

She grabbed the bag, took a calming breath, and sauntered into the open bathroom. Jake stood in front of the mirror with a thick, white towel wrapped around his hips. Playing it as nonchalant as she was able, Kaz set the overnight kit on the stone counter next to the sink and tried not to drool.

He'd looked good in worn jeans and a T-shirt, but wearing nothing but a towel, Jacob Lowell was absolutely magnificent. The plush Egyptian cotton stretched tightly across an absolutely perfect butt, covering his legs almost to his knees. His calves were beautifully shaped and muscular, dusted in dark hair, and he had long, narrow feet. Sexy as hell, but even sexier was the fact that, barefoot, he was still taller than Kaz while she stood tall in platform wedge sandals.

With his upper body naked she finally got a look at that impressive chest, confirming her guess that yes, while he was lean and rangy, he was strongly built with what she'd always thought of as a swimmer's body—broad shoulders, a smoothly muscled chest, and a flat belly. There wasn't an ounce of fat on the man. That and the rippled definition across his midsection were proof of either quality time in the gym or a damned healthy lifestyle—or both. He did have an intriguing trail of dark hair that circled his navel and disappeared beneath the towel.

Her fingers itched to follow it, even though she knew exactly where it led. Or maybe that should be *because* she knew exactly where it led.

"Thanks. I'll just be a minute."

Blinking herself back to the present, Kaz glanced up. The dark shadow covering his cheeks and jaw only added to the entire package, but the twinkle in his dark eyes let her know he'd caught her looking. She swallowed her need and prayed she wouldn't blush. "Don't shave on my account. I like the look. Sort of edgy and dark."

He tilted his head and studied her for a brief moment.

"That's what I liked about you the first time I saw you."
He set the razor back on the counter. "Edgy and dark, exactly the look I wanted."

"I'm glad you got it."

The moment the words were out, she felt the hot blush spreading over her chest and face, but she didn't look away.

He stared at her a moment and then lowered his gaze. "Will you show me the butterfly?"

She blinked. And then she shivered, almost as if she felt that searing gaze roving across her multihued tattoo. That wasn't what she'd expected to hear. Not yet, anyway. She had to swallow before she could answer him, all too aware how her voice sounded, sort of raspy. Needy. "How about later, after dinner? I'm starved." She glanced his way. Maybe he'd just think she was hungry, not terrified of sharing such a personal part of herself.

His smile slowly stretched across his face. "Works for me."

Oh, yeah. What was going on? She'd never felt an attraction like this. Of course, she'd never been in a gorgeous man's hotel room, fully dressed while he wore nothing but a towel, either.

He reached around her, his warm, muscular arm rubbing over hers as he grabbed the overnight kit. She sucked in a breath at a simple touch that left her shivering, needy.

"Toothbrush," he said.

There was no fighting her blush.

His smile just got wider. "If you're okay with the furry face, I'll just brush my teeth, get some clothes on, and we can go find food."

He'd expected her to want something expensive, something haute cuisine—she was a gorgeous fashion model after all, and this town was known for its quality restaurants—but she said she'd spotted a little Mexican dive on the way into town that looked interesting, and that's where she led him. They had to walk a few blocks from the trendier downtown area. He'd really wanted to grab her hand and hold on to her, but he wasn't sure how she'd take it. Then, when they got to the restaurant, she hadn't even paused to read the menu tacked beside the door—she was the one who grabbed his hand and dragged him inside.

An hour later, Jake was wiping his lips with his napkin, fully aware he couldn't eat another bite. "That was absolutely amazing. You definitely know how to pick 'em."

They could have been in Mexico, rather than an upscale wine-country town. The place was full, with conversations in Spanish and English flowing as easily as the beer. He eyed the few drops of salsa still left in the bowl.

"If you eat the last of that, I will not be responsible for you being up half the night belching." She laughed, reached across the table for the last chip, scooped up the salsa, and ate it herself. "See? I'm saving you from a night of misery. I hope you appreciate it."

"I thought models worried about their weight." Grumbling, he stared at the now empty bowl.

"Not usually. Fast metabolism."

She licked her lips and he followed the sweep of her tongue with his gaze. Then she neatly dabbed her mouth with the napkin.

He blinked to break the connection. "Right. You'll watch me starve while stealing the last of the chips and salsa, and you want me to feel grateful?"

"You mean you're not?"

"Not in the least."

The waitress brought the tab to their table and Jake handed her his credit card.

Kaz smiled at him. "I guess I'll just have to owe you."

"That you do." He couldn't help but smile back. She was nothing like the other models he'd worked with over the years, and he wasn't thinking only of the way she looked. They'd talked about everything from politics—which they'd mostly agreed on—to sports. Kaz was a sports fan, and while she liked baseball and approved of his Giants T-shirt, she absolutely loved basketball. Neither of them had traveled as much as they wanted, and they both liked Mexican food and good beer. She read mysteries and romances, he liked biographies, but they both read the *San Francisco Chronicle* daily from cover to cover. And she was so damned quick, with a sense of humor that meshed with his own rather warped view of life. In fact, they'd spent the entire meal laughing and smiling, even as they'd argued about every topic imaginable.

Unique really did describe Kaz.

He signed the bill and left a twenty on the table, stood at the same time as Kaz, and they walked to the door. She paused just outside the restaurant.

It had grown dark while they ate, but the overhead lights from the parking lot cast a golden shimmer across her dark hair. She smiled at him.

Good God, that mouth. It took everything he had not to lean close and kiss her.

"You tip heavy," she said. Her brows crinkled a bit as she frowned. "Our whole meal barely cost twenty bucks. Plus, you could've put the tip on your card, but you left a twenty on the table. How come?"

He shrugged. This wasn't the conversation he'd imagined, but then his imagination had been running a bit wild tonight. "Just making sure the money goes to the ones who earned it."

She nodded. Then she laughed outright. "Sorry. It's that damned business degree I'm still paying for. I pay attention to the pennies." Her smile slipped and she glanced away.

He wondered what she was thinking as he tugged her

arm through his, and it bothered him, in a way, how much he wanted to understand her. To get to know her. Hell, he just wanted to be with her. She wasn't like anyone he'd ever dated before. Part of what made her unique was her height. He wasn't used to looking eye-to-eye with a woman. It felt as if that level gaze of hers demanded honesty.

He was still thinking about that when they crossed the street to check out some of the different storefronts as they headed back to the hotel. There was a section of antique shops with interesting window displays, so they took their time, pausing to look, to tease and joke around. The night was cool, and Jake was so damned aware of her. The way she walked, the soft swing of her short hair when she turned to speak, the sensual curve of her lips. His primary thought should be how to transfer her look, her style and mood to photos, not hoping she noticed him as a man, that she wouldn't consider a kiss out of line.

Or even more. Damn, it had been a long time since he'd been with anyone. Not that women weren't interested, but rebuilding a life took time and energy. There was no time to meet women, especially anyone who fascinated him the way this one did. Most of the single women he met were models. Beautiful packages, nothing inside. Not like Kaz.

She filled the space around them with energy—so much energy that he felt it sizzle across his skin.

They'd almost reached their hotel when she paused in front of a store that carried designer clothing. Jake stood beside her, much too aware of the way men noticed her when they walked by. All of them were checking her out— the same way he'd been watching her. He slipped his arm around her waist, silently laughing at himself and his cave-man reaction.

"Look at all the color." She turned her head and smiled up at him, but she didn't pull away from his hand resting lightly on her hip, so he left it there. "I love store windows with lots of color." Laughing, she shook her head and then sighed. "Yet you look in my closet, and almost everything is black. Why is that?"

"Your closet. You tell me." His gaze rested on a long silk scarf dyed in colors across the spectrum. Slipping from black to darkest purple, through shades of teal blue and turquoise, it melted perfectly into a soft almost translucent shade of sky blue.

Jake pictured Kaz wrapped in the shimmering silk, pictured dark nipples sparkling with diamonds peeking through the folds, and the image filled his mind until he had no choice but to grab her hand and drag her inside the store. The clerk was at the register, sorting the day's tags and receipts.

"Hello." Raising her head, she smiled at them. "I was just getting ready to close. Did you need something in particular?"

"I do." Jake reached into the window display and grabbed the scarf. "This, please." He turned to Kaz, held the scarf against her cheek. He loved the way her eyes lit up. "For the shoot tomorrow," he said to her. "The color is perfect."

Business first. This was a business trip. That didn't mean he couldn't imagine slowly peeling the filmy scarf off of her, exposing that beautiful honey-colored skin inch by inch. Smiling at the saleslady, he reached for his wallet.

"Do you mind sticking this in your purse?"

She glanced up to catch Jake smiling at her, holding the small bag in one hand. "Sure." She took the package and carefully placed it in the side pocket of her oversized shoulder bag. Not a gift, as she'd first thought. A prop. She stroked her fingers over the small bag. A prop with infinite possibilities. Her nipples tightened, imagining the feel of Jake's big hands adjusting the silky fabric over her breasts, maybe even between her legs. All to display the jewelry, of course.

"Thank you." He was nodding to the clerk as once again he grabbed Kaz's hand and headed outside to the crosswalk that led to their hotel. She tightened her grasp around his fingers, felt his light squeeze in return, then smiled when he glanced down and caught her looking at him. She wasn't used to walking hand in hand with a man. She'd never held hands with a man like Jake.

There was live music playing somewhere—guitars and drums so loud, they must be close. They were good, too, and the music had Kaz sort of nodding along to the beat. She was tired, but not entirely ready to call it a night.

Jake leaned close, and it was like he was reading her mind. "I like the sound of that music," he said. "The hotel's got a cocktail lounge. No band, but the concierge said there's a really talented guy playing piano tonight. We can't stay up late with such an early start, but have a drink with me."

She glanced at him, fully aware that a very feminine part of her wanted to show off this guy she was with, business companion or not. She'd teased him earlier about cleaning up really well, but in black jeans, boots, and a snug, black long-sleeved T-shirt that showed off his exceptionally fine body, she hadn't been kidding.

He still held on to her hand, and it was such a unique experience, actually to feel small beside a man. A drink sounded good, and a quiet hotel bar made more sense with tomorrow's early schedule. A drink in the lounge was a terrific idea.

She bumped him with her hip and said, "After the day I've had?" Laughing, she glanced at their hotel on the opposite corner and focused on the second-floor balcony she was almost certain opened to their room. Then she tucked her arm through his and tugged him toward the crosswalk. "You'd better believe I'd like a drink."

There wasn't any traffic to speak of, but they waited for the light to change. As soon as it did, Kaz stepped off the curb. Jake glanced up at the sound of a revving engine. A dark car, with no headlights on, flew toward the crosswalk.

"Kaz!" He jerked her back so hard she stumbled. Wrapped his arm around her waist, held her tightly against his body, and spun the two of them to safety behind a stout light pole—barely ahead of the speeding car.

Tires screamed. The car bounced up on the sidewalk, sideswiped the pole, and skidded sideways through the main street, forcing a smaller vehicle over the curb. Pedestrians scattered. A young man jumped out of the way, cursing. The driver who'd caused the mess got control of his vehicle—an older BMW—but not before spinning a full circle in the intersection.

The sedan came to a halt, tires smoking, broadside to their corner. The driver's window was open. For the briefest moment, Jake and the man made eye contact. Then the guy hit the gas, burning rubber as he flew down the almost empty street. The few cars in his way dodged to one side or the other. People on the sidewalk hid in doorways; someone screamed.

The BMW blew through the red light at the next intersection, skidded into a left turn from the center lane, and disappeared down a side street. People converged from all directions, but Jake held Kaz close as those old memories slammed into him—damn, it was like he couldn't catch a break.

Thank goodness, this time there was another outcome. His body vibrated with an overload of adrenaline, but Kaz was in his arms. She was trembling, but she was safe. She was here, holding him every bit as tightly as he held her.

There was no one lying dead in the street. No one bleeding, no one screaming at him.

Nothing but a few stunned pedestrians staring in the direction the car had gone.

A policeman pulled to a stop across the street and a few of the people went to him, reporting what had happened. Still hugging Kaz, Jake buried his face against her neck. He really didn't want to get involved with the police. Questions led to answers he couldn't give. There were too many secrets he had to keep.

He thought of the latest text. He'd only had a chance to glance at it, a preview on the screen of his phone when Kaz had handed it to him earlier. Was the bastard who called him RJ driving an older, black BMW? Was something in Jake's past screwing with his present?

He glanced at the policeman taking statements from various bystanders. No one seemed to notice Kaz and him standing here, and no one appeared to be hurt. Kaz still held him tightly, trembling against his chest as he took one deep breath after another. He fought to control his anger, to get his emotions under control. Kaz gazed up at him.

"Are you okay?"

She nodded, but she didn't make any attempt to pull free of his embrace. "He must have been drunk," she said. "Or on drugs. He sure doesn't have any business driving."

"No kidding." He hugged her even tighter. He had to think, damn it. Why was that bastard aiming at them? There was no doubt in Jake's mind—either he or Kaz had been targeted, but why? He flashed on the driver's face. He looked familiar, but Jake was certain he'd never met the man. Still, the feeling persisted.

A second squad car arrived and the crowd began to thin out as folks went back to whatever had brought them into the small town on a Tuesday night.

After a moment, Kaz raised her head and gazed at Jake.

Her expression was haunted, and yet she was absolutely stunning—a woman both exquisitely strong and yet achingly vulnerable. "That man, the one driving the car? I think I saw him earlier."

"What?" He grasped her shoulders, anchoring himself as much as Kaz. "When? Where?"

"When you were filling the car up with gas. He was standing by the bank of pumps across from us. I didn't get a good look at him and don't know what kind of car he was driving, but . . ." Her lips tilted in a shaky smile. "He looked like the same guy I saw at the coffee shop, too. Sitting across from us, but . . ." She paused, glanced away. "No. Never mind. I saw a middle-aged guy with dark hair staring at your Escalade. He looked like he was reading the logo on your door. It couldn't have been him. I don't know why I thought it was the same guy."

"You're sure?" He hugged Kaz close.

"No." Her laugh was still shaky. "That car just missing us was scary. I'm not even sure of my own name."

"Still want that drink?" he asked. He managed a smile, hoped it didn't look more like a grimace. The last thing he wanted to do was frighten her.

She nodded, studied him a moment, then returned his smile. "Most definitely. Preferably in the hotel lounge where the room is only an elevator ride away. This place is more exciting than it looks."

Chuckling softly, he took her hand and, skirting the cars and the lingering activity in the intersection, led Kaz across the street to the hotel, to the quiet lounge on the ground floor.

CHAPTER 4

There was an older guy at the piano playing some really nice, lazy jazz, but Jake's mind was still spinning, not yet in sync with the gentle rhythms filling the quiet lounge.

Tonight's close call had brought so much back, so many memories he'd tried to bury. Funny thing about those memories. They tended not to stay buried.

He'd watched that car flying their way and he'd remembered that horrible night so long ago. Was that what the young mother saw before she died? A big, dark car with two stupid-ass kids inside, sliding directly at her, out of control on a rain-slicked road? She'd tried to shove her little boy out of the way, but she hadn't been fast enough. Jake could still hear the horrible sounds, feel the cold rain as he'd raced from the car to check on the woman and child.

It had been too late.

A warm hand grasped his, startling him out of the past. He glanced at Kaz's slim fingers wrapped around his.

"This was a good idea," she said. "Thank you. That was really scary."

He nodded, drawn back to the present by her soft voice. "I know. It's not every day some guy tries to run you down."

"Did it feel as if he was aiming for us?" She tightened her grasp on his hand. "I want to think it was just an accident, but . . ."

"That's all it was. Probably some jerk having a really bad day, and too much to drink."

"I hope that's all it was."

So did Jake, but he had a horrible feeling it was more. A lot more. He'd been trying to remember the man at the coffee shop. He'd been vaguely aware of an older guy who came in shortly after Jake. He'd gotten his coffee, found a place in the corner, pulled out a tablet. Then Kaz had arrived, and nothing else mattered.

Had the guy left before them? Afterward? He didn't know. Hadn't cared. Then.

He pushed the thought aside to concentrate on now, on the fascinating woman across the table from him. He sipped his glass of port, nodding along with the music, caught in the rhythm, the perfect tempo filling the room, the warmth of her hand holding his. He squeezed her fingers. "Thank you, by the way. Jazz is supposed to be mood music. It's either the jazz or you, but I think my adrenaline overload is settling down." He smiled at Kaz and wished he could explain how much her touch meant. It hadn't been the music that had taken him away from the discordance of broken memories and past mistakes. No, it had been her gentle touch and her voice that opened the way, that allowed the soft notes to wrap around him like a silken cocoon.

The music, though? The music had him thinking of smooth sheets and soft skin—and tattoos.

Specifically, a monarch butterfly tattoo.

It was so close, hidden beneath the fuzzy sweater draped artfully off one slim shoulder. Did Kaz have any idea what an aphrodisiac her hidden butterfly was?

Would he ever have a chance to show her?

She was easily the most fascinating woman he'd ever met, as well as absolutely beautiful, and sitting close enough to touch.

The same gorgeous woman he'd be sharing a room with tonight.

Damn. He stared at the drink in front of him, a stemless wine glass that still held a few swallows of some of the best vintage port he'd ever tasted.

It had been Kaz's selection, another surprise. He'd been planning on a shot of good whiskey and had her tagged for a dirty martini or maybe a margarita, but she'd carefully studied the wine list before choosing a rich dark red port that went down like velvet.

Watching the subtle ripple in that long, smooth throat of hers after she took her first sip, held the wine in her mouth for a moment with a look of absolute bliss on her face, and then finally swallowed, had him hard as granite.

Just like that.

He wanted to blame it on the long day, the frustration and then the absolute relief after his search for the perfect model, the adrenaline from that speeding car almost hitting her, but he knew it was more. It was Kaz. This entire day, since the moment he'd first seen her, had been magic. Pure, unbelievable magic.

Even the chance to drag her to safety, to feel her trembling in his arms. It had scared the crap out of him, but at the same time, that fear they shared had forged a connection. Something beyond the mere act of pulling her out of harm's way.

Except that connection had a darker side. If the guy in the BMW was the same one sending him texts, the same one Kaz had seen earlier, he was putting Kaz in danger. But when she'd gone into the restroom while he waited for their port, he'd had a chance to check the text he'd gotten earlier, the one he'd told Kaz was business.

Same blocked number. Same greeting. Not nearly as friendly a message.

Hey, RJ. Where'd you go? Sneaky bastard, aren't you?

Who the hell was it? This text had come before the incident tonight, but he hadn't gotten another message. There was absolutely no reason for anyone out of his past to want to hurt Kaz. None at all.

If anyone tried, he'd do whatever it took to stop them. She was already that important to him. But what of Kaz? Was he right to think he saw it in her eyes, felt it in the touch of her hand, the quiet glances? The sense that she was thinking of him beyond the job, beyond the fact that she was here as his employee?

Except he wasn't the right man for her, and it wasn't the right time. It would never be the right time. There was no way in hell he'd ever be able to reconcile the pain in her past with the horrible mistakes in his.

The phone in his hip pocket vibrated. Kaz was watching the piano player, so Jake took a quick look at the text.

RJ, buddy . . . you need to be more careful crossing the street.

Fuck. It was him. Who the hell was that guy? He pictured the man's face, the way he'd glared at Jake, but he didn't have a clue who he was, or why the bastard was stalking him. At least this was proof Jake had been his target, not Kaz. Thank goodness.

He glanced at her, at the serene profile as she watched the guy at the piano. He couldn't let her know, didn't want to worry her, but he'd have to watch carefully. At least now he knew who to look for.

She looked his way again and smiled. He sipped his wine, looped his fingers in hers. She didn't pull away. He rubbed his thumb over the back of her hand and thought about the night ahead, about sharing a room.

If she was willing, they could at least enjoy their time together. Really enjoy it. The visuals alone had him hard. Again. He smiled.

She tilted her head and frowned. "What's so funny?"

"Sorry. Meandering thoughts." Scrambling for something that would explain his expression, he said, "I was thinking of your protective roommates. Please don't tell them we're sharing a room. They might hire a hit man."

She tilted her head and studied him, nodded, and then very seriously said, "That might explain the jerk who almost hit us. Do you think Mandy and Lola sent him?"

The laugh burst out of him without warning. Others in the quiet lounge turned and stared, but Kaz, obviously biting back a laugh, merely shrugged. "Just a thought," she said. Then she calmly took another sip of her port, but her eyes were twinkling.

Jake thought he could sit here all night just watching her, but then he glanced at his watch about the same time Kaz yawned. She covered her lips with her fingertips and blushed.

"I really don't want to leave," she said. "But unless you want a droopy-eyed model in the morning, I need to get some sleep."

He stood and held out a hand. "Bring your glass." He grabbed his own; it was still half full.

Kaz nodded, slung her handbag over her shoulder, and picked up her glass. Jake took her free hand and led her to the elevator. The ride to the second floor was silent.

He was thinking about the tattoo.

He wondered what was on Kaz's mind.

For whatever reason, tonight she was ultra-aware of the tiny silver loop through the hood of her clit. Of the way her cami lightly abraded the matching loops in her nipples and her waistband softly rubbed the one in her navel.

Everything was so sensitive, she could have sworn she felt the frickin' butterfly. Was that all he wanted to see?

How much was she willing to show?

She loved the way the silver looked against her honey-colored skin as much as she appreciated the added sensitivity. According to Wilhelm, the huge, scary-looking pussycat of a tattoo artist who'd done her butterfly tattoo and all her piercings, the nipple and clitoral hood piercings would take sex to a whole new level.

Whether that was true or not was still up for debate. The only ones who'd ever seen her body jewelry were her roommates—who were more appalled than appreciative.

Jake opened the door to their room and flipped on a single low light just beyond the entrance. "After you."

She shot him a quick smile, nervous now that they were actually here. She walked across the shadowed room to a small table and a pair of chairs by the balcony door.

Standing there, staring at the dark sky beyond the balcony, she took another sip of her port and then set the glass on the table. Jake turned on another light, equally dim, but closer to the table. He moved past her and closed the shades, enclosing the two of them within the privacy of their room.

Even with the lamps on, the walls were lost in shadow. Kaz took a deep breath and softly exhaled when she realized Jake was standing close beside her. She wasn't ready. Not yet.

"I really need a shower." She spoke quietly and glanced up, startled by the feral intensity in Jake's gaze. She should be frightened, at the very least a bit unsettled to see that blatant look of need on his face.

She wasn't. Instead, it made her hot. Her feminine muscles clenched and fluttered, an unfamiliar, visceral reaction to the man standing so close. She reached for her glass, took another swallow of her port. "I'll be quick. I don't want to disturb you if you want to get some sleep."

"I'll be awake." His features relaxed a bit, though the intensity was still there when he smiled at her. "I guess I'll have to wait until you're out to see that tattoo."

She nodded with a short, sharp jerk of her chin. Then she was almost scrambling to grab her small makeup kit with her toothbrush and a comb, and a soft cotton maxi that was as much sundress as nightgown. Quickly she locked herself inside the bathroom.

It wasn't until Kaz was getting out of the shower and finger-combing her short hair that she realized she hadn't thought to bring clean underwear in with her. The only way to show him the tattoo would be to pull the hem of the gown all the way up or just take the damned thing off.

It took her a few seconds more to realize she was hyperventilating, but she sucked in a deep breath, held it, felt her heart rate slow to normal, and then let it out.

This was a job. Jake was her employer. He'd hired her to model intimate body art. She'd signed the contract, and she needed the money. So what if he was funny and smart and drop-dead gorgeous? He was still her boss until the shoot was over.

Softly muttering, "This is just a job," she stepped out of the bathroom and into their beautiful hotel room that was more shadow than light.

Most women took forever in the shower. Kaz walked out of the steamy bathroom in less than ten minutes, wearing a body-hugging, ankle-length navy blue dress with her wet hair combed straight back from her face.

Jake almost choked on his last swallow of port.

She was outrageously gorgeous, even without makeup, her hair slicked back, and her body covered in a long clingy gown that hugged every dip and curve of her tall, slim frame before ending in an uneven hem just above her ankles.

He'd photographed enough beautiful women to know that the thing she wore would look like a sack on anyone else. On Kaz it merely emphasized the perfect symmetry of her long legs, wide shoulders, and small breasts.

She set her overnight bag on the floor beside the bed she'd chosen and glanced about nervously. Then she folded her arms across her chest almost defensively, and tilted her head to one side. "I know this gig is to show off body jewelry. I figure if I'm going to show you the tattoo, you might as well see what else I've got so you can figure out the shots you want, though I'll admit I'm not all that comfortable with at least one of them making a public debut."

She laughed, obviously nervous. It bothered him— they'd both been totally relaxed with one another since their trip began. He looked into those deep brown eyes and merely shrugged. "We can work up to the more intimate shots. Maybe once you feel more comfortable with me?"

This time, Kaz was the one who shrugged. Was she faking it as well as he was, or did she really see this as a professional request, not the personal one it had become?

At least for him.

She bent at the waist, reached down and grabbed the uneven hem of her gown, then tugged it over her head. There was nothing staged about the display. She didn't tease him as she quickly drew it up and over her body, but he reacted just the same.

Immediately, almost viciously, his dick was so hard he hurt, and his breath caught in his throat at the pure and simple beauty of her. But she'd stripped off the dress to show him the tattoo, so he forced himself to focus on the art.

It was amazing; the brilliant orange and black butterfly

looked alive, as if it might take flight, its wings carrying it away from the soft curves of her body.

Trapped in the color, in the moment, he moved closer and went to his knees to get a better look. "How long ago did you have this done?" He ran his fingers lightly over the glistening colors, almost expecting to come away with the dust from live wings on his fingertips. He glanced up in time to return her smile. "It looks brand-new."

"A little over a year ago, shortly after my seven-year-old sister died in a car accident. It took a number of sittings, but I did it for Jilly." She ran her fingers over the upper wing. "The piercings, too." She touched the silver loop in her navel and then brushed over the matching loops in both nipples.

Jake clasped his fingers into tight fists to keep from touching her breasts, following where Kaz had so casually stroked.

She glanced away, sighed softly, and then looked his way again. "She'd wanted so badly to get her ears pierced, but Dad said she wasn't old enough, that she had to wait until she was ten. I'd gotten mine done when I was seven, but Mom was still alive, and she wasn't as strict as Dad.

"I was nineteen when Mom died, but Jilly was still a baby, so I raised her. I always figured I was the closest she had to a mom, and I didn't agree with my father's decision. I'm so glad that I went against his wishes and took Jilly to get her ears pierced. I knew he'd get mad at me, not her, and he did, but he got over it. It wasn't long after that when she was killed. She was gone so quickly. Later, Dad thanked me for taking her when I did."

She shrugged. Then she touched the tiny turquoise stud in one ear. "We got matching earrings. It was my one act of rebellion, but Jilly loved those turquoise studs, almost as much as she loved breaking the rules with her big sister. She's buried with them."

Kaz turned closer to the bed and sat, throwing the gown across her lap, covering her lower half. But her breasts were bare, and the tiny silver loop in her navel winked at him in the low lamplight.

He'd never seen more perfect breasts in his life. High and firm and not at all large, they were absolutely right for her.

She smiled and glanced away. "Doing that, going against Dad and doing something totally special was a good lesson, a reminder to take whatever joy we can find in life whenever the opportunity exists."

Was she trying to tell him something? She cocked her head to one side and looked at Jake. Still on his knees, he sat back on his heels, touched his fingertip to the loop in her navel, and lightly tugged. "This wasn't for Jilly, was it?"

Shaking her head, she laughed softly. "No. Well, yes and no. Growing up without a mom turned Jilly into an old soul. She would talk about things most seven year olds aren't interested in, about dying, about the things that Mom might be missing here and what she'd found in heaven. Jilly wasn't all that sure that heaven really existed, so she made me promise that if anything ever happened to her, that I would still have a wonderful life, enough for both of us, and do lots of exciting, outrageous things so I could share them all with her."

She glanced away, eyes sparkling with tears, then a moment later she seemed to shake off the emotion. "Now I wonder if somehow she knew her time in this life would be cut short, but heaven or not, I truly believe I'll see her again. She was such a powerful force. I can't believe her energy died with her body. When Wilhelm pierced our ears, he was so kind and gentle with her that I went back to him for the tattoo. I told him what Jilly had said. He's the one who suggested the nipple and navel piercings. He

said they were outrageous enough that Jilly would probably love the fact I had them. She would have, too, mainly
because they were something that Dad wouldn't approve
of. She loved to push his buttons, but she adored him.
When he finally told Jilly that her earrings were pretty, she
was as thrilled that he liked them as she was that we'd broken the rules and gotten away with it."

She smiled at Jake. "My father still doesn't know about
the nipple or clit piercings. There are some things fathers
really don't want to know about their daughters."

"What made you decide to pierce your . . ."

She laughed when he hesitated. "My clit? I'm not
really sure. I'd broken up with my boyfriend shortly before Jilly died, and we'd had a less than satisfactory relationship, so when Wilhelm told me that piercing a
woman's clitoral hood was supposed to enhance sexual
pleasure, I . . ." She shrugged and glanced away. "I guess
I was on a roll."

Jake's gaze flicked to the soft folds of her gown covering the top of her thighs and his mouth went so dry it was
hard to swallow. He'd been so intent on the tattoo, he'd forgotten to look at that one when he'd had the chance.
Finally he managed to ask her, "Well? Does it?"

"I don't know." Her laughter was soft, sort of embarrassed. "The only ones who've even seen it are my roomies
and Wilhelm, and no, I'm not having sex with any of
them."

He chuckled, but his mind spun with her words. She'd
had them done over a year ago, and she hadn't had sex?
From her sexy look, the way she moved and walked, the
voice that promised so much more, he'd thought . . .

Obviously, he'd thought wrong.

He was constantly revising his original opinion of her,
and there was no doubt in Jake's mind—each revision
made her even more fascinating. More desirable. He raised

his head and gazed at her for a long moment. She was just so fucking sexy, yet the sweet, almost vulnerable look in her eyes was the thing that made it hard for him to breathe. "I'd like to at least see it," he said. His voice was so gravelly he cleared his throat. "There are some pieces designed for more intimate use, though I'm not really sure how we could photograph them in a way that would be acceptable for advertising."

It wasn't easy, keeping a straight face, talking about viewing the ring in her clit as if it were a business-related question. Not when he was on his knees, his hands resting on her firm thighs. Practically salivating with the need to use his lips and tongue, even his teeth on her.

She laughed out loud this time. "Well, I'm not really sure about advertising my clit, for what it's worth."

She was killing him here, and she didn't have a clue. "It could be worth quite a lot," he said, "but I don't know if they're quite ready to push the ad campaign in that direction." Then he laughed. "Screw the job, Kaz. I'd really like to see. Will you show me? Just for me."

"Ah. I should have known." She raised an eyebrow and gave him a look he wasn't quite sure how to read, but then she tugged the soft folds of her gown aside and tossed the garment on the bed.

He really hadn't thought he could get any harder. Obviously, he'd been wrong. He carefully adjusted his jeans as Kaz slowly parted her legs. The small silver hoop glistened at the top of her sex. She must've waxed recently, and her legs and pubic mound were smooth as satin. Color bloomed across her torso, and from the catch in her breathing, he was almost certain it was arousal and not modesty that had her skin so perfectly flushed.

He couldn't have kept his hands to himself if his life depended on it.

For a moment he thought that, just maybe, it did.

He reached out, tentatively, with the small finger on his right hand and slipped the very tip into the loop. Kaz gasped a soft, almost wondering, sound. It didn't stop him.

He would have known. When she parted her slim legs just a bit more, there couldn't have been a more obvious invitation.

He glanced up. Kaz was focused on his fingers. He tugged lightly on the silver hoop again, and ran the pad of his thumb between her labia, watching her face, not his hand. She was hot and slippery, moisture spilling at his touch.

She raised her head, focused on him, and the eye contact was a visceral wrenching of his soul. So much need in her eyes, in the soft hitch to her breath, the even softer yet totally unexpected whimper that passed between her lips.

She came across as strong, so self-confident, and yet . . .

He parted her thighs gently with both hands, leaned forward, and used the tip of his tongue to tug at the loop. This time there was no ignoring the soft moan of pleasure, the sharp scent of her arousal, the harsh catch in her breath. Giving up all pretense of merely looking, Jake slipped his palms beneath her thighs and shifted her long legs over his upper arms.

He grasped her hips, pulled her close, and twirled his tongue around the warm, silver loop. She lay back, opening herself to him, and he used his mouth, his lips and tongue, and even his teeth, nibbling at her, licking deep, and then sucking the tiny ring between his lips and gently tugging.

She was hot and wet and tasted of spice and woman. He lost himself in her flavors and textures, returning time and again to the tiny silver ring. He used two of his fingers, slowly thrusting in and out of her warm, wet sheath until her muscles clenched around them in a spasm of need.

He stopped breathing when he felt her body quicken.

She arched her hips, pressing her slick folds close against his mouth, but he kept his eyes open, watching her, mesmerized as she tugged at the small rings in her nipples with both hands, tasting her as she climaxed against his mouth. He kept licking and nipping, his fingers still thrusting in and out, dragging against the tight clench of rippling muscles. Her legs tightened around his back and she cried out again, arching her body forward, curling up and over his head, sobbing.

"It's too much. Too much . . . I can't . . ."

"You can." He stroked her gently with fingers and tongue, and within a few, short seconds she came once again. Licking slowly, softly, he brought her down. Calmed her with low words and gentle touches. Then he slowly stood and turned Kaz so that she was lying in the middle of her bed. The sheets were already drawn back. He lifted them to cover her feet, pulled the blankets up to cover her breasts.

She gazed up at him. He was so tall, so strong and yet beautiful, leaning over her as she lay there in the bed, her body finally still after an orgasm that had lasted forever. She'd never felt so replete, so completely enervated after sex, but she didn't think she'd ever come that hard in her life. Never before tonight.

But what of Jake? He'd made love to her with his mouth, with his hands. She'd felt so safe with him, but she knew he hadn't found any kind of release at all. It didn't seem right. Those thoughts were drifting slowly through her mind when he leaned over and kissed her, licking into her mouth. She sucked lightly on his tongue, loving the taste

of him. Loving the deep groan that vibrated against her
lips.

He kept kissing her, stroking her hair, murmuring soft
words against her lips. She wanted to give him pleasure,
but he kept kissing her so softly, touching her gently, his
strokes over her hair soothing, relaxing her completely. She
was vaguely aware of him tucking her in as if she were
just a child.

He was such an amazing man. Gentle, kind, funny. He'd
made her laugh, and good lord how he'd made her come.
She rolled over, thinking of all they'd done in the few short
hours since she'd met him, of the laughter they'd shared,
of the intimacy of his mouth on her. All for her. Amazing.
Recalling his touch, his gentleness, she drifted into that
space between waking and sleeping. Drifting . . .

Jake stood beside the bed, watching Kaz as she fell asleep.
He was hard and he wanted her, but not tonight. Tonight
she needed her sleep, but that didn't mean he had to sleep
alone.

Quietly he stripped down to his boxers, leaving his
clothes on the unused bed. Then he turned off the lights,
slid between the cool sheets, and gently pulled Kaz close
to his chest. She rolled over and buried her nose against
him, sighed, and snuggled trustingly into his arms.

Breathing in her scent, Jake held her close, absorbing
her warmth, remembering her taste. Still aroused, he welcomed the sense of need, the warm desire pulsing in his
groin. It made him feel close to Kaz, a woman he knew
intimately, and yet hardly at all.

He had no doubt that would change over the next few
days. For now, though?

Now, giving her pleasure had been a high all on its own.
She felt absolutely perfect in his arms. More perfect than

anyone he could recall. He tried to remember if there'd ever been another, and woman after woman passed through his thoughts until he fell asleep on old memories.

When he awoke before five the next morning, Kaz still held the place of honor among them all.

CHAPTER 5

"C'mon, sleepyhead. Time to rise and shine."

Slowly Kaz opened one eye and glared at the man leaning over her bed. "I knew that port was a bad idea." She groaned and rolled over on her belly, hiding her face in the pillow, mumbling into the soft down. "But damn, it was good."

"I agree, but it's almost five. We need to be on the site before six in order to get good morning light, and it's at least a fifteen minutes' drive to the vineyard. How much time do you need?"

"More than I've got." She rolled over and was at the point of tossing the covers back when she realized she was naked between the sheets. "Where's my . . . ?"

She clamped her mouth shut as the memory washed over her. His mouth between her legs, his tongue tugging at the loop on her clit, her climax.

Make that multiple climaxes.

Flushing hot and cold all over, she sat up with the sheet and blanket pulled almost to her chin. "Well. This is awkward," she said.

Smiling, Jake handed her the blue maxi dress and turned away. He grabbed a couple of his bags of camera gear and headed for the door. "I'm going to take my stuff down to the car, and we can make a quick stop for coffee and something light to eat on the way." With one hand on the door, he turned to her and asked, "Is that okay with you?"

"Um . . . yes. It's fine."

And then he was gone. Kaz scrambled out of bed and raced for the shower. She felt wonderful—energized as if she'd already had her coffee, though it had to be Jake. Jake and the memories that slammed full-blown into her brain as she rinsed off under the hot spray, washed and rinsed her hair with the products supplied by the hotel, and finger-combed the shaggy cut.

Drying off quickly, she put on a loose pair of silky black hip-hugging yoga pants, a snug tank top, and a warm sweatshirt, and then slipped her feet into comfortable old flip-flops. The clothes she'd brought specifically for the shoot were in a separate tote, one she'd left in Jake's SUV.

She thought of the morning ahead, imagined posing for Jake. Not for Jacob Lowell, photographer, but for Jake, the one who had shocked Kaz with the power of her sexual response. The one who had made her feel so much, on so many levels.

She'd never before posed for anyone she'd been intimate with, and it didn't get a whole lot more intimate than what she and the sexy Mr. Lowell had been up to.

Or at least what he'd been up to.

Unless he'd taken care of himself after she fell asleep, Jake hadn't gotten off at all. She sucked in a quick breath. How would he see her today? As a tease? As a woman he wanted, one he was well aware responded to him on way too many levels?

A shiver raced along her spine. She could do this. Definitely. After last night, she figured she could do just about anything.

She went to the balcony, opened the door, and stepped

outside. It was still fairly dark this early in the morning, with a light fog misting around the outdoor lamps, but it wasn't cold. She shut the door and tossed the rest of her belongings into her overnight bag, setting aside the tote with her makeup. That bag went next to her handbag on the end of the bed.

A knock on the door startled her. "I'm dressed," she said, but then she had to bite back the giggles. He'd seen everything there was to see last night. It was a little late for modesty.

Jake stepped into the room, looking pleased that she was ready to go. "Leave anything you don't need here," he said. "I got the room again for tonight. Reservations at the B and B start tomorrow night."

"What do I need?" She held up her makeup bag. "I left the tote with my clothes for the shoot in the car. Anything else you can think of?"

"You've still got the scarf?"

She pulled it out of her bag and handed it to him.

"I've got everything then, but yeah, take your makeup." He stared at her a moment. "Are you wearing makeup now?"

"No. Wasn't sure what look you wanted."

His sexy smile curled her toes. "You look pretty darned good right now." Then he tilted her chin with his fingertips, as if he was checking the different angles of her face, but he leaned close and kissed her before she realized what he was planning.

"You ready?"

She nodded, licking her lips. It was truly gratifying, the way his dark eyes tracked the sweep of her tongue across her upper lip.

After a moment he blinked, almost as if he'd lost track of what he was supposed to be doing.

That was sort of gratifying, too. She picked up her small

tote and handbag, and slung them over her shoulder. She loved how sexy he made her feel. Sexy and feminine.

Perfect for the job ahead.

"Let's go." He held the door open and stayed beside her as they walked to the elevator. The lobby was empty this early in the morning. Neither of them spoke as they reached the ground floor, exited, and went out the back door to the parking lot.

Jake unlocked the car and held the door for Kaz. She got in, tossed her bags on the floor, and buckled her seat belt as Jake took his seat behind the wheel. He turned and gazed at her a moment, his expression lost in shadow.

Then he leaned over and kissed her once again, a slow, lazy kiss that had her leaning into him, tugging against the safety belt to wrap her fingers around the back of his neck. His lips were firm and he tasted of minty toothpaste and memories of last night, and when he ended the kiss, Kaz sighed.

And then she blushed, because Jake must have heard her. She opened her eyes and looked directly into his. He stared at her for a long moment. Then he blinked and the spell seemed to snap, like a rubber band pulled past the breaking point.

"I've wanted to do that all morning." He smiled, drawing the edge of his finger across her cheek. "I wasn't sure if it would be as good as it was last night."

She tilted her head. "Well? Was it?"

Slowly he shook his head. "Nope."

She touched her fingers to her lips. They felt swollen and tender, and she thought it had felt pretty damned good to her, but Jake was still staring at her. She cocked one eyebrow in his direction.

"Not at all." Slowly he shook his head. "This was way better." The smile was back. "Damn."

With that enigmatic comment, he turned the key in the

ignition and backed out of the parking space. The sky was showing the first hints of light through the morning mist as they headed out on the two-lane road to the vineyard.

They made a quick stop for coffee and a couple of muffins on the way out of town. Kaz sipped from her cardboard cup and nibbled on the blueberry muffin, but even the beauty of dawn over the vineyards couldn't stop her from catching quick glances at the man sitting beside her.

She actually enjoyed watching him drive—there was confidence in everything Jake did, whether driving this winding two-lane road taking them out of town, or making love to her with so much skill her body still shivered at the memory.

What he'd done. What she wanted him to do more of.

The muscles between her legs clenched and she looked away. There wasn't much traffic this early in the morning. Field hands headed to work, and they passed a tractor hauling some sort of equipment that neither she nor Jake could identify.

"I dunno," he said. "Time machine maybe? It looks like something out of one of my old comic books."

"Comics?" She almost snorted her coffee. Typical man. She's remembering his tongue teasing the ring in her clit and he's thinking comic books.

He didn't say much—just drove the big SUV with one hand on the wheel, his left elbow propped on the window frame. They passed row after row of grapevines, stretching across the valley floor and crawling up the low hills on either side, even growing around stands of redwood trees filling some of the narrow canyons. They'd driven out of the fog within the first five or so miles, and now only tendrils of mist drifted through the rows of vines shadowing the small canyons and lying against the hillsides. Wildflowers grew along the roadside and in among the vines, masses of white daisies and tiny yellow flowers that glowed like gold dust in the growing light. She let her thoughts drift, caught entirely in the beauty around them.

Jake glanced at Kaz when they turned onto a narrow road and crossed the creek. She was watching the scenery, and all he wanted to do was watch her. He'd been hard when he woke beside her this morning, harder still when he'd stood next to the bed and watched her sleep in that brief moment before he'd had to awaken her. She'd been so beautiful, lying there on her back with one arm resting on the pillow above her head, the other bent across her chest, her fingers curled against her sleep-flushed cheek. He'd wanted to crawl back into bed with her, forget the shoot, forget anything but making love to her.

He'd even thought about taking her picture, but it was much too intimate a scene to photograph without her permission. Even so, his fingers had itched to grab his camera.

What would it be like to actually make love to her, to feel the tight clasp of her body around him? He doubted if sex just once would be enough to douse the fire that had simmered since he'd first seen her. They would definitely be doing it before this shoot ended—two people didn't have this kind of chemistry and just ignore it—but he'd have to be careful. It couldn't go beyond the job. When the job ended, so would whatever was happening between them.

He couldn't forget that.

The person sending him texts wouldn't let him forget. He'd checked his phone. Nothing since the one last night, but he'd been there, in town. Watching?

Or driving an older, black BMW?

He forced his mind back to the drive as they went north, up the long valley. The road here was narrower, the area more rustic, and this early in the day, the wildlife was active. The sky was growing light while he waited impatiently for a flock of wild turkeys to cross the road. He'd barely started moving again when Kaz touched his knee.

"Look." She pointed at a doe with two speckled fawns grazing between the vines, their earth-colored bodies almost lost in the wispy fog.

Jake glanced at them before speeding up. "We have to hurry," he said. "I don't want to miss the light."

They turned off onto a narrow dirt road and stopped in front of a locked gate. A sign was posted—TASTING ROOM CLOSED UNTIL APRIL 22. He dug a set of keys out of the center console.

Kaz held out her hand. "Do you want me to get that?"

"Thanks."

He handed the keys to her and she got out of the car. The air was chilly but completely still. Not a breath of wind ruffled her hair, and the soft purr of the engine, the morning chatter of birds, and the rush of a nearby creek were the only sounds she heard.

Kaz unlocked the gate, held it open for Jake to drive through, closed and locked it, and got back in the car. They drove past a house and a cottage. Both dark, the buildings looked empty in the early-morning shadows. A few hundred yards beyond the gate, they drove by a row of olive trees and Jake parked the Escalade to one side of them. An old barn lay nestled beneath a couple of huge oaks that had grown over and around the structure, but all was cloaked in shadow. Birds chirped—a counterpoint to the steady rush of the creek, hidden by thick trees and blackberry vines.

He pulled a couple of large bags out of the back of the SUV, then stopped a moment and concentrated on Kaz. "I'm really thinking we'll do more test shots than anything today, just to get a feel for the light, for what you're comfortable doing. There's no one here right now. The man and woman who own the cottage and house we passed are away this week—that's why the tasting room is closed—so we're assured of privacy. Are you going to be okay with some seminudity?"

"Yeah, as long as I don't have an audience other than the photographer. He's already seen all of it." She sounded cocky when she said it, but there was no hiding that delicious blush flowing over her throat and face. She quickly ducked her head as if she'd embarrassed herself, grabbed her makeup bag, and followed Jake to an area near the barn.

Her offhand comment stayed with him. He had seen all of it. He wanted to see it again, but the fact that she'd blushed while joking about it was actually kind of cute. She wasn't nearly as confident as she'd led him to believe. He was trying hard not to laugh as he headed straight for a weathered old wooden fence with dark green ivy growing up the post. It was surrounded by lush green grass and purple lupine, an ideal setting for the Intimate jewelry—and Kaz.

Then he opened a small, locked box. Curious, he waited for Kaz's expression when he lifted the lid. Smiled when she caught her breath. The pieces really were beautiful. Marc Reed had every right to be proud of himself—the designs were all his. Gold and silver rings and tiny barbells, some with diamonds and what looked like rubies or garnets, others studded with green emeralds, blue tanzanite, and purple amethysts, sparkled on a bed of black velvet.

A second box held intricate chokers and matching bracelets, a jeweled collar to wear around a woman's throat and across her shoulders in a stunning cape of color. Today, though, it was about the more delicate pieces, the ones for ears and nose, nipples and navel, and maybe a clitoral hood if he could figure out how to frame it to make an acceptable ad.

Jake lifted out a pair of tiny gold rings with deep purple amethyst stones. A fine gold chain ran between them. "Let's start with these."

"They're beautiful." She reached out and touched one of the stones as Jake held them for her appraisal. The gold looked so fragile in his big hands, the stones almost fluorescent in the growing daylight. "They'll definitely work."

She pulled her sweatshirt over her head and draped it on the fence, then stripped off her tank top. It landed on top of the sweatshirt. The air was cool and her nipples immediately beaded up—or maybe it was Jake's intense observation as she carefully took the jewelry from him, slipped the tiny rings out of her nipples, and replaced them with the Intimate designs.

The gold chain brushed the curve of her breasts, links so fine and light there was little more than a whisper of sensation, but it was a pretty effective whisper because her nipples tightened even more. She'd never worn anything like this, and there was something inherently sensual in the way the gold chain tickled and teased her sensitive skin. She was almost afraid to look at Jake, afraid he might be watching her as she inserted the hoops, but when she finally raised her head, he wasn't even paying attention.

Instead, he was going through his bag of props for the shoot. After a moment, he pulled out the scarf and threw it over his shoulder. "Is the grass too cold for you to lie down in it?" He pointed to a spot where the sun was just beginning to glimmer in the dew-covered grass.

"Here? With the flowers behind or beside me?"

A patch of tiny blue wildflowers blended into a raised edge of dark purple lupine.

"Right there." He pointed to a grassy patch between the

two colors. It was cool but not too cold, and the wisps of fog were already burning away from the hillsides.

"Yoga pants on or off?" She shrugged when he raised his head and looked at her. "I'm wearing a thong, but I'd be more comfortable with long pants on in the damp grass, if that's okay." She laughed. "Ya never know what sort of many-legged critter might be crawling about."

"Good point. The pants are low enough on your hips. They should be fine." He held up a light meter and took some quick readings. "I may have you tug the waistband down a bit, but I won't be shooting below the butterfly." He stared at her belly and shook his head. "Damn. I love that tat. It couldn't be any better."

She loved the fact that he was admiring the tattoo on her belly, and not her bare breasts. Somehow that took the sexual angle out of being naked with a man who'd had his mouth between her legs last night. Today he was totally professional.

He dragged the scarf off his shoulder, shook it out, and draped it around the back of her neck and over her right shoulder, studied it a minute, and then looped it down to circle her left hip. The yoga pants rode low enough and the scarf disguised what little of the waistband might have shown. Jake fiddled with the silk, made a few more adjustments, and then stepped back.

Kaz found a position she knew she could hold while Jake continued setting the scene. The scarf as much as his purely professional touch made her feel sexy; the way the colors swirled and blended perfectly into the blue and purple wildflowers gave the setting a truly sensual vibe. She wondered if Jake had imagined she would feel this way when he picked it out.

She glanced at him and smiled. She hadn't expected to feel like this, just watching Jake work. The fact that there was nothing of the lover from the night before made everything he did sexy. He'd slipped so easily, so quickly into his professional persona that Kaz found herself doing the same. She held the position he set her in, turned her head, tilted her chin.

Yet her mind was in another world altogether, as if they shared an explicit secret. Yes, this was a job and they were both professionals, but she knew what he could do with those hands. That mouth. It kept her body humming, aroused.

He stepped back and studied her, reached forward and fluffed her hair back from her face. He frowned, reached into her makeup kit and grabbed a lip gloss, opened it and checked the color. Leaning closer, he held the tip in front of her mouth, waiting. She pursed and then parted her lips, remembering his kiss this morning. His throat rippled as he swallowed, and without even asking, she knew he was thinking of that same kiss as he brushed the slightest hint of shimmer over her lips.

He carefully smoothed the gloss with a callused fingertip. Kaz sensed the slightest hint of a tremor in his touch. Shivering in response, knocked entirely out of professional mode by that simple contact, she raised her eyes, curious to see if any of what she felt showed in Jake's expression. When she glanced at him, Jake had moved on to adjust the scarf near her breast. He was working. This was his job. The sensuality of the scene, the arousal she'd imagined him feeling, it was all in her head.

She forced herself back into her role as startling rays of sunlight broke over the hilltops and Jake took his first shots. He had her add a matching ring to her navel, another fine length of gold chain. He turned her to face into the first full flash of light and caught the shadow of the chain on her flat belly, with the gold glistening across a brilliant butterfly wing.

So quickly she slipped out of her fantasies and into his

rhythm, the quiet suggestions for poses, the simple requests for different expressions, the adjustment of the chains, changes in jewelry.

It was a dance. A dance between Kaz and the camera. For now, at least, Jake ceased to exist.

As Jake adjusted the scarf just above the dark areola of her right breast, he glanced at the sunlight streaming through the trees east of them. "We're not going to have this morning light much longer. Let's go with these." He handed the diamond earrings to her. Before she had time to do more than take them, he was gently switching out the amethysts in her nipples, removing the dark purple stones and replacing them with diamond-studded rings.

Her skin flushed when her nipples tightened, responding to his touch, but Jake seemed oblivious, working quickly as he added finely wrought chains, connecting her nipples and navel, his gentle touch entirely professional.

Her hands were shaking as she removed the amethyst earrings and added the diamonds. Once the jewels were in place, he posed her as if she were a piece of furniture, positioning her torso, tilting her head, all to catch the sun glinting through the multifaceted stones.

How did he do it? Stay so totally focused on the job, while she felt rattled from his oh so distant yet terribly intimate touch?

She waited for the click of the camera, but when she raised her head to see why he wasn't shooting, she caught him staring at her, the camera held loosely in his hands. His lips were parted, the expression on his face one of absolute need, but then he blinked, gave her a lopsided smile, and reached out to adjust the scarf over her shoulder.

Good. He looked like a little kid, caught with his hand in the cookie jar. She was really glad she wasn't the only one struggling to hang on to professional behavior.

It made it easier to keep working, to slide into the zone and concentrate on her poses.

The sun moved higher and Kaz reclined in the warm grass, teasing her lips with wildflowers as Jake took more pictures, this time focusing on tiny golden barbells studded with rubies, another set with emeralds, a matched set for ears and breasts. Another for her navel.

He paused at one point and brushed some soft blush across her cheekbones and freshened her lip gloss, but he didn't ask her to add more makeup.

Kaz had never been all that comfortable with the semi-nudity that the modeling business often required, but as the morning wore on, the shots became more intimate. He touched her breasts, her nipples, easily changing the jewels for her, adding the chains. For a group of shots he added a chain to her own silver clit ring, hiding her labia and the ring itself beneath the drape of the scarf, but allowing the chain to loop sinuously over her abdomen before disappearing beneath the folds of silk. He'd told her he wanted a warm, sensual feel to the pictures, but he didn't want to lose the edge, either.

That particular series, with Kaz standing in partial shadows that hid the color but not the shape of her breasts, her head bowed, and gossamer chains shimmering in the sunlight, disappearing beneath the silk scarf draped around her hips, straddled a very fine line of what most publications would allow.

Jake promised filters if any of them went to print.

Piercings were, by their very nature, dark and edgy, but he left it to Kaz to interpret the vision he'd tried to paint for her. Giving her that freedom had her finding new ways to showcase the jewelry that she might not have agreed to, had they been Jake's ideas.

She stripped down to jewels and a pale peach thong at Jake's request. Then she took it a step further. When she stretched her leg along the top board of the old fence, Jake paused.

"How did you know that would work so well? Damn."

She tilted her head. "In what way? Tell me what you like—that helps me."

"Okay—here, you're working the contrasts of boards weathered almost black against smooth, honey-toned skin. Leaning forward like that lets the chains catch the light. Perfect."

He took a number of shots, stopped, looked around, and pointed toward a huge valley oak. Wearing nothing but the peach thong and the scarf around her neck, Kaz walked through the vineyard and positioned herself against the rough trunk. Jake tilted her face just enough that her features were lost in shadow, the sun glinting off the earring, the chains, and the loop in her nostril.

He followed her lead when she went into the vineyard and gathered trailing vines against her bare breasts, with only the jewels peeking out. The fact that he left so much of it up to Kaz had her pushing her personal boundaries beyond anything she'd ever done. The more pictures he took, the more comfortable she grew. His fingers lovingly worked the camera, and she thought about what those fingers had done to her last night, how they'd made her cry out in absolute uninhibited pleasure.

Kaz was almost certain she would do anything he asked.

She was vaguely aware of the increasing sounds of traffic on the main road across the valley, the voices of men working in the fields on the far side of the creek, but here all was quiet, all was private, and the isolation felt complete.

No one but Kaz and her photographer.

Kaz Kazanov and Jacob Lowell, separated by the lens of the camera, drawn together by the changes of jewelry, the familiarity of this man she'd only met the day before, a man who'd had his mouth between her thighs just last night, his tongue teasing the ring in her clit, his fingers plunging deep inside her. He'd taken her to unimaginable heights of pleasure, and now he was helping her switch out the jewels in her nipples, the rings in her navel, the studs in her ears.

She almost laughed as she imagined trying to explain the day to Lola and Mandy.

At one point she was bedecked in chains—fine gold mesh running between her nipples and creating a triangle pattern of finely wrought gold from breast to breast, from nipples to navel. A crown of jewels circling her head like a multihued headband, a gold chain draped from a ring in her nostril, across her cheek to her ear. She thought of adding another to the ring in her clit, but she wasn't ready.

They didn't speak very much. Occasionally Jake gave her a direction, but mostly she merely did what felt right. She stretched and turned and bent, pulled the scarf across her lips, over her breasts, along her rib cage, always keeping the jewelry in mind, the drape of the chains, the shimmer of stones.

Her growing arousal was a subtle thing, affecting the shots, the poses she took. Each move felt like a choreographed step in a dance, a move to the right, then one to the left, following directions only she heard, not even sure if they came from Jake or if they were all a part of her own internal rhythm, patterns of her own design.

Her mind wandered as she worked, her body moving instinctively, her thoughts straying to the night before, to the beautiful man making love to her with those same hands that held the camera, that mobile mouth, lips pursed in concentration now as he focused on the scene he'd helped her set, lips that had taken her to heights she'd only imagined.

Her arousal spiked and she moved in a more sinuous pattern, arching her hips, thrusting her breasts forward. The steady sound of the camera as Jake recorded every twist and turn made her impossibly wet.

It hadn't been her intention when they'd begun the shoot, but Kaz realized she'd been subtly seducing him throughout the morning. Did he realize what she'd only now discovered?

She thought of what he saw, physically separated from her by the lens, and she arched her back, setting the scene for him as her mind filled with that first image of Jake when she'd awakened this morning—him standing so tall and strong beside the bed. He'd already been dressed, and all she'd wanted was for him to take off his clothes and crawl back in with her.

She'd noticed before they left that only one bed had been slept in, and it was hers. She hadn't even sensed him beside her during the night, but he'd been there.

"What are you thinking right now? I love the look you've got." He laughed and she heard the whir of the camera.

She fluttered her eyelashes. "I'm not going to tell." But tonight she'd make sure she knew exactly where he slept.

"I see."

The rapid click of the camera continued. He was shooting high speed on his digital, and she knew that every flicker of her eyes, every subtle twitch of expression was recording. She licked her lips. Pouted.

Click. Clickclickclick.

Right now, she was almost certain she wanted him in her bed, but would she feel the same later, after the shoot was over for the day? After the jewels were put away, the cameras stowed, when they'd be dealing with each other once again in what she thought of as the "real world"?

She ran her fingers across her chest, tangled them in the

chains linking from a diamond-studded slave collar to her breasts. The real world could wait.

Posing was, in so many ways, a fantasy. She projected the fantasy that the marketing people wanted for their product. Jake wasn't seeing the real Kaz. He was seeing the product through the lenses of his cameras, seeing Kaz as the display for those products. He needed her to be alluring, to project a look that would make someone seeing the ad want to buy the jewelry.

Her nipples ached, her breasts felt heavy and tender, and the tender skin of her inner thighs felt irritated and sore. Were the rough boards of the fence where she'd posed to blame?

No, it wasn't the fence at all. She brought her memories into focus and realized Jake hadn't shaved last night. She'd ended up with razor burn!

She'd never had razor burn between her thighs before.

Her inner muscles clenched in a quick spasm of need.

"I like that. More."

She certainly hoped he meant her seductive expression and not her rippling vaginal muscles. Fighting a laugh, she forced her thoughts away from Jake, away from graphic memories of last night, but it didn't help. Her body was suffused with heat, with too much sensation. She bit back a moan as Jake leaned close and adjusted the chain dangling between her nipples. His knuckles brushed the underside of her breast, his breath warmed her throat. The pads of his fingers were rough, and though she didn't think he was stroking her sensitive skin on purpose, every touch as he adjusted the jewelry sent a shock of sensation straight to her clit.

When he tugged the chains connecting her nipples, she might as well have had one of the chains attached to the tiny silver ring between her legs.

He backed away with a soft caress that trailed over the silky skin at the underside of her breast and she caught herself leaning into his touch.

His head jerked up, his gaze trapped hers, as if he'd caught himself doing something unexpected. As if he wondered what her reaction would be.

Her breath caught in her throat, her gaze locked with Jake's. Time stopped—a heartbeat, a year—and Kaz slowly turned her head away, slipped into another pose.

One where she wasn't looking into those darkly curious eyes.

CHAPTER 6

A moment later it happened again. This time, his startled reaction when the back of his hand brushed her aroused nipple barely concealed beneath the silk scarf, Kaz had a feeling he'd just made the same connection she had—that she was practically naked and he'd been touching her intimately all morning long.

They'd sure named this jewelry right. Intimate. She and Jake had been intimate for hours, and they still had hours to go. She took a deep breath and scrambled her thoughts. She had to think about something, anything but the man behind the lens.

The man whose gentle fingers were carefully adjusting the drape of gold chains beneath her breasts.

She snapped up the first nonsexual thought that came to mind.

Jilly.

She hadn't started modeling until after her baby sister died. What would Jilly think of her big sister now? Jilly would love Jake and his wonderful sense of humor. She'd probably make typical little kid gagging noises over the nitty-gritty aspects of modeling, though she would jump all over the chance to wear fancy jewelry or fashionable clothes.

Jilly had epitomized "girly-girl," and she would have had a true appreciation for a smart, handsome, funny guy like Jake.

Except Jilly would never know him.

She glanced at Jake, focusing on the good times with Jilly, smiling into the lens and probably ruining the shot.

"I like that smile," he said.

She breathed a soft sigh as he kept snapping pictures. Relaxing further, she continued the slow but steady movements that would give him more choices, more angles with the jewelry.

Then Jake's voice gently interrupted her thoughts. He'd been leaving the poses up to Kaz, but his words weren't at all jarring or intrusive. Instead, they heightened the connection, the sense that she was seducing the man behind the camera. Seducing him, and he didn't even know it.

"Brush your fingers over your right breast. Just the fingertips. Yeah. That's it." His whispered instructions reminded her of her yoga instructor's words as he led them into meditation, soft enough to let her stay within her own little world yet directing her thoughts all the same. She did as Jake requested, brushing her fingers across her breast, trailing them down the chain, circling her navel.

"The gold is warm from the heat of your body. From the sun. What does it make you think? What would you like your lover to do with those chains?"

His soft words had her concentrating on the sensual feel of the metal, imagining the source of the slight tension when she tugged on the chains and stimulated her nipples was Jake. He was pulling the chains, rolling her nipples between his fingers. She'd been holding the sound of the creek in her mind, but now she imagined the sensual rhythm of the music they'd listened to last night. It helped her find the rhythm she needed to create the dark and edgy, yet sensual look Jake wanted.

Unfortunately, it was much too easy to think of this job in sensual terms, and once again she was back there, remembering last night. Remembering the way it felt when Jake teased the ring on her clit with his tongue, when he'd filled her with those beautiful, long fingers of his.

She wanted more of him. She wanted to feel his body covering hers, wanted the stretch and sting of his cock thrusting deep, filling her. It had been so long since she'd been with a man, and never had there been a partner as attractive, as much fun, as Jake. Or as sexy.

She really should tell Wilhelm that he was right. That yes, the tiny ring in her clit definitely increased sexual pleasure, but the thought of going back to the big, burly tattoo artist and piercing specialist, admitting to him just how right he'd been, made her blush.

Damn. She was so fucking perfect. The whispered suggestions he'd given her had upped the sensual feel of the pictures, as if she'd taken his instructions and internalized them. Jake focused once again, catching the line of her jaw, the curve of her breast and the taut nipple pierced with a ring of yellow gold set with blue tanzanite.

A dark rose spread over her honey-colored skin. Jake snapped a few quick shots, pointed the lens down, and laughed out loud. "Okay," he said. "What are you thinking?"

Blinking, she stared at him as if he'd hauled her out of a daydream. "Thinking? Why?"

"Because you just blushed the most delicious shade of rose. It's going to give the pictures an entirely new feel. I love it. So spill. What was going through that devious brain of yours? I want to know so I can get it back."

She blushed even darker, the deep rose creeping over her skin and across her breasts. If he didn't know better, he'd think she was sexually aroused, but she seemed much too professional to let her mind go that far away from the job at hand. Even so, he remembered that color from last night.

"That's even better," he said, and he took more shots.

Kaz dipped her head. She pulled her knees close to her chest and wrapped her arms around them, until everything he wanted pictures of was completely hidden.

Then she totally shocked him. "Actually, I was thinking of last night." She raised her head, and the intensity of her gaze had him hard in an instant.

He'd been thinking of last night since . . . well, since last night. He lowered the camera. "You were?"

She nodded, and sat up a little straighter.

"What were you thinking?"

Kaz shrugged, and he clutched the camera to keep his hands to himself. The scarf had fallen away from her breasts; her nipples were flushed from the changes in jewelry and from the warmth of the sunlight spilling over the meadow.

And maybe from memories? If she felt anything like he did, her mind didn't need to be engaged for her body to recall sensation. To recall and react.

He was certainly reacting. "You can't stop there," he said, fully aware his voice had gone deeper, huskier. "It's not fair to leave me hanging."

She tilted her head and smiled at him, but her cheeks were still rosy. "I was thinking that Wilhelm was right. The little ring on my clit really does enhance sexual pleasure."

"Really?" He set the camera down. It had connected them all morning, but it had shielded them as well. Now that shield was gone. Without the lens between them, it was Kaz and Jake, and the connection between them felt as intimate now as it had in that hotel room last night.

He focused on her lips. Was she remembering when

he'd slipped the tip of his tongue into the ring in her clit? That was something he hadn't been able to get out of his mind. He'd never been so turned on in his life as when he'd tugged at that tiny silver ring oh so gently with his tongue.

He was never again going to find anything as sexy as that ring. He'd nibbled and nipped, but the ring gave him a focus, something quite literally to hang on to. Her reactions had been so sensual, so deeply erotic that he couldn't even think of her now without getting hard.

Hell, had there been a time since he'd met her that he hadn't been aroused? "What did it feel like?" He went down on one knee in front of her, putting himself at eye level. "I've never been with a woman before who was pierced the way you are. I was so afraid of hurting you."

"Oh, God." Laughing, Kaz covered her eyes with her hand and looked down. "It was amazing. Sparks of sensation. I can't even explain it, but somehow, when you tugged on the ring, I felt pulses deep inside."

She glanced up, and the blush was back. "It felt like the ring in my clit was a conduit sending energy inside me, just a delicious pulse of heat." The blush spread across her cheeks.

Jake could barely draw a breath, so focused on Kaz he forgot the simple things like breathing. Then she licked her lips, and he almost choked.

Good Lord, the pheromones surrounding them must be off the charts. Her pupils narrowed, and he figured his were probably slits right now, but all he could really focus on was her mouth.

She nibbled at her lower lip. Jake blinked slowly, mesmerized by her straight, white teeth teasing at the fullness of that perfectly shaped lip.

The artery at the side of his neck throbbed, beating a steady tattoo. He swallowed, fully aware that Kaz was watching the ripple of muscles along his throat. Something in her heated stare had him reining in his growing arousal, the pounding desire that wound his entire body tight, curled his fingers into fists.

He glanced away and took a deep breath. Let it out, drew in another, and felt his muscles begin to relax. His heart slowed its rapid cadence, as slowly but steadily he regained control.

When he looked at Kaz again, she'd also shuttered the desire that must have been raging through her body, racing at breakneck speed with his.

When he felt as if he could make a coherent statement, Jake chose not to comment on what she'd said. "You ready for a break?"

Kaz blinked. Then she laughed. "Oh. Sorry." Blushing, she added, "I sort of go into my own little zone during a shoot. I totally lose track of everything but the job. I mean, I'm thinking of all kinds of stuff, but it keeps me in the moment, in whatever mood the photographer is looking for." She sucked in her lips and then blew them out, laughing. "Unfortunately, it also takes me a while to come back, because I think I'm totally disconnected from reality."

He stared at her a moment, and he knew he probably shouldn't say anything, but he really couldn't help himself. "Is that what you call it? A zone?" Personally he thought it was more like a lesson in seduction.

She straightened her shoulders and actually glared at him. "Yeah," she said. "I do. What time is it?"

"Almost noon. I'm starving."

She seemed to relax, and this time her smile was as easy as if that momentary lapse hadn't occurred. "I had no idea. No wonder I have to pee so bad!" Her eyes went wide and Kaz slapped her hand over her mouth. "Oops. Sorry." Laughing out loud, she sat up and stretched. "For what it's worth, there are no filters in my zone. My mouth speaks without connecting to my brain."

Jake stood and held out a hand. Whatever had just happened between them was obviously over, but he wasn't the only one who had consciously shut it down. "No problem. There are actually modern restroom facilities inside. They use the barn for wine tastings on occasion, and Marc has quarters upstairs for when he's in town. C'mon. I'll show you where."

She tossed the scarf over her neck with the ends hanging down over her breasts to cover herself, and pulled the soft yoga pants back on, but it was so private out here, she didn't appear to be worried about putting her top back on. What was the point? He was the only one who would see her, and he'd spent all morning up close and personal with her breasts.

With luck, she wouldn't know how hard it had been for him to act professionally. He certainly hadn't been thinking like a pro, but he kept up the act as he casually took her hand and led her across the grass to the old barn. She followed quietly.

Knowing exactly how she looked, there was no way in hell he could turn and actually watch her. Bare-breasted, barefoot, bedecked in jewels and gold chains and swathed in silk, with those soft black yoga pants riding low on her slim hips, she was every man's wet dream.

She was most certainly his.

He'd always been good at connecting with models, at least on some level. He was damned good at his job, but he'd never connected with anyone, on or off the job, the way he had with Kaz.

If he didn't like her so much, he'd be scared to death of her, of what she could do to him. Thank God she wasn't looking for a serious affair any more than he was. She'd said this wasn't the right time for a relationship, that there was too much on her plate to even think of putting out the effort to forge any kind of permanent bond with a man.

She hadn't said anything against having fun with someone she liked, though. Why couldn't the two of them explore what this thing was that seemed to be growing between them? Explore it and enjoy it, at least while they were working together on the shoot.

They still had three nights of hotel and B and B reservations. Three more days of photos in some of the most beautiful, romantic country he'd ever seen. Three nights and three days to explore the warm sense of intimacy growing between them, what had to be purely sexual need that was keeping his body strung taut.

They were both adults, both aware of the pleasures and the pitfalls to be had in a straight-up sexual affair. But would she be interested?

He glanced over his shoulder and knew that if he didn't kiss her soon he was going to explode. "Through there," he said, and almost laughed when she jumped. Obviously, she was daydreaming as much as he was.

Kaz blushed. Again. Usually, her daydreams and fantasies took her a million miles away, but right now they had her focused on the rough calluses of Jake's palm, the way his fingers felt wrapped around hers.

The way they'd felt stroking between her legs last night, across her breasts today.

She hadn't realized they'd already reached the barn. She paused at the door he held for her, and smiled.

His answering smile told her he knew she'd been totally lost in her thoughts. As long as he had no idea what those thoughts were, she was good to go.

"When I called Marc yesterday," he said, "to tell him I'd found the perfect model . . ."

She turned and pointed her forefinger at her chest. "And that would be me, of course."

"Of course. Who else?" He laughed as he followed her

into the barn. "Anyway, now that we have that settled,
Marc said he'd make sure there was something for our
lunch in the refrigerator. If not, we can make a quick run
back to that little store we passed. It's got a terrific deli."

"Sounds good," she said. Then she escaped into the restroom he pointed out to her.

Jake watched the closed door for a moment, not even
trying to wipe the stupid grin off his face. Then he went
behind the counter, where there was a good-sized refrigerator, big enough to handle everything for the events held
out here at the vineyard.

This had once been a dairy barn. The inside had all
been redone and painted to look old and weathered, but
obviously everything except the shell of the structure was
new. To the right of the main door were a leather couch,
comfortable chairs, and small tables. Four stalls on the
back wall were filled with fresh straw with colorful wo-
ven horse blankets thrown over the short walls between
them. All very upscale, yet traditionally comfortable and
colorful.

To the left of the door was a complete kitchen with a
long granite counter for simple food preparation and that
well-stocked refrigerator Marc had mentioned. It was filled
with packaged meats, cheeses and dips, a bag of fresh veg-
gies, and chilled fruit juice. More than enough to keep
them going for a few more hours. A matching granite bar
opposite the counter was set up for wine tasting.

He washed his hands at the huge stainless sink, and by
the time Kaz came out of the bathroom a few minutes later,
he had a feast sitting on the bar.

Kaz had washed her face and finger-combed her dark
hair back from her eyes, and he knew he needed more
shots of her like this, almost starkly bare, but undeniably
beautiful. Without makeup of any kind, she would showcase

the jewelry with an entirely different look from the one she had earlier, when her hair had been falling loose and tousled around her face.

She still wore the jewels in her earlobes and the stud in her left nostril, but she'd wrapped the scarf around her back, crossed it over her breasts and tied it behind her neck. It covered her breasts completely, but the fine gold chains hung beneath the loosely tied scarf, swinging gently against her flat belly as she walked.

The butterfly tattoo shimmered with every step she took.

Jake bit back a groan. Damn. Was she trying to kill him? Ignoring his raging libido, he pulled one of the tall stools out from under the counter for her.

"Eat something. I don't want you keeling over from starvation."

She gave him a bright smile as she settled herself on the stool. "Wow. This looks wonderful." Then she grinned and fluttered her eyelashes. "And he cooks, too!"

He chuckled and grabbed paper plates for each of them. "Actually, he can slice cheese, make cute little piles of lunch meat, and put prepared stuff on a plate. That's about the extent of my culinary talent."

She swept a sprig of fresh broccoli through a tub of creamy dressing. "Works for me," she said, and popped it into her mouth.

Jake watched her chewing for a moment, realized he was concentrating on her lips, and had to look away. His feelings were all over the map, none of them familiar, or even remotely comfortable. He really needed to get a grip on whatever the hell was happening.

"I'm getting some great stuff today, more than I expected and way beyond test shots. I think tomorrow we'll do some pictures in town. I want to work on the more visible pieces, emphasize the ones in your navel, nostril, and ears. We'll do the more traditional designs as well—collars, necklaces, wrist and ankle bracelets. They're designed to pair up with the more personal jewelry. I'm thinking we could use places around the plaza, maybe in front of some of the local businesses. Then I want to come back out here another day, too. Maybe something down at the creek. It's really pretty this time of year."

"I like the idea of shooting in town, though I am not doing any breast or clit ring shots in public." Then she laughed.

He waggled his eyebrows. "Even if I ply you with really good wine?"

"Especially then." She covered her eyes with her hand and shook her head, laughing. "It's scary even to think about it."

"Okay." Sighing dramatically, he added, "I promise." His mind was suddenly filled with mental images of that tiny silver ring on the hood of her clit, and the things he wanted to do with it. Damn. He had to look away.

His gaze rested on a window, one that Marc had just had installed, though it was designed to look old-fashioned. Softly tinted glass with dark grillwork made it look as if it had small, individual square panes—old-fashioned in appearance, but the latest in double-paned, shatter-resistant glass.

Something moved, a dark shadow at the lower corner. Jake slowly turned away. "Stay here," he said, speaking softly. "Don't move, don't react, but I want to check on something."

He leaned close and whispered, "Something moved at the window. I'll only take a minute. Hopefully it's just a shadow from the trees, but I want to be sure."

Kaz flashed him a bright smile. "Okay," she said. Then her smile wavered. "If there's someone out there, don't play hero, okay?"

"I promise." Then he walked toward the restroom and slipped around a corner where he knew he'd be out of sight of anyone looking through the window. He took a last glance at Kaz, who went on eating as if nothing was going on. She didn't know about the texts and he wasn't about to tell her, but he hadn't been able to get those creepy messages out of his mind.

He was almost certain he'd seen a face at the window.

Quietly, Jake unlocked the small back door that opened to an area behind the barn. He glanced around and slipped through the door. There was no one near the window. He checked for footprints, but the area under the window was covered with fresh gravel. He circled the entire barn. Nothing appeared out of place, but he couldn't shake the feeling someone was out here.

He circled around to the door again, and noticed a large branch near the side of the barn. Shadows danced across the glass. He watched the shifting shadows for a moment, satisfied that was all he'd seen, but before he went back inside, he checked his messages.

Nothing new since last night. He slipped the phone back in his pocket.

His imagination was obviously a bit overactive, but it was probably his inner caveman asserting himself. After all, he had a beautiful, half-naked woman to protect. Chuckling, feeling sort of silly over his reaction to an imagined danger, he stopped beside Kaz and shrugged. "Just the shadow from a branch. Sorry to interrupt your lunch."

"It's okay," she said. "Actually, I think it's pretty cool. It makes me a lot more comfortable, knowing you're watching out for me."

But was he? Really? He slid onto the stool beside hers and they bumped shoulders like a couple of old friends, but he couldn't stop second-guessing his decision not to tell her about the messages. This was his past coming back to haunt him, his future being threatened, not hers. He didn't want to worry Kaz about something that was all about him, about the horrible things he'd done, but as long as they were together on this job, he needed to watch out for her.

No way in hell was he going to relax.

Just in case.

CHAPTER 7

"If I eat another bite, you're going to need to cover my stomach for the shots." Kaz patted her flat belly, pushed back from the counter, and picked up her plate and Jake's.

"We can't have that." He grabbed the tray of munchies and loaded everything onto a smaller plate, wrapped it up, and stuck it back in the refrigerator, while Kaz dumped the used paper plates in the trash and wiped off the counter.

She tossed the towel to Jake, he draped it over the counter with a melodramatic twirl, and they went outside. She hid her feelings well—no way was she going to admit that Jake had absolutely shocked her, that something totally mundane had seemed so spectacular. The two of them had just completed the cleanup like they'd been together forever. Her old boyfriend, the jerk, hadn't raised a finger to help with anything, and like an idiot, she'd waited on him. She'd been stupid. Just stupid.

Jake stopped just outside the door with his hands on his hips, staring at the wildly overgrown riparian area along the creek. The sun was high in the sky, the day already warmer than Kaz had expected, but she was used to San Francisco's cool ocean breezes and heavy morning fog.

Here, the fog had burned off shortly after sunrise, and

the brilliant shadows and contrasts had faded away as the sun moved higher in the sky. The colors in the vineyard and along the hillsides weren't nearly as intense as they'd been all morning, and the once vivid blue sky now had a hazy, dusty look.

Jake turned and slowly surveyed the area. His gaze stopped when it landed on Kaz. He stared at her a moment, one hand on his hip, the other rubbing the back of his neck, then he let out a deep breath. "Why don't you get a shirt and some shoes on. Let's take a look at the creek, see if there's anything there we can use as a backdrop. The light's not very good right now, but I'm not ready to leave. I want to hang around long enough to see what the afternoon shadows look like."

"Okay." She carefully removed the silk scarf, folded it, and stuck it in the side pocket of Jake's camera bag. "I need to take the jewelry off, too. I don't want to snag it on anything."

"Ouch." He smiled at her, and she felt it right behind her breastbone, that punch to the solar plexus that hinted she might be in more trouble than she'd thought. She had to look away as he grabbed the box he'd brought the jewelry in, so she concentrated on carefully removing the gold rings set with blue tanzanite from her nipples. The chains fell loose, still attached to the ring in her navel.

Kaz handed the nipple rings to Jake and he cleaned each one carefully in alcohol before putting them away. She was actually sorry he hadn't offered to help her remove them. She shivered, remembering the sensual sweep of his large, rough hands brushing against the sensitive underside of her breast, the sensation of those surprisingly gentle fingers removing the rings from her nipples.

Most of his assistance during the shoot had been as impersonal as if she'd been nothing more than a store mannequin, but she'd been fascinated by the way he'd handled both her and the tiny jeweled pieces and chains almost as fine as spider's silk with such care. He'd touched her so gently, with such sensitivity, that it was truly appealing.

Probably too appealing. In fact, it had been terribly arousing, if she'd only admit the truth, and his professional manner had slipped a couple of times as well. She really had to stop lying to herself.

The last thing she wanted to do was send him mixed signals. It was hard, though. He was just so damned sexy behind the camera. She couldn't remember this kind of on-going, simmering arousal with any other man. Curiosity alone had her wanting to pursue that feeling, to see where it might lead.

Behind the camera . . . of course. He probably acted this way with all his models. He wanted that sexy vibe? He knew exactly how to bring it out during the sessions. Why hadn't she realized that? He'd told her when they met in the coffee shop that relationships, even dating, weren't on his schedule—in fact, they'd both been pretty clear, talking in general terms about relationships, that this wasn't the time for either of them to get involved with anyone.

Now, if she could just convince her blasted libido.

While Jake finished cleaning the expensive jewelry and putting it all away, she replaced her own simple pieces—the turquoise studs in her ears and nose, the silver rings in her nipples, the matching silver ring in her navel.

He didn't look her way at all. Instead, he grabbed the camera cases and the jewelry, put everything in the Escalade, and shut the back, while Kaz slipped on a pair of flip-flops and tugged a snug black cami over her head.

He clicked the automatic locks on the vehicle and they headed down to the creek. Weaving along a narrow path through a thick stand of wild blackberry vines, Jake ducked beneath the low-growing branches of a redwood and took a grassy trail leading to a lower flood plain between the vineyard and the creek.

Kaz followed close behind, ducked beneath the same branches, and stepped into what looked and felt like an entirely different world from the neatly trellised vineyards filling the valley.

Alder trees grew thick along the bank, more widely spaced across a broad, flat area that obviously flooded regularly. The dark loam was muddy and mossy in low places, but ferns framed the trail, making it easy to follow. Shrubby willows and scraggly bay trees reaching for sunlight created an almost impenetrable forest, filled with birdsong and the rush of water splashing over rocks in the nearby creek.

Light filtered through the alders. Their fresh aroma mingled with the sharp tang of bay trees filled Kaz's senses. She stopped, soaking up sounds and smells, and the striking visual of sunlight splintered over dark green leaves and the pale bark of the trees.

A crackling in the brush had her turning just in time to see a doe lunging up the bank from the creek bed. A matched pair of tiny, speckled fawns followed, scrambling awkwardly to keep up.

Almost as a reflex, Kaz opened her hand and Jake caught her fingers in his. She turned and smiled at him, fully aware he'd been reaching for her, even as she'd reached for him. Jake merely glanced at their hands, so tightly entwined.

They stood quietly, waiting until the doe and her babies had crossed the low area and climbed the bank to the level of the vineyard. Kaz watched the two fawns until they disappeared between the vines. "Absolutely gorgeous."

"I agree."

But when she turned to smile at Jake, he wasn't looking at the deer. No, he was looking directly at her.

Only at her.

His free hand cupped the side of her face, and she knew he was going to kiss her. She wanted him to kiss her, and it seemed the most natural thing in the world to turn into his embrace and wrap her arms around him. Tangling her fingers in the thick, dark waves of his unruly hair, she pulled him close.

His kiss was soft at first, almost tentative, but then he licked the seam between her lips and Kaz opened for him. She tangled her tongue with his, taking as much as she gave, giving as much as Jake wanted.

He groaned. She tasted his passion. Her own. And the next sound, a soft whimper, was all Kaz. But the need? Both of them, arousal shared, compounded, and expanded as she pressed closer, as Jake demanded more.

His hand slipped beneath her cotton cami. He cupped the side of her breast and rubbed his thumb over the silver ring in her nipple. She groaned, arching into his touch, then whimpered again as he tugged on the ring and blinding lust exploded in her veins, in her breasts, her womb, across her skin. Every greedy inch of her sizzled with heat and passion and she wanted to crawl inside him, wanted to wrap around him and never let go.

She raised her left leg and draped it over his right hip. He wrapped his long fingers around her thigh and pulled her even closer, holding her so tightly against him that she felt the searing heat of his body and the thick length of his erection pressing almost painfully between her legs, riding against that ring of silver over her clit.

And all the while he was kissing her, his mouth moving over hers as if he couldn't get enough, as if their tongues and lips and teeth were conduits for every moment they'd spent together wanting and waiting, avoiding the obvious.

Avoiding desire.

Remaining professional.

Jake was the one who broke the kiss, pressing his forehead tightly against Kaz's, sucking in great draughts of air while she stared blankly at his face, too close to hers to focus on his features, too overcome to understand why he'd stopped.

His snort of laughter wasn't what she expected, but once his breathing had settled down, he laughed again, and then, in a surprisingly tender move, kissed her lips so gently she barely felt his touch.

And still that kiss made her shiver. Made her want him even more.

"I am not going to take you up against a tree in the middle of a bog like some Neanderthal."

She stared at him, imagining exactly that, and shuddered. She was wet, her sex swollen and lush and so ready, her heart thundered in her chest, but he kissed her again, a little more firmly this time. "Protection, Kaz. I've got some in the camera bag in the car. I hope."

He set her away from him and took another deep breath. Kaz was still trying to focus on the man who was looking at her as if she'd hung the moon and the stars, while at the same time telling her he didn't want her, and doing her best to make sense of him. But before she could call him out on whatever he was trying to say, Jake put his hands on both her shoulders and stared at her.

"I want you, Kaz. I want you like nothing I've ever wanted in my entire misbegotten life—but not here. Not shoved up against a tree, worrying someone might catch us. I want to bury myself as deep inside you as I can. I want to enjoy those beautiful silver rings, and I want to take my time finding them. Discovering each one."

"You found a couple last night. Quite effectively, I might add." She'd meant that to sound light, teasing, but she barely got the words out.

He sounded rough, almost angry when he answered.

"That I did. And it's all I've been able to think about all morning."

She stared into those dark, dark eyes of his and saw her own need reflected back. She grabbed his hand. "There's a lock on the barn door, blankets in the stalls, and fresh straw."

He cocked an eyebrow. "Have you ever had cowboy fantasies?"

Raising her head, she fluttered her eyelashes. "Hasn't every girl?" She glanced at the bulge in his jeans and raised her eyebrows. "What about you? Any particular fantasies?"

"At the moment? Only you."

Tilting her head, she kissed him. "At the moment, that works perfectly."

He stopped at the side of the Escalade, unlocked the back, and reached for his camera bag, hoping like hell he had condoms in the side pocket. Nothing. He checked a couple of zippered pouches—empty. Damn.

Kaz, in the meantime, had grabbed her handbag. "If you're looking for protection, I've got some, and the date's good. I told you I'm not looking for a long-term relationship, and that definitely means I'm not about to risk getting pregnant. C'mon."

"Good," he said. "That's good." Except his mind was spinning, and not in a direction he'd expected. He wasn't looking for a long-term relationship, so why did it bother him when she reminded him—again—that she wasn't, either? And why in the hell did she have him twisted in knots?

He was still staring at Kaz when she slung her handbag over her shoulder and turned toward the barn. "Are you coming?"

"Oh, yeah." He laughed and caught her hand. "I'm glad one of us is prepared."

She winked at him, and let out a dramatic sigh. "Only because Lola and Mandy both threatened me." She reached into her bag and held up a smaller zippered pouch with pink lips printed all over the outside. "Lola's stash. She forced me to bring them. Really."

His reaction bothered him. It shouldn't matter to him who she'd been with in the past. There was no reason for him to feel jealous when he thought of her with another man. He shoved that inconvenient thought aside, cocked an eyebrow, and tapped the lip-covered bag in her hand. "Is she going to count them when you get home?"

Kaz slanted him a glance. "I'd already planned to re-stock, if we used any. Before I return the bag." She held up the little pouch. The painted lips on it seemed to be laughing at him. "With any luck, we'll need to buy more, right?"

Oh, yeah. He locked the car and followed Kaz into the barn. She went straight to the stall at the back, grabbed the colorful blanket off the partition, and threw it down over the clean straw.

Jake shut the barn door and locked it, and then he realized his hands were sweating. *It's just sex, right?*

Sure. Just sex.

Sex with the most beautiful woman he'd ever seen. The most fascinating, brilliant, funny, amazing woman he'd ever met.

One he'd brought to climax multiple times last night.

No wonder he was so blasted horny. She'd gotten off. He hadn't. That was it. That had to be it.

She waited for him, sitting cross-legged in the middle of the colorful striped blanket covering a bed of fresh straw. They hadn't turned on any lights, and the barn was shadowed and dark compared to the bright sunshine outside. It took his eyes a minute to adjust, and then he couldn't stop looking at her.

She'd tossed her handbag to one side. Her flip-flops lay beside it, but she held the little bag covered in painted lips in her hand. Her hair was still tousled from their frenzied kisses a few minutes ago, her lips still swollen.

And Jake was hard as a rock. He grabbed the side of the stall door for balance and toed off one shoe and then the other. Tugged his socks off, walked the few steps through the straw barefoot, and then knelt in front of her on the striped blanket. Sitting back on his heels, he stared at her.

"Why is it," he said, saying each word with a depth of feeling that left him shaken, "that you look even sexier like this, more desirable, more beautiful, with your hair all mussed and your lips swollen from kissing?" He reached out and ran his fingers through her dark bangs, through hair sleek as silk.

She shrugged and then grabbed the hem of her cami, tugged it over her head, and tossed it aside. "Probably these." Without any pretense, without embarrassment, she touched the silver rings in her nipples. "It's one thing to take pictures of them, but altogether another to know they're under my shirt where you can't see them. Better, now?"

"Oh, yeah. Better. Even sexier, though. God, Kaz." She was right. Jake swallowed and forced himself to look at her face. "It's a good thing you can't read my mind." He reached out with both hands and lightly moved her fingers aside, grasped the rings. Tugging gently, he pulled her close, and she came to him, straddling his waist as he stretched his legs out, pushing him down against the blanket, controlling him even though he was the one holding on to the tiny silver rings, tugging at her dark nipples.

"And if I could read your mind, what would I see?" She hovered over him now, hugging his hips with her thighs as he continued to keep a gentle pressure against the rings.

He laughed, not the least bit surprised when it sounded

more like a frustrated bark than laughter. The effect she had on him was almost scary, the intensity of feelings pouring through him right now enough to scare the crap out of him. She was too perfect, too right for him, but he couldn't have her. Couldn't tell her the truth, couldn't live with the lies.

He went for what honesty he could. "In all reality, you'd probably see a slavering idiot tripping over his own tongue. You drive me crazy. I hope you realize that."

She leaned over and nipped his throat. The sharp sting from her very sharp teeth had him raising his hips, pressing his denim-covered dick up close against her crotch.

She didn't pull away. No, she pressed back, just as hard. He let go of the rings and pulled her head down, brought her mouth into contact with his, before rolling her over, changing their positions until he straddled her, still kissing her—wet, open-mouthed kisses she returned with more fervor, more fire than he'd ever experienced.

Kissing was never like this. Not such drugging, mind-numbing pleasure. He wanted more. He wanted everything. Sitting up, he ripped his shirt off over his head. Kaz was right there with him, undoing the snap on his jeans, lowering the zipper, helping him shove the worn denim down his legs, grabbing his sleek-fitting boxers at the same time, until he had to roll away from her just to get the pants over his feet and off.

He had a brief thought that he was showing damned little finesse, but Kaz didn't seem to mind at all. She had a big smile on her face and that silly pouch with the pink lips in her hand when he knelt between her knees, grabbed the legs of her yoga pants, and tugged them down her long, long legs.

She kicked her feet free, and the pure, honest beauty of her slammed into him. So much color with that vibrant monarch soaring across her torso, the sparkle of the silver rings in her nipples and navel, the smooth, golden glow of her sleek, soft skin.

The frantic rush they'd shared just moments ago, those deep kisses and heart-pounding needs, simmered just beneath the surface, held captive now by the knowledge that she was his, that he would finally have her. Jake blinked, pulling his gaze away from her eyes, moving across the vivid lines and colors of the monarch tattoo, slowly perusing every inch of her sleek body. She wore a tiny bit of lace, a pale peach-colored thong that covered her smooth pubic mound with fabric so fine, the silver ring at the top of her clit showed through the lace.

Remembering the way it had felt to tug that tiny silver ring with the tip of his tongue, he had to taste her again. Leaning forward, he nuzzled her belly and nipped at the narrow top band of her thong, but he didn't pull it down. Instead, he opened his mouth over the silky lace covering her pubes and licked her through the fabric.

She was wet and ready for him, the lace soaked with her cream. Her scent filled his senses, the sweet taste of her through the silk; her breathless groan left him smiling and his cock standing high and hard against his belly. Slipping his hands beneath her firm buttocks, Jake lifted her. Sat back on his heels and held her up to his mouth, tasting her through the lace, laving her with his tongue while she whimpered and twisted in his grasp. In spite of the alarm bells going off in the back of his mind, he filled himself with her taste, her scent, the very essence of a woman he doubted he'd ever grow tired of.

CHAPTER 8

Ohmygodohmygodohmygod . . . Sobbing, entirely overwhelmed by Jake, Kaz twisted in his strong grasp, but he held his mouth between her legs, his lips creating a seal over her clit and her labia, and then he merely exhaled. Warm moist air followed by the pressure of his tongue, but she still had on that damned thong and she wanted—no, she needed—him to touch her, flesh to flesh.

His tongue, his lips, even his teeth, but he breathed in and then exhaled again and she couldn't stop the whimpers, the soft cries, because she needed so much more. Her panties were sopping wet, and she knew it wasn't all from Jake's warm breath. The subtle contractions deep inside were a pretty good indicator that it was time to take a little control here.

She needed the fullness of Jake pushing deep inside, not his lips and tongue teasing her. Not merely hinting at what the two of them could be together.

She might not be ready for forever, but she could sure as hell use a little "right now."

And so far, sex with him was just plain fun. Lowering her legs, Kaz pressed her feet flat to the blanket, leaned forward, and pushed him back, moving so fast she caught him by surprise. She followed him, laughing, kneeling over him, grasping his hip bones in both hands and holding him flat to the blanket.

He gazed up at her, his expression one more of surprise than lust. She was going to have to work on that. "Looks like all that yoga Mandy makes me do has paid off."

Jake still had a rather dazed expression on his face, his lips and chin shiny with her fluids. She'd planned to put a condom on him and just sort of impale herself, but kneeling here this way, with her legs spread over his and that absolutely delicious erection in front of her, Kaz decided to show him exactly why his teasing was making her crazy.

She leaned over and licked the velvety crown, smiling when she heard his sharp intake of breath. She paid extra close attention to the tiny slit at the top, licking, teasing.

Tasting.

Then she opened her mouth and slowly took him inside. Not all the way, just sucking the smooth glans, still tracing the sleek contours with her tongue. She slid him deeper into her mouth, close enough to scrape gently with her teeth, then licking, soothing what she'd nipped.

He reached for her, tangling his fingers in her short hair. He didn't try to force her, but she felt the tremor in his hands and knew she was taking him close to the edge. She sucked him deep, as far as she could, though it was barely half his length. Felt her cheeks hollow with each sucking pull until his fingers tightened in her hair. He tugged gently.

She glanced up, watched his face. His intense gaze sent shivers along her spine.

"As much as I want you to keep doing this, mainly because it feels so damned good," he growled, "if you make me come now, the party's over."

She took her time, slipping him out of her mouth, tracing his length with her tongue. She tasted the salty drops of fluid and knew how close he was to losing control, but she still licked the very tip again as she carefully freed him from the clasp of her mouth.

Sitting back on her heels, she folded her arms beneath her bare breasts, conscious of how she must look to him right now, as if she was putting herself on display.

Which she was. "Hmmm . . . over? We certainly can't have that."

This kind of confidence with such an unbelievably gorgeous man was something completely new. In front of a camera? She was perfectly at ease. But this? Only with Jake.

Kaz leaned back and reached for the little pouch, flipped the top open, and pulled out a foil-wrapped packet. She tore it with her teeth and removed the condom.

Jake held out his hand, but she shook her head. "Allow me."

He merely raised one eyebrow and propped himself up on his elbows to watch.

Kaz winked. "The pressure's on, eh?" She studied his cock, so tall and hard, standing perpendicular to his flat belly, and tried to look as if she did this sort of thing all the time.

Except she hadn't. Ever. And there really wasn't any point in lying. "I've, um, never dressed a man before."

His laugh and soft curse sounded a bit strained.

She sat there a moment, giving her heart a chance to settle down, controlling her breathing so she wouldn't hyperventilate. After a moment, she wrapped her hand around the thick base of his shaft, but instead of sliding the condom over him, she slipped her other hand beneath and cupped his balls.

Jake hissed. Warmth pulsed beneath the hand holding his cock, and she felt the thick length of him swell within her grasp. This time Kaz was the one raising an eyebrow.

"Handle with care," he said. He wasn't smiling at all,

and it wasn't just his cock that was rigid. His entire body appeared to be made of stone, all angles and edges, and a light sheen of sweat across his chest and forehead was proof she'd probably pushed him far enough.

Shrugging, sighing as if she wasn't at all ready to stop playing, Kaz carefully rolled the condom over Jake's erection, smoothing it with her fingers as she went.

And gave thanks for the fact it went on the way it was supposed to, though it felt tighter than she'd expected.

"My turn." There was more than the hint of threat in that deep voice of his, and it sent another pulse of needy shivers racing along Kaz's spine. "Lose the thong, Kaz."

He looked at her as if he could eat her alive. His dark eyes blazed and all thoughts of humor, of laughing with him, at least for the foreseeable future, fled.

Still on her knees, she tugged the panties down, sat back on her butt, and pulled them off one leg, then the other— slowly, carefully—before tossing them aside. Then she lay back on the blanket, ignoring the rough texture of the weave, the scratchy straw beneath her feet, and raised her hands as Jake came over her. His broad shoulders and lean waist, the muscles that rippled with each move he made— the whole perfect package was more than she'd ever seen, much less loved.

Except this wasn't love. It couldn't be, though it was most definitely a friendship. One that appeared to be taking on a life of its own, growing and tangling the two of them together.

That was okay. She could work with that.

He knelt over her, his knees between her legs, elbows planted on either side of her face, hands tangled in her hair, and his big body so close she felt the heat pouring off him.

"What you do to me, Kaz . . . what you do." He kissed her.

She arched into him, taking the thrust of his tongue, the

firm pressure of his lips, and giving it back, but the control belonged to Jake and her body was all his.

He slipped lower, kissing her throat, her chest, the hard ridge of her collarbones, trailing his lips from right to left with a short pause to concentrate on the sensitive dip at the base of her throat. Working his way slowly to her left breast, he sucked the nipple between his lips, tugging the tiny silver loop with his tongue.

She felt the burn between her legs and whimpered.

Then it was a different burn, a sense of urgency as he pressed the broad head of his cock between her thighs, pushed deep into the slick, wet heart of her, filling her, stretching her with one long, hot thrust.

Bowing her back, she tilted her hips, giving him better access. The smooth crown of his penis slid across her cervix deep inside, his thick shaft stretched her tissues until she burned with such intense pleasure it caught her breath.

The crisp hair at his groin tickled her smooth pubes and his balls pressed against her butt, their bodies so tightly connected, he could go no deeper. Stopping, Jake lowered his head and took a deep breath. Let it out, then took another. His body trembled. Kaz felt his struggle for control, knew the moment he'd mastered himself.

One more breath, and he slowly withdrew. Then, with agonizing slowness, he pushed forward, his body angled so that the upper side of his penis slid against the ring in her clit.

Pushing in. Pulling out.

That bit of silver forged a direct line to her womb, a link transmitting sensation and feeling back and forth, from one erogenous zone to another, confusing Kaz with her body's alternating needs. She wanted him now, wanted the flash of arousal and the shocking conclusion. Even more, she wanted this to last.

As Jake had said, she didn't want to ruin the fun. Not

now. Not when she felt as if she hovered on the edge of something unexplainable. Something she'd always wanted, couldn't name, couldn't describe.

She wanted Jake. That would have to be explanation enough for now. Raising her legs, she wrapped them around his hips and he lifted her, settling back on his heels, filling her so perfectly she knew their bodies had been designed to fit this way.

She arched her back, pressing her pubes tightly against the hard root of his shaft. He leaned over her, cupped one breast, lifting it to his mouth, catching that silver ring between his teeth and tugging in perfect rhythm with their bodies.

She whimpered, so close to the edge, a leap she'd never once taken with any man during sex. During foreplay, or after if she'd been left wanting, but this time, the pressure was rising so fast, her body responding so quickly that her climax hit before she was ready, slamming into her with breathless power.

The scream surprised her, her sharp cry a counterpoint to the shock of sensation that flashed through her body, contracted her muscles, sensitized every inch of her skin. Seconds later, Jake's harsh shout, his short, fast, powerful strokes, and the rigid strength in his arms as he held her close sent Kaz into a second climax.

It seemed to take forever before her muscles stopped clenching, before her breasts and her clit, even her lips, stopped tingling and pulsing. Jake eased her down, and then came down over her, supporting himself on his forearms, his forehead pressed against hers, their bodies still intimately connected.

"I knew we'd be good together, but damn." He raised his head. From the glazed expression on his face, he seemed as stunned as she was.

"It probably sounds rather clichéd, but I had no idea it

could feel like that." Her blunt honesty seemed to surprise him, but he didn't move. No, he kissed her, long, sweet, sucking kisses that had her arching against him. Finally, he backed away, reached between them and pulled free of her still tightly clenched muscles, carefully holding the condom.

Taking care of her.

She watched him walk back to the restroom, that perfect butt of his scored with marks from her rather short fingernails. He returned a few minutes later carrying a warm, wet washcloth.

And though they'd used a condom, he carefully bathed between her legs, so carefully that she didn't even feel embarrassed—well, not too embarrassed, though she'd never had a lover do anything like that. She watched him as he washed her, and when he looked her way, his expression wasn't what she'd expected.

She felt like laughing. Like doing backflips through the vineyard. But Jake looked so serious. As if something had happened that he hadn't quite figured out yet.

Neither had she. Kaz stared after him as he walked back to the restroom with the washcloth. She'd never felt more confused in her life, but one thing she was sure of—she really wanted to know where they went from here.

Stunned didn't come close to covering the way he felt. Jake rinsed the washcloth off in the bathroom sink and hung it over the edge of the hamper. He'd grabbed his pants on the way back. Now he slowly put them on. What an idiot—he could procrastinate all he wanted, but he couldn't avoid going back in there. Back to Kaz.

It shouldn't be this hard, but he hadn't expected the connection they'd made. Not last night, and certainly not this. Not now—not with all his baggage. Not when he carried around enough secrets to overload an airport carousel.

His phone vibrated in his back pocket. He pulled it out, then almost dropped the damned thing. With his gut clenching in a painful knot, he read the brief text.

Hey, RJ. You always were a fast son of a bitch.

Fuck. Who the hell was this bastard? And fast, how? Swimming?

Kaz? Having sex with her so soon after meeting?

Had that shadow on the window been more than a branch? Was the bastard actually watching them? His hand shook as he shoved his phone back into his pocket. He took a deep breath, waited a moment longer until his racing heart had quieted, and walked back to the stall.

Kaz was already dressed, though he liked the fact that her face was still flushed, her hair still a tousled mess. He glanced at the windows, skin crawling, heart pounding once again.

Kaz watched him, a wary look on her face.

"Here, you missed some." He pulled a couple of pieces of straw out of her dark waves.

She raised her head and gazed at him, and then just as quickly looked away. That hesitation, the way she couldn't look him in the eyes, disturbed him. He caught her chin with his fingertips and turned her to face him once again. He really had to think of Kaz. This wasn't all about him. Not at all.

"You okay?"

She smiled, nodded. "I am. Better than okay." Her hesitant smile turned into a full-fledged grin, but it wasn't enough to hide the blush that slowly suffused her face, her throat, the exposed part of her chest. "That was, um . . . pretty spectacular."

He should have said something flip and funny, something to diffuse the tension in the air. He didn't think. He reacted, cupped her face in both his palms, held her, kissed her.

Okay. He really shouldn't have done that. He couldn't believe that just one kiss would have him hard again. Especially this soon, especially with the threat of someone watching, knowing what they did, but he couldn't deny his body's reaction. Or Kaz.

"Beyond spectacular, if you want my opinion." He stared at her a moment and sighed. "Which is why I put my pants back on. This is supposed to be a work day, but all I could think about was coming back here and doing it again."

She shrugged, blushed again, and glanced away. "It could have been work. You know, getting your model in the mood to sell sexy jewelry? It's your job, isn't it? To make sure I can feel the vibe, act the part? You know . . ." Her smile turned into full-throated laughter and she did a little swivel that started at her hips and ended at the top of her head. "Feel the heat?"

"Any more heat and I'd self-combust." He muttered the comment beneath his breath but Kaz obviously had excellent hearing. Instead of coming back with a quip, though, she stopped her dance and just looked at him for a long, slow moment.

He had absolutely no idea what was going through her mind, but he wasn't sure he really wanted to know. He was such a fucking coward, waiting for the next text, hoping like hell it never came. Wanting Kaz. Knowing he couldn't have her. "C'mon." His words were sharper than he'd intended, but he barged ahead. "We need to get back to work."

"Yeah." Such a softly spoken word before she turned away, but he caught the glittering shine in her dark eyes. Damn, he was acting like an absolute bastard.

He really should apologize, but what was the point? Had the ground shifted for her, too? He wasn't used to this . . . this . . . whatever this was. Too much, too fast. His head was spinning. He wanted her again. He had to get away from her, put as much distance between them as he could to keep her safe. His presence in her life, the danger of someone watching him, could spill over onto Kaz.

It scared the crap out of him. He hated it.

Jake raised his head and she was right there, as beautiful, as perfect as no woman had a right to be. She was everything he'd ever wanted, but he'd screwed himself out of ever having a woman like Kaz in his life. Not now, not ever.

Not when his past included the deaths of two innocent people, and almost six long years behind bars. Not when someone who knew of that past was bringing it all back, making it so much worse. He really thought he'd finally pulled his life together.

He'd always pushed the ugly memories away, but they never went far enough—a constant reminder that the bad choices of his past had totally fucked his future. The messages merely underscored his stupidity.

He'd handle it. He always handled it.

Only now he knew what he'd be missing, and it hurt. A lot.

Kaz still watched him. "I have to go comb my hair, get my model face on. Do you still want to get some shots near the creek before we shoot in the vineyard?"

All business. Voice sharp, body totally in control. How the hell did she do that when he was a twisted mess inside? "Yeah." He glanced at his watch, more to stall than to check the time. He knew exactly what time it was. "It's only a little after two. We'll get shadows in the valley early, because of the hills on the west side, but we've got time to get a few shots in that overgrown area by the creek. The emeralds should work in that light."

She smiled, but it wasn't the free, natural look he'd come to expect from her. Had they totally blown their working relationship? Even more important, what of their growing friendship? It didn't make sense. How could the best sex he'd ever experienced screw up anything?

Except it wasn't the sex screwing things up. It was him. All by himself.

"I'll be back in a minute," she said.

Then she was gone, leaving Jake standing in a stall filled with straw and a rumpled blanket. And memories he knew would haunt him for a lifetime.

Kaz stared at her rumpled self in the mirror and frowned. "Okay, Kazanov. What the fuck just happened?"

She had no answer, obviously, but something had certainly shifted between them. What did he mean about self-combusting? It could have been a joke, except he hadn't said it like he thought it was funny. It might have been flirtatious, except he'd sounded absolutely furious—but with her or himself? And why?

Then telling her they had to hurry and get back to work? Who the hell was he, treating her like a cheap lay? Because that's exactly how he'd made her feel. But why?

She got her hair wet and combed it back. He'd said earlier he'd liked the look, and she might as well go for it now. She tilted her chin, and checked for razor burn. Other than her lips looking fuller than usual from all the kissing, she looked okay.

Adding just a small amount of lip gloss, she grabbed her things and left the bathroom. Jake wasn't in the barn, so she stepped outside into the warm afternoon sunlight. He waited by the Escalade, leaning against the side of the big SUV, staring out across the vineyard.

She'd wadded up her thong and stuffed it in the side pocket of her handbag rather than put on a pair of wet underwear, and now, as pissed off as she was, she still had to worry about the rush of moisture from merely thinking of their lovemaking.

No. Not lovemaking. Sex, pure and simple. It was just sex.

"You ready?" Jake stepped around to the opposite side of the SUV and grabbed one of his camera bags and a heavy tote bag out of the back.

She nodded.

"I'll lock the barn. Got everything you need?"

"Did you want me to take makeup?"

He paused and stared at her. She felt more naked under his assessing look than when they'd been fucking. That's how she'd think of what they'd done. Fucking. That's all it was.

At least, that's what it had to be.

"No. You're okay like that." He shook his head, abruptly turned away, and locked the barn door. Clicked the key lock on the Escalade and hoisted his heavy camera bag over his shoulder, along with the other bag filled with equipment for the shoot.

She didn't offer to help him carry anything. Not this time. Instead, she followed him down the trail, both hands free. He walked fast. She hurried to keep up, realized what she was doing and slowed her pace. Damned if she'd run after him. He led her a little farther than they'd gone earlier, to a patch of emerald green grass surrounded by ferns and willows covered in new, brilliant green leaves. Tiny yellow monkey flowers grew along the edge between the grass and a patch of wild blackberry vines.

He dropped the tote and stared at the place he'd chosen. Without looking her direction, he said, "Watch for stickers. Blackberry vines are everywhere."

All business, to the point of being insulting. None of the laughter they'd shared. None of the camaraderie. Just as well. She could do this.

Jake pulled a towel out of the tote. "Sit on this. I want to concentrate on the earrings and the stud in your nostril, but with you low enough that you'll have the ferns for backdrop. We'll use the emerald set."

He opened the box and held it steady. She lifted the pieces out. This time he didn't offer to help her, but that was okay. She didn't want him touching her. Not like this. Cold and distant, not even making eye contact; he was acting like a total jerk.

She glanced at Jake and caught him watching her, but this time he didn't look away, and she really couldn't stand it. Not knowing was making her crazy.

"Jake? What the fuck happened?"

He let out a long, pent-up breath. Glanced away, and then turned slowly and focused on her. "You don't mince words, do you?"

"Should I? We had great sex. Really great sex. Then you turned into . . ."

"A jerk?"

"Yeah," she said. "An absolute jerk."

He shrugged. Looked away, up this time, as if he needed to assess the treetops. Then he turned, and this time he didn't turn away, but he didn't look very happy. "Truth? It was good. Too good. I like you, Kaz. A lot. But you were looking at me like . . ."

"Like I wanted to do it again?" She planted her hands on her hips and glared at him for a couple of heartbeats. "Is that what made you so uncomfortable?"

He nodded. "Yeah. Stupid, I guess, but I wanted you again. I still want you. I can't do that."

"Can't have sex, or can't get involved?" She stepped close enough to breach that personal space bubble most people had. "Well, Jake, I thought I'd made that clear. I don't want to get involved, either. I'm trying to build a career and I don't have the time, energy, or interest in a long-term relationship. Yes, I want to get back into living, but the last thing I want is to get seriously involved with anyone, including you. Especially you, if this is how you act after sex."

She stepped back and stared at him for a long moment, long enough she could tell he was feeling uncomfortable. Good. He deserved it. "That doesn't mean I don't want to have sex with you again, because I do, but not if you're going to freak out and think I plan to tie you down. Yes, while I'm with you I certainly expect it to be exclusive, but I'm not looking for a serious boyfriend, nor do I hear wedding bells, okay?"

He watched her for the longest time. Maybe she'd overdone it, but to be perfectly honest, she was still pissed off. She'd never said anything to make him think she wanted more from him than he was willing to give. Not a thing, beyond telling him the sex was good.

And he'd agreed. *Beyond spectacular,* he'd said. Well, damn it, it was.

Finally, he frowned. "You're okay with that? With an exclusive relationship that's not going anywhere? Just while we're here on the shoot?"

Okay, so he wanted a limit. She could do this, but he looked so serious, so conflicted, she laughed. "You are such a dork. It's called friends with benefits. And yes, that's all I'm looking for."

Giving her a wide-eyed, innocent look, he slapped his hand over his heart. "You call me a dork and then you expect exquisite sex? I don't know about that."

"I didn't ask for exquisite. That's the platinum package. I'm only asking for spectacular." She finished putting the jewelry in place, but she had to bite back a smile. It felt as if they were slipping back into that comfortable space she thought they'd lost. He pointed to a dry spot on the grass, and she posed with the brilliant green ferns behind her face.

"I see." Jake adjusted his camera, pulled a portable light stand with a battery pack and a reflector screen out of the bag, adjusted it, and checked with his light meter to make sure all was the way he wanted it. He concentrated on his equipment. Didn't even glance her way. "We're running a special this week. You can get the platinum service for the same price as the gold."

"And that is?" She tilted her head, better to show off the gold chain snaking from her earlobe to her left nostril.

Jake took a couple of quick shots, adjusted the light, and then flipped the strap from her cami off her left shoulder. Frowning, he ruffled her damp hair a bit, bringing a few tendrils down across her brow. Kaz held the pose.

Jake stopped and stared directly at her, the camera hanging from his hand as if he'd forgotten he held it. "The price is you ignore me when I act like a jerk, or a dork, or any other kind of idiot." He knelt, putting himself at eye level with her.

"Honest truth? The sex was so good it scared the crap out of me. I didn't behave well and I'm sorry. I looked at you and for a minute I wanted more, and I know you don't want that and I can't do that. Not for a long time, and I panicked. Then I took it out on you. I won't do that again."

"Good." She smiled at him, knowing she'd just been given a rare gift—a truly heartfelt and honest apology—but she wasn't about to rub it in. "Now that that's settled, I think I do want the platinum package. And we're running out of daylight."

"Yes, ma'am." He saluted, and they went back to work. But Kaz couldn't stop thinking about what Jake had said. That after they'd made love, he'd wanted more.

No wonder he'd panicked. Thank goodness he didn't know she'd started thinking the same damned thing.

CHAPTER 9

"The sun goes down awfully fast, doesn't it?" Kaz watched the shadows deepen and finally merge with the hilltops on the eastern side of the valley as Jake drove back into town.

"It does." Jake glanced her way and smiled. "I'm anxious to see how the photos look when I can load them on my laptop. The contrasts in those last few shots could be really interesting."

"We still on for more pictures in town tonight?" She was exhausted, whether from the long day, the emotional highs and lows and in-betweens, or just the fact she'd had to be "on" all day, posing, holding position, changing position, changing jewelry.

Watching Jake and wondering what he was thinking.

"No. I think we've done enough for one day." This time his sexy smile left no doubt what he was thinking about. "Did you bring a swimsuit?"

She shook her head. "No. Too tired to swim, anyway. I'm beat."

"I was thinking of the spa. A perfect little pool . . . all those jets of hot water? Bet your muscles would whimper in ecstasy. They serve you wine while you're turning pruny."

"That's mean. Teasing me with a vision of heaven."

"We'll get you a suit."

She groaned.

"Picture a black bikini—doesn't have to be all that brief, but enough to show the navel ring and tattoo. Steam rising behind you. If the lighting is right, it would be spectacular."

"You said no working." She pouted.

He merely shrugged. "It's the visual I've got. Not to shoot—it's how I see things."

"Okay. I've got a black bra and panty set that would work—I've gone swimming in them before and no one knew I wasn't wearing a swimsuit." She gave him a very tired smile, so glad they were back to the more relaxed connection they'd started the day with.

"Crap." Laughing, he said, "I'll know."

"Good. I'll wear it then."

They stopped at a little market on the way into town where Jake said he'd eaten the best deli food in his life. Everything smelled so good that Kaz was embarrassed when they checked out.

"You just spent a fortune on takeout. Wasn't that a bit much?"

He merely laughed and opened the door to the SUV for her. "You won't say that once you taste it. Besides, part of the bill was a bottle of good pinot."

"I noticed."

But he was right, and they were both scraping the bottom of the containers an hour later, sharing tastes, once again comfortable together. Kaz changed into her black bikini panties and matching bra, and the set really did look like a swimsuit. Sort of. It certainly showed off the butterfly tat to perfection. Jake asked her to wear the diamonds, "just in case." Ears, nose, navel. They were gorgeous—flashy without looking tacky. She liked them. A lot.

"You sure you don't want the nipple rings? They're just under a full carat each."

"You said no pictures, but I notice you have your camera bag. Fine, but we are not photographing nipple anything in public."

He winked. "Killjoy."

"Damn right." She tried to look ferocious, but after such a good meal, sharing a bottle of wine and a lot of laughter, it was hard to be ferocious about anything.

The spa was next to the pool, and there was no one around other than a young man in a hotel uniform at a station near the door. Jake stopped to speak with him while Kaz walked over to where steam floated above a bubbling pool. She left her robe on a nearby chair and got into the water. Slowly. It was deliciously hot.

Jake knelt beside the edge, and she tilted her head back to see him. Blinking lazily, she smiled and said, "You're even pretty upside down."

"Thank you. I think." He nodded toward the young man he'd spoken with. "Josh will be here all evening unless we ask him to go. Do you mind if I take a couple of minutes to walk across the parking lot to the grocery store?"

"What do you need?"

He kissed her nose. "Condoms in a little larger size. Lola's boyfriend was, um . . . not as generously endowed."

"I see. And you're assuming you're going to get lucky tonight?"

"I hope so. If I promise not to act like a jerk?"

"Then you just might. I'll be here."

He set the rest of the bottle of wine and two plastic cups on the deck beside her. "Ten minutes. Behave."

"What trouble can I possibly get into in ten minutes?"

He was laughing when he left. Kaz merely smiled and let her body go limp. This was the perfect way to end a long day. A long, confusing, hopefully productive day. Her eyes drifted shut.

"Kaz? Hey, Kazanov. What the hell are you doing here?"

"Wha . . . ?" Blinking, she stared at the man kneeling beside the tub. Not Jake, that's for sure, though he was every bit as handsome. He was one of the models she knew from Top End. "Marty? Hi. I'm on a job. What are you doing here?"

"Same as you." He stripped down to a pair of very skimpy trunks that left absolutely nothing to the imagination and stepped into the tub. "Tim's here, too, and a new kid the general hired this morning. Hey, Tim, look who I found! Steve, this is Kaz Kazanov. She works at Top End, too."

"Hi, Steve." Awake now, Kaz smiled at a very young, very handsome young man. He looked about eighteen, Asian with dark eyes and coal-black hair tipped with magenta highlights. She knew the agency didn't send anyone under twenty-one out on overnight jobs, so he had to be at least that old, but he was almost too cute to be a grown-up. His smile was shy, but she figured after a little time around Tim and Marty, the shyness wouldn't last.

A third man joined the group, fair where Marty was dark, but even larger, more muscular. Definitely sexy. "Hey, Tim. I haven't seen you in ages. How've you been?"

"Busy. Been taking some business classes and they've cut into my work time. What job are you on? Lola didn't say anything about you being out of town." He got into the tub and leaned over for a kiss.

Kaz kissed him, and got another from Marty. "You only get a handshake, Steve." She laughed. "I never kiss on the first meeting." But she flashed on Jake, and what they'd done their very first day. All her feminine muscles clenched in reaction.

Steve sighed as he got into the small spa between Marty and Tim. "I guess I'll survive."

Laughing, Kaz leaned back against the smooth side of the spa and turned to Tim. "You didn't hear about the job I'm on because it's not through the agency. The general fired me. One of the clients had trouble with my, um . . . attitude."

"Fired?" Marty gaped at her. "That bastard fired you?"

"He did." And she proceeded to tell them the whole story, though she carefully left out the more intimate details. That was between her and Jake and was no one else's business.

Jake walked back from the drugstore, went up to the room, and dropped off the box of condoms. He checked his phone. Other than a couple of texts from Marc that he'd already answered, there wasn't anything new.

Even so, he took a quick look out the window with absolutely no idea who to look for.

Sticking the phone in his camera bag, he headed back to the spa.

He heard laughter as he rounded the enclosure to the pool area. He'd been gone longer than he'd planned—almost twenty minutes—but he certainly hadn't expected Kaz to be having a party when he returned.

Especially not a party with three buff-looking men. One of them sat awfully close to her. He had his arms stretched out along the rim of the small pool, one behind the guy next to him on his left, the other too damned close to Kaz's shoulders, which shouldn't have bugged Jake.

But it did. He stopped in the shadows, fingers curling into fists as he watched Kaz laughing and talking with three strange men as if she'd known them forever. Just the way he'd felt with her—as if they'd known each other forever. Was she like this with every man she met? Damn. He shouldn't have to remind himself that she worked for him, that they were friends, not in love. No reason for him to be jealous, right?

But she'd said she expected an exclusive relationship while they were sleeping together. What was going on in that hot little pool of water didn't look exclusive from where he was standing.

He took a deep breath, got his unexpected emotions under control, and walked across the deck. Kaz looked up and smiled. "There you are. I thought you got lost."

He paused beside the pool and tossed his towel onto the chair beside his camera bag. "No. I didn't get lost."

She frowned, and then her mouth spread in a wide smile. "Jacob Lowell, I want you to meet Marty Reynosa, Tim Milbank, and Steve." She laughed. "Sorry, Steve, I don't know your last name."

"It's Chen. Steve Chen."

"Gotcha. Steve Chen. They're all models at Top End. I was just telling them about the general's meltdown yesterday."

Models. They were friends from work. The sense of relief sweeping over him didn't make any more sense than the jealousy. He'd rather not think about that. He got into the spa, and Marty moved aside to give Jake his spot next to Kaz. "It's nice to meet you guys. You here on a job?"

"Yeah." Marty shook his hand. "An online touring company that caters to gay travelers is doing a full spread on the Sonoma wine country—print and film. We fit the demographic, so it's perfect for the three of us. Fletcher Arnold is directing." He glanced at Kaz. "Kaz was just telling us about your shoot. We've all seen your work. I'm definitely a fan."

Tim interrupted. "And she's been showing off the bling.

Gorgeous stuff. That's something that would appeal to a lot of our crowd. If you think about doing any ads with guys, we know a few models with piercings."

Kaz laughed out loud. Jake found himself smiling in response. "What's so funny?"

"I'm trying to picture you photographing some guy's Prince Albert. Brain won't go there."

"You've lost me. Why am I almost afraid to ask?"

"Because you're an intelligent man," Marty said. "A Prince Albert is penile piercing, as in drilling holes in the privates for the purpose of adornment."

Jake grimaced and then laughed. "You're right. My brain won't go there. Ouch."

"Thank you," Marty said, but it was obvious he was trying not to laugh. "Not my idea of a good time, either." He lay back in the hot water. "This, however, is."

An hour later, after much laughter and some great stories at Kaz's expense, with their skin wrinkled and pruny and not a single picture taken, Jake was ready to call it a night. Kaz had fallen asleep with her head against his chest while the four guys talked.

Jake had thoroughly enjoyed himself, sitting in the spa with an arm wrapped around Kaz. The three models were intelligent and well-read, and they'd found a surprising number of common interests.

Not what he'd expected when he first saw Kaz surrounded by three strange men.

He helped her out of the water, put her robe on her as if he were dealing with a three-year-old, and looped his camera bag over his shoulder. "I think I need to take my model upstairs," he said. Then he swung her easily into his arms, surprised at how light she felt. How perfectly she fit against his chest.

"Crap," Marty said, looking at the camera bag. "You

were planning to do shots down here. Why didn't you say something? We could have cleared out of the spa for you."

"Not really. Kaz threatened me. She's off the clock, but it's hard to go anywhere without it. I think it's my security blanket." Then he glanced at the woman in his arms. She was out like a light. "Besides, I've had a really good time tonight. It was great to meet you. And I promise to let you know if we need any Prince Albert pictures."

He grinned at Marty and then crossed his eyes. The guys all laughed. "I'm sorry," Jake said, biting back a laugh. "I can't even say that without wanting to cross my legs."

Steve, quite seriously, added, "Well, it's supposed to enhance sexual pleasure."

"I'll have to take your word for it. G'night, guys." But as he carried Kaz into the hotel and up in the elevator, Jake couldn't help thinking of that tiny silver ring between Kaz's thighs. And what she'd said happened when the two of them made love.

Had sex. This was nowhere near love.

He really did have issues. But tonight, he also had Kaz.

It was the sound of Jake unlocking the door that jolted Kaz awake. She was in his arms, and Jake was carrying her into their room. He sat her on the bed and she blinked at him, frowning as she gazed around the room and then down at her wet panties and bra.

"Did I fall asleep?"

He knelt in front of her. "That you did. Here, let's get these."

He grabbed the waist of her panties, and she lifted her hips so he could slide them off. She released the front catch of her bra, and Jake helped her tug the straps over her shoulders.

Totally oblivious to her nudity, Kaz stood and walked to the bathroom. "I smell like chlorine. Need a shower. I'll be quick."

Half asleep, she stepped into the bathroom and shoved the door part of the way closed.

She left him there, holding her wet bra and panties, his mind spinning with all that had happened today. After a minute, he slipped his own swimsuit off, carried the wet clothes into the bathroom, rinsed them quickly in the sink, and hung them on a towel rack.

He saw her clearly behind the glass shower door, standing beneath the spray, head tilted forward as it hit her from behind. The condoms were in the bedroom, but he was here, now. They didn't need to have sex, but he needed to touch her.

Maybe reinforce his . . . what? Claim?

Where the fuck did that come from? He didn't want any claim on Kaz.

He watched her a moment longer. Then he turned away and walked out of the bathroom, leaving Kaz to finish her shower alone.

Kaz got out of the shower and dried off. She could barely keep her eyes open, but she was almost sure Jake had been in the bathroom while she showered. Yeah, their wet clothes were hanging on the towel rack, so he'd been here.

But he hadn't joined her in the shower. She wasn't sure if she was relieved or hurt over that, which meant it was probably just as well he'd left her alone.

Wrapping a towel around herself, she brushed her teeth, and then turned out the light. Jake had left a small lamp burning at the far end of the room, but there was no sign of him.

The clock beside the bed said 9:17, but she didn't care how early it was. It was time to put an end to a very long, confusing yet exhilarating day. Crawling into bed, Kaz pulled the blankets up over her head and closed her eyes.

She awoke once during the night, aware of a heartbeat that wasn't hers. Her face was pressed against a man's warm chest, her legs tangled with a familiar, hair-roughened pair, and a heavy arm lay across her back.

She didn't open her eyes. Feeling safe and warm, she slept the rest of the night through.

Kaz didn't awaken until Jake waved a fresh cup of coffee under her nose. He was already up and dressed, and the only proof she had that he'd slept in her bed was the fact that the other one was still covered with his camera gear and their overnight bags.

"Thanks." She took the cup he offered and glanced at the clock. "Good lord! I slept almost twelve hours."

"I figured you needed it, and it's really foggy out, so an early start wouldn't have mattered. Light's not an issue because there isn't any." He gave her a lopsided smile. "Yesterday was . . ." He glanced away. "I owe you an apology, Kaz, and I'm sorry I was such an ass."

She waved a hand to stop him. "It's over. I'm okay with whatever happens as long as you are."

He laughed. "Are you always the grown-up in the room?"

This time it was Kaz's turn to laugh. "Only when forced."

"Sorry about that." He checked his watch. "How long before you can be ready?"

She shrugged. "Fifteen minutes?"

"Amazing. Meet me in the plaza. It's kind of cool and breezy out, so dress warmer than you did yesterday. We'll get some breakfast and figure out where we're going to get our shots."

It was closer to twenty, but she found him by a pond in the center of the plaza. The wind was blowing, and big clouds scudded across the sky. The morning was brisk but not uncomfortable, and she couldn't believe how hungry she was, after all the food the night before.

Jake turned as she drew closer, and he absolutely took her breath. So tall and lean, dressed in a worn pair of Levi's that hugged his butt and sat low on his hips, he'd traded the black T-shirt for a dark maroon button-down shirt with the sleeves rolled back at his wrists. When he spotted her, his face lit up with a wide smile, and he walked toward her as if she was the only woman around.

She heard a long, low wolf whistle and glanced toward the street. A couple of young guys standing near a flashy car grinned at her. One waved. Rolling her eyes, she turned toward Jake just as he reached for her, wrapped his arm around her waist, and lifted her to his mouth for a long, very satisfying kiss.

Then he buried his face in her hair and whispered, "That was terribly caveman of me, but those two really pissed me off."

She leaned back within his embrace. "Friends, remember?"

He sighed. "I know, but don't hesitate to remind me. Let's get something to eat."

He led her across the street to a small restaurant tucked in among a row of boutiques. Stepping inside had her mouth watering.

They were just finishing breakfast when Marty, Tim, and Steve walked in with a fourth man.

"Good morning, Kaz. Jake." Marty headed their way.

"I'm glad we found you. Jake, I think you know Fletch, the dude we're working for."

"If you can call it work." Laughing, the man stepped forward and held out his hand. "Haven't seen you in ages, Jake. Glad you called last night. How've you been?"

Jake stood and shook hands with Fletch, and then introduced him to Kaz. By the time introductions were made, Kaz realized that Jake and Fletcher Arnold weren't that far apart in age, but the other man's solid build and snow-white hair made him look years older.

"It's the work," he said, obviously aware of the impression he made. "I direct film commercials, and when you have to work with dunderheads like these three . . ." He laughed when Tim threw a napkin at him. "How long is this gig going to run, Jake?"

"Two more days of shots, and then I have to get them to Marc's art department. But Kaz is a pro. We got some great stuff yesterday."

Fletcher studied Kaz, long enough to make her uncomfortable. "You ever do any voice work, Kaz?"

She shook her head. "I've had some training, but no actual work in front of a camera."

"I've got a project next week, should be, oh, six to ten days, if you're free. You're the look we've been talking about—young, beautiful, sort of edgy. I had one woman interested, but then a chance to shoot a commercial in Maui came up before she'd signed a contract." He shrugged. "Hell, I'd have taken it, too. We'll be filming in San Francisco." He named a restaurant, one that was way out of her price range, and added, "It's for a winery in the South Bay that's making a push to go national, so you'll need to do an audition Monday morning. There are a few lines, not a lot, but the final choice of model-slash-actress is up to me. You've got the look I want, your voice is great, and you come highly recommended by your camera-toting boy-friend. Are you interested?"

She glanced at Jake and raised an eyebrow. Boyfriend? Recommended?

He shrugged. "I've known Fletch for years, and when the guys mentioned him last night, I thought I'd let him know about you. This job's going to be ending this week-end, and . . ."

"Thank you, Jake, and yes, Mr. Arnold. I'm interested." Was she ever! She'd heard of Fletcher Arnold. His com-mercials got national distribution—some of his models had gone on to huge careers. "As long as Jake's gotten everything he needs for his project."

Jake nodded. "We've got all day today and tomorrow and should be heading back to the city by Saturday after-noon."

"Perfect. Thanks, Jake." He winked.

She swung around to face Arnold. "Just tell me when and where, Mr. Arnold, and I'll be there."

"Fletcher, please." He handed one of his cards to her. "Take this. I wrote the address where we're doing the first few days work on the back."

She liked him. He was relaxed and yet very organized. They worked out the details. Jake didn't say anything while she and Fletcher talked—she couldn't sense his feelings on what she was doing, but this was a bigger break than she ever could have gotten while still working for Top End.

A break, it appeared, that Jake had made possible for her.

"You got everything you need?"

Kaz nodded. "I think so. Fletcher?"

"We're good. I'll call you Sunday afternoon. We can set up a time for a quick audition on Monday and the costume gal can get your measurements then, but wear something high-end and sexy looking, just in case. We're supposed to showcase some designer's fashions along with the wine. I think she's the winery owner's girlfriend, but you didn't hear that from me." He laughed. "Wear something for a night on the town in San Francisco. That's the look we're going for."

Jake stood and pulled Kaz's chair back for her. She and Fletch shook hands, but she got kisses from Marty and Tim, and even Steve, though he definitely blushed. Jake paid for breakfast, and they left the restaurant.

For whatever reason, he didn't say a word.

CHAPTER 10

Jake paused at the edge of the plaza and glanced around. He'd quickly gotten in the habit of scanning his surroundings, looking for anyone who appeared to be watching them. Everything looked quiet, but he was keyed up. He took Kaz's hand. "Let's go back to the room so I can grab some of my gear, and then we can check out a few of the local tasting rooms." When Kaz raised an eyebrow, he laughed.

"Not to taste. It's a little early for that."

"Good. I agree."

"What?" Still holding on to her hand, he turned her to face him. "Wine on top of a spinach omelet doesn't appeal?"

"Yuck." She stared at him, smiling, and then she pressed her palm to his chest. "Jake? Thank you for calling Fletcher. I had no idea . . ."

"I'm glad it paid off. When the guys said they were here working with Fletch, it seemed like a good idea. He and I go back a while. He's a good man, has an excellent reputation. Between Marcus Reed's ad campaign and the media blitz Fletch is working on, your career could get a real boost."

"Thank you." She kissed him. "You went above and beyond."

"You're welcome." Then he winked. "You might consider wearing some of Marc's jewelry for the shots."

"Ah. I should have seen your angle. But thank you, and yes, I will."

Her eyes sparkled. She was so beautiful, it was hard to watch her, to realize their time together was passing so quickly. As they crossed the plaza, he forced himself to look away from Kaz, from her laughter and her sparkling eyes, from that beautiful, tall, athletic body. It was the only way to keep from holding on to her.

He glanced at the people around them, at young mothers with babies in strollers, an older couple walking a very old dog, two young men sitting close together on one of the benches, heads bent low over their mobile phones. Other couples strolled hand in hand, a couple of city workers did something near the pond in the middle of it all, laughing and teasing while they worked.

There was a brisk breeze, but the sun was shining, and Jake couldn't help but be aware of all the life around him. Life the way it should be. It was beautiful, in fact it was perfect, except it forced him to see what he didn't have.

What, most likely, he would never have. The lifelong connection of the older couple, of the mothers and babies. Of friends working together, sitting together in the sun.

Would he ever be able to accept that it wasn't possible for him to expect his own slice of normal? RJ would haunt him for the rest of his life, and he'd damned well better get used to it. He glanced down at their hands, at the way Kaz wrapped her long fingers around his, and it was like a punch to the gut. So close, and yet totally out of reach.

They stopped at the crosswalk to wait for the light. Kaz

stood close beside him. Close enough for Jake to feel the heat from her body, to pick up the light scent of whatever shampoo she'd used—probably the same stuff he had, the one provided by the hotel. Why did it smell so much better on Kaz?

He held tightly to her hand when the light changed, and they started across the street. Held on while glancing in all directions. That speeding car, the text messages, all horribly personal. Either the bastard had seen the car that almost hit them, or he'd been driving it. Jake would bet he was the driver, but why?

He'd gotten a good look at the man right after he spun out in the middle of the road. He'd looked familiar. Had he been the guy Kaz saw in the coffee shop? He hadn't paid close enough attention to be sure, but if it was, that meant the bastard was following him.

"What do you want me to wear?"

It took a minute for him to change gears. He glanced at Kaz, trying to wrap his mind around her wardrobe while obsessing over the incident Tuesday night, the message he'd gotten shortly afterward.

RJ, buddy . . . you need to be more careful crossing the street.

"Sorry. Mind was a million miles away. I'm trying to remember what you've got that would showcase the ruby set, the one that goes from ear to nostril with the three chains. That's more apropos for daytime wear than the diamonds or tanzanite."

She smiled at him. Eyes, face, lips. Little crinkles at the corner of her eyes—the whole package in that smile. "I like that set. How about that dark brown, almost black silk top with the wide neckline? I brought it because it's almost exactly the color of my hair, and I'm vain." She laughed. "Actually, I think it must look good because it's one thing I wear that always gets lots of compliments, but that could be because it fits snug." She rolled her eyes at that. "Are you doing whole body or upper only?"

"I'm thinking of posing you at one of the tasting room counters, elbows on the counter, glass of wine in your hand. Face to the camera. I want to find a wine that matches the color of the stones. The shirt sounds perfect. Understated. Are any of your lipsticks that dark red, like the rubies in the set?"

They paused at the hotel entrance.

"I think so. We should be able to make a good match. If not, I can blend colors."

"Perfect." He liked what she'd said, though he wasn't thinking of lipstick.

We should be able to make a good match.

Kaz released his hand and headed toward the elevator. Jake stared at his fingers a moment before raising his head and catching Kaz watching him. "Go on up," he said. "I want to see what time we have to check out."

The elevator doors opened. She waved and stepped inside, but Jake stared at the empty spot where she'd been. In just a couple of days, he'd gotten so used to having her beside him that he felt her absence as a physical loss. He had no one to blame but himself—this was the future he'd chosen, the one he'd mapped out for himself.

Alone, but for the occasional meaningless relationship. He hadn't minded before, but there'd never been anyone like Kaz. He doubted there'd ever be another, but the connection she'd made with Fletch this morning was proof she wasn't meant to stay with Jake.

She was smart and beautiful—a dangerous combination for Jake's peace of mind. She was destined for so much more than he could offer. A natural in front of the camera, she had perfect instincts for playing a scene, and a sexy voice that would work beautifully for commercials.

A voice he knew he'd be hearing in his dreams for

years. When the Intimate campaign went national in just a few short weeks, Kaz was going to be everywhere. She didn't seem to realize what changes were ahead of her, the true scope of the campaign. Marc had a lot of ad space booked—an international media blitz that only someone with Marcus Reed's resources could afford—and Kaz's face would be at the heart of the promotion. Fletcher's commercial, should she end up doing that, would give her even broader national media attention.

Commercials would expose the world to more than her absolutely perfect body—they'd get to hear that sexy voice of hers. How was he going to handle that, never again hearing those deep-throated cries of pleasure, or her soft, husky whispers, begging for more?

A shiver ran across his spine; already he felt the loss. He shook himself out of it and got into line at the front desk. It looked like this might take a while.

He pulled out his phone to look at the pictures again, slowly scrolling through shot after shot of Kaz. She was exquisite, absolutely breathtaking in every single shot. The jewelry didn't make her look prettier—she showcased the jewels in a manner that was going to put Marc over the moon.

He paused at one where she'd been nude from the waist up, but the combination of light and shadow and the multihued scarf had turned the photograph into art, acceptable for commercial use by anyone's standards. Another showcased the chains shimmering from nipples to navel with the monarch butterfly filling the frame. It was spectacular, not merely because of the brilliant colors, but also because of the perfect lines of Kaz's sleek body.

He had no doubt, over the next few months, Kaz Kazanov was going to explode onto the modeling scene. As the photographer, Jake could stay in the background, but her life, and anyone she was connected to, was going to face close scrutiny. Jake couldn't handle the possible attention if he were still a part of Kaz's life.

He could already see the headlines of the online gossip sites, comparing the death of Kaz's little sister to Jake's time locked up for the same type of crime that had cost Jilly her life. They'd pull out his history as an Olympian, his fall from grace. They'd squeeze the story until there was no blood left, but then it wouldn't matter anymore.

The minute Kaz learned the truth about him, as soon as she realized he'd lied to her, if only by omission, the only thing she'd want from Jake would be for him to leave.

Kaz had most of her things packed when Jake finally came up to the room. She raised her head, fighting a powerful need to stand here and just stare at the man as he stepped through the door. Instead, she welcomed him with a smile. "Hey! I thought you got lost."

"I know. They were busier than I expected. Sorry I took so long."

He walked over and stood beside her. She had the skinny jeans and dark silk blouse lying together on the bed.

He looked at them for a minute, and said, "We don't need to vacate until two. The people who have this room for the rest of the weekend aren't due in until late tonight, or we'd have to be out earlier, but two should work great. Gives us a few hours to poke around, look for some good settings in town before we check into the B and B in Geyserville and head back out to the vineyard."

"Two works for me." She gestured at the clothing. "Well? Does this work?"

"It does."

"Good. It's my favorite of everything I brought." She smiled at him, and then she was biting back laughter. She couldn't stop smiling. Felt like laughing her head off. She hadn't been able to stop since meeting Fletcher Arnold this morning, knowing she'd be able to pay her bills for at least a little longer.

"What about lip color?"

"I need to see the jewelry in order to match the lipstick. What about nail polish?"

"Keep your nails the way they are. If you used polish, you'd have to add fake nails."

"Ya think?" She glanced at her short nails with their clear polish and just shook her head. "It's funny that I ended up as a model. Makeup and all that girly-girl stuff just isn't me. Jilly got all the family girly genes. She loved the glam."

Jake turned and frowned. "How did you end up modeling?"

She almost snorted. "I was a horrible waitress. I couldn't find a job in banking, which is what my father was pushing, but I didn't try very hard. Marty and Tim were friends in college. They dared me to apply, and I got hired. I've been lucky. I've got a look that's popular right now, the money's been steady, and pretty good. It's almost worth having to wear makeup."

"You don't wear much."

She shook her head. "Not if I can avoid it. Only what the shoot requires."

"I guess you're lucky you don't need it." He grabbed a box off the bed. "See what you can do with these."

He opened a black box to show her the jewelry. She'd seen them before, and of all the jewelry Jake had brought, this set called to her. It was absolutely beautiful. The necklace was more of a collar, a beautiful band of gold and rubies that would be perfect above the wide neck of her blouse, but the earrings were exquisite. Three dark red rubies hung from fine gold chains in gradually longer lengths, all attached to ruby studs for each ear. Three more chains ran from one of the earrings to a single small ruby set in gold, designed for facial placement, whether cheek or lip or, like Kaz, for her nostril.

Put all together, it was a beautiful set but, unlike the diamonds, perfect for daytime wear.

"Those are absolutely gorgeous. Such a deep, dark red."

Jake laughed. "They're called pigeon's blood rubies. The color is darker than the traditional brilliant red. Makes them more valuable."

She wrinkled her nose and frowned at him. "Well, that's gross. And I'd rather not know what the set's worth. It might make me too nervous to wear them." She couldn't stop staring. "These really are beautiful, not fragile looking at all." She glanced at Jake. "It's jewelry with a sense of power, in spite of how fine the chains are. Makes me want to meet your friend Marc. I'm curious about a man who can design something like these."

She grabbed the box and the brown silk shirt and went into the bathroom. The shirt went on first, and then she slipped the earrings into place and looped the gold chains across her cheek when she added the stud for her nose.

The effect was not only stunning, it was sexy as hell. The way the chains sort of rolled across her cheek when she moved had a truly sensual effect. Tilting her head one way and then the other, she decided this was definitely her favorite of all the pieces she'd modeled.

She'd washed her face and added a translucent moisturizer before Jake got back, and now she found a perfect lipstick match in her makeup case and carefully painted her lips.

She glanced at the lipstick wand and shivered. The color was called ruby midnight. That sounded better than pigeon's blood, thank goodness, especially since it went on her mouth.

Her hair was its usual tousled mess—she ran a brush through it, fluffed her bangs, and walked back into the room. She'd picked a pair of super-tight black skinny jeans and dark bronze flats that almost matched the blouse. It was a good look.

Jake stood by the window, gazing out over the plaza, hands crossed over his chest, head tilted as if he watched something or maybe someone.

She watched him just as intently for only a moment, but somehow it felt important, as if she might be holding on to this view of him—turned away from her, his long, tall frame and dark hair, the broad shoulders and lean hips an image of strength.

Except, strength wasn't what she thought of, seeing him this way. What filled her mind was how lonely he looked. How utterly and completely alone.

"What do you think?"

Jake forced himself to look away from the man on the corner. He'd been wishing the guy would turn around so he could get a look at the guy's face, but Kaz's soft question was enough to pull him away from the window. When he turned, he actually caught his breath. She was beautiful. Absolutely amazing. "Come here, in the light. Lord, Kaz . . ." He cupped her chin, turned her to the sunlight streaming in through the open window.

The brilliant shaft of light added fire to the dark rubies. The gold glistened against her honey-toned skin, and the shimmering silk truly was the same color as her hair. "Hold that, okay?"

She merely smiled. Jake grabbed his camera off the bed, switched out the lens with long practiced ease, and went back to Kaz and a sunbeam that was apparently intent on turning him into a slavering idiot.

He didn't need grapevines and wildflowers. All he really needed was Kaz. She was the flawless canvas Marc's beautiful designs deserved. He snapped a few shots, tweaked his settings a bit, and took more. No need for a flash—the golden light shining through the window couldn't have been better. She'd matched the lipstick perfectly to the dark rubies.

Pigeon's blood. He almost laughed. Damn, he hoped that wasn't the name of her lipstick, but then she tilted her head and smiled, and it was quite literally a punch to the gut. If he caught that look, he'd have the money shot, though how could he possibly limit himself to one?

After a couple of minutes, the sun had moved just enough to lose the focused spotlight effect. Jake lowered the camera and gazed at Kaz, at the questioning smile in her eyes, at the quiet joy in her smile, and he had to shake himself, remind himself that it was all in the look, that her smiles weren't for him, they were for the camera.

"I think I got some good ones," he said. He turned away to pack up the gear he wanted to take when they wandered through the tasting rooms and shops. Kaz's hand on his forearm stopped him.

"What were you looking at?" she asked.

"What?" He turned and she was gazing out of the window, frowning.

"Nothing. Why?" He walked over to stand beside her. Stared at the corner he'd been watching earlier.

"There was a guy down there, in front of the store where you bought the scarf. I swear he was staring right at me while you were taking your pictures."

Crap. He really didn't want to hear that, but he didn't want to upset Kaz, either. "The guy in the gray shirt? I didn't see his face. Looked like he was waiting for someone. He probably glanced this way, saw a beautiful woman posing in front of an open window, and just stopped to watch."

She turned again and took a quick look at the plaza, then down the main street in both directions. "I dunno,

Jake. I might sound totally paranoid, but I could swear it was the same guy who almost hit us the other night. Looked just like him."

Jake looked out the window, made a point of checking out the plaza, watching sidewalks in both directions along the main street. He didn't want to tell her he'd thought the same thing. Wondered if he'd seen the same guy. "What was he wearing?"

"Dark pants. Light blue or gray shirt. Dark hair, probably in his forties or fifties. Looked too grungy to be a tourist, really. He was alone."

"Let's go down. We're going to be around the plaza; we can watch for him. I think I'd recognize him if I saw him." And he'd definitely be looking for the guy.

"Okay." She rubbed her hands over her arms and then laughed. "I sound like a real freak, don't I?"

"Not at all. What happened was pretty scary. The fact that, after he almost hit us, he stopped and glared at us like we were at fault . . . now that was freaky."

Not nearly as freaky as the texts. No way in hell was he saying anything about the texts.

They went to three different tasting rooms around the plaza while Jake took what felt like hundreds of pictures. Everywhere they stopped, women asked Kaz about her jewelry, and she easily told them what she knew about the designer and the designs. Jake teased her about taping the conversations for Marc, told her Marc might start thinking in terms of film commercials for the company once he heard the sales pitch she was giving.

"You keep that up, I'll have to put Marc in touch with Fletcher," he said.

Even though he laughed when he said it, Kaz wondered if he might be serious.

Finally, Jake packed his cameras away and they wandered through a couple of wonderful, trendy little dress shops, playing tourist. Kaz had finally begun to relax when she realized the guy she'd thought was watching her was nowhere to be seen. He'd made her nervous. It was just creepy, as if he'd expected her to show up in that window, like he'd been waiting for her, but then she'd always had an active imagination.

It was almost time to head back to the hotel and check out of their room when Jake dragged her into one final store. "This is the last one. I promise."

"You said that at the last one." She was laughing when she said it, but the novelty had worn off after the first store. Prices were high, and for a woman without a steady job, the last thing she wanted to do was spend money on clothes she didn't need. Jake kept telling her he'd buy whatever she wanted, but that wasn't going to happen, either.

Jake pointed to a darkly beautiful skirt and top on a mannequin just inside the shop. "I have a clothing allowance for this project. If they have this in your size, we're buying it. No arguments. It's perfect to display the tiger eye set. That's the only non-precious gem group in the entire catalog, but it's Marc's favorite stone, and the one that gave him the idea for the entire line. Those pieces and that outfit will look gorgeous in the vineyard setting."

Kaz had to agree. The skirt was gauzy and shimmery, patterned with dark bronze grape leaves over a black background, designed to sit just below the waist. The cropped cami top had the same colors and design, though the leaves were smaller. The back of the top was longer and would sit right at waist level. In front, it would float just beneath her breasts, exposing a flash of her butterfly tattoo.

"Could we add the gold chains?" She was trying to see the shot through Jake's lens. "The way the top is cut, if I didn't wear a bra I could use the plain gold nipple rings with the chains attached to the one in my navel. That would hint at the tiger eye stones without actually showing them."

She didn't give Jake a chance to answer. Instead, she looked through the rack, found her size, and took the skirt and top into a dressing room.

It really was stunning. She stepped out and almost ran into Jake. He waited impatiently, standing in front of the small curtained room with his arms folded across his chest. He stared at her, wide eyed, and then slowly shook his head. He sounded almost reverent when he said, "Turn around."

She spun slowly, aware of the gauzy fabric floating above her ankles. She hadn't noticed the attractively un-even hem at first, but she loved the way the fabric hugged her hips and thighs and yet still seemed to float away from her ankles on the nonexistent breeze.

The top barely covered the lower curve of her breasts, but she was a lot taller than the average shopper. Things never fit her the way the designs were supposed to, but in this case, it was all to Kaz's advantage.

She felt sexy in this outfit. From the look on Jake's face, he agreed. The salesclerk wandered over, though her gaze was focused entirely on Jake. She barely seemed to notice Kaz, standing there in almost eight hundred dollars' worth of designer outfit.

Kaz couldn't blame her.

She'd watch Jake, too, but the man was in a hurry. She knew he hadn't packed yet, and his gear had been all over the room. "Look, why don't you go on ahead. I'll get changed and be right behind you."

"No, I don't . . ." He glanced toward the front of the shop.

"We haven't seen that guy at all. If you do see him, come back and get me. Here, take these." She handed him the tags off the top and the skirt. "You're buying." She leaned close and kissed him. "It's almost two, and I'll be right there. There are people all over the place, and it's just half a block, Jake. That's all we are from the hotel."

"Okay. Keep your phone handy, and pay attention. I'm going to worry about you."

"Don't. Now go."

Jake took the tags. "You're sure you're okay walking back by yourself?"

"Definitely. Be there in a couple of minutes." She leaned over and kissed him on the nose, loving the way he looked so nonplussed by the silly act.

Jake wrapped an arm around her waist and pulled her against him. His lips moved over hers much too quickly. When he ended the kiss, she stood there, staring at him, her heart pounding, her lips tingling from his kiss.

Then he kissed her on the nose and walked up to the front of the store to pay for the clothes.

Kaz took her time changing, thinking of that kiss, as well as the idea of walking back to the hotel alone. Neither of them had noticed that strange man anywhere on the plaza, and they'd both been looking for him. She decided he wasn't an issue.

No, the issue was that she'd practically been glued to Jake's side from the moment he'd picked her up in San Francisco. A walk—even a short one—by herself sounded really good right now, if only to give her a chance to think about the last couple of days and what Jake meant to her without his powerful male presence affecting her thoughts.

Would she ever find another man like him? Did she really want to? He was totally male, and in so many ways, totally overwhelming. He wasn't a guy any woman could easily forget. When they were close, he filled her senses. When he wasn't, he filled her thoughts.

But he'd been very clear—there was no future for them. She needed to be just as clear, and the way to do that was to remind herself that this job was important to her career. The exposure to a national audience was a huge leap for her. Even with all its hassles, she loved modeling. She loved the freedom it gave her, the chance to meet new people, to do really fun projects, even improve her acting skills if this job with Fletch worked out, all with relatively little risk.

Except, her focus had shifted over the past couple of days—and had steadied with all the certainty of a compass pointing north. Hers pointed toward Jake. Misquoting Hamlet, she muttered, "And therein lies the risk."

Unfortunately, she was fully aware that it was her sense of self-preservation facing the biggest risk of all.

CHAPTER 11

Jake parked in front of the B and B, a beautifully restored Victorian on the main street in town. It was another beautiful day—no sign of the rain Jake had mentioned the day he hired her. They'd had such a terrific time today that she decided not to call him on it—if he'd lied to get her to come with him, she wasn't going to complain.

He held her hand as they went inside. A young couple was ahead of them, listening to an older woman in the lobby. "I'm sorry," she said. "I found the note our part-time girl wrote down about your call for a room, but we don't have any vacancies at all. We've been booked for weeks. This is a busy time of year."

The man stared at the beautiful woman next to him. They looked so young. Kaz didn't think she'd ever been that young, that innocent.

"I'm sorry, sweetheart." He faced the older lady. "We must have misunderstood. She assured us we had a reservation."

Kaz glanced at Jake. She knew Jake had reservations for two rooms, and she was absolutely certain they only needed one.

"Excuse me." He stepped closer to the young couple. Kaz thought their wedding rings looked awfully new. "I have reservations for two rooms, but we only need one. Are you guys on your honeymoon?"

The girl nodded. Jake spoke to the older woman. "Can you give our extra room to these folks?"

That was all it took.

Sometimes things were meant to be.

But now they were walking hand in hand, back to their shared room after a lovely dinner in the little town of Geyserville. It was a place she'd driven past more than once, but had never stopped to explore.

"That was a really good dinner," she said, but she wasn't thinking of the salmon she'd eaten. No, it was all about getting back to their room, getting naked. She wondered if he realized she was wearing the rubies tonight. All of them.

"It was." He squeezed her hand, glanced at her from the corner of his eye, and she had a strong feeling his mind was moving parallel to hers.

"So tomorrow," he said, swinging their hands together, "I want to go back to the vineyard, get some shots among the vines, maybe a few more down near the creek."

"What?" She fluttered her eyelashes. "None in the stall?"

His soft chuckle sent shivers over her spine. They'd had sex only once, yesterday in the barn, and she'd thought of it constantly until her explicit memories—visual and tactile—played an infinite loop in her mind and left her with one entirely inescapable conclusion: once wasn't nearly enough.

She had two more nights with Jake. Two nights and two days, but the days would be all about work. About finishing the job.

She had a snarky thought and doubted he'd penciled in time to get naked with his model, but she couldn't blame Jake entirely for the chemistry that practically exploded between the two of them. She was well aware of the effect arousal could have when she was on a job. She'd learned to work it, to project that sensuality in a way that left no doubt in the minds of consumers. They would look at her picture in the ad, feel her desire for whatever product was the focus, and know, without any doubt, that they, too, could feel that way, look that good, even experience that kind of excitement and sensual fulfillment if only they purchased whatever product the ad was trying to sell.

Manipulative and probably unfair, but it was a job she loved, and what her role entailed. She earned her living selling products by making them look so desirable that the consumer couldn't live without them.

Except Jake made her forget all about the job. When she smiled at him, whether he held a camera or not, she was smiling at the man, not the camera. Somewhere around the middle of that first day with Jake, she'd moved well beyond the lens.

But the ones looking at her image wouldn't understand. They wouldn't know that all of Kaz's desire wasn't focused on them or on the product she was touting, that what they saw was her response to Jacob Lowell. No—they'd see the product and the look of need in her eyes and that's the connection they'd make.

And wasn't that exactly what Jake and his client wanted?

Of course it was. For all she knew, his fascination with her was merely his method of getting the job done. Okay, so that would hurt, but she couldn't hold it against him. Now all Kaz had to do was keep reminding herself that sexual desire, even arousal, was perfectly okay, as long as it enhanced the shot.

It was not okay if she personalized it, if she lied convincingly enough to herself and ended up believing her own sales pitch. Keeping that thought in mind, Kaz walked through the door to the B and B when Jake held it for her.

Walked up the stairs to their room, her mind free to enjoy whatever the night might bring.

No strings. No permanent attachment.

Then she blew it. She glanced at Jake, caught him watching her, and there was so much need in that dark-eyed gaze that shivers raced over her arms and her nipples tightened against the gold rings she wore.

The best of plans, the very best of intentions, all swept away in that one intense look from the man still holding on to her hand. Was she reading more into Jake's look than he meant?

Or was she a complete idiot, believing she could spend more time in his bed and then blithely walk away, un-scathed?

Except she had to walk away. The deal with Fletcher Arnold was huge, a chance to take her career to an entirely new level. Jake had put them in touch; he'd understood that she was serious when she said she didn't have time for a relationship. He'd made it perfectly clear he wasn't inter-ested in more than the next couple of days.

He smiled at her, tugged her hand, and they continued down the hall to their room, but the truth was an uncom-fortable weight lying heavily on her chest, most likely in the vicinity of her heart. Lying there with the half-truths she'd allowed him to believe.

She'd been lying to herself as much as to Jake, and she was absolutely terrified she'd never, ever get enough of him. She'd better make tonight count—make every minute with Jake count—if only to give herself as many memo-ries as she could. They might be all she'd have of him to keep.

And wouldn't that just absolutely suck.

For whatever reason, Jake was a wreck. They'd had such a great day together—dinner had been terrific, he knew he'd gotten some gorgeous shots in town today—and yet he felt out of sync, as if he was making some horrible mistake.

But what?

Marc was going to be totally blown away by the photos he'd gotten so far. One more series out among the vines, and they'd be done.

Kaz would go her way, Jake would go his. Once they were apart, she'd be safe.

Hell, he'd never dreamed he'd be putting her in danger on this trip, but as long as that bastard was out there, watching him, she was at risk.

He hadn't gotten any texts today, though there was no doubt in his mind the guy outside their hotel room was the one who'd been sending them.

What the hell did he want? And how did he know about RJ?

Screw it. He'd wait for the next one, and concentrate on Kaz, on tonight and tomorrow night making love with an amazing woman, knowing that what they had would end when he took her home. He'd concentrate on that, not on whoever was out there waiting for him to do something stupid.

Jake used the old-fashioned key to unlock the door to their room. It was decorated in Victorian chic, overdone as most places like this were, but with the subtle glow of one small lamp, the big bed against the far wall, the polished oak plank floors, and the plush area rug patterned in black with pink roses, somehow it worked.

And somehow, Kaz fit right in, even dressed as purely modern as could be. Wearing black skinny jeans and a tight black turtleneck sweater with knee-high red leather boots, she looked glamorous and sexy as hell.

Locking the door behind them, Jake turned to pull her into his arms. She fit perfectly, eye-to-eye with him in those high-heeled boots of hers. He'd given her the rubies to wear tonight, but she'd never said whether or not she'd worn the entire set. Keeping him guessing had added a layer of arousal he'd not expected, but he reined in his inner caveman and gently kissed the curve of her jaw before settling on her lush mouth.

Kaz opened for him, sucking his tongue into her mouth, pressing herself tightly against his groin. He knew it was impossible for her to miss how hard he was as she rubbed against him.

"I like this," she said. "Knowing you're all ready for me."

He ran kisses over her cheek, across the gold chains that draped from her earlobe to her nostril. He tickled behind her ear with the tip of his tongue. She scrunched her head to her shoulder, laughing.

He pulled back and looked into her dark eyes. "I've been ready since last night." He ran his tongue around the shell of her ear. "But you fell asleep."

Laughing, she pulled back and rested her forearms on his shoulders. "And you're never going to let me forget it, are you?"

"Never. Besides, it's incentive to get you naked and under me as soon as I can. At least, while you're still awake."

"What if I want to be naked and over you? What if I want you at my mercy, begging?"

He raised an eyebrow. "Hadn't thought of that. How about some particulars. Plan of attack, that sort of thing?"

She kissed his chin, his left cheek then his right. "A good general never gives away her battle plans. Now strip." She stepped back and folded her arms across her chest.

Jake let his gaze run slowly from her head to her toes, settling longer on her breasts, at the *V* between her legs.

"Well?" She tapped her toe.

"I'm trying to decide if submission is the better part of valor."

She leaned close and ran her finger from his sternum to the band at the top of his jeans. Then she tugged at the snap, popped it open. "Submission might be the difference between getting laid tonight. Or not."

He slowly unbuttoned the top button on his shirt. Then the next. "That's a fairly good argument."

"I thought you'd see things my way."

He slipped the shirt off and hung it over a chair, then toed off his shoes and socks. Unzipped his pants and stepped out of them. His sleek black boxers hugged his package, but there was nothing subtle about the firm arch of his dick against the snug fabric. He glanced at Kaz and had to bite the inside of his lip to keep from laughing.

She started with his chest and he watched her eyes slowly track downward until her gaze reached his groin. Her eyes went wide, and a sensual smile curved her lips. Then she shocked the hell out of him when she went to her knees. Blood pulsed along his shaft, and his balls went tight. Her focus never left his crotch. She hadn't touched him, hadn't said a word, but he was hanging on the edge of climax merely from the look of lust in her eyes.

Her tongue slipped between her lips, swept across her top lip, then the bottom. She caught her bottom lip in her teeth and gnawed on it a moment. Jake's whole body tensed. His balls drew up hard and tight between his legs.

Kaz slipped her fingertips into either side of his shorts and gently tugged. When the waistband caught on the curve of his erection, her lips spread in a wide smile, but she never raised her head, didn't look anywhere beyond the goods between his legs.

Jake wanted to tangle his fingers in her tousled hair and press her against him, wanted her to pull his shorts all the way down and just do something, anything, as long as it involved her mouth and his dick. The suspense was driving him nuts. He heard himself breathing, realized his breath was coming in short, sharp pants, but Kaz seemed perfectly happy, moving at a snail's pace, driving him slowly insane.

She leaned close and ran her tongue along the fabric covering his shaft. He groaned and clenched his hands, fully aware he was shaking like he had some sort of palsy, his entire body trembling while she nibbled the head of his dick through the slick fabric.

Abruptly, she sat back on her heels. "It's getting hot in here." Glancing up at him, she drew her black turtleneck over her head. The lacy bra she wore was the same color red as her boots. The same red as the rubies peeking through the lace. She'd worn the ruby studs in her nipples, and the gold chains snaked from her tits, down over her rib cage, across her flat belly, and over the monarch butterfly tattoo, where they met at the gold ring with the matching ruby in her navel.

He reached for her. She stopped him with an arched brow and a stern look. "Don't move. I think you should grab your wrists behind your back. That might keep you out of trouble."

"You're killing me here." He grabbed his left wrist with his right hand behind his back.

"Good. Payback's a bitch." She sat back on her butt and unzipped her boots, slipped them off, and tossed them aside. Then she unsnapped and unzipped her jeans and slid them down her long, long legs.

Leaving her wearing nothing but a lacy red thong, a matching red bra, and . . . *Holy shit.* A gold chain running from her navel to the ring in her clit. Jake groaned. Kaz tilted her head and smiled up at him. "I thought you'd like that."

"Oh, God. I really don't want to stop, but I need a picture of you like this. I really do, Kaz. You are so fucking hot."

"I am not ready to advertise my clit." She sat back on her heels with her arms folded across her chest, which pushed her breasts higher, plumped the rounded curves until they practically spilled out of her lacy bra. Jake's mouth went dry.

"For me, sweetheart. Just for me. You still have a bra and the thong, and I want you to leave them on." He laughed. "For now, anyway. Kaz, you're so beautiful. I want to be able to see you like this. When you're off somewhere on a big shoot with some multinational company, I'm going to pull out my pictures of you for consolation."

Shaking her head, Kaz laughed. "Well, when you put it like that."

He reached around behind her and grabbed one of his cameras off the bedside table, leaned back to fit all of her in the frame, and snapped a couple of shots. He got down on one knee to get a picture straight on, and she posed for him, hooking her thumbs in the top of her thong and shoving the waistband down even lower on her hips, rolling the band to just above her sex. The gold chains disappeared in the red folds of silk between her legs.

"Got what you wanted?"

"Not yet." Then he put the camera away and, once again, stood in front of her with his hands behind his back.

Kaz flipped the tiny catch at the front of her bra, slipped the straps over her shoulders, and dropped it on the floor. Her breasts were perfect—softly rounded and very firmly in place. She was lean and muscular, with the look of a woman who worked out regularly. He wondered if she was a runner.

Another thing he didn't know about her. Wanted to know.

The rubies on their gold rings piercing her nipples gave him something to focus on. *Stare at the jewelry,* he thought.

If he stared at the fragile-looking chains, maybe he'd be able to hold on.

He'd never experienced this level of arousal. She hadn't freaking done anything yet, but his shorts were already damp from the pre-cum he couldn't control. Then she ran her finger over the curve of his shaft and he almost lost it.

"You're horribly overdressed, don't you agree?"

"Oh, yeah." He had his boxers off in a heartbeat. Stood straight again, but with his hands at his sides, clenching and unclenching his fists. He couldn't remember ever being this hard, and he'd been hard a lot around Kaz. His dick arched up and touched his belly. His balls ached.

Did she have any idea what she was doing to him?

She raised her head and looked directly at him, and the expression on her face was one of stark need.

And with that one look, he knew Kaz could take all the time she wanted and do whatever she damned well pleased with him. Anything at all.

Planting her palms on her thighs, Kaz sat back on her heels and openly admired Jake's impressive package. Then she glanced up at his face. His jaw was clenched, his dark eyes narrowed as if he struggled for control. "Just thought you might want to know that I've never really done this before."

"Done what?"

"This," she said, waving her hand to encompass his midsection. "My life hasn't been at all conducive to this sort of thing. You know, kneeling in front of sexy men."

No exaggeration there, not when she'd been raising her sister, worrying about her dad, worrying about finishing school. "I don't see myself as naturally submissive, but I think I like this." She ran her finger along the underside of his erect cock. He rolled his hips forward, groaning. Kaz ignored the sound, even as her own body clenched with need. "I mean, I might be on my knees, but I'm still the one in control. It's hot. Totally hot."

"No argument from me."

She bit back a laugh. Jake was having trouble getting the words out. Whatever she was doing, it must be working. She scooted closer on her knees, cupped his sac in her palms, and once again stroked the stark, powerful curve of his erection. His breath hissed out as she palmed the rounded head. She thought she heard him whimper when she ran her tongue the full length of his penis, from root to tip. His hips jerked, so she did it again, but when she got to the end, she grasped the base in her free hand, held him still, and licked the velvety crown.

His breathing sped up. She wrapped her lips around the end, then tightened her fist around his thick base, holding him in place so she could slide him deeper into her mouth. Slowly, she slipped her lips along his length and then stuck her tongue in the tiny slit at the top. He must be turned on, because she tasted the first drops. Salty and almost bitter, they really shouldn't have tasted as good as they did.

She wanted more. Wanted everything.

Running her tongue across the smooth curve again, she wrapped her lips around the plum-shaped head. It was deceptively firm beneath the soft skin. She lightly sucked, sliding her mouth over him again, taking him deep inside. She hadn't been exaggerating—she'd never really gone down on a guy, hadn't liked what little oral play she'd tried in the past, but there was something so special about Jake that she realized she was getting turned on by the taste of him. By the way he felt on her tongue and against her lips, his hard shaft and the silky skin covering him, and even the musky scent that was all Jake, unique to him alone.

She sucked him deep, then slipped her mouth back to the rounded tip. She nibbled just a bit, scraping gently with her teeth. Then down again. His fingers tangled in her hair, and she heard his soft voice, whispers, really, a steady litany of "Oh, shit, don't come. Oh, shit . . ."

Which, of course, was all the incentive she needed to make him do exactly that. She found a rhythm, in and out, her tongue working over his skin, teeth scraping gently along his shaft. She let go of him, gave his sac one last stroke, and rested her hands on his hips, squeezed his buttocks, pulling him close to her mouth.

He groaned, and since she took that for an affirmative, she squeezed him again, and then ran her hands across his hips, down the strong muscles of his thighs, and then back up. Once again she wrapped the fingers of her left hand around the base of his shaft, which left her right hand free to cup his balls.

He tensed when she wrapped her fingers lightly around him, but when she began massaging the two orbs in her palm, his hips jerked, and his fingers tightened in her hair.

"No more, Kaz. I can't . . ."

She slipped free of him. "More," she said. "I want you to come. It's my turn."

"But I don't—"

"Shut. Up."

And then she went back to work—like it was such a tough job. She stroked his balls, ran her middle finger over his perineum, laved the full length of his shaft with the flat of her tongue, then nibbled at the crown with her lips and teeth.

She felt his legs trembling, his hands clutched her hair and dug into her scalp almost frantically. She'd never taken oral sex this far before.

She'd never felt so sexually powerful in her life.

He groaned. The sound tore from him as his body tensed, his hips bucked. She caught the first pulse of his seed and more. She took it all, sucking him quickly at first, then gently, continuing to cup his balls in her left palm while milking his shaft with her right until he was through, until his body stopped jerking and his cock no longer pulsed between her lips.

Sitting back on her heels, she finally raised her head and looked at Jake. His head was bowed, his eyes closed. He'd moved his hands to her shoulders, and his erection had subsided a bit, but not entirely. His shaft glistened, the sleek skin wet from her mouth, from his ejaculate. She figured he probably felt about the way she had that first night—totally wrecked.

"You okay?" She gently stroked his thigh until he opened his eyes and stared at her.

"I think I need to lie down before I fall over."

"That works." She stood and tugged his hand. He followed her to the bed. Gently, she shoved him down. "Be right back."

She went into the bathroom and found a washcloth, rinsed it in warm water. Brought it back into the room, knelt between his legs and began to carefully wash him, the way he'd done for her.

"Kaz, sweetheart. You don't need to do that."

"Yes I do. Because I want to." Gently, she ran the cloth over his balls and then along the length of his shaft. In less than a minute, he was hard again. She smiled at him. "I figure it's the only way I'll get my turn. Be right back."

Jake was laughing as she headed back to the bathroom.

Well, she'd just officially ruined him for any other woman. Jake lay back on the bed, thankful that the comforter had been turned back so his collapse had taken him directly to the sheets. He didn't think he had it in him to move.

She walked into the room after dumping the damp cloth, still wearing nothing but that tiny red thong. The chains from the ruby jewelry caught the light from the one small lamp in the room, and he couldn't not stare at the chain leading beneath the tiny red triangle of her thong, running from her navel to her clit.

She'd had that on tonight, while they were at dinner. While they'd sat in the bar waiting for their table, talking with the owner of the restaurant. She'd been her usual funny, chatty self.

Yet all that time, she'd been wearing a ring through the hood of her clit. A gold chain linking to her navel, to her breasts.

She'd flirted with the owner, complemented him on the decor in the restaurant, and Jake had never suspected.

She'd been wearing that perfect ruby atop her clit, and he hadn't had a clue. Yeah, he'd thought she might be wearing the ones in her nipples, but he figured she would have left the navel ring and chains off because her tight jeans would make them rub.

He'd never dreamed she'd wear all the chains, all the jewelry, but knowing that now made it hard to catch his breath. He was going to have to tell Marc that somehow they needed to emphasize the jewelry's effect on the male libido as part of their ad campaign.

And why the fuck was he thinking about work when he was here, in a bedroom, with an almost naked, gloriously beautiful woman ready to crawl into bed beside him? Under him. On top of him.

Hell, did it really matter?

Kaz stopped beside the bed and hooked her thumbs in the waistband of her thong. "Well? Did I give you enough time to recover?"

Laughing, he grabbed her hand, sat up, and helped her

tug the thong down her legs. "I think so, but you might have to check to make sure."

"Oh . . . I love the checking part." She pushed him back on the bed and straddled his hips. His dick arched up and over his belly, and even though she'd just given him about the greatest orgasm he'd ever experienced, he was hard and wanting again.

Wanting Kaz. Damn. He rubbed his hands over her thighs and considered begging, but then she rose up on her knees, scooted forward, and wrapped her fingers around his erection.

His whole body jerked when she touched him. Damn, he was so sensitive he felt like he might fire off at her slightest touch.

"Got those condoms handy?"

"Oh, shit." He laughed. "No. They're in my camera case."

"Lost in the moment?" She crawled off his legs and walked across the room.

He stared at her perfectly rounded butt, her tiny waist, the long, sleek line of her thighs, the firm muscles in her calves. He sighed while she unzipped the case and found the box of condoms.

"Extra-large? In the economy-size pack?"

Her laughter pulled him out of the moment. "Hey, the one we used yesterday was uncomfortably tight. And a man can hope, right?"

Raising an eyebrow, she held up the box and then very carefully opened the package and removed one foil-wrapped condom. "He can. I guess."

Walking back across the room with an exaggerated sway of her hips, she once again straddled his legs. Only this time, she carefully slipped a condom over his erection.

When she settled the roll at the end over the base of his

shaft, he groaned. When she leaned over and kissed the latex-covered tip, he bit back a whimper. And when she rose up on her knees and then slowly lowered herself down over his full length, Jake wasn't sure whether he wanted to weep or cheer.

CHAPTER 12

Wisps of fog drifted over the vineyard as they pulled in beside the barn just before sunrise. Jake took a careful look along the road and vineyard, watching for an older, black BMW. He'd awakened to another text this morning. It must have come late last night, when he and Kaz had been otherwise occupied.

Hey, RJ? Where the fuck did you go? We were having so much fun today and then poof . . . you're gone. But I'll find you. You can't hide. Not anymore.

He was actually glad he'd not seen it until he got up this morning. Glad nothing had ruined what had been an absolutely spectacular night. It was going to be so damned hard to walk away from this woman.

But with crap like that going on, what choice did he have? At least for now, anyway, it appeared the bastard had lost them.

Kaz grabbed the thermos of coffee and bag of muffins the B and B had provided, while Jake unlocked the barn and carried his camera gear inside.

He glanced up as Kaz walked through the door. "Now aren't you glad I told you to wear warmer clothes?"

"I don't get it. It was sunny just over that little hill." She glanced at the gray surrounding them, at the ghostly images of vines through fog.

"That's what creates the different microclimates this valley's known for. Cool, foggy mornings and warm, sunny days. Warm hillsides on the east, cooler on the west. The grapes love it."

"Half-naked models prefer the sunbeams. Just sayin' . . ." She grabbed a couple of paper plates and some napkins out of the cupboard over the sink and set them on the counter beside the bag of muffins.

"Looks good." Jake took a stool beside her and looked through the selection. "I'm hungry."

She leaned over and kissed his cheek. "Probably from all that exercise you got last night."

He turned and gave her a slow, lazy, incredibly sexy smile. "You, my dear, are a slave driver. And no, I am most definitely not complaining."

She felt the blush rising from her chest to her collarbones. "You'd better not be." Yawning, she covered her mouth. "Though I hope you're really good at tweaking the photos. I'm sure I have bags under my eyes."

"Your eyes are perfect. Just like the rest of you."

"You're making me blush." She dipped her head as heat suffused her face.

"You were already blushing. I can only assume you were thinking of last night."

She gave him a long, assessing glance. "How come it doesn't make you blush? Are you so jaded that—"

He shook his head. "Not at all. It's just that I'm too busy trying to figure out how to get you to do all that again tonight to actually waste energy on blushing." Taking a big bite of his blueberry muffin, he winked.

Kaz glanced away, sipping her coffee. It would be so damned easy to fall in love with this man. Too easy, and that alone was warning enough to back off, at least emotionally. Men who seemed too good to be true, generally were.

Taking a sip of her water, Kaz stretched and then stared at the remnants of lunch. It had been a really busy morning, but the time had flown. The skirt and top Jake had gotten for her yesterday worked beautifully, making it even more fun to find innovative poses. It was important to show off the jewelry—and her tattoo, when possible—without getting shots too risqué for most magazines.

She'd been so caught up in the poses, she hadn't realized she was even hungry until Jake mentioned it was already after noon.

Now he stood, shoved the stool back under the counter, and began gathering up the disposable trays and plates. There were still cheeses and sliced meats left, but they'd eaten most of it. Jake hadn't said whether they'd need to come back tomorrow morning.

He'd certainly taken a lot of pictures. She watched his hands as he stacked the plates and stuffed everything into a plastic garbage bag. Those hands had done amazing things to her body last night.

Things that had her nipples tightening around their rings, sending a charge of arousal straight to her sex. Those gorgeous gold chains linking nipples to navel to clit were like superconductors for sexual sensations.

Her abdominal muscles—and lower—clenched in reaction.

Jake glanced her way, and her first thought was that she'd said something aloud, which had the beginning heat of a blush spreading across her chest and up her throat.

"I'm going to toss the rest of this stuff," he said. "It's been here since Tuesday when Marc had the place stocked for us."

"Probably a good idea." Relieved he'd had no idea where

her mind had been headed, Kaz stood, wiped off the counter, and then leaned against the granite. "What now?"

Jake pulled a thin tablet out of his camera bag. "I want to take a look at the shots we got this morning. If they're good, we won't need to come back here tomorrow. I thought we might get some at the B and B." He glanced her way and raised an eyebrow. "I found our room to be quite inspirational."

She snorted.

"Are you casting aspersions on my lovemaking?"

Laughing, Kaz held up her right hand. "Never. I swear."

"Good."

At least he was smiling when he turned away and loaded photos from his camera onto the computer. Kaz stood beside him, quietly watching while he flipped through picture after picture. They all looked so similar to her, but she knew that Jake saw things in them she was totally unaware of.

"Damn." He went back to a photo and enlarged it. "That blanket is just too busy. Between the pattern on your dress and all the shadows from the leaves, it's too much. Do you mind reshooting a few of these? I think with the sun overhead and fewer shadows . . ."

His voice drifted off, and she knew he was thinking light settings and lenses and composition. "Not a bit," she said, reaching beneath the counter and grabbing her bag. "Let me fix my hair and lip gloss. Be right back."

Once in the small bathroom, she splashed water on her face and brushed her teeth. Then she touched up the light makeup she'd worn for today's shoot, added lip gloss, and fluffed her hair.

It took about five minutes. When Kaz got back to the main room, Jake was going through a cupboard filled with towels and what looked like sheets.

"Feel like sprawling in the vineyard on a tablecloth?"

"Beats weeds and bugs. What color?"

"I'm thinking the dark red. You're still wearing the tiger eye set, right?" He glanced her way when she nodded, and stared at her ears, at the tiny stud in her nose.

"Perfect. Those stones with the bronze leaves and the black background on your dress work really well. Can you carry this?" He handed the dark red table cloth to her. At the last minute, he reached in and grabbed a black one, too.

"Here." He pulled out a bottle of deep red wine with the Intimate label, along with two glasses, then picked up a pretty wooden tray and a small plate. "Any of that cheese left?"

"You tossed it."

"Damn." He rummaged through the trash and found some intact slices of yellow cheddar cheese, a triangle of Brie they'd hardly touched. A few crackers.

"I'm not *that* hungry." She stared at the foods he'd retrieved.

"Me, either, but they'll look okay for the shot. I'm thinking of you lying on the tablecloth between the vines, the bottle of red wine open, two glasses filled, looking at the camera as if it's your lover joining you for an afternoon tête-à-tête."

She tilted her head and gave him her best "come hither" smile. "And will my lover be joining me for a tête-à-tête?"

"He might. If he gets the shots he needs."

The sun was high in the sky, the valley surprisingly quiet. They found a spot at the edge of the vineyard with the riparian area in the background. These were older vines, all gnarled and twisted with shoots already spilling out in all directions, unlike the younger vineyards with their careful trellising and neat rows.

"This section belongs to the winemaker and the vineyard manager, but we have permission to use the property while they're away for the week. Marc told me that some of these vines are over a hundred years old."

"They're beautiful."

"So's the wine. That bottle you've got? It was made mostly from grapes off of these old vines. Look at the label—it's called Field Blend Red for a reason. A lot of the families who settled here came from Italy, and they loved their wine. During prohibition, the farmers could make wine for themselves and their families. They'd have a field of red wine grapes and a field of white, all different varieties, but same colors."

He held up the bottle filled with a dark plum shade of wine. "They'd blend all the white ones for their white wine, and all the red for the red wine. These are mostly Zinfandel, but there's some Syrah, a few Carignane, Sangiovese, and Barbera, even some Cabernet Sauvignon. When this field is harvested, the grapes are all dumped into the stemmer-crusher together. You put them together, in the percentages that come out of the field, they make magic. Wait until you taste the wine."

His face grew animated when he described the wine and the process to make it. She loved how he talked with his hands in motion, his eyes sparkling. "You love this, don't you?" she said. "You said you were one of the owners, right? You must have worked a harvest before, but you sound like you really love the whole process of wine making."

He stared out over the vineyard for a long moment. "I do. There's something timeless about making wine. Even with all the fancy equipment and the science that goes into creating good wine, growing good grapes, the best wines are still made with grapes picked by hand, and the best winemakers are right in the middle of the vineyards and the harvest, taking part in the whole process."

He glanced her way. "And yes, I do own a very small

part of the larger vineyard." He laughed. "About three vines' worth, though I'm not part of Marc's jewelry line. That's all his."

She held up the bottle she'd been carrying. "Did you help make this one?"

He glanced at the date of the vintage. "Not this one. The ones I worked on are still aging. Believe me, it's hard work. There's nothing glamorous about the crush, what they call the harvest. You're up there at the crusher fighting off the yellow jackets. Those damned bees love the sweet juice. You end up covered with it, and you're trying to keep up with the pickers, who are really fast, and dodge the bees, who are even faster." Laughing, he said, "I've never worked so hard in my life."

"Sounds like good work, though. You have something really special to show for it." She paused beside a twisted vine surrounded in tiny white daisies. "Is this spot okay?"

He nodded. "Looks good to me."

He helped her spread the tablecloth out between the vines. "Sometime, I'd love to experience that," she said. "I imagine it would make me appreciate my glasses of wine a lot more."

He gazed at her with such a soft smile on his face, it made her nervous. Finally, he nodded. "I'd like that," he said. "I'd love to bring you back here during harvest. If you're not in the Bahamas on some important shoot, or maybe the Swiss Alps."

"I don't ski well enough for the Alps. They'll have to find someone else to model their après ski wear." She laughed, and then realized she'd done a lot of laughing with Jake. Her gaze landed on his mouth, on the curve of his lips.

Almost as much laughing as kissing.

She held up the plastic bag with the cheese and crackers. "How do you want this?"

He seemed to shake himself. Maybe he'd been thinking what she'd been thinking. Their thoughts were so often aligned.

"Let's arrange the tray with a few grape leaves. Here's an opener if you want to get that cork out and pour about an inch in each glass. I'm going to set up a couple of reflectors to even out the shadows."

It took them about ten minutes. Kaz arranged the tray with the glasses and wine bottle surrounded by grape leaves and a few wild daisies, then she positioned herself on her side, resting on one elbow with her knee bent forward, the other leg stretched out, the glass in her hand.

She tilted her head, blinked slowly, and smiled seductively at Jake.

He stopped, dead in his tracks. "Can you hold that look?"

She licked her lips and batted her eyelashes slowly. Deliberately. Lowered her voice and whispered, "Give me a good reason. I'm sure I can."

"You're trying to kill me, aren't you?"

"Never. I want you alive. And hard. I really want you hard." She licked her lips again.

Jake crouched down to get the shot lined up. Then he groaned, stood, and rearranged himself in his loose-fitting cargo pants before going down on his knees once again.

Still looking through the lens, he added, "Kneeling to take a shot is a lot easier without a boner. Just sayin' . . ."

"Then don't look at me." Kaz twirled a grape leaf across her lips.

"I have to. That's what Marc's paying us for. I look at you, you look gorgeous."

She laughed. It really was fun to tease him. "I'm doing my job. Just lying here . . ."

"Looking and talking way too sexy for your own good. And mine, too." He tilted his head and studied her for a moment. "I'd like to see more of the chains. Can you arch your back so the underside curve of your breasts will show more? That way the chains have a nice flow to the visible ring in your navel, and it shows off more of your tat."

She arched, probably more than he expected, but she'd always been limber, and it was fun to throw him for a loop. The steady click of the camera had her shifting her position, using her imagination to come up with poses that showcased the tiger eye stones to their best advantage.

She slowly shifted until she was sitting upright with one knee up, the other folded beneath her, and her head turned to one side, her cheek resting on her knee. From that she stretched out on one knee with her other leg bent until her toes almost touched the back of her head.

The camera clicked steadily as she slowly went back into the original position, lying on her side with the glass of wine in her hand.

Jake snapped a few more shots, checked the screen on his camera, and smiled. "You are absolutely magnificent. I think I've got exactly the ones I needed."

Then he looked at her again, and this time there was so much heat in his eyes that Kaz imagined the slow sweep of his gaze leaving scorch marks across her skin.

"Of course, there are more I want," he said. His voice was even hotter. "I'd love to have a few of you for my personal stash."

"Anything in particular?" She lifted the cropped top high enough to expose her breasts.

She heard the hiss as Jake sucked in a breath, but his camera was up in an instant.

Glancing around, she made sure there was no one working in the vineyard, then slowly pulled the top over her head.

Jake didn't say a word, but the steady sound of the camera let her know he was still shooting. Slowly, she slipped the skirt over her hips, taking her thong along with it. Naked, lying beneath the brilliant spring sunshine, she felt stronger, more self-confident than she could ever recall.

It wasn't the fact she'd exposed herself to the man and his camera. It was all about choice. He hadn't asked her to do this. She'd made the decision on her own, to give him this gift, a bit of herself to remind him of what they'd shared.

There was no sound. The camera was on the tablecloth beside Jake's knees. She tilted her head and raised an eyebrow. "No more pictures?"

He shook his head. "I wanted to see you with my eyes, not through the filter of a lens. You're beautiful, Kaz. You're beautiful and you make me laugh, and you make me so damned hot. I will never forget these past few days."

She rolled over to her hands and knees and crawled close to him. "Well, if you do, you'll have pictures. And I certainly hope you keep your promise not to share those, or I will be forced to hire a hit man. And they don't come cheap."

"Never. Though after this ad campaign and the commercial you're doing for Fletch, you should be able to afford one." He pulled her forward into his lap, and she wrapped her arms around him, locked her legs behind his back. "I will never share them with anyone." He kissed her, sealing the deal.

She kissed him back.

Then he lay beside her on the red tablecloth, stroking her side, her flank, the curve of her bottom, until her skin tingled and her nipples ached. It didn't take him long to get rid of his clothes, to dig through his camera case and find the condoms, but she was more than ready for him when he finally rolled on top of her and filled her with a single long, hard thrust.

They'd tried all kinds of crazy positions last night, some so absurd they'd ended up giggling. Then there'd been the absolute showstopper that gave Jake a cramp in his leg. They'd decided not to try that one again.

Kaz liked this best, though why they called it the missionary position made no sense at all, unless she thought of making love with Jake as a religious experience. Which it was.

Dear God, it really was.

It was definitely perfect for making love in a vineyard. She looked up into those dark, dark eyes and the tousled hair falling across his cheek, at the sheen of sweat on his perfectly muscled chest and the way his biceps flexed as he held himself above her, and she knew it couldn't get any better.

They fit together perfectly, his long legs tangled with hers, his narrow hips nestled between her thighs. The ground beneath the cloth was covered in thick grass, but it was still rocky and rough. Kaz no longer noticed. They might have been lying on the softest bed in the world rather than a tablecloth hidden between rows of ancient grapevines.

When her climax took over her body, when her mind and her heart, her entire being, was suddenly thrust into a connection with Jake she'd only dreamed of, Kaz was inordinately proud of the fact she didn't scream the words lodged in her heart. She didn't blurt out the truth and admit something she'd been trying to deny, that in a very brief few days, she'd fallen head over heels in love with R. Jacob Lowell.

That wasn't in the contract. Not part of the deal at all, but she'd treasure these past few days, this perfect time with him.

"Damn. I didn't expect it to be so crowded." Jake glanced around the full restaurant, at the busy staff and the line of people waiting to be seated.

"Hey, Jake! Hi, Kaz. Good to see you back."

He and Kaz turned at the same time. It was Luke Borelli, the owner who'd been bartending the night before. He was a fan of Intimate wines, in fact, he featured them quite proudly on the wine list.

"This place is hoppin'." Jake shook his hand.

"Tourists. There are always events on weekends. You and Kaz here for dinner?"

"We were hoping to, but I didn't make reservations. It looks like a long wait. We're both beat, so we'll probably go grab a pizza or a sandwich."

Luke poured a beer for Jake and handed a glass of Chardonnay to Kaz. "On the house," he said. "And if you don't mind a table in the bar, you can be seated right now. We've got some great specials."

Jake glanced at Kaz.

"Hey, it works for me," she said. "I need food, and it smells wonderful in here."

"You got it. C'mon." Luke led them to a small table in the back, a semiprivate booth out of traffic.

Kaz slid in against the wall, and Jake took the seat across and smiled at Luke. "Thank you. This is perfect. I'm surprised no one grabbed it."

"It's where I sit during the day and do my paperwork. The bar isn't crazy then. I think I'm going to be too busy tonight to sit, so for now it's all yours." He handed them each a menu and went back to the bar.

Almost two hours later, after consuming more excellent food than either of them probably needed, Jake covered his mouth to hide a yawn.

Kaz laughed. "I think that means I'm beginning to bore you."

"Actually, it means I haven't been this relaxed in ages." Relaxed, if he didn't count the simmering arousal that had kept him at a low burn all evening. He was certain his blood pressure had gone down as his contentment level went up.

Kaz had the better seat for people watching, and she'd kept up a steady commentary about the diners coming through the bar, which appeared to be the main entrance to the restaurant. She'd worn a cropped top that showed glimpses of her butterfly tattoo if she raised her arms at all. Jake was really going to miss that tattoo. He couldn't tell if she'd worn any chains.

Then Kaz yawned and they both laughed. Jake stood and helped her to her feet, paid for their dinner, and they both thanked Luke before heading down the street to their room. As they walked through the quiet evening, he thought of their conversation tonight, about the combination of his ad campaign and Fletcher Arnold's for the South Bay winery.

Whether she was ready or not, Kaz could easily become a household name after both campaigns went public. He already thought about her as if she were his, but that wasn't going to happen. He'd worked so hard to build a new life, one free of RJ Cameron and his awful choices. If he and Kaz ever became an item, his secret would be out. He had no doubt he'd be judged and found guilty. Again.

He didn't want to lose her. Couldn't keep her. But neither could he keep himself from saying what he was thinking. "Ya know, Kaz, I'm thinking your little sister would be loving what you've done with your life so far. How do you think she'd take the news of your doing two major ad campaigns? And your mom, too."

Kaz tilted her head and stared at him. Then she sighed and her eyes sparkled with unshed tears, but she didn't look away.

"Jilly would love every minute of it. But Jake? I've been

lying to you." She let out a deep breath and bit her lips together. Then she said, "My mother isn't really dead. She's in prison. She's a drug addict. She snatched Jilly out of the front yard and was driving away when she ran a light and a truck hit her car. Jilly died. My mother survived, but she had a number of priors and ended up with a twenty-five-year to life sentence. She won't be eligible for parole for years."

Too stunned to say anything, Jake held tightly to Kaz's hand. She told him more, staring at the ground as they walked back to the B and B.

"She was in and out of my life. When I was little, I wanted so much for her to love me, but she always loved the drugs more. I was ashamed she was my mother. I hated her. The last time she came back to Dad, she was pregnant and homeless. The child wasn't my father's, but he told my mother she could stay if she'd submit to regular drug tests. Things were pretty good while she was pregnant, but within weeks after Jilly was born, she was using again. Then she left when Jilly was a few weeks old."

She slanted a sweet smile his way. "Those were the best years ever. They lasted until Jilly died, but I was so lucky to have my little sister for those seven years. I hated my mother so damned much, but then I realized she wasn't worth the wasted energy. Hating someone takes up too much space in your heart."

They'd reached the B and B. At the top of the stairs, Jake turned and pulled Kaz into his arms. There really were no words. Nothing to answer her grief, nothing that would fix what she had gone through.

The loss of the little sister she'd loved so much.

How the hell could he ever tell her his story? Kaz's honesty was a painful thing. She deserved the same from him, but the minute she realized the whole truth, that in some ways he'd been no better than her mother, she would despise him, too. He wouldn't be able to blame her.

But he wanted more from her. Wanted to know more of the story, even as he debated how little of his own he was willing to share.

He was such a fucking coward.

CHAPTER 13

"Why?" Jake stopped in front of the door to their room, looking as perplexed as a man possibly could.

Frowning, she tilted her head and stared at him. "What do you mean, why? Why did I raise my sister? Why did my father ever take the woman back?" She laughed.

It was either that or cry. She missed Jilly. Missed the life they'd built after her mother abandoned the family for the . . . what was it? Seventh? Maybe the eighth time?

"Why did you tell me your mother was dead?"

He unlocked the door and she stepped ahead of him into the room. "That's the simplest 'why' to answer. Because it was easier than having to explain the whole story. Jake, I've never told anyone what I've told you tonight. We never even told Jilly her mother was alive. The saddest thing is, Jilly might be alive if we had. Dad and I agreed that was our biggest mistake, not telling her the truth, that our mother was just gone, that she was sick, that if she ever came back, she wasn't safe, and that Jilly was never to go anywhere with her without asking Dad or me, but we had no reason to believe she'd ever return. It took her over seven years to come back, and that was the day she stopped in front of our house and saw Jilly playing in the front yard with her friends."

Kaz set her bag down on a table and then sat on the edge of the bed. Remembering was painful, but she felt as if she owed Jake the truth.

"Jilly must have recognized her—Dad kept pictures in Jilly's room so she'd know who her mother was, but we'd always told her that Mommy was dead. After so many years, she might have been, for all we knew. The fact Jilly recognized our mother is the only reason she would have gotten in the car with her. She knew better than to go with a stranger."

"Do you think your mother planned it?"

Kaz shook her head. "She said she didn't, that she would sometimes drive by the house in the hopes of seeing one of us. She was just curious, you know, how we'd turned out, but she didn't really care to get involved with any of us again. She saw Jilly, knew it had to be her, and she stopped the car. It was an impulse, not a plan. Everything my mother ever did was an impulse. She has no self-control. She called to Jilly and told her she was her mother. Jilly recognized her from the pictures and went to her. She said she only wanted to take Jilly for an ice cream, but she was high. She ran a red light just a couple of blocks from our house, and a garbage truck plowed into the passenger side of the car. Jilly had a seatbelt on, but she was small enough to still need a booster seat. She shouldn't have been in the front seat, either, though the whole side of the car was crushed. I doubt anything would have saved her."

"I'm sorry. Kaz, I'm so damned sorry."

She grabbed a tissue and blew her nose, then realized her mascara had probably smeared all over her face. "I'll be back. I need to wash my face."

And have a good cry while she was at it.

Her last night with Jake, and she'd ended up dumping a story on him that would have most men running for the hills. Closing the bathroom door behind her, she stared at her raccoon eyes for a minute.

This was going to take more than a washcloth.

Quickly stripping out of her clothes, she carefully removed the tiger eye jewelry she'd worn to dinner and replaced the pieces with her own simple silver rings and studs. Then Kaz turned the water in the shower on really hot, waited for the room to fill with steam, and got under the spray.

She hadn't cried over Jilly for a long time.

Tonight, though, why did she feel as if she wept as much for Jake as for the little sister she'd lost?

It was cool this evening, so he cranked up the gas on the fake fireplace and parked his butt in a chair in front of it. He was such an ass. He'd sat there listening to Kaz's heartbreaking story, holding on to secrets of his own that were so damned ugly. Kaz and Jilly had been victims.

The only thing he'd been a victim of was his own stupidity and a healthy case of hubris. So certain his admission of guilt to protect Ben would get him, at the most, a slap on the wrist from the court, but he'd been willing to do anything for Ben. Anything to regain his brother's love.

So what had his great sacrifice earned him?

Nothing but disappointment. Jake sighed. As much as he wanted to blame his brother, Jake knew he was every bit as guilty. In his own way, Ben had to be suffering, too. But Jake had been in that car; he'd been having a wonderful time until everything went terribly wrong.

The young mother and son who died that night had lost everything. During the trial, it was revealed she'd been a victim of abuse, that she was running from her husband after years of torment. Jake had killed her dreams every bit as thoroughly as he'd killed his own.

His Olympic dreams were dead. His already pathetic

relationship with his parents, who blamed him for the wreck and their unexplained estrangement from Ben, had died as well. And Ben? Ben hadn't been home since he'd enlisted in the army before the trial had even ended, before Jake was turned over to the California Youth Authority for almost six years. Choosing multiple deployments to Iraq and Afghanistan rather than return to his family was a good indication of Ben's mental health.

Two families totally screwed by one night of teenaged stupidity.

He heard the shower go on, pictured Kaz under the spray, and his body reacted, but not the way he expected. Yeah, he was hard and he wanted her, but this was different, and pretty unsettling.

He felt a sense of longing, and it was unlike anything he'd ever experienced, a feeling that what he faced losing here tonight was worse than the loss of his freedom. Worse than the destruction of his Olympic potential.

But how do you lose something you've never really had? Kaz was poised to see her career go through the roof. He'd known from the beginning that this—whatever this was they had—was going nowhere.

Because he couldn't tell her the truth. At least not the whole truth, but maybe, if he told her a little, the secret wouldn't weigh so heavily on his soul. Or in his heart.

She'd washed her hair, cleaned the makeup off her face, but she still wasn't ready to get out from under the streaming water. She'd cried a little, though not as much as she'd feared she would. Tears weren't going to bring Jilly back.

Tears certainly weren't going to keep Jake in her life, either. She was stronger than that, strong enough to enjoy this last night with a truly special man and then move forward.

She heard a knock at the door. "Kaz? You okay?"

It was nice that he worried about her. At least for now. "Yeah. I'll be out in a minute."

"Do you mind if I come in?"

"It's not locked." She stuck her head under the water to rinse the conditioner off her hair, but a blast of cold air had her spinning around so fast she almost fell.

Jake's strong arms came around her from behind, and he pulled her close, her back against his chest, her legs brushing his hair-roughened thighs. Nuzzling her throat with his scratchy chin and its five-o'clock shadow, he planted a kiss along the edge of her jaw.

"I've been worried about you. Are you okay?"

She turned in his arms and pressed her forehead against his shoulder. "I think it's just been an emotional week for me. Getting fired, meeting you." She laughed, but it sounded more like a sob. "The sex?" Shrugging, she tried for humor. "It's been a long dry spell." Then she sighed. "Too many highs and lows. I think my mother was the pro-verbial straw, ya know?"

He chuckled and nuzzled her wet hair. "I'm almost afraid to ask if I'm a high or a low."

Raising her head, she shot him a cheeky grin. "Right now, you're a high." She glanced down. He was beautifully erect. She ran her fingers over the sleek length of him. "Very high."

"Turn around." His voice was so rough and deep, it sent shivers along her spine.

"Bossy, aren't we?" She turned and planted her palms on the slick tiles. His fingers slipped between her legs, teasing her, barely entering and then withdrawing. Bracing herself, she glanced over her shoulder. He tugged at the tiny ring between her legs, then slipped his fingers inside her again. When he withdrew them, she watched him sheathe himself, felt the broad head of his penis separating her folds, sliding slowly, deeply inside.

He filled her so perfectly that she groaned and pressed her bottom against his groin. He found both her nipple rings and tugged them, just the right amount of pressure that had Kaz clenching her inner muscles around his thick shaft, holding him when he tried to withdraw, tightening even more when he surged forward.

The water pounded on her back. Steam rose all around, and Jake whispered in her ear, things he wanted to do to her, with her, things that made her blush, made her hot and hotter still, while the steady in and out slide and glide of the hard and hot length of him filling her sensitive sheath left her panting.

"Now, Jake. Now!" She thrashed within his grasp, so close to the edge, so ready for the fall.

"Not yet." He palmed her breast with his right hand, tugging almost painfully on the silver ring. His left hand slipped low, cupped her pubes, and flicked the ring in the hood of her clit, flicked it, tugged it, twisted, oh, so gently, and that was all it took.

She arched her back and cried out against the heavy pulse deep inside. Jake flew with her, the two of them going together in a climax that left her seeing stars.

Hanging there, her hands pressed against the tile, her body shivering from the aftermath of orgasm and the cooling shower as their hot water finally ran low, Kaz felt the tears hovering close again.

This was their last night. Tomorrow, he'd take her back to the city, back to a new job, and their idyllic break from reality would end.

Wrapped in a thick white towel, Kaz walked back into the bedroom a few minutes after Jake. He'd put on a pair of black sweatpants but no shirt, and sat by the fireplace, staring at the flames.

It reminded Kaz of how her dad would stare at the fire

at home—a wood fire, when she was a kid—and look as if he were a million miles away. As an adult, she understood some of the things that might have been going through his mind, but as a kid she just thought he looked lonely, and she'd crawl into his lap and hug him, so he wouldn't feel so sad.

She felt like she should do that with Jake, but instead she sat on the floor beside his feet and leaned back against the overstuffed chair, feeling replete and somewhat sheepish.

Staring at the burning log, she sighed. She really had to say something, if only to feel less fragile, more in control of her emotions. "I'm sorry I fell apart earlier. I'm usually a little more together." She sighed again. "It hit me really hard tonight, and all at once."

His fingers tangled in her damp hair. "You don't owe me an apology. I've been sitting here, trying to figure out how I can apologize to you, but I'm not as brave as you are. You face the things that hurt. I bury them."

She tilted her head back and looked at him. Even upside down, he was gorgeous. Gorgeous and horribly sad looking. And lonely, too.

"What's hurt you, Jake? Whatever you say won't leave this room. I can promise you that. I can offer a nonjudgmental ear to listen."

He tilted his head back, sucked in a deep breath, and then exhaled. "That's probably more than I deserve. I've been wanting to tell you but wasn't sure how. I spent almost six years in the CYA. From the time I was sixteen until I turned twenty-one."

She frowned, still looking at him upside down, but what he said made no sense, so she turned around and faced him. "CYA? All that means to me is 'cover your ass.'"

He laughed. A great burst of laughter that sounded as if he really needed it. Then he leaned over and picked her up, towel and all, and settled her in his lap. That always amazed her, how easily he could lift her. She was over six feet tall, but he was so strong. So comfortable with his size and strength.

"Sorry. That was not the answer from you I was expecting. The CYA is the California Youth Authority. It's a hellhole of a detention center for kids who screw up bad enough that they need to be locked away. I was locked away."

It took longer than it should have for that to register, to make any sense at all. Jake? But he was one of the smartest, nicest, gentlest men she'd ever met. She shook her head and touched the side of his face. "I don't get it. What for?"

He sighed and glanced away. "Sort of a long, convoluted story, but basically it happened because I idolized my older brother. Ben was like a god to me, but we had issues. We'd been really close, and then we weren't. I was into hero worship and he saw me as a pain in the ass punk kid. One night he got drunk and stole a car. He never would have done anything like that sober. At least, I don't think he would. I thought it was the coolest thing in the world when he asked me to hang out with him. Long story short, we had an accident and got caught. Ben convinced me to tell the cops I was the one driving. Since I was a kid, we figured I'd get off with a warning. He was nineteen and could have gone to prison, so I went along with it."

"But you didn't get off, did you?"

He shook his head. "No. There was a new DA and he threw the book at me. I was sentenced to the California Youth Authority where I stayed until I turned twenty-one."

"But your brother? He never fessed up, never told anyone you were innocent?"

Jake shook his head. "But I wasn't, really. I was in a stolen car. Even though I didn't know it was stolen, I should have. It was wrong. So damned stupid, but it cost me everything. My parents blamed me for messing up Ben's life.

I haven't heard from them since the bailiff led me out of the courtroom. Ben joined the Army before the trial even ended, long before I was sentenced. He hasn't been home since. He's dealing with his guilt his way, I guess. Back to back tours in Iraq and Afghanistan, from what I've heard. The point is, what we did was wrong. I paid in my way, Ben in his. Our parents apparently wrote us both off."

"Parents don't do that. At least, the good ones don't." She had a hard time believing what he was telling her. It made no sense. None at all.

He shrugged and stared at the fire. "Mine did. They live in Marin, not twenty miles from me. I haven't seen them since I was sixteen."

"They never came to see you when you were locked up?"

"Nope. But then I never contacted them after I got out, either."

"I don't blame you. I think if I ever saw them, I'd end up making a scene. Good parents don't ignore their kids, especially when those kids need them."

"Obviously, they missed that day in parent class. They weren't horrible parents, but they weren't the best, either. At least I hope I won't make their mistakes, should I ever end up having any kids. Doubt that will happen, though."

"Why not?" She felt so warm and comfortable, snuggled in his lap, her head on his shoulder, but his answer was more jarring than it should have been.

"Because I'll never marry, and I don't believe in purposefully bringing kids into the world without two parents. Besides, with the training I've had, I'd probably make a horrible father."

He was such an idiot, and Kaz thought about telling him so, but he didn't want to hear that. Someday he'd find a woman who was right for him, he'd fall in love, and he'd

want to marry her and have kids, but until he found that
woman, she knew he wasn't going to change his mind.

   And since that woman obviously wasn't her, she refused
to agonize over it or try and correct his misconception.
What she did intend to do was enjoy every moment of this
last night together.

Saturday seemed so anticlimactic, after their deep conversation the night before. After hours of the best sex she'd
ever experienced. Jake had definitely ruined her for any
other man, ever.

   She wondered what kind of nun she'd make.

   Probably not a very good one. She loved sex too much,
at least with Jake. They packed up their stuff, Jake got a
few more shots around the B and B, and then they checked
out around eleven.

   They'd skipped breakfast to get some photos around
town, stopped in Santa Rosa for a quick lunch, and then
headed south on Highway 101 to San Francisco.

Traffic was mostly headed north to the wine country, so it
was a fast trip home. Jake found a parking spot right in
front of Kaz's house and helped her carry her things up
the stairs. They'd talked about the shoot, about what she
should expect from Fletcher Arnold when he called her on
Sunday. Other than that, he might have been with any
model after a short job.

   There'd been no mention of their conversation last night,
of the amazing sex afterward. Why couldn't he tell her that
she'd changed his life? That he wanted her more than anything, but he didn't want to hold her back?

   That he'd lied to her about his past? He hadn't told her
the part that really mattered.

   He followed Kaz into her house, waited while she

greeted Rico the basset hound and fondled the dog's droopy ears before heading down the hall to her bedroom. It was as neat and utilitarian as if she were in the military. The only picture was one of Kaz laughing with a beautiful little blond-haired, blue-eyed girl.

He picked it up. "Jilly?"

"Yeah."

"She's almost as pretty as her big sister."

Kaz turned and rested her forearms on his shoulders.

"You are such a smooth-talker, Mr. Lowell. I'm going to miss you."

He kissed her nose. "You're going to be too busy to miss me. Will you let me know how it goes with Fletch?"

"I will, when I see you at the Intimate launch. You still want me to wear the black and bronze outfit I wore for the photos? With the tigers eye set?"

"I'd rather you wear the diamonds. Unless you can think of something better to show off the jewelry, I'm leaving the diamond set to wear with the black and bronze, and I slipped the rubies and the tanzanite sets into the box, too, in case you have a chance to wear them in the commercial. Marc wants the more expensive stones showcased at the launch. I got to thinking that if you had something bright red, or even in black, that's as revealing, feel free to wear it instead of the bronze. I want you to be in something comfortable, but sexy as hell. Something that shows off the tat, too."

"I can do that."

He stared into those dark coffee-colored eyes. How the hell was he ever going to walk away from her? He knew they'd be together in two weeks, but a lot could happen in two weeks.

His feelings for Kaz were so powerful, so unacceptably strong, he couldn't trust them. He'd never been in love. Didn't want to be in love, but the entire ride home from the wine country, his only thought was how he could possibly keep her in his life.

And the truth was, he couldn't. Not until he was willing to tell her the full story of his arrest, which he obviously couldn't do. Her sister had died because of a DUI. He'd spent almost six years locked up for killing a young mother and her son, even though it was his brother's DUI. Guilty by association, if nothing else. Case closed.

He pulled Kaz close and kissed her. He put everything he felt, everything he wanted, all that he couldn't have into that kiss. And then he stepped back, took her hands in his, and held them, as much to keep her from touching him again as to hold onto her.

"For what it's worth, Ms. Kazanov, I'm going to miss you, too. Good luck with Fletch, don't take any crap off the bastard, and knock 'em dead."

"Gotcha. Thank you, Jake. For everything."

"You, too. For giving an absolute stranger a chance."

"Works both ways." She shrugged and sort of smiled. "And, for what it's worth, we're not strangers anymore."

He nodded. "No," he said. "We're definitely not strangers." He closed his eyes for a brief moment and then somehow managed a smile. "I'll see you in two weeks, okay?" He turned before she answered and walked away. His cell phone vibrated in his hip pocket. He didn't check the text. He just kept walking, out the front door, down the steps.

It felt worse than that day almost twenty years ago when the bailiff had led him out of the courtroom to begin his sentence.

Kaz watched Jake walk down the hall and out the door. She stood in the doorway to her bedroom, watching him until the front door shut behind him. Then she had to force herself not to run to her bedroom window to watch him drive away. Instead, she shut her bedroom door and leaned against it.

"If it's meant to be, it will happen. If not, this will be a wonderful memory."

And if she said that at least a gazillion times, maybe eventually she'd believe it.

Who the hell was she kidding?

Standing there, alone in her bedroom, she laughed, but the laughter broke, and she was sobbing. Sobbing as if her heart were breaking.

And maybe, just maybe, it was.

CHAPTER 14

Kaz glanced up from her book when Mandy and Lola got home around four. She'd done her crying in the shower, accepted Rico's undemanding sympathy while she lay on her bed with an ice pack on her swollen eyes, and had finally thrown on a slinky old dress that somehow made her feel relaxed, comfortably frumpy, but still in control.

Sort of. Jake was gone, and she had a new job already lined up. She'd see Jake in two weeks, after the most amazing four-and-a-half days of her life. Remembering—even wallowing in—all the crazy emotions of that time was okay.

Rico raised his head and howled, a long, mournful note that suited her mood while announcing someone coming up the stairs.

Mandy threw open the door, rushed across the room, and gave her a hug. "You're home! You didn't call. We've been worried."

Lola dropped her purse on the couch, stood over Kaz with her arms crossed, and glared at her. "You should have called."

"I . . ." She grimaced as the truth rolled over her. Jake had filled her senses in every possible way. "I never even thought of calling. I'm sorry."

Mandy grabbed her hands. "You always let us know how a job's going. We didn't want to call you and interfere, but we really were worried." Then she winked. "This guy must be something special."

There was no doubt in Kaz's mind. "He is." Her roommates were the best friends she'd ever had, the two she'd met shortly after losing Jilly, who, without even realizing, had helped her through the worst time of her life. "But no, don't get your hopes up. He's got a busy career and I . . ." she paused for dramatic effect, "I'm expecting a phone call tomorrow with details about an audition with Fletcher Arnold for a commercial."

"Fletcher Arnold?" Lola's eyes went wide and she slapped her hand over her chest. "He's like the biggest thing around here. I just sent Marty and Tim and a new kid out on a job with him. We were all shocked he'd come to Top End for models. How'd that happen?"

Mandy flopped down on the arm of Kaz's chair. "Even I know who Fletcher Arnold is. He's won a bunch of awards for his commercials. Remember that one with the tiny little kitten and the Great Dane?"

"Or the old, old man and the little girl? That one just made me cry." Lola sighed. "So what's the interview for? What's the commercial?"

Kaz shrugged. "Lucullan Cellars. It's a South Bay winery that wants to build its brand. It's a speaking role. I met him in Healdsburg when I ran into the guys." She told them what little she knew, and answered most of their questions about her four-and-a-half days with Jacob Lowell. But she didn't answer all of them, and she decided to let them think what they wanted.

Her feelings for Jake were too new, too fresh. Much too fragile. She knew he cared, but they'd agreed it wasn't the right time. That didn't mean that it would never be the right time. That what they'd begun this past week might not actually be something they could build on. Sometime. She'd hang on to that, for now at least. But she couldn't help but wonder if he thought of her at all.

The way she couldn't stop thinking of him.

Jake shoved his chair back from the desk and rubbed his eyes. He glanced at the clock on the wall. Three in the morning wasn't the best time to be working, especially since he'd only had a couple of hours' sleep last night. He never should have read that damned text after dropping Kaz at her house.

Hey, RJ! Did you enjoy the ravioli? I knew I'd find you. What's on the menu tonight?

The bastard must have followed them to the restaurant. He'd been that close, and Jake hadn't known it. He'd been so damned pissed off, but after he'd calmed down enough, he'd worked until after midnight going through photos from the shoot.

Spending so many hours staring at images of Kaz had been its own kind of hell, especially when he'd crawled into bed and realized how quickly he'd grown used to her long, lean body beside him at night.

He hadn't left his apartment all day today, but in a way, he'd been back in wine country, watching Kaz through the lens of his camera. Her brilliant smile, the sassy sparkle in her dark brown eyes, the soft, contemplative looks that left him wondering what she was thinking as he'd shot photo after photo, each one better than the last.

She had an amazing ability to focus on the lens as if it were a living, breathing person, which translated into an intimate relationship between Kaz and whoever viewed her image. Images he'd captured in what he now realized might have been the most important four-and-a-half days of his life. Professionally and personally.

Every single shot was absolute gold. He'd been trying

to choose the best ones to deliver to Marc's art department, but it was impossible to find favorites. Somehow, he was going to have to go through all of them again and again until he was able to narrow the hundreds of pictures he'd taken down to a dozen or more.

He missed her so much he ached.

He hadn't had the balls to look at the personal photos. The ones Kaz had allowed him to take with the promise that no one but Jake would ever know about them, much less see them. That promise held its own intimacy, the fact she'd trusted him enough.

Viewing her face on the oversized flat-screen monitor in the professional shots, with her perfect cheekbones and long, narrow-bridged nose, the lips he'd kissed—the same lips he would forever see wrapped around the hard length of his dick—had almost killed him.

He wasn't ready to view the ones they'd done together. The ones that would forever make him think of the most amazing experience he'd ever had. Pictures out in the vineyard on the tablecloth, shots of her smiling that seductive smile with her breasts entirely bare, the sensual curve of her hip, the barest glimpse of the smooth pubic mound between her thighs with the tiny silver ring in the hood of her clit . . . no. He wasn't ready for that.

Nor was he ready for the photos he'd taken in their room at the B and B, less revealing but even sexier for what they didn't show. Merely thinking of them made him hard.

Made him remember that night—a night he should try to forget though he knew he would always remember. He hadn't been ready to discover what "making love" actually felt like. What happened with Kaz was no ordinary sexual experience.

He wasn't ready for love.

Staring at the monitor, at Kaz's beautiful smile and the

devilish twinkle in her eyes, had him reaching for his cell phone. Was she awake like he was? Thinking of him the way he thought of her?

Then he remembered it was already Monday. In a few more hours she'd be going to her audition with Fletch.

His phone chimed, startling him so badly he dropped it. It was the middle of the night. Kaz? Maybe she'd sensed he was thinking about her. He grabbed the phone off the rug and flipped it over to see what she'd sent him.

It wasn't Kaz. Not with a fucking blocked number.

I've missed you, RJ, but I understand. Not when you had that hot little number keeping you so busy. Hope you enjoyed the wine country vacay.

He stared at the screen. There was a name this time. *Fanboy.* Number still blocked. Who the hell was it? More important, what the fuck did he want?

Kaz's face still watched him from his monitor. The text message on his phone mocked him. He turned off the phone and then flipped off the monitor and shut down the computer. But he couldn't shut that creepy message out of his mind.

Around four he sent a text to Marc. Marc had a security department—maybe they could figure out who this guy was. He forwarded all of them, along with the info to allow Marc's people access to his online account.

Even Marc didn't know the whole story about Jake's arrest. Damn, his life was so filled with secrets. Once upon a time, he'd kept them out of loyalty to his brother. He couldn't use that excuse anymore—not when he hadn't seen or heard from his brother in almost two decades.

So what was his excuse now?

He was such a fucking coward. He shut out the lights and forced himself to concentrate on that last shot of Kaz that had been up on the monitor. She was so fucking beautiful . . . but even with her visual behind his eyes, the text was in his mind.

It was a long time before he fell asleep.

Late Monday afternoon, after a long day shooting the first of the winery commercials for Fletch, Kaz slipped into a comfortable pair of yoga pants, a faded crop top, and her flip-flops for the short walk home. Their first day had been at a gorgeous restaurant less than six blocks from the house she shared with Lola and Mandy.

Fletch had paired her up with Tim Milbank, the model from Top End. Their chemistry was surprisingly good, and the entire day had been fun. Exhausting, but fun. Tomorrow's shoot was scheduled at a beautiful home on Ocean Beach.

She tucked the address into her bag and headed home. Walking by the coffee shop on the way, she spotted Mandy working inside. Kaz made a quick about-face and stepped through the door. The screech of tires and a cacophony of honking horns spun her around. Horrified, she watched an old pickup truck jump the curb and plow into the wall right where she'd been before she turned back to come into the shop.

Patrons inside the coffee shop scrambled to safety as the big, plate-glass window exploded, throwing glass around the room. Mandy screamed. Kaz yelled at her, "You okay?" Mandy nodded, and Kaz raced out of the shop to check on the driver.

Half a dozen cars were scattered about the street, but no one appeared to be hurt. Just as Kaz reached the truck, the driver climbed out through the shattered windshield and took off running. Within seconds he reached the far side of the road and disappeared down an alley.

"Wow." Mandy and all the patrons in the shop had come outside to watch. "He just missed you."

"I know." Kaz stared after the kid, long gone now. That had been way too close for comfort, and reminiscent of that night in Healdsburg just last week. A cold chill swept over her arms.

A police car arrived. The officer got out and directed traffic around the truck. Kaz stepped back inside the shop and helped Mandy clean up the broken glass, while the shop owner called about repairs. After the bulk of the mess was cleared away, Kaz took a seat by the wide-open window where she could watch the excitement. Mandy brought her a caffè mocha and took the seat across from her.

"My shift's over," she said, sipping her latte. "That was too damned close for comfort. Seconds, Kaz. Two seconds and you'd have been squashed like a bug." She shook her head. "I wonder what made him lose control?"

Kaz shrugged. "It's probably stolen. He didn't look old enough to drive. He sure didn't hang around for long." She sipped her mocha, thinking of last Tuesday night, of the car bouncing off the light pole, Jake pulling her to safety.

She finished the coffee, took Mandy's empty, and then got up and carried the mugs to the counter. A tow truck was hooking up to the pickup as she and Mandy stepped outside. The policeman was writing his report, using the hood of his cruiser like a desk.

Kaz stopped beside him. "Any idea who it was?"

The cop raised his head, but before he could speak, Mandy said, "He almost hit Kaz. It was like he was aiming for her."

He straightened and took a closer look at Kaz. "Is she right? Do you think it was intentional? Something more than an accident?"

She shook her head. "No. Not really. It was just too close for comfort. I don't think he was very old, more like a kid, but I didn't get a good look."

"The truck was reported stolen last night. Probably just out joyriding." He gave her another appraising glance. "I'm glad you're okay."

"Thanks. Me, too." She turned to Mandy. "C'mon. Let's get home."

Later that evening, she picked up her phone to call Jake. Stared at it, and said, "Funny thing happened today, Jake. I almost got squashed when a truck skipped the curb."

And then what? She put the phone down. There really wasn't anything to report—it was a skinny kid driving this time, not the same man from Healdsburg, so all the call would accomplish would be to worry Jake for nothing.

The rest of the week turned out to be so busy, the "almost getting squashed" incident lost importance, as Fletch had her take on a larger speaking role in what turned out to be an entire series of commercials he was filming. The days sped by while she and Tim worked on the neat sets Fletch lined up. The spots grew more involved as Fletch took advantage of the chemistry between Tim and Kaz. He expanded their speaking parts, turning the short commercials into mini-stories filled with a gentle humor Kaz found really appealing.

They spent a couple of days at the house near Ocean Beach and then filmed in Golden Gate Park. That shoot required an impromptu picnic on a red tablecloth—carefully orchestrated—that reminded Kaz much too much of the most exquisite lovemaking ever in the vineyard in Dry Creek Valley with Jake.

Everything she did reminded her of Jake, but she couldn't bring herself to call him.

Instead, she lay awake for hours each night, thinking of him. Missing his long, strong body beside hers, his soft, sexy laughter, his amazing kisses.

Missing Jake.

* * *

Late Friday night, Jake sat in his darkened office, still going through the pictures of Kaz. It was impossible, choosing the best of the best, because every single shot was pure gold, but at least he'd managed to send a half-dozen stellar shots to Marc's art department for posters for the launch. He had to get his ass in gear, though. Marcus Reed wanted to see more.

Reed was thinking long-term with Kaz.

Jake had delivered enough shots for the printed booklets to Marc a couple of days ago, and then had had the pleasure of standing beside his friend while the man exclaimed over the perfection of Jake's model. He'd loved everything about the photos showcasing his jewelry.

It only hit Jake later that, as the photographer, he'd been more proud of Kaz than of the pictures he'd taken. It was impossible to get a bad shot of her. Absolutely impossible.

His phone chimed. He was expecting a text from Marc and welcomed the chance to interrupt his depressing musings about Kaz. He grabbed the phone off the charger, glanced at the screen, and a chill raced up his spine.

Fanboy. Fuck.

Hey, RJ! Had a good week? I'm glad one of us has. Figured out who I am yet? We go back a long way. You're a smart boy—make that a smart-ass. You'll figure it out.

Another text came through. Marc. He was obviously still awake. Jake called him. Marc answered immediately. "What's up?"

"I got another text from the bastard. Any info on who it is?"

"That's why I'm calling you. Heard back from my head of security. Bill says he's using burner phones—no way to trace them. You buy them cheap with prepaid minutes, use them, and then toss them. He could be anyone, anywhere."

"Crap." He'd been counting on Marc. He ended the call after answering a couple of questions Marc had about the ad campaign, and realized he was staring at Kaz's image on his computer once again.

Damn, but he missed her. He'd picked up the phone to call her too many times, and like the coward he was, set it back down again. It sounded clichéd, but he just wanted to hear her voice, make sure she was okay, that Fletcher was treating her well. He wondered what actor or model she'd been paired with—was it someone she could laugh with? Someone she liked?

Someone without a lifetime of baggage weighing him down?

He ran his finger over her image on the screen, and it felt almost as if she turned to look at him, her dark eyes condemning him for the idiot he was. But what other way could he have handled it? The truth would end any chance he might have of Kaz ever loving him. Hell, did he even know the truth anymore?

His entire adult life had been spent denying what he'd done, who he'd been, and now his worst nightmare was coming true. Someone had found him, someone who, for whatever reason, was doing his best to drive Jake nuts. But why?

Kaz didn't know Jake at all. She only knew the person he'd allowed her to see.

That guy was a bigger jerk than R. J. Cameron had ever been.

Fletch had them working through the weekend, taking advantage of a high-end hotel suite that had opened up due to a cancellation. The dresses Kaz had been asked to wear, designed by the owner's girlfriend, had had to be modified to look even remotely attractive, and Tim's critique of each outfit had her fighting the giggles through too many shots. Even Fletch had gotten into the teasing, but after seven straight days of filming, they were all a little punchy.

"Okay, kids. That's it for today." Fletch rubbed his hands together and grinned like a little kid. "Tomorrow, AT&T Park by seven. That's seven in the morning, children. There's a game at one, but we've got the Hall of Fame Suite for two hours pregame for filming. Kaz? My gift to you? You may choose your own outfit."

She gave him a magnanimous bow. "You are too kind. Sounds like a skinny jeans, poet's shirt day for me."

"Do it in orange and black and we're good to go."

"You promoting the Giants or the wine, Fletch?" Tim Milbank carefully settled his orange and black cap on his perfectly styled blond hair.

"Both. We get the box for free as long as my models dress 'appropriately.' So dress appropriately, okay?" He sent them off laughing.

Tim walked with her as far as the Muni station. They'd developed a closer friendship working together during the past hectic week than they'd ever had at Top End. She'd miss him when this job ended. She'd almost told him about Jake—Tim would understand—but something kept her from saying anything.

He gave her a quick hug before his train arrived. "I've had fun this week," he said, echoing Kaz's thoughts. "But I want to tell you before you hear it from anyone else. I'm leaving Top End. Fletch offered me a spot in a pilot he's filming for an investment group that wants to break into the cable TV market."

"Tim! That's wonderful. But you'll have to tell me more about it tomorrow. Your train's pulling in." She sent him off with a quick kiss and crossed to the platform to wait for her ride.

The light rail cars were just pulling in when something hit her hard from behind.

Kaz screamed and tumbled toward the tracks.

A strong arm wrapped around her waist, jerking her out

of the path of the train so quickly she slammed back onto her rescuer, knocking both of them to the raised platform, mere seconds ahead of the oncoming train.

Gasping, sucking air as if she'd run a mile, she slowly rolled away from her rescuer, dragging in deep breaths. People moved past and around them, boarding and exiting the train, but Kaz was barely aware of the activity. She focused on the man who'd saved her, noted skin the color of dark chocolate, black sweats, and a sleeveless T-shirt showcasing more muscles than she could recall seeing on any single body.

"Thank you. Ohmygod." On hands and knees, she dragged in another breath before she was able to turn, sit on her butt, and hang her head between her upraised knees. "You saved my life." She swallowed, shuddering. "Thank you. Did you see who pushed me?"

He stood slowly, shaking his head. "Not sure. You were the tallest in the crowd. I was on your left, heard you scream, saw you jerk forward. Thought at first you'd stumbled, but a guy took off, running like hell, the train was coming . . . didn't look real good." He chuckled as he took her hand and helped her to her feet. "One of those split-second decisions: chase the ugly white dude or be a hero and rescue the gorgeous woman from certain death. The woman won."

"And I do appreciate that." She brushed her hair back from her eyes. "Did you get a good look at him?"

"Not really. Average height, white guy, maybe dark hair, but he was wearing a hoodie. I couldn't see his face. Security cameras might have something. I'd say report it to security, have them check."

Kaz glanced at the empty tracks. Her train had come and gone. She was still shaking. "Can I buy you a cup of coffee? Or a drink? I owe you big time."

"You don't owe me a thing. I'm glad I could help, and

if I didn't have a beautiful wife and an even prettier brand-new baby boy home waiting for me, I'd take you up on your offer."

Smiling, she held out her hand. "Kaz Kazanov, and I am truly in your debt."

"Martin Jackson." He shook her hand. "Now you be careful. That guy who pushed you? He's either crazy as a loon or he has it in for you. Keep your eyes open."

She was still thinking of Martin's comment when she caught the train a while later. She'd left a brief report with the security officer working in another part of the station. He'd missed the incident, but she told him about what had happened, that she'd been rescued by a quick-thinking fellow passenger, and left her contact info in case they were able to ID the guy.

She didn't mention the car in Healdsburg or the truck at the coffee shop, but still, three strange incidents in less than two weeks was a bit too much to be coincidental.

When she finally got home, Mandy met Kaz at the front door with a glass of wine. "How'd your day go?"

Kaz took the wine and drank about half of it down. Mandy stared at her while she swallowed. "That bad, eh?"

"You don't know the half of it. Is Lola home?"

"I'm here." Lola stepped out of the kitchen. "You're late. You usually beat me home. What's up?"

Kaz led them into the kitchen, reached into the refrigerator for the wine bottle, and refilled her glass before taking a seat at the table. "Okay, I told you about the guy who almost hit me in Healdsburg, and Mandy was there when the pickup truck hit the wall where I'd been standing. Today, some jerk shoved me in front of a Muni train."

"What?"

"Who?"

Kaz laughed. Sitting in her familiar kitchen, none of

this felt real. "What I said, and I don't know who. I didn't see him. The train was coming, and someone hit my lower back—it felt like he used his shoulder—hard enough to launch me off the platform. Then the biggest dude I ever saw snatched me out of the way before I fell." She took another, slower, sip of her wine. "He said he had a split second to decide—chase down the ugly white dude or rescue the beautiful woman." She tapped her chest. "That would be me, of course."

"Good God." Lola stared at her as if she'd grown a second head. "You okay?"

Kaz gazed into her glass and sighed. "I'm alive. I wouldn't have been if Martin Jackson hadn't stepped in and saved me. I didn't really get scared until I was on my way home. It was so damned close—closer even than the pickup Monday or the car the week before."

Mandy covered Kaz's hand with hers. "Do you have any idea why anyone would—"

"No. None."

Lola shook her head. "There's got to be something. The guy in Healdsburg—did you get a good look at him?"

"Not really, though there was a moment, when the car skidded to a stop in the intersection, I could have sworn he stared right at us, as if he knew us. A couple of days later, I'm almost sure I saw the same man watching our hotel room window when Jake was taking some pictures of me. And Mandy? The day I met Jake at the coffee shop? Do you remember a dark-haired man in there, sitting opposite us? The man we saw in Healdsburg looked a lot like him."

"Sheesh, Kaz. I don't remember anyone from the shop. Do you think he was following you? A fan, maybe?" Mandy glanced at each of them. "You're in a lot of print ads, magazines and stuff."

"A fan wouldn't want to kill me."

Mandy shrugged as if this conversation were perfectly normal. "If he's crazy, he might."

"What if he's after Jake?" Lola frowned. "What if he's got a beef with Jake and he's going after you?"

"Why would someone mad at Jake attack me? Jake and I hardly know each other."

"Just a thought." Lola glanced toward Mandy. "I think she should call Jake, tell him what's going on."

"I agree." Mandy shot her a very dark glance. "Call him. Let him know what happened. Make sure he hasn't had any of the same shit coming his way."

"I dunno . . ." She wanted to call him so badly she ached, but not because she was afraid, not because somehow she'd become a target of all sorts of really bad stuff. She wanted to talk to Jake about good things, about the days they'd spent together, about the possibility of a future.

But she really wasn't ready for that talk. Neither was Jake.

They'd already planned to meet for the Intimate launch.

The call could wait. Not that she'd be ready by then to talk about possibilities.

Unfortunately—or fortunately as the case may be—neither would he.

CHAPTER 15

Kaz was ready to drop from exhaustion by Wednesday afternoon when Fletch jumped up on a small table and clapped his hands.

"Good news, people. To use an old phrase, it's in the can. Our client is thrilled with the results to date, and he's invited all of us to Fleur de Lys tomorrow night for a wrap party."

"Wow!" Kaz turned to Tim and almost laughed out loud at the stunned expression on his face. "They must really like us."

"No shit. That place is amazing. I hope I can bring Marty."

Which of course made her think about asking Jake, but she'd see him Friday, and she'd started thinking about the past two weeks as a test. Did she really miss him as much as she thought she did? Friday night at the Intimate launch would tell her, one way or another.

Tim picked Kaz up around six Thursday evening, and they drove across town to Fleur de Lys, where they met Marty. Kaz wore black silk pants that rested low on her hips and a matching crop top with an uneven hem that floated just beneath her breasts. The style was sexy as hell, very flattering, and set her butterfly tattoo on almost full display.

She'd worn the Intimate diamond studs and gold chains Jake had left with her. She'd left off the chain to her clit, debated on the one between her ear and nose before adding that one as well, and immediately she felt sexier. But was it the jewelry or the fact it made her think of Jake? It certainly reminded her she'd finally see him tomorrow night, and that thought gave her butterflies in her stomach as big as the one that graced the outside.

In some ways, the past two weeks had dragged, but in others, she'd been much too busy to really wallow in her misery. She'd managed to put her concerns about the nut at the train station in proper perspective—the city was full of crazies, and it had just been her turn to interact with one. Obsessing over stuff that made no sense wasn't going to do her any good at all.

Besides, she wanted to think about Jake. She'd never missed a man before. Not the way she still missed him. It wasn't just the exquisite sex that had her so impatient to see him. It was something more, something deeper.

Something she really didn't want to try and name until she actually saw him tomorrow.

Twenty-four hours from now.

She was really proud of herself after the event, when Marty and Tim dropped her off in front of her house. She got a kiss good-bye from Tim, and then Marty walked Kaz to her door and kissed her cheek just before she stepped inside. She waved to them from the open doorway as Tim pulled away from the curb. Then she carefully locked and bolted the door.

Yep, she was definitely feeling proud. She'd made it through the entire evening, having a wonderful time and not feeling sad. And while she'd thought about Jake, she hadn't let his not being with her ruin a perfect evening.

Well, almost perfect.

As she headed to her room, Kaz was already thinking of how much more fun tonight would have been, if only Jake had been her date.

Jake closed all his files and shut down the computer. Kaz smiled at him from the screen just a few brief seconds more before her image went dark. She'd been his screen saver for over a week now, a profile shot of her gazing over her left shoulder, lips painted a dark, ruby red, her dark eyes sparkling with reflected candlelight. She'd touched her lashes with just a bit of mascara, a shimmery black that gave her a dramatic flair without overdoing it.

Jake had chosen the jewelry for this particular shot—the blood-red ruby studs that perfectly matched her lipstick, and a fine gold chain that draped from the lobe of her left ear to a matching ruby in her left nostril. She'd worn a comfortable top for the shot, but he'd cropped the image across the upper curve of her breasts, which gave the illusion of total nudity. In the candlelight they'd used with reflector screens, her skin glowed a dark shade of honey.

It was much too easy to imagine that same color all over, even easier to imagine her giving him that "come hither" look while wearing nothing but the subtle jewelry. Marc had fallen in love with this shot.

These last two weeks had stretched on forever. He'd picked up the phone to call Kaz more times than he could count, but every single time he'd talked himself into walking away, into giving her time.

He'd never expected to feel this way, but he missed her. Missed her smile, missed the soft silences that were so easy between them. Most of all, he missed her laughter. He'd never laughed as much before Kaz.

Staring at the empty screen, Jake saw his life. A dead, black screen. Nothing there. No matter what he did, what he accomplished, it all added up to nothing if he didn't have the courage to tell Kaz the truth.

Not merely the bits and pieces of his fractured life, but all the filthy, cowardly details.

Which was probably the best way ever to insure that she'd not only walk out of his life forever, she'd walk away hating what had been the most perfect four days of his life.

He glanced at the clock. Almost midnight. Tomorrow by this time, he'd know for sure how Kaz felt about him. He'd call in the morning, offer to pick her up for the launch party, and be on his best behavior. If he got the slightest feeling that she felt for him even a fraction of what he felt for her, he would tell her everything.

His phone rang. He picked it up and glanced at the screen, blowing the brief burst of hope that it might be Kaz. Fletcher Arnold? Why the hell would Fletch be calling so late?

Kaz? Had something happened? "Fletch? Hey, man. It's late. What's up?"

"Jacob! I called to thank you. Kaz is amazing. She's absolutely perfect. I think—no, I know—I'm in love."

Jake's immediate, gut-deep jealousy shouldn't even surprise him at this point. He took a deep breath, let it out, and calmly said, "You're married, Fletch. How are we going to explain this to Janice?"

Fletch's laughter boomed in his ear. Jake held the phone away and set it on speaker. "Fletch? How much have you had to drink tonight?"

"Not nearly enough. Look, Jake, I called because I missed you tonight. I honestly thought you'd be at the wrap party with Kaz, and I planned to thank you then. She is a joy to work with, and I appreciate your introducing us. She and Tim Milbank were absolutely perfect for the series of spots my client wanted. Both of them are professional and adaptable. We ended up doing a few more commercials than intended. Point being, they're talking about offering her a spot as spokesperson for Lucullan Cellars, and I need to know what her contract with your client allows."

He had to think about that for a moment. "Marcus Reed has right of refusal on her for now, but I don't know if he has anything planned. The launch party for the jewelry line is tomorrow night. I'll check with him then and get back to you by Monday."

"Good. We're not going national with this campaign until mid-October. Let's keep in touch. Let me know what you find out."

Jake stared at his phone after Fletch disconnected. It was happening, just the way he'd thought it might.

She wouldn't need him. Didn't need him, not with all the fucking baggage attached to his ass. Damn. Jake stuck his phone back in the charger, stripped off his sweats, and got into bed.

He lay there, going over the conversation with Fletch, and the fact that it had come just as Jake was getting ready to tell Kaz the truth about everything. Fletcher's call shot his plans all to hell. He couldn't tell Kaz how he felt. Not now. Not with her career ready to explode.

Even if she forgave him, even if she could look beyond what he'd done, the last thing she needed hanging on to her arm was an ex-con with his ugly history. All he'd be was dead weight. Not good. Not when Kaz was ready to fly.

It was after ten before Kaz crawled out of bed and stumbled into the kitchen. She was greeted by a note on the counter in front of the cold, empty coffee pot. *Out of coffee—stop by for a cup this morning. My treat. Mandy.* She let out a sigh and headed back to the bedroom.

Twenty minutes later, after a quick shower and a change into yoga pants and a worn sweatshirt, Kaz walked to the coffee shop over on Irving.

Traffic was light, and fog hung low over the city. She shoved her hands in the pockets of her sweatshirt and walked quickly—to warm up as much as anything—though she was absolutely desperate for some caffeine. Last night had been more fun that she'd expected, but all she could think about this morning was Jake. She couldn't wait to see him again. Would he still look at her the way he had when they'd parted? Would her heart still stutter in her chest when he touched her?

Good Lord . . . if this wasn't love, she was badly in need of therapy. Had he thought of her at all while they'd been apart? If he had, at least he had pictures. She had nothing but her memories, and they'd been working overtime.

She still wasn't sure what she was going to wear tonight. The bronze skirt and top he'd bought for her in Healdsburg looked good, but she'd felt really sexy in last night's black silk pants and crop top. She could always go shopping, find something special just for tonight. Something that went well with the rubies. Jake had seemed partial to the rubies, but he'd suggested she go with the diamonds for Marc's big night. He'd really liked the tigers eye, too.

Except he hadn't left those with her, had he? Not flashy enough, according to Marcus Reed. So, diamonds or rubies? Black outfit or bronze? She'd felt really sexy in the bronze, and it rocked the wine motif really well. She glanced up, her nose twitching at the smell of freshly roasted coffee. Almost there, and she really, really needed her caffeine.

It felt weird, walking by the damaged wall where the truck had almost hit her. She paused a moment to get a better look, but as she turned away, the front of her sandal caught in a crack in the sidewalk. She stumbled, arms flailing to catch her balance.

A loud crack sent Kaz to her knees. Bits of stucco rained down around her and instinct took over. She rolled to one side as another shot hit the pavement where she'd just been kneeling. Sucking in a harsh breath, she raised her head and glimpsed a dark car she'd not even noticed spin out and race down the street.

The smell of burning rubber hung in the foggy air as she gasped for breath, one harsh cry after the next.

"Kaz! What the hell . . . ?" Mandy grabbed her by the arm and helped her to her feet. "What the fuck happened?"

It took her a minute to draw in enough air to speak. By then, everyone who'd been in the coffee shop had spilled out onto the sidewalk. An older man had his phone out, calling 9-1-1. Kaz clutched her hands together, but they wouldn't stop shaking. "That bastard shot at me. Twice!" She pulled free of Mandy's grasp and walked over to the wall. "Look. The bullet's still in there."

"Don't touch it." Mandy, the expert on all things *CSI*, grabbed Kaz's hand before she could touch the bullet to dig it out. "It's evidence."

"Oh. Yeah. Evidence." She glanced in the direction the car had gone. "Did you see what make it was? Get a license plate?"

"I got a partial." Eddy, one of the kids who washed dishes on the weekends, held up a scrap of paper. "I wrote down the first four digits, 5LRD, but I didn't get the rest. I think the next number was a seven, but I'm not sure. It was an older black sedan. No idea what kind, though."

"Better than what I got, which is nothing. Thank you." She grabbed Mandy's hand. "I need caffeine. Really, really badly."

"You got it." Mandy went back inside as the police car pulled up to the curb.

It was the same officer who'd responded when the truck almost hit her. Kaz shrugged and waved. "Uh, hi."

Frowning, the cop looked at her. "You again? What happened?"

As she explained the two shots and pointed first to the hole in the stucco and then the deep gouge in the sidewalk, he went very still. "That's two very suspicious events."

"Actually, it's four."

"You want to explain?"

So she did. The dark-haired man in the black BMW in Healdsburg, the truck hitting this same wall a week ago, a stranger pushing her in front of a Muni train. Two gunshots just now, in broad daylight, possibly the same car. She wrapped her arms around herself and shivered, while the officer took a couple of pictures, dug the bullet out of the wall, and carefully bagged it. He was putting it inside his vehicle when Mandy came out and handed Kaz a caffè mocha with a thick swirl of whipped cream on top.

She took it with a frustrated sigh.

Mandy stepped closer to the officer. "Why don't you come inside to talk to Kaz where it's warmer, and I'll bring you a cup of coffee."

He raised his head. "Is there an empty table?"

"There is." She waited while he grabbed a digital tablet and locked up his car. She led them inside to a table at the back of the small shop. A minute later, she brought him a cup of coffee, set a plate of muffins on the table, and then went back to her spot at the register.

It was almost an hour later before Officer José Macias had his complete report. At least Kaz's hands had stopped shaking, but he didn't make her feel any more confident about her safety. "I wish there was something positive I could tell you," he said, "but at this point, I don't think this was a random shooting. Neither, in my opinion, were the other incidents. If you think of anything at all, call me. And whatever you do, be aware of your surroundings."

She held up the card he'd given her. "I will. It's just . . ." Shrugging, she gazed toward the brand-new plate glass window, installed to replace the one the truck had broken last week. "I have no idea why anyone would be after me. I mean, I go to work, I go home. I haven't dated in months. I broke up with my last boyfriend because he was cheating on me. No jilted lovers in my past." She shook her head. "I was the one getting jilted."

"He cheated on you? The guy was an idiot, Ms. Kazanov." His radio crackled and he took the call. "That's for me. I have to go, but be careful. If you think of anything, anything at all, call me. José Macias. The number on the card is my mobile phone."

"Thank you." She watched him leave and wanted to lay her head on the table and have a good, long cry. None of this made sense. No sense at all.

Her phone rang. She answered without looking to see who it was. Jake's voice had her on the edge of tears again. "Jake? Hi."

"Kaz? You don't sound . . . are you okay?"

"Not really. Let me call you back." She ended the call, gathered her bag, and went over to the register to pay her bill. Mandy waved her off.

"No way. If I'd remembered to get coffee, you wouldn't have walked down here, and that jerk wouldn't have shot at you. Should I call you a cab?"

She shook her head. She just wanted to go home. Maybe she shouldn't go tonight. He wouldn't follow her to the launch, would he? Damn. She hated this. Absolutely hated it.

Mandy grabbed her by the arms. "Kaz? Don't be foolish. Someone is obviously after you. It's too dangerous."

Finally, it was just easier to let Mandy call the damned cab.

CHAPTER 16

The cab was out in front of the coffee shop in a couple of minutes. Five minutes later, Kaz was inside her house. She paused at the front door and looked up and down the street. It was empty except for an older lady walking her equally old poodle. Kaz unlocked the front door, stepped inside, and carefully locked it behind her.

Her phone rang again. This time she looked at the caller ID and answered. "Hi, Jake. I just got in the door. I was going to call you." She dropped her handbag on the floor and plopped down on the couch with the phone to her ear.

"What happened?"

She frowned. He sounded really pissed, which, for whatever reason, ticked her off. She gave him a snarky answer. "Other than someone trying to kill me? Not a damned thing."

At least the silence on the other end was gratifying. But only for a moment.

"Okay," he said, drawing out the word. "I hope you're making a really bad joke, Kaz, but I want you to know I'm not laughing. What the hell happened?"

She went through the entire scenario again, beginning with the pickup slamming into the coffee shop wall. When she ended the recitation, there was absolute silence.

Then he exploded.

"Good God, Kaz! Why the hell haven't you called me? Why haven't you gotten the police involved before now?"

She held the phone away from her ear and stared at it. Okay. So she hadn't heard from him in two weeks and all he does is yell at her? Not what she needed. Not now. She took a deep breath. Then she took another.

"For your information, Jacob, there was no reason to connect the pickup truck to the man in Healdsburg. It was a teenaged kid in a stolen truck, so the policeman who responded said he was probably just joyriding, but he took a report. I reported the incident at the station to Muni security, but I didn't see the man who pushed me. The only reason I knew it was a man is because the gentleman who saved my life caught a quick glimpse of him. But when a man in a black car took two shots at me today, there was no mistaking the fact he was aiming at me. For that I have made a report, we have a partial license number, and the police are now involved. I didn't connect the incidents until today. It all just felt like a very scary set of coincidences, and there was no reason to call you."

"No reason, Kaz?"

His soft answer infuriated her. The fact she was upset enough to be pacing back and forth pissed her off even more. "Well, Jake . . . did you call me at any time this past couple of weeks? No. You didn't. Not once." She was definitely pissed, so angry she knew if she didn't get off the phone she was going to end up crying. Anger and frustration usually had that effect on her, and she really didn't need it right now. "I'll see you tonight," she said, and then she quickly ended the call. Her hands were shaking so badly she dropped the phone.

It was ringing again when she picked it up. She didn't have to look to know who it was when she answered. "What?"

"I'll pick you up. Be ready by five-thirty. We need to talk before people start arriving."

"No. I've already arranged for a cab. I'll meet you there."

"Look, Kaz, there's stuff you don't know. I—"

"No. You look. I've had a really crappy morning, and you are not helping me one f'ing bit. If you want me to look good for tonight's event—which, as far as I know, is the only reason you want me there—you'll just leave me alone and let me do my job. I'll see you tonight."

She waited for his answer.

And waited. Finally, very softly, he said, "Okay. If that's how you want it. Try and be there before six. I really do need to talk to you. It's important."

There was another long pause before he added, "Understand this, Kaz. Looking good for the launch isn't the reason I want you there." Before she had time to think that through, he gave her the address and ended the call.

She stared at the phone in her hand for a long time before the tears finally won.

Jake stared at the phone in his hand. Then he set it aside and went into his office to get the photos Marc had called and asked for this morning, but even working with the pictures couldn't get him out of the crap he'd pulled with Kaz. How the hell had he managed to screw things up so badly? Was it because he'd fantasized about talking to her again? Was it because he was worried sick when she first answered the phone, her voice breaking and sounding like she was ready to cry?

He knew one thing. He was telling her the whole sordid story tonight. No hiding behind half-truths. He was still shaking, chilled inside and out after listening to her as she'd calmly explained all the crap she'd been through the past couple of weeks. Dangerous crap she'd been dealing with on her own. The truck could have killed her. She was beyond lucky the train didn't kill her, but today. Damn it, today someone tried to shoot her. Someone in a black car. It had to be the same guy. He'd bet it was a black BMW. Why didn't he think to ask her?

Was Fanboy the guy driving the BMW? Except that guy looked older—Fanboy just didn't fit. Why Kaz? That didn't make any sense, either—he was stalking RJ, and the fact that Fanboy was using that name meant he was someone out of Jake's past. Why would he be interested in Kaz? As far as anyone knew, the only relationship he and Kaz had was professional, not personal.

His gut knotted as more ideas, more scenarios flashed through his mind. What if Fanboy had figured it out? If he'd been there . . . Had he been watching them at the vineyard? A montage of images flashed through his mind— Kaz, stripping her crop top up and off, sliding that skirt down her long legs. Holding her arms out to him. Taking him deep inside.

If the bastard had been watching them . . .

Fuck. Kaz was no fool—definitely not as big an idiot as he was. She had to know all the so-called accidents were connected, that she was the target of some kind of psychopath. She had to be terrified.

But she didn't know about Fanboy. Had no idea Jake had been getting texts. There had to be a connection.

Crap. If anyone was a fool, it was him. One of the texts he'd gotten referred to the incident in Healdsburg, another mentioned the dinner he'd had in Geyserville.

Fanboy was after Kaz.

"You are such a fucking jerk, Lowell." He'd lost time, working and worrying and getting nothing accomplished. He stood up, shoved his hands through his hair, and tugged hard. He tried calling her back. No answer. He wanted to go see her, but Marc needed him to come by to go over some last-minute details for the event tonight. It was a huge deal—the media would be all over the place, and so much depended on Kaz.

The pictures were exquisite. She was exquisite.

And right now, she wasn't even speaking to him. Should he go to her? Force his way in, whether she wanted to see him or not? Except, what if he made her mad enough to quit? To decide not to show up? Crap. He'd see her tonight. Somehow he'd get her off by herself. He had to tell her everything. Holding back was killing him, but even worse, not knowing the truth could kill her.

That thought forced his hand.

He grabbed his laptop, locked his apartment, and ran out to his car.

Instead of going straight to Marc's office, he headed west. He'd go to Kaz, tell her about the texts, tell her about RJ, make sure she was safe. If she left him, if she decided she couldn't live with the jerk he'd proved he was, that would kill him. But at least he'd know that he'd told her the truth. No excuses, no lies of omission.

Barely ten minutes later, he pulled up in front of Kaz's house in the Sunset, raced up the front steps, and knocked on the door. He waited and knocked again, harder this time.

A door opened across the street, and an older woman stepped out on the porch and glared at him. Either Kaz wasn't home, or she just wasn't answering. He noticed the doorbell and tried that, heard the chimes inside, waited a little bit longer.

He checked his phone and then turned and went back down the steps. He'd meet with Marc. He hated to put more pressure on his friend, but he had to let Marc know about the connection, the risk to Kaz. Then he'd focus on the launch, on showcasing Kaz Kazanov as the star he knew she was going to be, but he had to at least warn her. He got back into his car and dialed her number, let it ring until it went to voice mail. "Kaz? It's Jake. This is really important. There's crap going on you don't know about, but it could be connected to the attempts on your life. Call me."

She'd been honest with him, and he'd lied to her, treating her like she didn't have any sense. She had plenty of sense, and if she was thinking straight she was probably running as fast and as far away from him as she could possibly get.

Kaz had a glass of wine with an early lunch. She never drank during the day, but it was the only thing she could think of to make her hands stop shaking. The shooting had terrified her, but Jake had flat-out pissed her off. He'd been angry, she'd been upset, and she figured both of them had totally overreacted.

Tonight, with any luck, and if she could get there early enough, she hoped they could talk things out, get all the crap between them fixed. She was almost sure that Jake loved her. She'd been trying to convince herself that's why he'd gotten mad. He was afraid for her, right?

She was positive she loved him, though right now she felt more like strangling him.

Officer Macias had called. They'd gotten a couple of possible matches to the partial license plate that might or might not be the shooter. He'd asked her if she recognized the names, a woman named Sondra Franklin from Malibu and a guy named Russell Norwich from Oakland.

She'd never heard of either one, and neither of them had reported a stolen car. She'd written their names down and planned to ask Jake.

Jake. She really had to get her head on straight before she met up with him tonight. Finishing her wine, Kaz stuck her glass and dishes in the dishwasher and headed to her bedroom. She had to figure out what she'd be wearing, and really needed to get ready.

A long soak in a hot tub sounded like a good place to start. She filled the tub, turned the music up, stuck her headset on, and put everything out of her mind.

An hour later she got out, with wrinkled fingertips and toes and a better feel for the evening ahead. She checked her phone, noted a message from Jake, and decided not to listen to it. There was no way she was going to give up her relaxed state of mind.

There'd be more than enough drama later. She was positive on that count.

By four, she'd decided on a totally different outfit than the ones she'd originally considered, a dark teal blue silk cropped top with matching harem pants that sat low on her hips, hung in soft, flowing folds, and gathered in at her ankles. The look was totally retro, but it showcased the monarch tat perfectly, only clipping off part of the lower wing, but the best part about it was the fact she felt sexy and confident when she put it on.

She'd never worn it out in public before. There hadn't been a reason to dress this outrageously. Usually, the last thing she wanted was to be the center of attention.

Tonight she wanted to shine. She decided on the diamonds and the finely wrought gold chains from earlobe to nostril, from nipples to navel. She loved the way the chains swung beneath her breasts and across her belly, the way the silk abraded her sensitive nipples.

"Well, crap." She stared at herself in the mirror. She was already aroused, and Jake was nowhere around, but she couldn't blame it on the outfit. Not entirely. Yes, she loved the feel of the chains drifting over her cheek and torso, and the way the silk caressed her skin. She'd had these same feelings when she dressed for each shot, knowing full well that Jake would be focusing on her for the next few hours.

Would he focus on her tonight? Or would he decide she was just too much trouble? For that matter, did she want him to? He'd acted like a complete ass this morning. That phone call still had her wanting to strangle him, but her reaction was so over-the-top, that it had to be something else.

She had a feeling she knew exactly what it was.

Staring at herself in the mirror, Kaz made a face. "Life was so much easier and a whole lot less complicated before you came along, Jacob Lowell. Way easier and definitely not as stressful." She tilted her head to the right, felt the chain slide across her left cheek. Thought of Jake trailing kisses beneath her ear, his lips nipping at the chains beneath her breasts, and practically moaned.

Turning away from the mirror, she whispered, "But not nearly as entertaining."

She went back to her room and grabbed a pair of sandals the same color as her outfit. The soft teal leather and the matching platform heels added to her height and her confidence.

Tonight, Jacob Lowell wasn't going to know what hit him.

She'd lied when she'd told Jake she'd already arranged for a cab. It was almost four-thirty, so she took one last look in the mirror, grabbed a small handbag with a narrow shoulder strap that couldn't be more apropos—light teal silk with hand-painted monarch butterflies swirling over the fabric—and headed out to the kitchen where she'd left her phone. It rang as she reached for it. Lola's name popped up on the screen.

"Hey, sweetie. What's up?"

"Kaz, you have to come to the coffee shop. Right now.

Mandy can't leave but we have something you need to see before you go to that launch tonight."

She glanced at the clock on the wall. "I'm ready to go, and Jake wants me there early. Said he wants to talk, but I'll see if I can get a cab."

"I'll just bet he wants to talk."

Lola sounded absolutely furious. "Lola? What's going on?"

"Just get down here. Now. I'll wait."

Lola ended the call. Kaz called for a cab, and the dispatcher said he had one dropping off a passenger just two blocks over. Kaz grabbed a black shawl that would work with her outfit and met him out in front less than five minutes later.

She asked him to wait in front of the coffee shop, got out, and went inside. The place was almost empty. Lola and Mandy were sitting together at a table near the back. Kaz waved as they raised their heads, and drew her hand down at the matching looks of fury on both faces.

She slipped into an empty chair. "What's going on?"

Lola shoved a manila envelope in front of her. Kaz glanced at the label. She didn't recognize the handwriting, but it was addressed to Kaz Kazanov in care of Lola Monroe at Top End. Frowning, she raised her head and looked at her two roommates, and then she opened the envelope and pulled out a thick folder with a note taped to the front.

After going through my pictures, I decided to use these. Wanted to let you know. RJL

"Oh. No . . . he wouldn't . . ." Kaz thought she was going to be sick. Slowly, with fingers trembling so badly she could barely open the folder, she flipped the top to one side. The first shot was a close-up of her shaved mound and the tiny gold ring and ruby sparkling from her clitoral hood.

The next was one of her bejeweled breasts, with the tigers eye this time. Her head was raised, and she looked directly into the lens. No disguising her identity, nothing to take away the almost pornographic look of lust in her eyes. She flipped through more of them, each one more explicit, more titillating than the last.

More heartbreaking.

How could he?

Her breath burst in and out of her lungs in heated gasps, and she grabbed the photos, stood them on end. She wouldn't—couldn't—look at the rest of them. Her gut ached, a horrible pain that could have been her lungs, her stomach, her heart. Nausea rolled through her. With shaking hands, she finally managed to get the pictures into the folder, the folder back into the manila envelope.

"What are you going to do?" Mandy grabbed her hand, held on tightly. "You never pose nude. You've always said that was something you'd never do. Those pictures are . . . they're just wrong, Kaz. They're awful."

Taking a deep breath, Kaz said, "I agree. They're horrible. I did not pose for them for any commercial use. I'm going to go and have a little talk with Mr. Lowell." She shoved her chair back and stood, holding the envelope tightly clutched in both hands against her breasts. She'd thought he was wonderful. Fun and smart, handsome and caring. She didn't know what to think.

Except that she didn't know Jacob Lowell at all.

The cabby was still waiting, the meter running. Two weeks ago she would have been in a panic over the cost. Not now. Not after the money Jake had paid her, or the even larger sum she'd gotten from Fletcher Arnold. No, money wasn't a problem right now.

Maybe that was part of the reason she felt so dirty. He'd promised her that the photos were for him alone, they were private and too personal to share with anyone. She'd been half in love with him when she posed, awash in her own sexuality.

No. Who the hell was she trying to fool? She'd been wholly in love with him. Convinced he was a man worth loving.

Maybe he figured that, since he'd paid her so much, he could do what he wanted with the pictures. Except, he'd promised, and she'd believed him.

Proof she was an absolute idiot.

It was after five, and traffic across town was horrible. She'd told Jake she'd be there early. It looked as if she'd barely make it by six. When they reached the hotel, she had the fare and tip already in her hand. The cab pulled up in front, she handed the driver the cash and got out. She'd barely entered the lobby when she saw Jake rushing across the expanse, black silk shirt, black slacks, a huge smile on his face.

She waited, holding the folder in her hands. As Jake drew closer, his smile faded. By the time he reached her, his brow was knotted, and his eyes looked wary.

"Kaz? What's wrong?"

She was so proud of herself. She didn't scream at him. She didn't cry. Instead, she held her ground and looked him in the eye. "You lying son of a bitch. How dare you?" She shoved the envelope against his chest. "You're going to have to handle your sacred launch without me, Mr. Lowell, but if you use any of these photos, my lawyer will be in touch."

She turned away before he said a word, practically ran out of the lobby, and looked for a cab. "Damn!" She should have asked her driver to wait. Spotting a couple of cabs at the curb near the end of the block, Kaz stalked toward them. She'd gone barely a dozen paces when a man ran past and grabbed her arm. Jerking hard, he pulled her off balance and covered her mouth with a hand reeking of cigarette smoke.

They were beyond the well-lit front of the hotel, near the exit from underground parking. No one was close enough to see or to help. She fought back. She was taller than him, she should have had the advantage, but he twisted her right arm high behind her back and shoved her into the backseat of a dark car, knocking her head hard against the door frame. Stars flooded her vision as he forced her to the floor and followed her in, closing the door behind them.

Stunned, frightened, she tried to lift herself, to dislodge his weight from her back, but she was on her knees with her left arm trapped beneath her body, her right still in his iron grasp.

She twisted, still trying to rise, and forced him back. He cursed, and then he punched her, hard, against her temple. Dazed, she tried to move but he hit her again.

She barely felt the pain. Then she felt nothing at all.

Moving like a man trapped in a horrible nightmare, Jake pulled the folder out of the manila envelope, flipping from one disgusting picture to the next. His first thought—that paparazzi had learned his identity—gave way to blind fury when he found the note. Not his, and neither were the pictures. But Kaz didn't know that. Dear God, she thought he'd taken these? That he would ever think of using anything like this?

They were horrible. Beyond the fact they were technically bad, the photos were pornographic in the extreme, but he couldn't stop looking, had to see every damned one, each more disgusting than the last.

Then he came to the last photo.

One of him covering Kaz, taken with a big lens from the back. His butt, his balls, her legs spread wide, heels locked against his lower back. Obviously, Kaz hadn't gotten this far, or she would have known. Hell, she should have known anyway. He'd promised her.

He didn't break promises.

Grabbing his phone, Jake called her number. It went straight to voice mail. He left a message and then walked to the main door. He'd go to her house, find out what the hell was going on, where she'd gotten the pictures.

"Hey, Jake. Been looking for you. Where's the model? People are arriving."

Jake glanced over his shoulder. Marcus Reed walked quickly across the lobby. He actually looked a bit stressed tonight, and if Jake wasn't worried sick over Kaz and what she had to be thinking right now, he'd be razzing Marc about his case of nerves.

"Marc, I hate to do this to you, but something has happened. It's Kaz. I'm scared it's tied into the texts, the attempts on her life. I need to find her. I'll make it up to you, somehow, but I have to leave."

Marcus stared at him for a moment and then nodded. "Go. Kaz is more important. I hope she's okay." He grabbed Jake's shoulder as he turned to leave and added, "I want to meet this girl. She's obviously managed to turn you inside out."

Jake nodded and raced toward the parking garage. Marc was right. She'd certainly done exactly that.

CHAPTER 17

The coffee shop was his first stop. He had a feeling that if her roommate was working, Kaz would head here first. He ran inside. No sign of Kaz or her roommate.

There was a young kid behind the register. Jake pulled it together, forced himself not to lose it on an innocent employee. "Have you seen Mandy or Kaz?"

The boy shrugged. "Mandy's shift ended at six. She's probably gone home. I haven't seen Kaz since around five."

"Home. Gotcha. Thanks."

He raced back to his car, but the fear was rising, certain he was running out of time. That Kaz was running out of time. It all had to be connected. The car in Healdsburg, the Muni train, today's shooting. Hell, even the truck. Fanboy was using Kaz to get to him, but why would someone from his past go after her? Who in their right mind would ever want to harm Kaz? He had to talk to her, tell her everything.

Tell her he loved her.

The girls' house was only a couple of blocks away. He found a place to park just three doors down and raced back up the sidewalk, up the stairs, and pounded on the door.

"Who's there?"

"Lola? It's Jake. Is Kaz here?"

The door flew open. Mandy and Lola stood together in the doorway, and Lola practically snarled at him. "She's not here, you son of a bitch."

"How could you?" Mandy's eyes were red. "She trusted you. She loved you."

"She's not here? God damn it! I think she's in trouble." He shook the envelope. "Where did these come from? They're not my pictures. I didn't take these."

"Prove it." Lola stepped aside. Jake shoved his way past Mandy and went straight through to the kitchen. As he pulled the folder out of the envelope, he said, "For one thing, I know she doesn't work at Top End anymore, and I don't know your last name, but it's sent in care of Lola Monroe. If that's you . . ."

He left the sentence dangling as he grabbed the last picture in the stack and threw it on the table. "There. That's me with Kaz. Someone was behind us in the vineyard taking these. As grainy as they are, he was using a cheap telephoto lens. How did she get these? Who gave them to her? Do you know anyone who might want to harm Kaz? An old boyfriend, an acquaintance from work, anyone?"

Breathing hard, he stared at the women, and he sure as hell hoped they had some suggestions, because if it wasn't someone out of her past, it had to be the bastard from his.

Mandy had her fist shoved against her mouth, but she shook her head. "No," she said. "No one. Everyone loves Kaz."

"She got the pictures from me." Lola stared at Jake. "A bike messenger dropped them off at the office a little before four. I didn't look at them right away, but the minute I saw the first few pictures and read your note, I called Kaz and told her to meet us at the coffee shop. I figured they were from you."

"Well they're not from me, the note's not mine, and I can't find Kaz. Do you have any idea where she is?"

"She took a cab to the launch," Mandy said. "She was really upset." She glanced at her sister. "We haven't heard from her since."

Cursing, he ran his hands through his hair. "Look, there's a very good chance that she's been kidnapped."

Mandy made a whimpering sound and covered her mouth. Lola cursed.

"Someone has been sending me anonymous text messages, bringing up shit that happened a long time ago. I hadn't said anything to Kaz because there didn't seem to be any reason to frighten her. I thought it was just someone out of my past trying to freak me out, but now I think he followed us to Healdsburg. I think it was the same guy who tried to hit us when we were there. Do you have any idea what kind of car the guy who shot at her was driving?"

Mandy glanced at Lola and said, "It was a black car with four doors. Eddy, the kid who works with me, thought it was an old BMW, but I don't know for sure."

"Shit." He bowed his head. "Same guy. It has to be the same guy."

He felt Lola staring at him. He raised his head, forced himself to meet her steady glare.

Finally, she said, "Then where the hell is she?"

"I don't know." He felt as if his legs might give out and sat down hard on one of the kitchen chairs. "She threw these in my face in the hotel lobby, turned around, and was gone before I had any idea what was going on. I've tried to call her, but she didn't answer. Her phone went straight to voice mail."

Mandy nodded. "That makes sense. She always sets it that way when she's going to a shoot or an event. So it won't bother anyone."

Lola shot a quick glance at Mandy. "Where's her tablet? Doesn't she have that app on it that'll find a lost phone?"

"She does." Mandy took off toward Kaz's room with Jake and Lola right behind her. She grabbed the slim digital tablet off the bedside table, waited a moment while it booted up, and then punched in the password. Once she was in, she entered another password and tapped the icon on the opening screen. A map of the Bay Area came up. A moment later, a little green light blinked on the freeway, just north of the Golden Gate Bridge.

Mandy said, "What's she doing there?"

Lola muttered a curse. "I have no frickin' idea."

Jake stared at the image for a moment, his mind spinning in useless circles. Why in the hell would she be headed north, unless she was going back to Healdsburg, maybe Dry Creek Valley? There was no other destination that made any sense. None at all.

Except, whoever had taken those pictures had been there, in the same vineyard, when he and Kaz were making love. If he'd been the one driving the black BMW, the one who fired two shots at Kaz this morning, then . . . "Fuck! I know where she is, where he's taking her."

"What?" Mandy grabbed his arm. "Where who's taking her?"

"She told you about the guy in the BMW who almost hit us, right? We both thought he was watching us at one point in Healdsburg, but we weren't sure. We had no reason to suspect anyone was after either of us then, but his car matches what little description you've got of the one from this morning, when the guy shot at Kaz. I think he's got her. I don't know who he is or why he's after her, but I think he's trying to get back at me for something. It's got to be him. Give me the password—I want to take this so I can use the app and follow them. We need each other's phone numbers, in case you hear anything. Or when I find her."

When, not if. Kaz was out there, in trouble. He was sure

of it. Just as certain it was his fault—someone wanted to hurt Kaz because of him.

Lola grabbed his arm. "Shouldn't we call the police?"

Frustrated, Jake raked his fingers through his hair and shook his head. "And tell them what? We think someone's after her but we have no idea who it is? We think she might have been kidnapped, but she was really pissed off at me and could just as easily have been mad enough to leave town? That her phone is headed north, but we're not sure she's got it? I don't want to waste the time trying to convince them. I'm going after her now. But if there's someone you can think of who might be able to help, then call them."

"José Macias," Lola said. "He's responded twice now, and he knows us and Kaz. Mandy? Do you still have his card?"

"Let me get this first," Jake said. Mandy took his phone and typed in their numbers. He grabbed one of his business cards and set it on the bedside table. "Call me if you hear from her."

Lola nodded. "And you'd damned well better call us." She glanced at Mandy. "The password for the tablet is *manilow*, all lowercase. It's the same for the app."

His head filled with the songs they'd sung together that first night on the drive to Healdsburg. He had to find her. Raising his head, he said, "Why am I not surprised? Thank you." Then he grabbed the tablet and raced back to his SUV. It was almost seven. She'd been gone for at least forty-five minutes, and Jake had never been more terrified in his life.

A cramp in her left arm dragged Kaz back to consciousness. She was still on the floor in the backseat of a car with her face pressed against the back of the driver's seat. Some-

one had thrown a musty smelling blanket over her, hiding
her from view. If it was the same man who'd grabbed her,
she was positive she was in the black car from this morning.

Maybe the BMW from Healdsburg? It made sense—if
any of this made sense.

There couldn't possibly be more than one person out
there who wanted her dead. But who? And why? Her hands
and feet were tied together with what felt like those plastic cable ties the police sometimes used as handcuffs.
She tugged, but the ties didn't give at all. Her jaw and the
side of her face hurt like hell. He must have hit her a couple
more times after she'd passed out.

Her left arm felt numb, but she was all twisted up on
the floor between the front and rear seats. Slowly, she
stretched out her legs, pressed her linked feet against the
door, and got enough leverage to roll until she was lying
on her back with her knees bent. As tall as she was, the
guy had folded her up like a damned pretzel to fit her back
here. With the blanket over her face, she couldn't see anything.

Kaz figured she should be terrified, but for whatever
reason, she wasn't. She was pissed off more than anything.
Frustrated because she didn't know why she'd been targeted.

Or why Jake had done what he'd done. Her stomach
rolled at the thought of those horrible pictures, at the terrible betrayal, at Jake's broken promise.

The car slowed, sped up, slowed again. From the
sounds, she figured they must be on a freeway, but she had
no idea where, what direction they were going, how long
they'd been traveling. The driver hadn't said a word.

She wasn't sure she wanted him to know she was awake.

Her thoughts took her back to Jake, to those horrible,
horrible pictures of her. How could he? Her eyes burned as

she thought of him, walking across the lobby in the hotel with that deceptively innocent, welcoming smile on his face.

Didn't he realize how much he'd hurt her?

Not if he didn't know anything about the pictures.

The thought slipped into her mind like a shard of ice—along with another image. Before they'd left Sonoma County, he'd shown her some of the photos he'd taken, brought them up for her on his laptop. They were beautiful—sensual without being at all trashy.

The pictures in that envelope were ugly, like something you'd see in a cheap tabloid. Out of focus, and grainy, not like Jake's work at all.

Not Jake's?

She hadn't looked at all of them, but she was almost positive they'd been taken in the vineyard. She wished she'd paid closer attention, but lying here on the floor now, trapped between the back and front seats with her hands tied behind her, she had nothing to do but think.

It didn't take long for her to become absolutely certain those weren't Jake's pictures.

Whoever was driving—what appeared in that one quick glance as she was shoved in through the back door to be a black BMW—was the same man who'd tried to run them down. The same one who'd taken shots at her this morning. Maybe even the guy who'd tried to push her in front of the train.

Could he have hired that kid with the stolen pickup?

It was too screwed up to make sense, too great a coincidence to ignore. But she wasn't ready to confront him. Not yet. She still had way too much to think about.

"Think, Lowell!" Jake pounded on the steering wheel, caught once again in stop-and-go traffic. He'd gotten through San Rafael faster than expected, but now he was sitting at almost a dead stop north of Novato. He glanced at the digital tablet on the seat beside him, tapped the screen, and refreshed the image.

"Shit." The app showed them almost to Santa Rosa. A space opened up in the lane to his right, and he shot into it. A short time later he saw the lights of an accident up ahead—a pickup truck had spun out in the commuter lane and hit the concrete barrier blocking northbound from southbound traffic. The diamond lane, designated for vehicles with multiple passengers, was wide open beyond the wreck.

As soon as he got past the crumpled truck, Jake cut across the lane to his left and slipped into the diamond lane. He hit the gas, and the Escalade surged forward. Hopefully, the cops would be too tied up with the wreck to pay attention to one lone passenger in the big SUV. Passing slower traffic on his right, Jake prayed to whatever gods might be listening to let him get to Kaz in time.

The worst part was her inability to judge time. How long had she been back here, stuffed between the seats with her head covered? It seemed darker than when she'd first regained consciousness. She didn't know if there'd still been a little daylight left when she'd come to. She'd left Jake in the lobby around six, well before the sun had set. It was definitely dark now.

Where the hell was she? And why? Enough. It was time to find out what the hell was going on. "Hey! Who are you? Where are you taking me? What the hell's going on?"

"Shut up. You want to stay alive a little bit longer, bitch, you'll keep your mouth shut."

That wasn't the response she wanted. Kaz shut her mouth and thought about Jake. Did he know she'd been taken? If he'd looked at the pictures, he'd know they weren't his.

She should have known, damn it. Should have paid attention.

Woulda, coulda, shoulda. How many times had she and her dad repeated those horrible words after Jilly died?

Why hadn't she looked at those pictures more carefully, thought about what she was doing before she'd confronted Jake? She'd totally screwed up the jewelry launch, and he was going to be so pissed. And Marcus Reed, the man behind the whole thing . . . what was he going to think if his model went off and got herself killed?

No. She wasn't going there. She refused to end up dead. Somehow she'd get away, and with any luck, Jake would be looking for her. Someone had to be looking.

"That goddamned RJ Cameron. Smart-ass son of a bitch. Gonna make him pay. Gonna take someone he loves. Show him what it feels like."

The man's voice—but who was he talking to? She'd thought he was alone, but . . .

"Some star he turned out to be. Winning all those races at the Olympics, making all that money. Thought he could get away with it, but I'll show him."

Was he talking to himself? The car had slowed until it was barely crawling along, so they must be in heavy traffic, but none of this made sense. She didn't know any Olympians, and the name RJ Cameron didn't ring a bell. Did this guy think Jake was RJ Cameron?

He was still muttering. She took a chance and asked him. "Who's RJ Cameron? What did he do?"

The muttering ended. Kaz held her breath. Was he going to answer her? If she could get him talking, maybe she could find out where they were going, what he was planning. While she lay there with her arms cramping and her head and jaw aching, she slipped her shoes off, tried to find her purse with her toes. Her cell phone was in it, but she had no idea where the purse had ended up. She leaned to one side, felt for any sharp edge with the tips of her fingers.

There. Under the driver's seat, part of the track for adjusting the seat. She started rubbing the tie holding her wrists together, back and forth over the bare metal.

The guy still hadn't said a word. The blast of a car horn sounded really close by, and the one she was in jerked forward. The driver cursed, a steady litany of profanity, as someone else honked, and they skidded to a stop. Another horn blared, to the right this time. The car she was in moved forward, slower but at least steady. For now.

Had her question thrown him off that much?

"So. He hasn't even told you who he is, eh? You're good enough to screw, but not enough to hear the truth. Ha! Sounds like him. Lying bastard."

Obviously, she'd gotten to him. He was breathing hard, as if he'd been running. Maybe she'd just made him really mad. That fit. He sounded mad—the insane kind of mad—and didn't that make for an interesting evening.

She kept her voice smooth, a little haughty, and said, "I don't know what you're talking about." She wasn't about to give him the gratification of knowing she was scared spitless.

Of course, he probably already knew that. Kaz twisted her head back and forth and felt the blanket begin to slide away from her face. Each movement sent pains shooting through her jaw and down her neck, but if she could just get rid of this damned blanket, maybe she'd see something familiar, anything that would give her a clue where she might be.

The blanket fell away from the left side of her face, but even with just one eye, she could tell they were passing through an urban area, if the amount of light meant anything. She concentrated on searching for her purse. The blanket had moved as far as it was going to.

"Listen up."

She stopped moving. Stopped rubbing the plastic tie against the metal. And listened.

"Almost twenty years ago, a well-known competitive swimmer who'd won big at the Atlanta Olympics was involved in an incident."

There was a lot of extra inflection on that final word. Kaz hated how curious she was. Hated even more what she thought she might learn.

"He went by the name of RJ Cameron, but his real name was Richard Jacob Lowell, now known as R. Jacob Lowell, photographer." He paused.

Kaz didn't say a word, but her mind spun in so many circles she felt dizzy.

"You're not gonna ask me what happened?"

He sounded almost gleeful as he added, "You don't want to know that your jackass lover was driving the car that killed my beloved wife? My beautiful little boy? That a fun night of joyriding in a stolen car took my Mary away from me forever? Huh? Not interested, sweetheart, that my son, my beautiful little Russell junior, just six years old, holding on to his mommy's hand to walk across the street in the fucking crosswalk, is dead because of your boyfriend?"

She didn't say anything. She couldn't. Jake hadn't said a word about killing anyone. Just that he'd been out joyriding with his brother, that Ben was the one driving, that Jake had served time instead of his brother.

Why hadn't he told her the truth?

Because I'd told him about Jilly. She'd talked so much about her little sister, how she'd died. Had he been afraid to tell her the truth? Afraid it would change the way she felt about him?

And did it?

She honestly didn't know. He'd not been honest, but she hadn't, either, not at first. Was that why he'd been so insistent about not getting involved? Because he didn't want to tell her the whole story? If so, his lack of complete honesty might well cost Kaz her life.

Not something she particularly wanted to dwell on right now.

"You're being awfully quiet back there, girly. He didn't tell you, did he? Didn't tell you about all those years in jail, about having to sit there in the courtroom and look at the pictures. Yeah, they had pictures—Mary all broken up so I didn't even recognize her. Little Russ almost as bad, while that pretty boy just sat there, slouched down in his chair like he was bored with the whole thing. Bored!"

He shouted the word and slammed his fist down on something, and the car lurched forward, picked up speed.

He was still talking, but not to Kaz anymore. He was muttering about the horrible pictures and his beautiful little boy, and he sounded as heartsick now as he must have been when they died.

When Jake killed them. Why did he lie to her? Was he too cowardly to tell the truth?

The man was slapping something—the dashboard? Talking in a singsong voice, the sharp slaps emphasizing his words. Something about the horrible pictures and how he'd wanted to kill the kid who'd done this terrible thing.

Then the slapping stopped. He sort of growled, and the sound actually raised shivery bumps along Kaz's arms.

"He took everything from me. Everything that mattered. Mary was mine! Russell, mine. Now they're gone." He moaned painfully. "That's why I have you, missy. I swore I'd make him pay. He took what I loved. I'm going to do the same thing to him."

"I think you've made a mistake," she said. It was hard to talk around the fear choking her words. "Jake doesn't love me."

"RJ. His name's RJ." Then he laughed, and Kaz really wanted to hit him.

"If he loved me," she said, "he'd have been around. I worked for him, but I haven't seen him in two weeks. Not until tonight when I took those disgusting pictures and threw them in his face."

"Disgusting? I thought they were pretty damned good." He sounded almost jovial. Upbeat. "You all naked out there in the sunlight, him just as bare-assed, fucking you like you were some cheap whore. I wasn't that far away, you know. It was so easy. I could have killed both of you then, but where's the fun in that? I want him to watch. Want him to see you all broken and bloody, just the way my Mary looked."

He was quiet for what felt like a long time. Then he laughed again. "Once I send him a text, tell him where to find you, I'll have more than enough time. Or maybe I'll just call. Yeah. It's time for me and RJ to have a little chat. I'll call, tell him where you are, and then I'll have all the time I need."

CHAPTER 18

Jake pulled off the highway north of Healdsburg and drove toward the winery. The last time he'd checked, the tracker showed Kaz's signal passing Healdsburg, so their destination had to be the vineyard. There wasn't even a glow of light in the western sky. He glanced at the clock on the dash, something he'd been trying really hard not to do, because it made him all too aware how fast time was flying. Despair took a tighter hold on his hope of saving Kaz.

The sun had still been up when Kaz tossed those damned pictures in his face.

It was after nine. A drive that should have taken two hours at the most had lasted almost three. How far ahead were they? And damn, what if he'd guessed wrong? Anxiety swamped him, the sense that he'd screwed up, that she wasn't going to be where he'd thought she was. The tablet had shut itself off so he pulled over at a wide spot and punched in the password.

It felt like it took forever to open. The battery was low, and he didn't have the fucking charger, but the moment the screen lit up, he punched in the same password for the app. Again he waited. A car sped by, and then another. His hands were shaking; his mouth was dry.

The green light popped up. The phone and—damn, he

hoped he was right—Kaz were exactly where he thought they'd be. Taking a quick glance in the rearview mirror, he saw the road was empty and punched the accelerator. The Escalade fishtailed and skidded back onto the asphalt. Frantic, now that he was so close, but what if he was too late? How long had she been there?

Who had Kaz, and why? Something about the man who'd tried to run them down tickled the edges of memory, but he couldn't place him. Who was Fanboy? Jake had gone back through all his clients, even guys he'd competed against in the Olympics. He'd dragged up memories of guys he'd known at the CYA.

Things had been rough when he was locked up. Rough and dirty. The rules the mostly teenaged wards lived by were more *Lord of the Flies* than any actual training to enable them to function on the outside, but he'd learned fast and he'd survived. It couldn't be anyone there—they'd known him as Richard Lowell, not RJ Cameron.

He felt his cell phone vibrate and dug it out of his pocket, glanced at the screen, and saw it was Lola. He answered, hoping like hell he wouldn't lose the signal as the road twisted and turned up the valley. "I'm almost there," he said. "Have you heard anything?"

"Maybe. Mandy found something on the kitchen counter, a note Kaz must have written earlier today. It says, 'Ask Jake re: Sondra Franklin, Malibu, and Russell Norwich, Oakland.' Do those names mean anything to you?"

"I don't know." His thoughts were scattered, his heart pounding. Norwich? Why did that name sound familiar? *Crap.* Not a clue. He was so damned close, but would he get there in time? "I'm not sure. Norwich kind of sounds familiar, but I don't know why. I'll be at the vineyard in about ten minutes. The app says they're already there. If I don't call right away, don't panic. Sondra Franklin and Russell Norwich, right?"

"Yes. I have no idea what the names are for. Oh, and Mandy called the cop who's been on two of Kaz's calls. He was off duty, and the officer she talked to wasn't much help. He suggested you call the sheriff's department in whatever county you think she's in. Call me as soon as you can. Good luck, Jake."

"Yeah. Luck." He ended the call. Racing into the darkness, he watched for the turnoff to West Dry Creek and the narrow lane that led to the Intimate vineyards.

"I'll be right back, girly. Don't go anywhere. Gotta cut the chain on the gate."

What gate? Bastard. Kaz heard the car door open and then quietly close. She kept her wrists shoved beneath the driver's seat and sawed at the piece of metal, but it didn't feel as if the plastic ties binding her wrists had weakened in the least.

She heard a dull *thunk,* a grating sound that must have been the gate opening, and a moment later her captor was back behind the wheel.

"Almost there," he said. His voice had gone all singsongy. Her fear factor moved up a couple of notches. The guy was crazy. No doubt in her mind. She flashed on the face of the man who'd almost run them down. He'd definitely looked scary.

She still hadn't seen this guy's face, but the gut feeling was growing stronger by the second. He had to be the same man.

The car moved slowly forward. She heard the sound of gravel crunching. It was all eerily familiar, and suddenly she knew. The sound of the gate, the gravel: he'd brought her back to the winery. They were driving through the service entrance to Intimate Winery, the same gate, the same road she'd driven with Jake.

But why? Why bring her back here? It didn't add up,

though somehow, knowing where she was helped ease some of her fear. There were houses here. Nate and Cassie Dunagan, the people who lived in the bigger house, had been away when she and Jake were shooting, but maybe they were back.

Their gate was on the opposite side of their property, but wouldn't they notice someone breaking in, driving down a lonely dirt driveway at night?

While she and Jake were working here, their house had been empty. Maybe this guy didn't realize that. Maybe he just thought the house was empty all the time. She rubbed the plastic tie harder.

She was still rubbing it against the metal edge when the car came to a stop.

"Not a sound, if you know what's good for you. Not a goddamned sound."

She heard the seat squeak, then it moved, as if he shifted his weight. She looked up. He was staring at her over the back of the seat. Light streamed in through the window from somewhere nearby—probably a security light on the barn—and illuminated his face.

"I knew it had to be you."

His head jerked back. "Had to be who? You don't know me."

Her mind was spinning with bits and pieces of information that suddenly fell together. Officer Macias's phone call this afternoon popped into her head. "Russell Norwich, right? You were in the coffee shop that day, and at that gas station, too. You're the one who tried to run us down a couple of weeks ago in Healdsburg, and then you took a couple of shots at me this morning. Was that you shoving me in front of the Muni train?"

He leaned fully over the seat. This time he looked pleased that she recognized him. "It was. That big guy came out of nowhere and hauled your ass back on the platform, or you'd have been dead. It would have been nice and messy, but it's good he saved you. I hope you appreciate all the effort I've gone to on your behalf." He winked. It made her skin crawl. "It's made all of this so much more entertaining, coming just. This. Close."

He held his thumb and index finger a fraction of an inch apart. Then he smiled, showing way too many teeth. "How come you know my name? Don't tell me Jacob figured it out. Jacob—what a pansy-ass name. He's RJ. Poor little rich kid RJ. I just feel so, so sorry for him. Did he tell you?"

"I got your name from the policeman who's working on my case. All those unexplained attacks were a little too coincidental. In case you're interested, you're their only suspect."

Chuckling softly, he got out of the car and opened the door behind her head. She'd hoped he'd go for the one by her feet, because she might at least have had a chance to kick him, but he wrapped his arms around her chest, snagging one of the gold chains attached to her nipples.

"That hurts. Be careful."

He laughed as he dragged her from the floor of the backseat. "Sorry, girly. But you're the one who put them on. It's not my fault your fashion sense is so impractical. Love the harem-girl look. Maybe I'll just keep you as my sex slave. You'd like that, wouldn't you? I'm sure RJ would approve."

His laughter left her shivering, but she kept her mouth shut as he grabbed her and flipped her over his shoulder, grunting with the effort. He wasn't very tall, but he was solid and obviously stronger than he looked.

He'd pulled around the barn and parked in back, so they were out of sight of the houses. The door he took her to was the small one that led to both the stairs to the upper apartment as well as to the tasting room through the back, past the restrooms and storage area. He set her on her feet and leaned her against the building. With her ankles and hands tied, she couldn't run. She could only stand there while he carefully picked the lock on the door.

She tugged at the ties holding her wrists. There seemed to be a bit more space between her arms. If she'd stretched the cable enough, maybe . . . She pulled her wrists apart as hard as she could, but the tie held.

Damn! She hated being this helpless, hated that she couldn't fight back, couldn't do anything to help save herself. Once he got her inside . . . He'd already told her he planned to hurt her badly before he killed her. At this point, she had damned little to lose.

He was bent over the lock, focusing intently on the set of picks he worked with both hands. Kaz jerked at the ties once more, and suddenly her hands were free. She couldn't run, but having her hands free gave her a chance. She sucked in a deep breath of air and cut loose with a scream. Norwich turned his head, and she clenched her hands together and hit him, hard, against the bridge of his nose.

Hard but not hard enough. She was still screaming when Norwich caught his balance and glared at her for a brief moment. She raised her hands to fight him off, but he punched her in the jaw. With her feet tied together, she tumbled to the ground.

His kick to her ribs knocked the air out of her, and then he was on her, punching and hitting, growing more incensed with each blow.

She knew she was losing consciousness. Knew she wasn't going to survive. Her last thought was of Jake, and how he'd never know that she'd figured out he hadn't taken those pictures. He'd never know how much she loved him.

Nate Dunagan, manager of the Intimate vineyards, was stepping out of the shower when his wife rushed into the bathroom. "Cassie? What's wrong?"

"I heard a woman scream. She's close—I heard her over the sound of the TV."

He grabbed a towel and quickly dried himself. "Where? North or south?"

"Near the barn, I think." She grabbed his arm as he slipped back into the dirty jeans he'd just taken off. "Be careful. I'll call 9-1-1, but it could take a while before anyone gets here."

He gave her a quick kiss and laced up his boots. "I will be. I'll have the gun and my phone. It'll be on vibrate, but call me if anything alarms you. Please stay inside, okay?"

"What if something . . ."

He stood and unlocked the gun safe, took out an older but fully functional revolver, and loaded it. "I'll be careful." He passed his hand over the slight protrusion just below her waist. "I've got too much good in my life to risk any of it."

He kissed her again and quietly slipped out the front door of the house, which faced away from the barn. It took a minute for his eyes to adjust to the darkness, and then he began working his way through the overgrown garden, moving quietly in the direction of the barn.

He heard an engine running and looked toward the road as a big SUV swung into the service driveway on the other side of the gate and stopped.

The gate was open. He'd locked it just a couple of hours ago.

Nate stood in the shadow of one of the big oaks on the property. It wasn't one of the sheriff's deputies, but the vehicle looked familiar. The car door clicked, the overhead light went on and immediately shut off, but he recognized the man in that brief second before he turned out the light.

What the hell was Jake Lowell doing here late on a Friday night? He'd finished the photo shoot two weeks ago, while Nate and Cassie were visiting family back east. Tonight was the launch of Marc's new jewelry line. He and Cassie had wanted to go, but there was too much work here to leave.

Nate waited in the shadows, just in case.

Jake opened the car door just as his phone vibrated in his pocket. He pulled it out and saw a number he didn't recognize, but he answered anyway.

"Is that you, RJ?"

The moment he heard that voice, Jake knew exactly who Russell Norwich was. The image of the man, staring at him all through his trial, made his blood run cold. Norwich had tried too hard to play the grieving widower, but the prosecuting attorney had made the point that, while Ben and RJ's car had killed her, not all of Mary Norwich's injuries had been caused by the accident. Her husband had beaten her so badly she would have been permanently scarred. The fact that she was escaping abuse to be killed by a kid out joyriding had added even more gravity to the crime.

"I thought you looked familiar, Norwich. Where's Kaz?"

"You do remember! Good boy. Hope you've enjoyed my little messages, but I thought a call was more appropriate this time. I'm not going to tell you where I took her. Not all at once, anyway. I want you to leave that fancy party of yours in San Francisco and head north. I will call you in half an hour's time and give you further instructions. You will not call the authorities, and you won't try and pull anything over on me. I have her, and I fully intend to hurt her. Badly. It's only fair since you love her, just like I loved my wife, you bastard."

Jake heard harsh breaths and a curse. "She's quite lovely, though I imagine she'll be much prettier after you clean the blood off. The gold chains are a nice touch."

"If you hurt her, if you harm her in any way . . ."

"Oh. I'm sorry. It's a little too late for that, RJ. Let's see how much more I can do before you get here. Drive north."

The line went dead. Heart pounding, Jake slowly, quietly got out of the SUV and slipped through the open gate. The chain with the lock still attached had been cut through and was lying in the dirt. Jake had blocked the driveway, so Norwich wouldn't be able to escape without going across the property to the entrance by the house. There was a light on at the big house. He hoped Nate and Cassie were home. He had a feeling he was going to need any help he could get.

Keeping to the shadows, he quietly ran down the driveway.

"Jake! It's Nate."

Jake turned as an arm snaked out of the shadows and grabbed him. "Thank God. Nate!" He slipped into the darkness beside the man.

"What the fuck's going on, Jake? Cassie heard a woman scream near the barn. I was headed down there to check on things when you pulled in."

"Shit. C'mon. Here's what it is." They slipped between two rows of old, twisted grapevines and worked their way closer to the barn. Jake whispered enough of the story to give Nate a good idea of what they were dealing with.

"You think he wants to kill her while you watch? That's sick."

"I know." Jake looked down at his hands. They shook so badly he clenched his fists to find some control. "The thing is, almost twenty years ago, I was in an accident where this guy's wife and son were killed. I served time for it, but I guess he's been waiting to find me after all these years. He's not entirely innocent, either. He'd beaten her badly. The night the car I was in hit her, she and the little boy were trying to get away from him. It was a cluster fuck any way you look at it, but he's twisted enough that now he's the grieving widower and I'm the bastard who killed his family.

"So why go after the girl?"

"He wants to hurt her because I love her."

They'd reached the side of the barn, away from any windows. Nate brushed Jake's shoulder and whispered, "Here's the key to the main door, but once you open that, he'll know we're here. I'll go in the back and try to distract him. I'm armed, but I really don't want to use a gun. Cassie's called for help. If we can stall him, keep him from hurting her until the deputies get here, we do that, okay?"

Jake nodded. None of this felt real. Kaz was in horrible danger, all because of him. This was his fault.

"Does he have a weapon?"

"I don't know." Jake leaned against the barn. All his fault. Everything. "He tried to shoot her this morning. He could be armed."

"Give me a minute to get inside."

"Yeah. Be careful, Nate. I've ruined enough lives."

Nate gave him a quick glance and then disappeared around the side of the barn. Jake moved toward the front. He knelt low to pass beneath the window that opened into the tasting room. Slowly he raised his head, looking through a corner where shadows hid him from view.

What he saw made him ill even as it scared the crap out of him. Kaz was tied to the opening of the same stall where they'd made love. Rope knotted around her wrists looped over the overhead beam, her legs were stretched wide, ankles lashed to the lower posts. Her head was down, her chin resting on her chest, and he couldn't tell if she was dead or alive.

All she wore was a tiny teal blue thong. The gold chains glinted obscenely from her bare breasts in the overhead light. The one that should have run from her ear to her nostril hung loose from her earlobe. Blood dripped from a head wound, falling in dark streams over her chest and belly, but the tattoo glowed brightly through it, almost as if the ink was lit from inside.

Norwich stood to her right with one hand on her tattoo. He appeared fascinated by the thing, tracing the outline with his fingers. Kaz slowly raised her head and glared at her captor. Blood ran from her nose and mouth; one of her eyes was swollen shut.

Thank goodness she was alive. He'd seen enough. More than enough. Jake dipped low and moved beneath the window to the main door. Quietly, he unlocked the door, and just as quietly, eased it open far enough to see through the narrow crack.

"If you're going to kill me, what are you waiting for?" Kaz's voice was breathless, her words garbled through swollen, split lips.

"You don't seem to get it, girly. I want him to watch. He won't be here for at least a couple more hours. You might have missed it, but traffic is terrible. We have plenty of time." His hand slid higher on her torso and rested just beneath her breast.

Jake sucked in a breath. He couldn't see Nate from here, didn't know if he'd gotten inside yet or not. He had to get Norwich away from Kaz. Then she spoke again.

"You don't honestly think he's going to stand by and watch you hurt me, do you?"

"You told me he doesn't love you. Which way is it going to be? I bet he's really pissed off at you, with you not trusting him to keep his promise and all. Maybe he'll want to help me rough you up a little. Now that's something I hadn't thought of."

Jake put his finger to his lips and slipped through the door with his eyes on Kaz. She glanced his way, obviously saw his signal and lowered her head once again. Norwich continued staring at the tattoo, running his fingers over the underside of her breast. Jake noticed there was blood on Norwich's face. Both eyes were turning black.

Had Kaz gotten in a punch? Damn. He sure hoped so.

Nate stood in the hallway with his gun pointed at Norwich, in full view should the man turn his way, but so far the bastard's concentration was all on Kaz. He was too close to her for Nate to get a clean shot.

Jake slipped closer and dipped down behind the bar. Somehow, they had to get Norwich away from Kaz.

The fact he might be armed made them more cautious.

As if she'd picked up on Jake's worry, Kaz spoke up. "Is that the gun you used when you shot at me?"

That's when Jake saw the ugly automatic in Norwich's left hand. He'd been holding it behind the post, out of sight. Now he held it up in front of Kaz's face. "Hollow points. In case anyone gets any ideas."

There was a metal corkscrew on the shelf behind the counter where Jake was hiding. He grabbed it and tossed the thing toward the partially opened door. It skittered across the concrete floor. Norwich jerked around and turned toward the clatter. Jake rushed him.

Norwich turned with the gun raised. Jake heard the explosion of gunfire, heard Kaz scream. Fire lashed his shoulder, but it didn't slow him a bit. Snarling a curse, arms outstretched, he dove at Norwich and took him down.

The gun slid across the floor. Nate kicked it out of the way.

"Jake! Be careful!" Kaz struggled against the ropes, then a man she'd never seen was at her side, releasing her feet and then reaching overhead to untie her arms. Her legs wouldn't hold her, and she crumpled. "Careful, honey. Here." He caught her gently before she could fall, and helped her down to sit on the blanket covering the straw.

"I'm Nate Dunagan," he said. "I live here." He shoved a gun into her hand.

"Take this, okay? The safety's on." Dizzy, maybe in shock, she stared at the revolver she was holding as Nate joined the fight. Jake had gotten a couple of punches in and Norwich was bleeding, but Jake was bleeding even more. Desperation had to be driving Norwich. He managed to free his hands and wrap his fingers around Jake's throat.

Nate grabbed Norwich from behind in a choke hold and pulled him back, but he was twisting and turning, kicking out and cursing.

And still choking Jake. Jake grabbed Norwich's wrists with both hands and pulled.

Kaz watched the fight as if from a vast distance. Jake was here, but how? He shouldn't be here for a couple more hours. That's what Norwich said, and then he'd told her he was going to hurt her. But he couldn't. Not anymore, because Jake was here. How'd he find her?

Her legs tingled and burned and so did her arms as circulation came back. She rubbed at her ankles as Jake broke away from Norwich while Nate held him back. Jake ran to her.

"Jake?"

She reached for him, and he took her hand, planted a kiss on her palm, and whispered, "Hang on, sweetheart. I'm sorry, Kaz. I'll be right back."

She was trying to process what was happening, why he was apologizing, when he grabbed the rope Norwich had tied her with and went back to help Nate. Norwich twisted and spun in Nate's grasp, and then Jake got back into the fight and punched Norwich a couple of times. Kaz was so woozy it was hard to follow the three of them moving so quickly, but Norwich was still kicking and cursing, and she was afraid he'd get loose.

Then Jake punched him again, harder this time, a right to his jaw, a left to his nose.

Norwich went limp when Jake hit him a third time.

"Well, that was certainly effective." Breathing hard, Nate took the rope Jake shoved into his hands and went to work tying Norwich.

"I'd rather kill the bastard."

"So would I, Jake, but I hear sirens coming up the valley, and Cassie would never forgive me if I ended up in jail for assisting in this bastard's much-deserved death."

"I hear them, too. Thanks, Nate. I owe you big-time."

"That you do, buddy." He raised his head and grinned at Jake. "Baby pictures when the little one arrives?"

"You got it." Jake slapped Nate on his back like they were old friends. Kaz remembered Jake telling her how he'd helped Nate and Cassie with the grape crush last fall. She blinked and tried to focus, but it looked like there were two Jakes coming toward her.

She sat there in the straw, propped against the side of the stall, knowing she looked like hell, feeling even worse. She wanted to stand up, to think clearly and process what was happening, how Jake had gotten here so fast, how he'd known where to find her, but all she could do was sit in the straw all crumpled and broken, covered in blood and bruises.

Jake was bleeding, too. Blood ran down his left arm and dripped from his fingertips, but he knelt beside her, and there was only one of him, thank goodness. One of him bleeding. She touched the back of his hand.

"You've been shot."

"I'm okay. Stings like a son of a bitch, but I think he just grazed my shoulder. God, Kaz." Gently, he gathered her up in his arms and held her close against his chest. The tenderness in his touch, the pain in his eyes, the blood covering his arm undid everything holding her together. She couldn't stop the tears. She cried softly, clutching his sides, twisting her fingers in his shirt, holding on to him for all she was worth.

He'd come for her.

Even when she'd been so awful, when she hadn't trusted his promise, he'd found her.

Except he'd lied, hadn't he? What was the truth? Had he really killed this man's wife and child? No. She wouldn't make guesses. She'd ask him later, but for now he was here, and because he was here, she was still alive. Kaz pressed her bruised and battered face against his beautiful black silk shirt, now wet and sticky with his blood, and sobbed.

She always cried ugly, but now? Now she really didn't care.

CHAPTER 19

Jake sat in the straw and leaned against the side of the stall with Kaz in his arms. His shoulder seemed to have stopped bleeding, but it still hurt. He held Kaz close against his chest while she cried, and he thought his heart would break. This was all on him. His fault. He kissed the top of her head and rested his cheek against her crown. "I don't even know where to start, sweetheart. This is all my fault. I did this, Kaz. God, I'm so sorry. So damn sorry. I should have told you everything from the beginning, but I was a fucking coward. This should never have happened."

But sorry wasn't enough. It would never be enough. He'd done this to her. His cowardice had done this to her.

"Jake?"

He pulled Kaz close to hide her nudity against his chest before he glanced up. Nate stood beside them. Norwich was hog-tied in the middle of the tasting room. Jake was sorry he hadn't killed him. "Yeah?"

"Your lady okay?"

Kaz nodded before Jake could answer. Hell, he had no idea if she was okay or not.

She sniffed, and he grabbed a handkerchief out of his pocket and wiped her eyes. She took it from him and carefully wiped the blood away from her nose and mouth.

"Nothing's broken. He beat me up pretty bad, but he said he was more interested in leaving marks and lots of blood than killing me. At least until you got here." She stared into Jake's eyes. Her left eye was no more than a slit. "How did you find me? How did you know?"

"Honestly? I was so stunned when you threw that envelope in my face and ran that it took me a minute before I looked at the pictures. I knew immediately they weren't mine. If you'd gone through all of them, you would have seen a picture of the two of us making love in the vineyard and known I couldn't possibly have taken it. But the note . . ." He shook his head.

"I know. I saw the note first, but didn't see a picture of the two of us. I couldn't look at them. They were so ugly, so wrong, but I read the note and didn't think. I'm sorry. If I'd really thought about it, I would have known they weren't yours. Your pictures are art. Those are ugly."

Jake gently brushed her hair back from her eyes. Her face was a mess, and yet she was still the most beautiful woman he'd ever seen. "You have nothing to be sorry about. This was all my fault. As soon as I saw them, I knew I had to find you, tell you they weren't mine. I promised you, Kaz. I will never share those pictures with anyone." He sighed. "But I guess you really didn't have any reason to believe me. I was still lying to you, even then, about my past.

"The day I met you, I'd started getting anonymous text messages from someone who remembered me as RJ. Nothing specific at first, but I figured he was stalking me, not you. Then he made references to things that were happening to both of us, but I was too thick to make the connection. When you told me about the attempts on your life, I figured it had to be the same guy. By then I'd gotten enough texts, I knew he'd been in Healdsburg, possibly driving the car. This afternoon I called and left a message on your phone that I needed to talk to you. I went by your house, finally gave up, and figured I'd see you tonight at the launch, tell you what was going on. Then you showed me the pictures. I tried calling and even went to the coffee shop, trying to find you. I finally went to your house, and Lola and Mandy were furious with me. I showed them the picture, the one of us together, and they finally believed me. That and the fact it was delivered to Top End. They know that I know you don't work there."

"But how did you find me?"

He brushed her hair back from her eyes and kissed her forehead. It was just about the only place without a bruise. "Mandy remembered your tablet with the app for finding your phone. That's how I traced you here, but until Norwich called me and I heard his voice, I didn't make the connection between the attacks and him. It's been almost twenty years since I saw him, and he's changed. He doesn't look anything like the man I remember."

He turned and stared at Norwich, lying all trussed up in the middle of the tasting room floor. What if he hadn't made it in time? What if the bastard had just decided to kill Kaz? He rested his cheek against the top of her head. "I'm so sorry, Kaz. Damn, just so fucking sorry."

Her fingers tightened their grasp on his shirt, and he held her tightly.

Nate walked across the room to check on Norwich. He was still tightly bound, though beginning to regain consciousness. "Sirens are getting close," Nate said. "You guys okay? I need to let the sheriff's deputies in. Your car's blocking the gate."

Jake fished his keys out of his pocket and tossed them to Nate. "Here. Go ahead and move it."

Nate caught them and walked out to meet the deputies.

"Let's get you covered up before they get here. Sorry

about the blood." Jake shrugged out of his shirt, and Kaz helped him peel the sticky silk away from his left arm.

"Sheesh, Jake. It might just be a graze, but it's left a divot at least a quarter inch deep. It's still bleeding." She used the handkerchief to apply some pressure against the wound while Jake helped her slip into the shirt. The black silk he'd worn for the event tonight was a bloody mess, but at least it hung all the way to her thighs. By the time the deputies stormed into the barn, she was decently covered.

Nate's wife, Cassie, came out to the barn when the deputies arrived. Jake had met her during last fall's crush when she and Nate were still engaged. She hadn't been pregnant yet. He'd thought she was beautiful then, but now she absolutely glowed.

She went straight to Kaz and introduced herself.

"I'm so sorry for what that man did to you. Promise me you'll go to the doctor. There's a good little hospital in town; let them take a look at you."

Kaz glanced away, almost as if she was embarrassed, but about that time the deputy walked over to talk to her. Jake sat behind her on the blanket. He didn't want these men looking at her all beaten and bloody. Didn't want them to see her wearing nothing but his shirt, but the deputy was both professional and kind.

"Ms. Kazanov, this wasn't a domestic, was it? You're not related to the man who's tied up?"

Kaz shook her head. "No. He's a stranger to me, though Jake—Mr. Lowell—knows who he is. But he's made four other attempts on my life. He tried to run us both down about two weeks ago when we were in Healdsburg. Then he hired a kid to run a truck into me in San Francisco, but the boy missed. He told me tonight he was also the one who pushed me in front of a Muni train at the station in front of AT&T Park a couple of days ago, and this morning he took two shots at me in front of a coffee shop near where I live. You can get information for the three attacks in San Francisco from Officer José Macias."

She waited while the deputy wrote down the information.

"There are police reports on all the incidents in San Francisco, and I'm sure there's some sort of record of what happened here in Healdsburg. The police were there, but Jake and I didn't realize it was anything but an out-of-control driver. Tonight, he kidnapped me, beat me up, and told me he wanted to kill me with Jake watching."

Her voice remained steady, her delivery sounded detached, almost professional. Jake felt sick.

When it was his turn, he told the police the entire story, about the accident when he was sixteen, the fact the woman who died had been badly beaten before the car ran into her, that he'd been arrested as the driver and spent almost six years incarcerated in the California Youth Authority system for the crime. He didn't mention that Ben was driving, nor did he bring up the fact that he was RJ Cameron, Olympic medal winner and media star, when it happened.

That would probably come out soon enough.

It was time.

There was too much for her to process. Kaz hurt everywhere. She kept telling herself she was lucky he hadn't raped her, but Russell Norwich had done a job on her just the same. Jake found her handbag and cell phone in Norwich's car, and that gave her something to hang on to. The deputies finally got their information, read Norwich his rights, and took him away. She declined an ambulance, and Jake helped Kaz to his car. Her outfit and shoes were in shreds—Norwich had actually cut the crop top and harem pants off of her, and then he'd gone on cutting up her wedge sandals.

The man was totally crazy, and she was damned lucky to be alive. Cassie had brought a clean T-shirt for Jake and a cotton maxi dress for Kaz that would at least cover her better than Jake's silk shirt, though she was loath to give up the shirt. It smelled like Jake. It was warm from his body, it was his . . . and wasn't that pathetic?

Still, she decided to keep the bloody shirt on and save the dress for something clean to change into after the hospital visit.

They called Mandy and Lola, and Kaz cried when she talked to them, and they cried, too, and she just felt so damned fragile. She wasn't fragile. She'd always been strong, but this past couple of weeks had totally screwed her over. She loved a man with more issues than dogs had fleas, and she wanted what she didn't need and possibly something he couldn't give her—she wanted him to love her back.

Her dad called her while she was in the ER waiting for the doctor to take a look at her injuries. Mandy had told him about what had happened, and she cried again, but it was okay because she was alive, and he wouldn't have to bury another daughter. It had been too close. Way too close.

Finally, after Jake's arm was stitched and wrapped, her ribs were x-rayed, a scan showed she didn't have a concussion, and her other cuts and abrasions were cleaned and bandaged, it was time to leave. She didn't question Jake. Instead, she let him lead her to his car and take her back to the same hotel on the plaza in town. Jake had called the hotel while she was getting x-rayed and scanned, and once again managed to find an available room.

She was dressed in hospital scrubs and still an absolute mess, and the young man at the desk couldn't help but stare at her when they checked in. Finally, he glanced at Jake and then again at Kaz and said, "Are you all right?"

She nodded. "I am now, thank you." She glanced at Jake, met his dark brown eyes, and softly said, "He saved my life."

Kaz sighed as he helped her to the elevator, and they went up to the second floor. She wasn't sure how to feel about tonight—either she was really lucky, or the unluckiest woman alive. She still couldn't believe Jake had found her in time. She'd expected to die, and then he was there. Norwich was in jail, and she was going to be okay, eventually. But she'd been in danger because of something out of Jake's past. Something he'd been unwilling to share with her. Not that knowing about his past would have changed anything.

Or maybe it would have changed everything.

They stepped into the room. Kaz noted the single king-sized bed and then headed straight for the bathroom. "I need a shower. I have to wash the feel of his hands off me, along with your blood and mine. This has been a rather messy evening." She left Jake standing in the room behind her and closed the bathroom door.

She was exhausted and hurting, but she wanted to know the truth. He owed her that much.

No. He didn't owe her anything. She had to stop thinking like that. He couldn't help it if she loved him any more than he could change who he was, what he had done. But she was still planning to ask him.

She stared at herself in the mirror. She looked more naked without her jewelry. One of the gold chains was missing, the one that had hung from her right breast. At least the diamond stud was intact. The chain from her earlobe to her nostril had broken, but the nurse had removed all of them at the hospital. Jake had the chains and the various diamond studs in a plastic bag in his pocket. She wished she had her plain silver rings. She felt naked without her jewelry. The only piece of her own that she'd worn was the tiny silver ring in the hood of her clit.

She heard Jake on the phone, but she didn't want to pry, so she turned on the shower and slipped out of the scrubs the nurse at the hospital had given to her. Everything still seemed to be moving in slow motion, but the steam rising from the shower called to her, and she got in and stood under the spray, letting it beat against her face and then her back and shoulders.

A few minutes later, she heard the bathroom door open, felt the change in temperature as cooler air drifted in, and then Jake was at the shower door. He was still dressed, obviously not assuming anything. Sex was the last thing on her mind, but she wanted him close. Wanted to know he was okay.

"Kaz? Are you all right?"

"I could use some help."

"Give me a minute."

It was barely that long before he'd stripped down and slipped into the shower behind her.

"You can't get your bandage wet." She touched the thick pad covering his upper arm.

He smiled and kissed her. "I'll keep it out of the spray. What do you need?"

She turned and looked at him and then cupped his jaw in her palm. She couldn't ask him for honesty if she wasn't willing to tell him the truth. "Just you, Jake. All I need is you."

He wrapped his arms around her and held her close. His body trembled and she thought he was crying, but that didn't make sense.

After a moment, he nuzzled her, rubbing his face against her hair. "I was so afraid I'd lose you, that I wouldn't get there in time. I had the tablet and that damned green light showing me where you were, and you were always so far ahead of me."

She kissed him. "But you got there in time. That's what counts."

"Not soon enough. He hurt you. I wish I'd killed the bastard." He rested his forehead against hers.

"I'm okay, Jake. I'm alive. Everything else will heal."

Gently, he kissed her cheek, where a bruise was probably turning all sorts of colors, and then her eye that was still swollen almost shut. Finally, he kissed her lips, again, so carefully. Norwich had punched her in the mouth. She was surprised he hadn't knocked out any teeth.

She took the washcloth and started working on her face, but Jake took it from her and washed away the blood and the stuff the ER nurse had painted over her cuts and scratches. He checked her all over, and she heard him cursing softly when he ran his fingers over her bruised ribs where Norwich had kicked her.

He'd been wearing cheap running shoes, or he might have broken her ribs. She was badly bruised, but there was nothing that wouldn't heal. Jake finally rinsed the washcloth and wrung the water out of it before hanging it on the shower rack.

Kaz watched him and then said, "I'm ready to get out." He hugged her tightly, reached behind her to turn off the water. Then he grabbed a thick towel off the rack beside the shower and carefully dried her arms, her legs, her entire body. He grabbed a fresh towel and wrapped it around her, but he let Kaz tuck in the ends to hold it close against her breasts.

He whisked the towel they'd both used over his arms, legs, and chest and wrapped it around his hips. Then he followed her out of the bathroom.

She spotted a bottle of wine on the small table by the

window, picked it up, and read the label. "This is the same port we got that first night. Thank you."

He shrugged. "I knew it was one you liked. Figured you could probably use a glass tonight."

She tried to laugh. It was almost successful. "Or maybe the whole bottle." She poured a glass for Jake, one for herself. Held her glass up to his for a toast. "My hero. You saved my life."

He glanced away. "If I'd been honest from the beginning, this might not have happened."

"You can't know that, Jake. Even if I'd known your past—which I still don't entirely know—I can't imagine I would have tied all the incidents together." She took a sip of the port and let the rich flavor roll over her tongue before she swallowed. "Will you tell me what happened? All of it?"

He closed his eyes for a brief moment, enough to tell her he really didn't want to, but then he opened them and smiled at her. "Everything. I promise. It may take a while."

She shrugged. "I've got all night. I'm too keyed up to sleep."

They ended up on the bed together with the pillows stacked behind them. Jake's first words weren't at all what she expected to hear.

"I won three gold medals in the Atlanta summer Olympics in 1996. I was sixteen years old, and all of a sudden I was a media star. Youthful, edgy Olympic swimming star RJ Cameron, headed for fame and fortune."

She turned and stared at him for a moment. "You don't sound very happy about it."

He shrugged. "My mother was the quintessential stage mother. She thought RJ Cameron sounded better than Richard Lowell. Cameron was her maiden name, and my success really was all about her. My job was to fulfill her dreams of fame and fortune. She had me bleaching my hair blond, coached me on how to talk to the media. I went along with it because I was a dumb kid and loved the spotlight. I was also an absolute jerk, and that just got me more attention. What I didn't realize was that my brother, Ben, had been the first great hope, but he wasn't as fast as me, so when I started winning, our mother essentially shoved him aside. He must have hated me, but he covered it well, because I continued to idolize him."

He took a sip of his port and then stared into the glass. "We had a really dysfunctional family, I guess, but when you're living it, you don't realize you're any different from anyone else. Looking back, our parents never hugged us, never played with us. The housekeeper hauled us to school and anything else before Mom got on her thing about having a star for a son. Ben was the source of any love I got as a kid. He's three years older than me, and I was his shadow, at least until I started winning races and got more famous. I was such an asshole after that—he didn't want anything to do with me. I can't blame him."

Kaz tried to imagine Jake as an egotistical teenaged heartthrob, because she knew that the girls must have gone crazy over him. She'd only been seven years old—not old enough to pay attention to a teenaged swimming star. "So what happened?"

"I hadn't seen Ben in weeks. He didn't attend the games in Atlanta, didn't come home, didn't want anything to do with me. I missed him so much." He shrugged. "I still do. He'd been the world's greatest big brother until the swimming came between us, but I guess he was going through a lot of issues with our parents—my dad was always busy with work, my mom was busy molding me in the image she wanted. It didn't matter to her how hard I'd trained, how important it was that I had beaten older swimmers with more experience. It only mattered that I was her ticket to Hollywood. She couldn't make it on her own, but she didn't mind using her kids, and her plan was to push the media interest into a movie or TV deal."

"What happened that night?"

"I was home alone. The parents were out. I can't remember where. Ben came home to get something out of his room, and I knew he'd been drinking. He was only nineteen. He saw me in the game room watching TV, walked in, and sat next to me on the couch.

"It was like old times. We talked for a minute, nothing special, and then he asked me if I wanted to hang out with him." He glanced at Kaz. "He hadn't spoken to me for almost a year, not since before the Olympics, and it was like my winning had driven a wedge that was even deeper between us. I jumped at the chance. I remember going out in front and he had a really cool new car, so I got in the passenger side and we took off. We'd only gone a couple of miles when he popped a beer and drank it while he was driving. It freaked me out. I was an athlete and I took diet and all that pretty seriously, but I was with Ben and he could do no wrong."

Jake glanced away, sipping his port. "He was my big brother. I knew he'd take care of me." He turned and smiled at Kaz. "Obviously, that didn't happen. We drove around for a couple of hours until it was getting late and I told him I had to get home. It was a school night. He was really plastered by then, and he swung a U-turn in the middle of a busy street, cut a couple of drivers off, and drove back toward Marin.

"It had started raining after a long dry spell, and the road was slick. I remember he spun out a couple of times on turns. I was getting scared. He was laughing, and I think he was enjoying the fact I was afraid of his driving at this point. We were almost home when he raced around a turn, going like hell just a few blocks from our parents' house."

Kaz hadn't said a word, but knowing what was coming next didn't make it any easier to hear his story. She linked her fingers with his, aware he needed a minute to get himself together.

"I can still see the trees whipping back and forth in the wind and rain, and the way the headlights reflected off the big drops. There was a crosswalk ahead with an overhead light. I saw the woman and the little boy, all bent over against the storm, walking across the street. She was dragging something, but I couldn't tell what it was. We found out later it was one of those suitcases on wheels, a big one. She had everything she'd been able to sneak out of the house, and she and her son were running away from her abusive husband, but we didn't know that then. I only knew we were going too fast, and Ben didn't even see her. I screamed at Ben to stop, but it was too late. We hit them. I can still see her . . . It was horrible.

"Ben hit the brakes, but the car skidded off the road and we hit a tree. He got out and started puking on the side of the road. I checked the woman first—she was a mess, her face all beat up. I thought the accident had caused it, but most of it was what Norwich had done to her. It was obvious she was dead. I ran to the little boy."

He swallowed convulsively and sucked in a deep breath. "Ben had run over him and he was all broken up, but he was breathing. I knew CPR, but there was nowhere to touch him that wasn't broken. He gasped a couple of times and I held his hand, but he stopped breathing before the police and the paramedics came. Ben managed to get to me and convinced me to say I was the one driving, that he was over eighteen and would end up in jail, but I was a kid and famous, and they'd let me off."

He shrugged. "There really wasn't any choice for me. I would have done anything for him, so I didn't even question what he asked.

"The police came and questioned Ben, and he said I'd been driving. I agreed, but even though it was a lie, while I was sitting there watching the paramedics with the mother and her little boy, I knew I was every bit as guilty of their deaths as Ben. They ran the plates on the car and it was stolen, so auto theft was added to the charges. There was a new district attorney, and he threw the book at me. Our dad bailed us out that first night, but after I was charged, I went back to juvenile hall to await the trial, and my parents refused to bail me out. My mom said I needed to be taught a lesson, but at least they hired a good attorney. When my case was scheduled for trial, I was positive Ben would come and tell them the truth, but he didn't. He never even came to the trial. I found out later he'd enlisted. I haven't seen him since."

Kaz tried to work her way through Jake's story, tried to imagine what kind of horrible person his brother was. "So you were charged and found guilty and sentenced to juvenile detention, and Ben just left?"

Jake nodded. "I imagine he's lived his own hell. At least my sentence ended and I could move on, though I'll never be free of that night. I can only imagine what it's done to my brother. I think he's still in the Middle East, moving from battle to battle as far as I know. The thing is, Norwich was there at the trial. He blamed me for killing his family, though he stopped coming when the prosecuting attorney brought up the history of spousal abuse. The prosecution wanted the jury to realize how awful her death was, that she'd been killed when she was finally escaping years of beatings."

His confession made her angry, at the circumstances as much as with Jake. "It was awful. It was a tragedy for all of you. I wish you had trusted me enough to tell me the truth." She twisted her fingers through his. "Why? What was the reason for holding back? I spilled my guts—told you everything. Why weren't you honest with me? You had plenty of chances."

"Because I was a coward." He'd been staring into his glass of port, but now he turned and faced her. "I was afraid of what you'd think. I knew about Jilly from the beginning. Lola had told me that day at Top End how you'd gotten the tattoo when your sister died, and she said at the time she hadn't known you yet, that she thought Jilly was killed by some kid out joyriding. I knew then that if I told you the truth, you'd never want to work with me. Then, as I got to know you . . ."

He looked down at their hands, clasped together now, and then at Kaz. "The lie took on a life of its own. Believe me, I've thought of all the mistakes I've made, how many times I could have told you what happened, but I was always afraid of what you would think. The more I got to know you, Kaz, the more I realized I was falling in love with you. That was the last thing I wanted—you'd already told me you weren't ready for a relationship, and I knew I could never tell you what I'd done or you'd leave in a heartbeat. At the same time, I knew there could never be any kind of relationship with you based on lies. I should have given you the chance to make that choice on your own, but I didn't. I was wrong, and I'm sorry."

She slipped her hands free, but her gaze never left his face. "I'm sorry, too, Jake. Sorrier than you'll ever know."

CHAPTER 20

Jake lowered his head. This was exactly what he'd feared, and it hurt even worse than he'd expected. He let out a long, slow breath. "I talked to Marcus while you were in the shower. The launch was a huge success. People couldn't stop talking about the photos, about you. He laughed when he said his only concern is that you made a bigger splash than his jewelry designs. Everyone agreed that you had exactly the perfect look to bring Intimate Jewels to the public. Marc can't wait to meet you. He told me he wants you to be the voice of Intimate, but Fletch told me that the other winery . . ."

"Lucullan Cellars?"

"Yeah. Fletch said they want you for the same type of position. If you take Marc's offer, and it's a good one, you'd have to work with me." He sighed and glanced away before turning back to her. "So you might want to consider Fletch's offer."

She tilted her head and stared at him for the longest time. Her eyes filled with tears, and when she spoke, her voice broke on the simple question. "Do you hate me that much?"

"Hate you?" He frowned. Where'd that came from? "I

love you. I think I will always love you, but you just said . . ."

She sniffed and then shook her head, a short, sharp jerk of impatience. "I said I was sorry you hadn't told me the truth, and I am. I'm sorry you didn't trust me enough to feel you could confide. I'm sorry you thought I couldn't love you if you'd done something stupid that turned into something horrible when you were young. I'm sorry we both spent so much time dancing around the truth, when the truth would have been so much easier. Jake, I think I was in love with you that first day in the coffee shop. I kept trying to tell myself I wasn't ready, that my career was more important, that you had said you weren't interested, but I was lying to myself. Everything about you . . ."

"Everything about you." He set his glass of port aside, took Kaz's glass out of her hands, and set hers next to his on the bedside table. Then he cupped her face in his palms. She was a mess, so battered and bruised, her eye swollen, her lips split, and it was all on him. If she'd never met him, this wouldn't have happened.

If he'd never met her, he might be facing the rest of his life without love. She was just that perfect, and he was self-ish enough to take what he hoped she offered. A lifetime? Damn, he hoped so. He brushed his thumb over her bottom lip and then very gently kissed the one spot that wasn't cut or bruised. He chuckled. "I just flashed on that scene in one of the Indiana Jones movies, the one where the hero-ine wants to kiss Indie and he's so battered she doesn't know where she can kiss him without hurting him."

Kaz smiled. "And he says, 'here,' and points to a spot on his face, and 'here,' and another, until finally 'here' is his mouth. Start here, Jake. Please?" She touched her lips and then pressed her fingers to his.

He kissed her. Gently, carefully, with love. "I hope you realize I want this for the rest of my life, Kaz. I want you.

I've missed you. I kept telling myself I hardly know you, but I've missed you every second we've been apart."

"I believe you, because I've missed you so terribly this past couple of weeks. I came home every night so excited about what I was doing on Fletcher's set, and there was no one to talk to who understood. Mandy and Lola were curious, but you would have known exactly what I was talking about." She laughed. "It was more fun than I imagined it could be. Fletcher obviously loves what he does, and that joy carries over to the set and everyone involved. It was amazing. The wrap party last night was wonderful. You would have loved it, and I'm sorry I didn't ask you to go with me. I wanted to, but I was looking at our two weeks apart as a test." She shrugged. "You know, if I still miss him, maybe I really do love him?"

"Me, too. I wanted to see if I still missed you as much at the end of the two weeks as I did at the beginning. It was worse. Then when I called and you told me about all the attacks . . . I'm so sorry. I was already uptight about the texts because they didn't make any sense, and when you told me what you'd been through . . ." He let out a deep breath. "Sweetheart, it scared the crap out of me, and I reacted badly."

"So did I. I was terrified, and then you were so angry, and I didn't even try to see it from your point of view. I just got mad. I'd really wanted you to come pick me up, but I told you I had a cab because I was upset and my feelings were hurt. Stupid, huh?"

He shook his head. "No more than me. Do you have any idea how many times over the past couple of weeks I picked up the phone to call you? And then I'd talk myself out of it." He sighed, thinking of the long, lonely nights. "I spent way too much time looking at all my pictures of you."

She brushed her fingers over his cheek. "I wondered. I don't have any pictures of you. Not one. I could have taken one with my phone, and I never even thought of it." She yawned and covered her mouth. Glanced his way and blushed. "I'm sorry. We're having a serious heart-to-heart, and I'm yawning. Not very flattering, is it?"

"Actually, it is. I know you're exhausted, but it also tells me you're relaxed around me. That's a good thing, considering the night we've had. You need to get to sleep, and so do I."

"Sleep?" She raised an eyebrow.

He shook his head. "I wish, but no sex. I didn't bring any protection. Next time you get kidnapped, we need to plan better."

"Excellent idea. Schedule the next kidnapping so we have clean clothes and condoms. I don't think so." She unwrapped the towel, tossed it on the floor, and slipped beneath the sheets. Then she stretched up on one elbow and kissed him. "I'm not going to finish the port. I can hardly keep my eyes open." She kissed him again. "I love you, Jake. So much. It feels so good to be able to say it." She lay down, pulled the blanket up over her shoulders, and closed her eyes.

She was beside him, naked, her body still warm and damp from her shower, and he wanted her so badly he ached. So he drank down his glass of port as if it were water, and then finished Kaz's as well. With any luck, the buzz would put him to sleep.

Kaz awoke to the sound of the shower running and the bed beside her empty. She rolled over and groaned. Every part of her body ached. She touched her face with her fingertips, opened her eyes and realized she could see out of the left one this morning. It had been swollen almost shut by the time she'd gone to bed, and she'd totally forgotten to ice it, but it felt as if the swelling had gone down.

She heard the shower shut off, and a minute later Jake

walked out of the bathroom. He'd wrapped a towel around his waist and was drying his hair with a smaller one. The heavy gauze covering his injured shoulder had been replaced with an oversized bandage the ER tech had given him last night.

He looked wonderful, and when he saw her sitting up in bed, he smiled. "You're awake." He leaned close and kissed her. "How are you feeling? I can see both your eyes this morning."

She fluttered her lashes. "I'm afraid to look in a mirror, but I have a feeling it's going to get more colorful before it gets better."

"Well, in case you're interested, you're working some nice blue, green, and purple this morning. Imagine it'll fade to yellow in a day or two."

"Gee, thanks." She threw back the covers and got out of bed.

Jake stepped back and looked her up and down in a most lascivious manner. She struck a pose and then walked into the bathroom with an exaggerated sway of her hips, but when she reached the mirror, she stopped. "I'm a mess!" She leaned close and wiped away the steam left over from Jake's shower so she could get a better look.

Jake appeared in the reflection, standing behind her. He put his hands on her shoulders and kissed the side of her throat. "You're still beautiful, Kaz. And this will heal, but it really pisses me off to see what he did to you."

He ran his fingers over her ribs. The contusions along her left side were almost black, and they still hurt like the blazes. Her face wasn't as swollen this morning, but there'd be no disguising the bruises.

"Would you mind very much if we didn't go home today?" She turned and looked at him, loving the way a smile slowly spread across his face, but she felt like such a fraud. He thought she only wanted to be with him, but she had to be honest—getting naked wasn't her reason. She felt like a total coward when she said, "I'm not ready to face everyone and all the questions they're going to have."

He kissed her forehead. "I'd love to stay here. Get your shower, put on that dress Cassie loaned you, and we can go buy some clothes and toothbrushes and stuff for both of us. Nate and Cassie offered us their guest cottage last night, but I knew we'd be late after going to the ER. I bet their offer's still open."

While Kaz took her shower and got dressed, Jake called Marc and let him know they'd be back Sunday rather than today. Then he called Nate, but Cassie answered. Nate was already out in the vineyard, and she said to come out any time. The cottage was clean, the bed freshly made, and she had plenty for dinner.

He heard the shower shut off as he ended the call, and a few minutes later, Kaz walked out wearing nothing but the teal blue thong and a huge smile on her face. "You washed my undies! That's sort of going above and beyond, ya know?"

He couldn't tell her the truth, that he'd known she'd need to wear them this morning to go shopping, and he didn't want her to have to touch anything that bastard had handled. "I knew you didn't have any others," he said. "If we tried to go shopping with you wearing Cassie's dress and nothing under it, I'd be trying to shop with a hard-on." He shrugged and gave her a devilish grin. "Or we could just stay here and take care of it."

She planted a kiss on his mouth, but when he tried to turn it into more, she laughed and spun away. "Not until we shop for those necessities, okay?"

Every hour he spent with Kaz strengthened Jake's opinion of her. She didn't go for the most expensive stores, and she wasn't as concerned as he'd thought she'd be about people seeing her badly bruised face. She picked up a pair of rubber flip-flops and a wide-brimmed hat at the drugstore, while he bought toothbrushes and toothpaste, a small pack of bandages to replace the one on his shoulder, and the most important necessity: condoms.

Neither of them had had dinner the night before, so they stopped for breakfast, and then Kaz found a shop with men's and women's clothes—they each bought things that were simple and comfortable enough to get them through the day.

She held up bags in both hands. "I've got enough stuff. Enough that I don't need to go home for at least a week."

He gave her a quick kiss. "Why don't you go on up to the room and get changed? I'll be there in a minute. There's a jewelry store I told Marc I'd check out as a possible retailer for the Intimate line."

Jake gave her the key card to the room. She kissed him, and he was ready to change plans and follow her, but they had to be out by eleven and it was already after ten. He watched Kaz walk away, her long legs visible through the gauzy skirt, the self-confident stride that even a kidnapping couldn't destroy, and it reaffirmed what he already knew—she was the one. The only one he would ever want, the woman he loved beyond anything he'd ever imagined.

He walked into the jewelry store, but Marc's line of jewelry was the last thing on his mind.

"Thank you. This has been a wonderful evening." Kaz held out her hand and let Jake tow her to her feet. An afternoon and evening of laughter, good food, amazing wine, and more laughter was exactly what she'd needed. "I'm so glad I got to meet you guys." She gave Nate a hug and then took both Cassie's hands. "Jake told me about you, about what happened. I'm sorry about your dad, but it sounds as if he would have scripted it that way if he'd had a choice."

Cassie blinked away tears, but she was smiling. "That's so true. He saved Nate's life and mine with his bravery; he had time to tell Nate to take good care of me . . ."

"Which I am." Nate wrapped an arm around her shoulders.

"Yes, you are." She smiled at her husband. "And he had a chance to talk to Mom before he died. Her spirit, anyway. They're both out there. We spread Dad's ashes near Mom's in the Mac and Melinda block of grapes that Marc gave us as a wedding present."

Nate laughed. "Actually, he gave it to Cassie. I had to marry her to get it."

"I knew you had an ulterior motive." She leaned against his shoulder, and the two of them shared a very private smile that made Kaz ache inside. Would she and Jake ever find that level of communion? That sense that their love was the forever kind? They'd known each other for such a short, intense time. Were their feelings real? Could they stand the test of time?

He'd said he wanted what they had for the rest of his life, but Jake still had so many demons to deal with—his parents, his brother, the lies that had hung between Kaz and him.

"C'mon, Wonder Woman. Let's get some sleep." Jake wrapped an arm around her waist and hugged her tightly against his side. "I know it's barely nine, but I'm beat, and our hostess is ready to fold."

"Actually, the real Cassie folded an hour ago. This is the blow-up version." Nate kissed the top of her head.

"And she is running out of air. I swear, the first three months of pregnancy would be better spent sleeping round-the-clock, but I'm so glad you guys can stay over. I hope you sleep well. The cottage is a comfy little place."

They left with promises to meet up for breakfast and more laughter. Nate was the one who'd tagged her with the Wonder Woman name, and Jake had picked up on it. Much had been made of the fact that she'd broken the restraints on her wrists and gotten in at least one good punch to Norwich's face. The deputy told them at the ER that he had a broken nose. She was sure it was from the punch Jake had given the man, but after the horrible things he'd done, she preferred to think it might have been hers.

The moon was almost full, the light shimmering off the grape leaves, giving the vineyard a ghostly hue. Jake held her hand and they walked toward the cottage, but then he veered out into the vineyard of very old, gnarled, and twisted vines.

"This is where Cassie's mom and dad's ashes were scattered." Jake stood between two vines that were over a hundred years old. "I wanted to see if I could feel anything out here. Nate said that when he plowed this section a few weeks ago, he was almost positive he saw a much younger version of Cassie's dad walking beside the tractor, holding hands with a beautiful woman. When he told Cassie what he saw, she said it had to be her mom and dad, that he'd described them perfectly, the way they'd looked when they first married."

"How neat for Cassie. It's as if she's got her parents close, even though they've both passed. I'm envious. It's obvious her mom loved her, that her father respected her work here at the vineyard."

Jake took both her hands in his. "Have you gone to see your mom since she was incarcerated?"

Kaz nodded. It wasn't a pleasant memory. "Yeah. Once. She told me never to come back, that she was sorry I'd ever been born. I guess that's closure of a sort."

"What about your dad?"

She leaned back, secure in the grip he had on both her

hands. "He's wonderful, in his own way. I know he loves me, but he doesn't quite get why I enjoy the modeling. He thinks I'm too smart to be a prop."

"You are, but you're a lot more than a prop. Damn, Kaz, I've never worked with a model as intuitive as you are. You can read the mood, project the emotion I need. You know exactly how to move, what way to look, how to give a photographer absolute gold with every shot. That's a very rare quality."

She laughed, well aware she loved him way too much, that he was quickly becoming so important to her that, when he finally moved on, as she figured he eventually would, she would be devastated. "Did you ever think that maybe the photographer had a little bit to do with this model's ability to project emotion?"

He kissed her. "One can only hope."

And then, suddenly, without warning, he was down on one knee in the freshly plowed vineyard. He held her hands against his heart and looked at her with so much love, Kaz felt her legs go all wobbly.

"I love you, Kaz. So damned much. I've been trying to think of how to say this, but I get all caught up between what sounds really cool and romantic, and what I feel." He kissed the backs of her hands and then raised his head. His dark eyes glittered in the moonlight, and the intensity in his gaze made her shiver.

"Kaz, sweetheart, we haven't known each other for very long, but you have to admit, it's been pretty intense. I've got to go with what I feel. You make me whole. You give me purpose, and I love you so much I can't imagine any kind of life without you in it."

Her legs weren't the only thing shaking, and she knew they wouldn't hold her. It was so much easier just to let them fold, until she was kneeling in the dirt, at eye level with a man she wanted to spend her life with. "I love you, Jake. So much."

"Will you marry me, Kaz? Are you willing to spend your life with an ex-con with way too many issues?" He laughed, but it was a harsh, painful sound. "You know that if you say yes, it probably means you need therapy."

"Oh, Jake. It only means I need you. Are you sure? You were so dead set against—"

He put his finger over her lips. "I was only against relationships because it would have meant telling you the truth. I figured the truth would make you turn tail and run."

"I'm not running. Not from you." She looked into eyes as dark as hers and thought of waking up next to him for the rest of their lives, crawling into bed with him every night, knowing that, no matter the jobs they did, they'd be coming home to each other.

She slipped a hand free of his grasp and cupped the side of his cheek. His beard was rough beneath her fingers because they'd forgotten to buy razors and he hadn't shaved.

Yesterday, at just about this time, she'd been tied up in the barn and wondering if she'd live to see the next day.

She hadn't had much hope of anything then. Certainly not this. "What else could I possibly say to you but yes? I love you, Jake. So much, but I thought it was too much to dream that you might love me back."

"Will you wear this, Kaz? Will you let me tell the world you're mine?" He reached into his pocket, and the next thing she knew, he was slipping a ring onto her left hand.

It was an absolutely perfect fit. Sort of how Jake fit with her. "If I can tell everyone it works both ways. You're mine, Jake. All mine." The ring had a gorgeous stone that looked almost black in the moonlight. She laughed and took a wild guess. "Don't tell me . . . pigeon's blood, right?"

When he smiled and nodded, she hugged him. "It's beautiful! I want to go inside so I can see it."

She stood and tugged Jake to his feet.

He wrapped his arms around her and kissed her.

"I want to go inside where I can see you." He cupped her face in his hands and kissed her again. Then he took her hand and led her through the old vines to the cottage.

Jake's cell phone was blinking. He'd left it charging while they'd had dinner with Nate and Cassie, and he was perfectly willing to ignore the call until he saw who it was from.

"Why would Mandy be calling?" He called her back and waited a moment. When she answered, he flipped it on speaker so Kaz could hear.

"What's up, kiddo?"

"There's a man here, Jake. He looks like you, and he says he's your brother, Ben. I wanted to make sure that's who he is, since he needs a place to stay the night. We were going to give him Kaz's room, if that's okay. He said he's been trying to find you, that Marc Reed put him in touch with us."

Jake stared at the phone for so long that Mandy said, "Jake? You still there?"

Kaz leaned close and said, "I think he's just surprised. He hasn't seen Ben in years. And yes, please tell him to go ahead and use my room. Clean sheets are in the closet. We'll be home tomorrow, but not until after the commute traffic winds down. Hopefully, by noon."

They chatted a moment longer, but she didn't mention Jake's proposal. That was something they would share together. Tomorrow.

After Jake faced the brother he hadn't seen in almost twenty years.

CHAPTER 21

Kaz was still talking to Mandy when Jake went into the kitchen, hoping like hell Nate had left the bottle of Maker's Mark he'd bought during last season's crush. There, shoved to the back behind a bottle of cheap gin and an unopened six-pack of tonic water, was about half a bottle of that good Kentucky bourbon. He pulled the bottle out and poured some into a cocktail glass, moving on autopilot so he wouldn't have to think about Ben.

Except that was all he could think about.

Why the hell had Ben come back? Why now? Jake leaned against the kitchen counter and took a big swallow of the whiskey. The bite was strong enough to make his eyes water, so his next swallow was more of a sip, and it went down a lot easier. As soon as he swallowed, his thoughts raced back to his brother. It had been almost twenty years since he'd seen the guy. Twenty years since Ben had walked away on a lie and left his little brother to do time in a hellhole of a juvenile detention center.

"Jake?"

He raised his head and took another swallow. Kaz took the glass from his hand and set it on the counter. He reached for it, but she wrapped her fingers around his and said, "Later. After you talk to me. Then, if you want to drink yourself stupid, have at it."

She tugged his hand and dragged him back into the front room.

He managed to grab his glass on the way out.

Pulling him down beside her on the couch, Kaz turned and stared at him. There was no condemnation in her eyes. Curiosity, yes, but compassion wasn't what he'd expected.

He set the glass on the table beside the couch.

"What are you thinking, Jake? How do you feel about seeing Ben? Because you don't have to if you don't want to. No one can make you talk to him or even see him. That's your call. I need to know how you're feeling about the fact he's shown up like this, so I have some idea how we're going to deal with it."

Again, not what he expected, but he liked the way she included herself in his problem. If Ben's reappearance in his life even was a problem. "I don't know." He shook his head slowly, surprised by his confused feelings—feelings he'd not ever really analyzed. "Ya know, the first thought I had was 'thank goodness he's alive.' I've been worried after not hearing from him for so many years that he might be dead. I doubt my parents would have told me, but I always read the reports of battleground deaths, hoping against hope that Ben's name wasn't listed."

He stared at his hands hanging loosely between his knees. "I've missed him. I was so angry for so long, but then I started remembering the good stuff, the way we were before my mother got so caught up in shaping us into sons she could love. Ben's the oldest, so he was her first project, and he resented her from the beginning. Swimming wasn't his thing, but Mom swam competitively in college and got a bug up her ass that it was an acceptable sport, so Ben would be a champion swimmer."

"Was he good?" Kaz reached for his right hand and held it in both of hers. "Did he like it?"

"Hated it." He laughed, remembering the arguments between Ben and their parents. "He was good enough at the junior level, but he wanted to play Little League and be a regular kid. He used to talk about teaching high school— he was really good at math, and he figured he could be a math teacher and coach high school sports. Unfortunately, that was frowned on by both parents. Our dad because it wasn't a powerful corporate position, and our mother because she couldn't brag about her son the math teacher nearly as well as she could her son the Olympic champion. So Ben just bailed on all of it. He went to college and was doing okay working toward a business degree, with Dad figuring he'd go into finance and Ben knowing that he could use the degree to get him into the credential program for teaching."

"So he was still in college when the accident happened?"

"I'm not sure. By then, he'd quit coming home and had cut off all communication with the family. I don't know for a fact, but I think Dad might have stopped paying for his college. My training was really expensive, and we were never short of money to pay for top coaches."

He thought about that for a long moment, how he would have felt if his parents had openly favored Ben instead of him. He wouldn't have liked it. So much of his thinking about what had happened had changed. At first, when he'd barely gotten settled in detention, he'd been really pissed at Ben for not coming forward when it was obvious the charges against Jake weren't going to be dropped.

Over the years, though, Jake had started seeing things differently. He'd begun to realize what a jerk he'd been and where he'd been headed. He didn't like what he remembered of that egotistical, spoiled teen. He'd had so much promise, but he hadn't cared. He'd been a screwup in school, and the only friend who'd stuck by him had been Marcus Reed.

His phone rang again. He glanced at the name and answered. "Think of the devil, Marc. How's he look?"

"Rough. I hope I didn't make a mistake, sending him to Kaz's house, but damn, he looks like hell. He's really gaunt, fresh scars, like maybe he's healing from shrapnel wounds. I don't know how he found me, but he showed up at my office today. He said he had to see you, that it was time. What the hell does that mean?"

He'd never told anyone the whole truth. No one but Kaz, but she was right. It was time to stop hiding from it, but not until he'd cleared the air with Ben. "There's more to what happened that night of the wreck, stuff I've never talked about, but before I can tell you, Marc, I need to see Ben. Find out where he's been all this time, why he did some of the things he did. Then you and I need to sit down and talk about some stuff. I wasn't always honest with you, and it's time to clear up a lot of crap. You, of all people, deserve the truth."

"Whenever you're ready, Jake. You know I'll be here."

Marc's soft words almost unmanned him. He blinked back the sting of tears, the tightness in his throat. "A lot of the time, Marc, you've been the only one who was. And I will never, ever forget that. Later, okay?"

"Later."

He stared at the phone a moment before ending the call. Then he turned it off. If anyone tried to reach him, it could go to voice mail. He honestly didn't know if he could handle anything else. Not tonight.

He turned and took Kaz in his arms, holding her tightly against his chest, resting his chin in the sleek waves of her short hair. "I proposed marriage to you tonight, and you accepted." He laughed, a short, sharp bark with absolutely no humor in it. "If you want to back out, no foul. You can even keep the ring."

She leaned back in his arms and stared long and hard at him. "I hope you're joking, because I'm in for the long haul. And what you're suggesting is an insult."

He had to swallow a couple of times to get his voice to work. "You're an absolute treasure, Marielle Leigh Kazanov. I still can't believe you love me, even knowing—"

"Knowing what? That what you and your brother did was dead wrong? That people suffered—two people died because of what you did? It was wrong, and it was a horrible mistake, and it will always be part of who and what you are, but smart people learn from mistakes." She leaned close and kissed him. "You were a stupid kid, Jake. Most teenaged boys are." Then she backed off again so she could look into his eyes. He felt the intensity of her stare, as if she looked through him. Inside him.

"Thank goodness," she said, stroking her hands over his shoulders, "those stupid kids can grow up to be intelligent, caring men. What happened that night was terrible, but you and I both know that Ben didn't run over that poor woman and her little boy with malicious intent. It happened because Ben had been drinking and you were both too young and dumb to handle it well, but not because either of you were mean or hateful. You got locked up because you loved your brother enough to keep your mouth shut, even when it meant a hell of a long time away from everything you knew. I just hope Ben's worthy of that love. I wonder what he's here for, what's finally brought him looking for you. I really hope it's because he wants to make amends."

"I wish I knew. Hell, I don't even know what I feel anymore." He brushed Kaz's hair back from her eyes and then tucked her back under his chin again. "A month ago if you'd asked me how I felt about my brother, I probably would have said nothing good, that I hated him for not speaking up. Now though?"

He kissed her forehead. "I have you, Kaz. If I'd stayed on the same track I was headed down before the accident, I probably would have totally messed up my life. I wouldn't know you, wouldn't know what it felt like to love someone so completely, to know they love me. When I was sixteen, I didn't have the desire to work for a second Olympics, though I know my parents would have been pushing me. I don't know how well I would have handled it. I was already a jerk, and there's no reason to think I would have suddenly grown up and gotten my act together. Not without some serious intervention."

She tilted her head and looked at him. "Are you saying that what Ben did was intervention?" She chuckled. "That's stretching it, don't you think?"

"Maybe, but it worked. I took classes when I was a ward of the state. There wasn't much offered, but I figured out that getting an education was actually a pretty cool thing, and when I got out, the money I'd put aside in the bank from all the promotional deals I'd had as a kid was still there, still earning interest. It was enough for me to go on to college. I'd gotten my GED through a program while I was locked up, and went on to get degrees in computer science, business, accounting, and film studies. I never would have done any of that."

"Where'd the photography come from? You're amazingly good."

Damn, he loved the fact that she liked his photos. The one thing he did that was all his. "One of the social workers who came to work with us got me hooked. Photography was something that took me away from the sinkhole I was living in, even though I was still locked up. He showed me how to find beauty in the ugliest things. I'll have to show you some of my pictures when we get home."

"I'd like that. But you know what I'd really like now?" She kissed him, slowly. Thoroughly. "Think you can guess?"

"I certainly hope so." He stood, holding Kaz in his arms. Her bruises had faded a bit more, and her eyes actually twinkled. He didn't say another word. Instead, he carried her to the bedroom at the end of the short hallway, laid her down on the faded quilt, and slowly, methodically stripped out of his clothes.

Kaz watched him—not even trying to disguise the huge smile on her face with a more serious expression—as he crawled over her, trapping her neatly between his arms and his thighs. She loved the feel of him surrounding her, covering her with his big, strong, oh so warm body. Jake was a truly beautiful man, one she was learning had as much beauty inside as out.

The life he'd led made her heart ache for him. The fact he'd come through it strong and kind and still willing to open himself to love made her love him even more. He kissed her, his mouth sliding over hers, his tongue tracing the seam between her lips, teasing them open until she forgot everything that had worried her, forgot her bruised ribs and battered face.

He carefully eased the clothes away from her, unwrapping her slowly, treating her body like a precious gift. Finally, when they were both naked, he sat back on his heels and stared at her. His dark gaze was so hot she felt the burn.

Then he took her left hand, held it to his lips, and kissed her palm at the base of her ring finger. "I still can't believe Kaz Kazanov said yes."

"Of course I said yes. You can't possibly think I would have turned you down, can you? I am not an idiot, Jacob. I know a good thing when I see it."

He nodded sagely. "I had no idea you were attracted to emotional wrecks with lifelong commitment issues. I'll have to remember that."

"Actually, I'm attracted to intelligent, brave men who are klutzy enough to get shot protecting the little woman."

He snorted. "The little woman would be you?"

"I'd better be the only one you think of within those parameters, buddy."

"Yes, ma'am." He kissed her again. And again, until she lost herself in his kisses, in the taste of him, the textures, the all-consuming need his touch and taste so quickly built in her.

She came up for air, sucking deep breaths, cupped his face in her hands and held him while she caught her breath. "I hope you have those necessities close at hand."

His smile spread across his face. She felt his bristly cheeks crinkle beneath her palms. "I do. Hold that thought."

He took both hands and kissed each one. Then he carefully placed her hands over her breasts. "Keep those warm for me."

He leaned over the side of the bed, grabbed the pair of chinos he'd bought earlier in the day, and reached into a pocket. Frowning, he searched through the pocket with more drama than Kaz figured was necessary, but she was laughing when he finally pulled his hand out, triumphantly holding three foil packets aloft. "These necessities?"

She pretended to study them for a moment, fully aware of his erection curving high and hard, of the need growing deep inside while they played their silly game. "I think those will do. For now." She snatched one out of his fingers, tore it open, and carefully sheathed him. She stroked his full length, ostensibly to smooth the sleek covering over his even sleeker shaft, but she took a moment to cup the warm sac beneath just so she could hear him groan.

Knowing she had this effect on him was the most powerful aphrodisiac she'd ever experienced.

Knowing now that this man loved her enough to commit, that he'd asked her to be his wife, trumped even that. It even changed the way she felt when he entered her.

Knowing Jake loved her made everything better.

It must have been an unspoken agreement that they talk about anything but Ben on the way back to the city. Even so, the trip seemed to take half the time it normally did, and before Jake was ready to see his brother, they were pulling to a stop in front of Kaz's house. Of course, there was a parking place right in front, when any other time parking would have been at a premium.

He turned off the car and stared at the steps leading to the front door.

"What are you thinking, Jake?"

He shook his head. Hell, he didn't have a clue what he was thinking. His thoughts had never been so muddled before.

Kaz wrapped her fingers around his neck and stretched across the console to kiss him. "He's your brother. You've already admitted that you've missed him, that you forgave him long ago. Let's go in and see why he's here, and if you don't like what he has to say, we'll just leave, together, and go to your apartment. Is that okay?"

He turned and looked at her, so beautiful even with her fading bruises. He knew he'd never, ever grow tired of seeing her beside him. She made him realize he still had it in him to smile. "When did you get so smart?"

"Oh, about the time I figured out I'd be a damned fool

to let you go. C'mon. I imagine they're all looking out the window, wondering what's keeping us."

He took her left hand and looked at the ring. It really was perfect, a beautiful dark red pigeon's blood ruby set in yellow gold and surrounded by tiny diamonds. He kissed her fingers and took a deep breath. "Okay. But if I freak out, slap me, all right?"

She laughed. "My pleasure."

She laughed even harder as he mumbled, "I'm sure it will be."

Kaz felt surprisingly calm, but figured it must be because she knew that's what Jake needed from her. What a weekend this had been, from kidnapping and a near-death experience, to getting engaged, and now this.

She hoped she liked Ben. She really hoped he was here for good reasons, not bad, but she didn't let any of her concerns show as she and Jake walked up the stairs holding hands and finally stepped into the house.

Mandy was the first one out of the kitchen. "Oh, my God, Kaz! Your face! That bastard." She ran across the small living room and gently held Kaz's cheeks. "I didn't realize how badly he'd hurt you."

"It's okay. I'll heal, and he's going to be in jail for a long time. Knowing that goes a long way toward making it all better. So does this." She winked at Jake and held up her left hand.

Mandy's eyes went wide as saucers. She looked from Kaz to Jake and back at Kaz. "Is that what I think it is?" Kaz nodded. Mandy grabbed Kaz's hand and yelled, "Lola! Get your skinny butt out here. These two are engaged!"

Lola came flying out of the kitchen, and Rico lumbered along after her, practically tripping on his long, floppy basset hound ears, his excited bark more howl than anything. Lola and Mandy talked over each other, asking Kaz so many questions so fast it was impossible to answer. Jake stood off to one side, smiling at the three of them.

Kaz sensed Ben's entrance before she saw him. She turned and looked at Jake instead of his brother, and she knew immediately that everything would be all right.

Jake wasn't certain what told him Ben had stepped into the room, but when he raised his head and looked into his brother's haunted eyes, there was no doubt in his mind, no sense of estrangement as he'd feared. He left the three girls chattering a mile a minute and walked up to Ben. His brother's face was marked with healing cuts and old scars, his hair had grown out until it was as long as Jake's. He was smaller than Jake remembered, but at sixteen, Jake hadn't reached his full height. Ben had been six two with a heavier frame, but he was thin now to the point of being gaunt and a good four inches shorter than Jake.

There was no hesitation when he wrapped his arms around Ben and felt his brother's returning hug, nor was there any doubt. He loved his brother now even more than when they'd been kids. If Ben's appearance was any indication, the past nineteen years hadn't been easy on him— harder even than the years had been on Jake.

"God, Ben. It's so damned good to see you. It's been so long." He dropped his arms and stepped back.

Ben scrubbed at his eyes with the heels of both hands. "How can you say that, after what . . ." He took a deep breath. "Are you okay? They said you got shot, that . . ."

Jake shook his head. Kaz was right. It was time to move forward. "I'm fine. Just grazed my shoulder. But the other? It happened, it's over, and one of these days we can talk about it, but right now I just want to enjoy the fact you're here and alive, that maybe I'll have you back in my life."

Ben stood still, watching him. "I didn't expect this. I thought you'd hate me."

Shrugging, Jake said, "I did. For a long time I hated your guts, but I got older and a little bit smarter. I was an absolute jerk when I was a kid. Kaz has really helped me see things through a different lens. I'm in a good place now, but it's a pretty long story how I got here."

"I want to know it. I want to know all of it, because I would give anything to be in that kind of place." He sighed and watched the three girls who'd moved to the couch and sat all together, still talking nonstop. "What I did was so wrong, and I was too much a coward to admit it. I knew that if I didn't come back and beg your forgiveness, I'd be eating a bullet before long."

"That better not happen." The way Ben talked about killing himself had come out too easily, as if it was something he'd thought about in more than an abstract way.

"Then Lola and Mandy told me about your girlfriend, your fiancée now, I guess, that she'd been kidnapped by that poor woman's husband, that you'd been shot. Everything I did that night has screwed up both our lives, and the lives of the ones who love us. I'm so sorry. I was a dumb shit, a selfish prick thinking only of myself, and too many people paid."

"For what it's worth, Ben, Kaz and I talked about that very thing last night. She asked me if I was still angry at you, because God knows, for a long time, I was. But I realized I missed my brother more than I hated him, that my life now is pretty damned good, and if all that crap hadn't happened, I could have totally fucked myself up. The past is over. Kaz said we need to move forward. She makes a lot of sense. Can you do that?"

Slowly, Ben shook his head. "I don't know. I've been living with guilt for almost two decades. I don't know if I can leave it behind, but if that's what you want, I can try. Or if you want me to turn myself in, admit what happened, that you were innocent, I'll do that. It's your call."

"We were both in that car, both doing stupid shit, and an innocent woman and her child paid with their lives. I may have been the one in jail, but I imagine you've served as hard a sentence as I ever did. We can't undo what we did, but we can move forward."

"Okay. Yeah." He rubbed at the back of his head and stared at the girls again before turning to Jake. "There's one thing, though, that I want you to do."

Jake didn't say anything. Instead, he waited for Ben.

"Whether you go or not, I'm going to see the folks today. They need to know the truth. I went to them first when I got back to the States, asked them where you were. They told me they didn't know and didn't care, but they begged me to come home. I didn't know they'd written you off. I can't believe you never told them the whole story. Haven't you seen them at all since it happened?"

Jake shoved his hands in his back pockets. It was painful, remembering, but the image of his mother and father turning their backs on him was one he'd never forget. "The last time I saw our parents is when the bailiff led me out of the courtroom after the judge announced my sentence, which was to spend the next eight years at the California Youth Authority juvenile training center over in Stockton."

"Eight years? Aw, shit, man. I had no idea." Ben took a step forward, turned, and walked across the room. He slapped the wall hard and leaned his forehead against the back of his hand. A minute later he walked back to face Jake.

"I didn't do the whole eight, Ben. I was supposed to serve out the sentence until I was twenty-four, but I got out at twenty-one on good behavior. Mom and Dad didn't come see me once in all that time. I never got a phone call, not even a fucking Christmas or birthday card."

"I want you to come with me, RJ."

Jake laughed. "RJ's not going anywhere. RJ Cameron went into detention, but Jake Lowell came out."

"Lola told me you went by Jake now." Ben smiled at him, and Jake felt the years sort of slide away. This was the brother he remembered.

"Is Jake willing to face the parents? I know it's something I have to do. Maybe you, too." Ben glanced at his watch. "I think we need to set them straight, and then, personally, I don't care if I never see them again. I can't believe they're our parents."

Jake chuckled. "Probably explains why we're both so screwed up."

Ben rubbed Jake's shoulder, as if he needed the contact, the chance to physically connect with him. "You're probably right. Will you follow me to the car-rental place? I need to drop mine off. I'm actually going to buy a car, now that I'm back in the States."

"Are you here to stay?"

Ben looked at him. "Damn straight I am."

Nodding, Jake followed Ben across the room to where the three women still talked nonstop. "Not a problem," he said. "The trip into Marin will give us a chance to talk. I want to know what you've been doing for the past nineteen years."

Ben looked at him, but there was no way for Jake to know what he was thinking. Ben had changed. A lot. Finally, he nodded and said, "Same here."

Jake went straight to Kaz, pulled her up off the couch, and kissed her. "I assume from all the screaming I heard earlier you've told them our news."

"I did. And they've given their permission."

"Good. Two down, one to go." He kissed her again. "I still need to talk to your father. If he says no, the deal's off."

She returned the kiss. "I love you. And I imagine Dad'll

be happy to let someone else worry about me. Ben? I didn't get an introduction, but I'm Kaz, soon to be your sister-in-law."

Before Jake could say anything, Ben took her hand and planted a kiss on her cheek. He shot a cocky grin at Jake. "It's nice to meet you, Kaz, and I definitely approve. Do you mind if I take your guy away for a couple of hours?"

Frowning, Kaz glanced at Jake. He shrugged. "Ben thinks we need to go pay our parents a visit. I'm not so sure it's a good idea, but I figure I'm game if he is."

Kaz focused on Jake, giving him that look of hers that made him feel like the only guy in the room. "I think it's a great idea. Get back early enough so we can all go out to dinner. My treat, now that I'm an almost famous, highly paid commercial actress."

She looked so beautiful standing there, smiling at him even though he could see the worry in her eyes. "You're going to make me feel like a kept man."

"Good. You can earn the title later. After dinner."

"I'd rather start now." He pulled her into his arms for a kiss that shouldn't have felt so desperate, but he wanted to stay here, with Kaz, Mandy, and Lola. And Ben, too, for that matter, but the kiss would have to hold him. He made it dramatic and hot at the same time, bending her over like a cover model on an old romance. She played along perfectly, but they were both breathing hard when he finally turned her loose.

"Wow." He kissed her nose. "I think I'm going to love being a kept man." Then he laughed when—still caught in the power of one hell of a kiss—she didn't have a quick comeback. Jake brushed his fingers against his chest and preened a bit. They were all laughing when he and Ben said good-bye, but the laughter died the moment he closed the door behind them.

He wasn't looking forward to the visit with their parents.

He really didn't see anything positive coming from this at all, but it was so good to have Ben back in his life.

He'd do this for Ben. He wasn't sure why, but Jake had a feeling Ben needed him right now. Needed Jake a hell of a lot more than he was willing to admit.

CHAPTER 22

Kaz made a reservation for six at a little Italian place that was close enough for them to walk to if they wanted. Six, because she'd decided to invite Marcus Reed. She wasn't sure how well he knew Ben, but she felt like she owed the man an apology for not making it to the launch, though getting kidnapped probably made for a good excuse.

She called him, and he sounded really pleased to be included. Reservations made and Marcus invited, she went in and took a shower, did her nails, shaved her legs. After a couple of hours and still no word from the guys, she'd killed all the time she could by herself, and she wandered back into the front room.

Lola and Mandy were just pouring themselves a glass of wine. Kaz got one for herself and joined them in the backyard. It was a beautiful afternoon, and Kaz wanted Jake here to enjoy it with them. "I'm worried about Jake," she said. And then she told her roommates how his parents had treated him, but she left out what Ben had done so many years ago.

That was Jake and Ben's story to tell.

Lola squeezed her hand. "I know some of it. Ben and I talked after Mandy went to bed. He said he didn't even stay for the trial, just enlisted and left. I hope this meeting with his parents goes well, but I doubt it will. He feels horribly guilty. He had no idea Jake had been locked up, or that their parents had disowned him. Once we started talking, more and more of the story came out. I had the feeling it was the first time he'd ever told anyone. Kaz, it was just horrible. We were both crying by the time he was done, and he was so wiped out he went straight to bed."

Kaz stared into her glass, thinking of the pain Jake had lived with for so many years, the convoluted feelings toward parents who should have loved him and stood by him but didn't, toward a brother who had selfishly sacrificed Jake for his own freedom. His entire family had failed him, and yet he still remained positive, still had it in him to love his brother.

She didn't hold out much hope for his parents. The choice they'd made almost twenty years ago said way too much about their character.

Or lack of it.

They'd driven around for over an hour, revisiting old haunts, talking, neither of them quite ready to face parents who'd failed them on so many counts. They'd talked some about Ben's many deployments, though he'd obviously not wanted to discuss too many of the details, and, while Jake skipped over much of his time spent as a ward of the state, he'd told Ben about his photography and a little about his courtship with Kaz.

That was something Ben was interested in, along with what little Jake knew about her roommate, Lola. "She's sort of bossy," Jake said, laughing. "But she loves her sister and Kaz with equal intensity. The three of them are all pretty special."

He glanced at the street sign and turned left into a cul-de-sac. He'd grown up in this neighborhood. Shouldn't he feel some connection to the area? He didn't feel a thing. It could have been any street in any town. Anywhere.

There were no cars parked on the street, so the Escalade seemed out of place. The house hadn't changed all that much. The trees in the yard were much larger, the landscaping as perfectly manicured as it had always been. A fairly new Lexus sat beside a brand new Porsche Boxster in the driveway.

Jake glanced at his brother. "Looks like Dad still needs his fancy cars." When Ben didn't comment, he said, "You okay?"

Ben shook his head. "I keep thinking I should feel something for them. For this place. I don't."

Jake shrugged. "Me, neither, but it's probably because they never felt anything for us. Our parents are a perfect match—they both love their things more than each other. We were things to them, Ben. Not children to love or nurture. I'll be the first to admit that any nurturing I got came from you. To them, we were things they could show off as long as we performed."

Ben's smile surprised him. "You're right. Damn. That's exactly what we were. Are. Only we're not something they can show off anymore." He laughed. "It almost makes me look forward to the next few minutes."

Jake put his hand on Ben's arm and squeezed. It was so good to have him back. "They're not going to like the truth."

"I know. But I need to clear this up. It's time I moved forward, and until I tell them, at least give them the chance to apologize to you, I'm buried in this crap. You're right. Living in the past is a waste of time and energy. I'd be stuck there for the rest of my life if not for you."

He opened the door and got out of the car, but he waited for Jake to join him on the sidewalk. Together they walked up to the front porch.

Their father opened the door before either of them had time to ring the bell.

"Ben." He smiled. "It's good to see you back." Then he frowned, as if noticing Jake for the first time. His eyes went wide as recognition set in, and he glared at him. "You're not welcome here. Ben, I told you . . ."

"Andrew? Who's there?"

"Ben's brought RJ."

"Oh." She stepped into the foyer, and Jake's first thought was that his mother really needed a better plastic surgeon. She took a quick glance beyond them, probably making sure none of the neighbors were watching. "We can talk inside. Andrew? Close the door, please. Ben? What were you thinking? We told you, RJ—"

"Mother." Ben stared calmly at both parents. "Shut. Up."

Her mouth shut. She shot a quick, nervous glance at her husband.

Ben glanced at Jake, and the two of them stepped beyond their parents and went into the formal living room. As kids, they hadn't been allowed in here at all.

The house meant nothing to Jake. He gazed at his mother and father and realized he felt nothing for them, either. If anything, he'd hated them more than he'd hated Ben for all those long years, but now he knew they didn't matter to him enough for him to feel anything. He stopped beside Ben in front of the fireplace, the two of them standing close enough to show a truly united front.

Their parents stood awkwardly for a moment, and then Andrew took one chair and Brenda another. Jake thought of Kaz, of the need he had to be close to her, and he almost felt sorry for the ones who had given him birth.

At least he felt sorry until Ben told their parents what had really happened that night.

Their father was the first to speak. "You're saying you left your brother to serve a prison sentence that should have been yours? Ruined a promising Olympic career to save yourself?"

"I did. It was wrong, and I will carry that shame with me for the rest of my life, but it's time for you and Mom to know the truth."

"Truth?" Jake had been waiting to see what their mother would say. She stood and pointed at Jake, and said it again. "Truth? You fool! You stupid, stupid fool! You could have had it all, but you went to jail rather than tell the truth? All our time? The training, our money. All wasted. And for what?"

Jake folded his arms across his chest. For some reason, her response had been oddly satisfying. "Because I promised Ben." He turned to his brother and smiled. "You okay, bro?"

Ben actually returned his smile. "I'm done here if you are."

"Good. Let's go."

The two of them headed for the front door. Jake was surprised when their father followed, wondered what he wanted. Andrew opened the door, but he stayed inside when Jake and Ben stepped out on the porch.

"Before you go." His father took a long look at Jake. "I'm sorry I didn't recognize you, RJ."

Jake shook his head. "It's Jacob now. RJ grew up."

His father frowned. He obviously had no idea what his son meant. Then he glanced at the Escalade parked in front. "It appears you've done well."

Jake chuckled. "I'm surprised you didn't ask me if it was stolen."

His father seemed taken aback. "It's not, is it?" He glanced at the SUV and back at Jake, but it was more than obvious he had no idea Jake was teasing.

Ignoring him, Jake said, "C'mon Ben. We've been here long enough. You get what you wanted?"

Ben took a long look at their father. "Unfortunately," he said, "yes."

"Will you be coming back? I don't know if your mother can—"

"Tell her not to worry," Ben said. "I have no intention of coming back here."

"Me, either." Jake glanced once again at his father. He definitely looked older. Not very happy. He hoped the fancy car in the driveway delivered what the old man needed, but it didn't matter. Jake knew this was most likely the last time he'd ever see him.

Their father nodded, a short, quick jerk of his head. "Good," he said. "That's good."

Jake drove off without looking back. Ben stared at the house as they left. "I'm sorry. I never should have forced you to go back there."

Jake just laughed. He hadn't felt this free in years. "I'm not. I've felt guilty about not going to see them since I got out, thought maybe my anger was out of line. Now I know it's not. If that's not closure, bro, I don't know what is. What about you? You okay?"

Ben seemed to think about that for a while. "I'm disappointed. I figured they wouldn't want any more to do with me, but I guess I thought they'd be a little bit nicer to you."

"Nothing in it for them to be nicer. Kaz explained it pretty succinctly. When I told her I hadn't seen them since the bailiff led me away after sentencing, she said that good parents would have stood by me. That good parents loved their kids without reservation."

"In a perfect world, maybe." Ben turned to stare out the window. "Do you think you and Kaz will have kids?"

His question hung there. Jake glanced at him and shook

his head. "I don't know. We haven't talked about kids, but Kaz raised her baby sister, at least until Jilly died in a car accident. She was just seven. When Kaz talks about Jilly, she absolutely glows. Don't be surprised if you end up as an uncle one of these days."

Ben merely grunted. They were heading down Nineteenth, almost at the turnoff to the girls' house, when he said, "Ya know, one of the guys in my unit told me we were his family, that the one God gave him absolutely sucked, so we were his brothers. He was right. It's not always the family you're born into that's the one that sticks by you. It's the one you build."

Jake thought about that as they got closer to the house. Without being conscious of the fact, he'd done that with Marc Reed and now with Kaz and her roommates—built his own family. He felt as if it was finally complete, now that Ben was back.

They were the family that mattered, not those two cold, unwelcoming people who'd raised him. He couldn't wait to get home to Kaz. He really wanted to hold her.

Later, after a wonderful Italian dinner, no mention of the visit to the parents, and a lot of laughter with people who mattered, Jake and Kaz took the elevator to his apartment.

"This was an excellent idea." Kaz clung to Jake's arm and smiled at him. "I hope Ben didn't mind you choosing me as a roommate over him."

He knew Ben was perfectly happy sleeping in Kaz's bed again tonight. "If his curiosity about Lola means anything, he'd rather stay there. Did you notice the two of them?"

She shook her head. "Not really. I think I only noticed you." She waited while he unlocked the door to his apartment. "I'm glad you and Ben told Marc the truth together. He's a terrific guy. I can see why you're such good friends." Then she put her hand on his arm, stopping him as he stuck his key in the lock. "Are you really okay with the way things went today? You and Ben didn't say much when you got back, but from what you did say . . . well, I can't believe your parents."

"I like Mandy's take on things," he said. They'd told her the story as well, after taking Marc aside and speaking privately with him. Opening the door, he stood back for Kaz to enter and realized this was the first time she'd been to his apartment.

"Which take? She said a lot—mostly involving illegal acts of retribution."

He closed the door. Locked it. "When she said we should merely think of them as the sperm and egg donors, because they weren't really parents. That's the truth. We were raised by housekeepers and nannies. I know Marc understands that. His parents were divorced, fought over custody, and then, when his father won, he was raised the same way Ben and I were. Paid help."

"I really like Marc. He's so self-contained, like an island amid all the emoting that was going on." She actually blushed, and he couldn't help himself. He ran the backs of his fingers over her warm cheek. He loved to see her skin turn that deep burnt umber shade. Only a few of his photos had caught that beautiful color.

"I didn't expect you to cry when you told everyone about my proposal." He tilted her chin up, kissed her lips. "You even had me tearing up."

"I'd say I'm sorry, but I'm not. I love you, Jake. Every time I look at the ring on my hand, I want to cry because it makes me feel so complete. You make me feel complete."

Damn. She was doing it to him again.

"It's still not official, though." He lifted her hand to his lips, kissed the backs of her fingers. "We still have to go talk to your dad. What if he doesn't approve?"

Laughing, she shook her head. "Are you kidding? He'll

be thrilled. Once he knows I'm yours, it means he can quit worrying about me."

"Does that mean you're going to be trouble?"

"I certainly hope so." She unbuttoned the top button on his shirt.

He covered her hand before she undid the next one. "I need a shower."

"Want someone to scrub your back?"

"You offering?"

"I am. Which reminds me . . . from now on, if another woman offers, you do not accept."

"Got it." Crazy woman, thinking any other woman would be of interest. He led her through the bedroom, straight to the bathroom. She'd worn a form-fitting cotton knit dress that did amazing things to her curves, the dips and swells of her perfect body. He ran his fingers across her shoulders, along her arms, and somehow ended up cupping her totally flat stomach.

She glanced at his hand on her belly and slowly smiled. "What are you thinking?"

He was almost embarrassed to tell her—they might be engaged, but he hadn't known her very long, and yet . . . "I was thinking how you'll look with our baby growing there. We've never talked about children, and my father wasn't a role model, but I hope . . ."

"Me, too. I'm definitely interested in motherhood at some point, but not yet. We've got time, but Jake . . ." She looped her arms over his shoulders and gazed directly into his eyes.

"Yes, Ms. Kazanov?"

"You're going to be a wonderful father. There's no doubt in my mind."

He shook his head. "How can you be so sure?"

She smiled, kissed him quickly, and then laughed. "Because you know what not to do."

"There is that." He glanced down as she slowly began unbuttoning his shirt. He reached for her, and she gently batted his hands away.

"Stand still."

He took a deep breath. Let it out. "That's not very easy when I really want to . . ."

"Not tonight. Tonight is about what I want."

She kissed him and then went back to those damned buttons. The slightest touch of her fingers against his chest had his body reacting. His breathing quickened, his muscles tightened, and he had to clench his hands to keep from touching her. And slowly, so damned slowly, she unbuttoned each button.

Then she slid her hands beneath the fabric, pushed the shirt back from his chest, and pulled it off his shoulders. He held his hands at his sides, fighting everything in him that said he needed to hold her, to bring her close and show her just how much he loved her.

Except, this was showing her as well. Standing here as Kaz drove him slowly insane. Grumbling, he said, "I really hope I get points for this."

She laughed as she tugged his undershirt up over his head, taking care over the big bandage on his shoulder, following the soft cotton with kisses over his ribs, across his chest. Teasing his nipple with the tip of her tongue just about drove him over the edge. He'd never thought of that as an erogenous zone—at least not on his body.

He practically salivated, thinking of tugging on hers, of the way that taut little bud felt between his lips, against his tongue.

But her hands were fumbling with the button on his pants, her warm fingers sliding between the waistband and his belly. There was no hiding the fact he was hugely aroused, especially when she shoved his pants down his legs and there was nothing between Kaz and his dick but a thin layer of sleek, stretchy boxers.

She raised her head and watched him as he toed off his shoes and lifted first one leg and then the other, obediently stepping out of his slacks and socks. She tossed them aside, and then, instead of pulling his boxers down, she went to her knees in front of him.

He groaned. "You're trying to kill me, aren't you?"

"Never." She rested her cheek against him, sliding over the smooth fabric, and then holding her mouth over the thick curve of his erection, teasing him with the heat of her breath, the knowledge that she was so close and yet still separated by the soft underwear covering him. He thrust forward, not a lot and not on purpose, but he had so little control with Kaz. Would it always be this way? This deep, mind-numbing pleasure when they were together?

She ran her fingers up the tight leg of his shorts, stroked the curve of his butt, and then ran her fingers under the fabric, between his legs, cupping his sac. He grabbed her shoulders as his knees went weak, but she wasn't through.

Slowly tugging his shorts down over his throbbing penis, she nuzzled the thick patch of dark hair at his groin and placed her lips against the curve of his shaft. He was so damned close, but it was too soon to allow himself even to think about coming. Kaz slipped his boxers over his feet, as he lifted them, one at a time.

Concentrating on not falling on his ass helped him gain a bit more control. He started to say something, had to clear his throat to find his voice. "How come I'm naked and you're not?"

She gazed up at him from those dark chocolate eyes and gave him a bright smile. "Because usually it's the other way around. It's my turn. But if it'll make you happy . . ."

She stood and whipped the cotton dress over her head.

The bruises had mostly faded, but she'd worn the rubies tonight, and he hadn't even known. Her nipples, her navel, the one in her clit, visible through the fine lace of her tiny pair of panties, all of them connected by fine golden chains.

And that beautiful monarch butterfly, its wings spread across her torso as if ready to fly.

This time, when he finally got the words out, he might have been talking through gravel. "It's probably a good thing I didn't know you were wearing these."

He wanted to drop to his knees, but she held him up. "Not yet."

Instead, Kaz again went to her knees, so strong and lithe, her body glowing in the overhead light that would have made any other woman self-conscious. Not her. She'd been just as proud and beautiful yesterday, shopping in town with all the wine-country tourists, her face bruised, her eye swollen. She was a woman who made her living with her looks, and yet she'd thrown on a floppy hat, a pair of cheap rubber flip-flops from the drugstore, and a borrowed dress and still carried herself like a queen.

Yet she loved him. A man so damned flawed he didn't deserve what she offered, but he'd be a fool to tell her that. She gazed up at him and then wrapped those beautiful lips around the length of him, licking and nibbling, sucking and blowing soft puffs of air over his sensitized flesh while he stood there like a damned fool, mentally going through his collection of quality digital cameras by model number and megapixel rating to hang on to the last thread of his control.

He'd never played Little League. Batting averages and home runs scored wouldn't work.

Nothing was going to work. There weren't enough cameras on the face of the earth to take his mind off what Kaz was doing to him right now. "Kaz?"

She smiled around her mouthful.

"Stop. Now. Shower."

He didn't think it was possible to pout while taking charge during oral sex, but she managed. "I don't think so. Not yet."

The power was a rush all on its own. The fact he'd so easily turned it over to her made Kaz love him even more. Everything about Richard Jacob Lowell made her want him and convinced her that, yes, even though they'd not known each other a month, she loved him. She could so easily picture herself spending the rest of her life with this man.

Having children with him.

Growing old with him.

She drew him into her mouth, used her tongue to tease the sensitive crown of his penis. She cupped his warm sac in her right hand while her left held on to his hip, pulling him closer to her mouth as she sucked him deeper. There was something so sexy about this position, kneeling in front of the man she loved, taking him in her mouth, pleasing him in such a submissive position.

She loved it. Loved the taste of him, the textures, the fact that he was willing to stand here with his legs trembling and the breath rushing in and out of his lungs while she took her own sweet time bringing him right to the peak.

She might be the one on her knees, but there was no doubt in her mind she was the one in charge, especially as she held him there, balancing him at the edge.

But going no farther. Slowly, even regretfully, she slipped him out of her mouth, letting the long, thick length of him tease her lips. Then she stood, rubbing against him as she stretched up long and tall, flowing against his lean body. His arms came around her, she felt the thick curve of his erection against her belly and hugged him close.

"Shower?"

He let out a deep breath. "Thank you, Lord!"

They made love in the shower and again after they'd crawled into bed. Kaz looked ready to fall asleep until Jake decided to kiss her bruises and got sidetracked by the rubies and gold chains. They made love again, and while it seemed impossible, each time was better than the time before. He'd never imagined anything like this.

He lay beside her, every muscle lax, his body sated, trying to catch his breath, while Kaz ran her fingers through his hair. She leaned close, kissed him, and said, "I hope Marc realizes he's going to make a fortune with his jewelry."

Jake didn't even open his eyes. "Marc's already rich. This was just a fun project."

"Do you think he has any idea what effect those gold chains have on the male libido?"

He chuckled softly. "Don't know. Marc doesn't have a girlfriend."

"I know." Kaz flopped over on her back. "Why is that? He's gorgeous, he's funny and smart, and the guy has a bazillion dollars."

"All true. So why are you here with me?" He missed the warmth of her lying across him and realized that was probably a really stupid question to ask. What if she thought about it? Realized she'd made a huge mistake with him?

"Because I love you, silly, not Marcus. Somebody else will love him, but it won't be me."

Was it really that simple? Kaz snuggled close against his side. Her lips pressed against his neck and the tip of her tongue made a quick lick beneath his jaw. "You taste so good," she mumbled. A few minutes later, her body relaxed in sleep.

He lay there for a long time, absorbing the sense of Kaz lying beside him. Her scent filled him, a subtle perfume all her own. Their bodies fit together perfectly—the first woman he'd ever dated who met him eye to eye, at least when she wore heels.

She made him laugh, had even made him cry. Hopefully, she would continue to make him a better man. Somehow, when Kaz was beside him, the flaws that had weighed him down for so long, the mistakes he'd made, the horrible failures in his past—all were surmountable.

He closed his eyes and buried his nose in her tousled curls. Drew another breath filled with the sweetness of this perfect woman he hadn't even known a few short weeks ago.

Something was different, but he couldn't quite figure out what.

Until he realized what it was he'd been missing for so long. What Kaz gave to him with her fierce hugs and her forgiving nature, with her trust and her unwavering love.

For the first time in as long as he could remember, Jake knew peace. All the disparate parts of his life had finally come together, here and now, because of the woman sleeping so trustingly in his arms.

With that thought in mind, he closed his eyes and held her close. The way he fully intended to hold her for the rest of their lives.

Read on for an excerpt from the next book by
KATE DOUGLAS

REDEMPTION

Coming soon from St. Martin's Paperbacks

CHAPTER 1

San Francisco, CA—April 30

Wind whipped the branches overhead, rain pounded the roof of the car, and dark leaves slapped against the windshield. RJ, the little shit, sat in the passenger seat, turned with his back to the door, seatbelt cinched tight, eyes wide. Staring at him. Ben took another swallow of his beer. He already had a buzz so he didn't really need it, but it was worth the sour taste in his mouth just to watch his kid brother squirm.

His kid brother . . . the family golden boy, at least as far as their parents were concerned. He used to hold that title. He'd been the one Mom was grooming to be the star, and then along came perfect little Richie, subsequently christened RJ because it sounded better. More in tune with the superstar image dear old Mom wanted the kid to have. Why not? He had everything else. Everything RJ touched turned to gold—including the three Olympic medals he'd won.

A small branch hit the hood of the car and skittered up against the windshield. RJ flinched. "Scared ya, huh, kid?" Laughing, Ben punched it, and the black Dodge Viper leapt forward, fishtailing on the wet asphalt. At least when he boosted a car, he got good wheels.

This baby was fast.

He wrapped his fingers around the gearshift. Really a sweet ride.

"Ben! Look out!" RJ braced his hands on the dash.

Ben snapped his attention back to the road, just in time to see the stricken face of a young woman, the wide, terrified eyes of a little boy. And then the child disappeared beneath the front of the Viper and the woman rolled across the hood, slammed into the windshield and flew off to the right, her body twisted, arms and legs flailing like a broken doll.

RJ screamed, and he kept screaming, and that was the last thing Ben heard until he lurched forward in the bed, his heart thundering in his ears.

He sat there in the dark, shivering from the blast of air conditioning hitting his sweat-soaked body, thoughts scattered, wondering if he'd made any noise, if any of the guys had heard him. He raised his head, realized he was alone in a quiet hotel room.

He wasn't in Kabul, not down at Spin B.

"Thank God." He bowed his head, ran his fingers through hair that had grown well beyond his regulation military cut. He wasn't in the Middle East; he was in a hotel just north of the airport in San Francisco, where he'd grabbed a room after his delayed flight finally got in around three this morning. All of his belongings would soon be headed for storage at Camp Parks—all but what he'd thrown into his duffle for the trip home.

Except, where the hell was home? The Army had been his home for almost twenty years. He hadn't communicated with his parents in all that time, hadn't heard from his brother.

Not that RJ hadn't made his presence known. Those

damned dreams had kept the kid sufficiently involved in Ben's life ever since the last time they were together.

The night Ben Lowell totally fucked up his life, his brother's life, and the lives of two innocent victims.

Because of him, a talented young Olympian's career was destroyed.

Because of him, a young mother and her child had died.

Their blood would forever be on Ben's hands. Somehow, before the nightmares won, before he took another cowardly way out—a more permanent one—he had to try and make this right. He wasn't really sure where to start, but sometimes the most obvious steps were the best.

Telling the truth after all these years was going to kill him. But he had to do it, had to admit what a fuck-up he'd been. He'd been dying inside for the last twenty years. Looking around the hotel room, listening to his own breath rushing from his lungs, the racing cadence of his heart, he knew he had to find the courage to take that first step, one apology at a time.

Lola Monroe checked the temperature on the oven, turned it down a notch and then poured herself a glass of wine. Mandy should be home in a few minutes, so she poured an extra glass of Chardonnay for her baby sister and carried it into the living room, careful not to trip over Rico. Their aging basset hound liked to sleep in major pathways throughout their house. It made it easier for him to keep track of them.

She'd just settled into the rocker by the window when she heard Mandy's key in the lock. Lola held out the chilled glass as her sister walked through the front door.

"Oh, thank you. You must have heard me wishing for this." Mandy took the glass, dropped her tote bag on the floor by the sofa, and sat. "I'm beat, but it sure smells good in here."

"Lasagna. I'd planned to have it ready when Kaz and Jake got home."

Mandy took a sip. "I thought they'd be here by now."

"Nope. They're spending the night at Cassie and Nate Dunagan's in Sonoma County. I really thought they'd be coming back tonight, but Kaz called, said they wanted to stay over another night. There's no reason we can't eat it."

Slipping her sandals off, Mandy took another sip of her wine and leaned back against the soft cushions. "I was hoping they'd come back. I need to see Kaz to be sure she's okay. It's just awful what happened to them. I mean, she said the bullet just grazed him, thank goodness, but . . . crap, Lola. They both could have died!" She stared into her glass for a moment and then gazed over the rim at Lola.

"I know. I couldn't sleep last night. I kept thinking about what happened. What could have happened."

"Yeah." Mandy stared into her glass. "I imagine they need some time together without anything else to worry about. Jake's got to be feeling pretty guilty over the whole thing."

"He's not the only one." Lola stared into the golden liquid in her glass. "It's my fault."

Mandy was across the room and grabbing Lola's hand before she finished her sentence. "No it's not. You had no way of knowing Jake didn't take those horrible nude pictures of Kaz. They were awful. I was as mad at him as you were."

"Hon, I should have looked closer at those pictures before giving them to Kaz. I had no idea Jake hadn't taken them, but I should have. They were terrible, and he's a talented photographer, but all I could think when I saw them was that I didn't want her to go to that premiere and see them on the walls. If I'd only looked at all of them, I would have known they weren't his pictures."

If she hadn't freaked out and given them to Kaz, none of this would have happened. Not Kaz getting kidnapped or Jake getting shot. None of it. But she'd given Kaz those damned photos, exactly as that psychopath out of Jacob's past had planned.

Furious, Kaz had gone to the reception where she and Jake were featured—the beautiful model and her sexy photographer and an expensive new line of body jewelry—except Kaz had thrown the envelope filled with disgusting shots in Jake's face and stalked out of the reception, directly into the waiting arms of a madman.

"But Jake saved her, Lola. Don't forget that. She's okay and so is he, and I would guess that if they've decided to stay up there for another night in spite of their injuries, it's because they want to be together. It's been pretty intense between them, and it could be they just need to explore what they're feeling. That's a good thing. Kaz deserves some happiness, don't you agree?"

Lola raised her head and managed to smile. "Yeah, she does. But ya know what? So do we. There have got to be a couple of decent men left out there."

Mandy giggled. "Well, if you find one, let me know."

"There's always Marcus Reed." Lola raised an eyebrow. Mandy had been lusting after him since long before they knew Jake, who was Marc's best friend. She still had a picture of him on the bulletin board in her bedroom, one she'd cut out of *People Magazine.* He'd been named one of the year's sexiest young millionaires.

Mandy merely shook her head. "Yeah. Right. The drop-dead gorgeous multi-gazillionaire is going to fall for the dorky little barista at the neighborhood coffee shop."

"Have you ever seen him in person? Kaz says he's a real sweetheart."

"I thought I saw him go by the coffee shop on a bicycle one time, but I doubt it was him. This guy was all by himself on an old Schwinn. Not the sort of wheels you'd expect a rich dude to have."

"Probably not." Lola stood. "C'mon. Dinner should be ready. We need to keep up our strength in case some good-looking, smart, nice, single guy shows up at the door."

"Yeah. Like that's gonna happen?" Laughing, Mandy grabbed her hand and dragged Lola into the kitchen.

"Well, if he does," Lola said, "as the older and wiser sister, I get first dibs!"

Ben walked away from his parents' Mill Valley home, got into the rental car and drove a couple of blocks to a small cemetery. He'd been here once before, the night before he left for boot camp. It had been right after he was cleared of any charges in that terrible wreck, before RJ had told anyone what really happened.

Another car pulled in behind him and parked near the entrance to the parking area—a dark sedan with two men sitting in the front seat—but other than that, he was alone. He went to the spot he remembered, toward the back of the cemetery where the graves were small and marked with flat headstones, and parked in a shady space beside a redwood tree. He didn't get out. Instead, he stared blindly at the dashboard.

He couldn't believe it. RJ'd never told the judge the truth. When Ben knocked on the door at his parents' home, wondering if they still lived there, if they'd even speak to him, his mother had opened the door and greeted him like the prodigal son. He was welcomed home with hugs and questions about where he'd been, why he'd stayed away so long. Then she'd called his father, and the man who never put his sons ahead of his job had rushed home from work to see for himself that his lost son had come home.

His parents weren't the most forgiving sort—the last thing he'd expected was to be welcomed home. But their response when he'd asked about RJ had left him angry and speechless.

They didn't want to hear his name. His parents had disowned their youngest son, hadn't heard from him since the trial ended and he'd been sent away.

Not since he'd been found guilty of involuntary manslaughter for killing two people while driving a stolen car. The car Ben had actually stolen; the one he—not RJ—had been driving that night.

His mother had sounded disappointed that the stolen car charges had been dropped. Ben hadn't known what to say, so once again he'd taken the coward's way out and kept his mouth shut. In his defense, he had a lot to process. He'd been so certain RJ, when faced with any kind of jail time, would have told the truth, but he hadn't. Not one word to anyone, as far as Ben could tell.

No matter how it worked it out in his head, it came out all wrong. Made him an even bigger dick. The kid brother he'd dragged with him, the sixteen-year-old Olympian he'd resented so much, had never fessed up. He'd stuck to that story Ben asked him to tell, that RJ was driving the stolen car because Ben was too drunk to drive. That RJ'd been the one to kill that poor woman and her son.

He never said a word. Not to his parents, not the arresting officer, not the judge. He'd been sentenced to the California Youth Authority, sent away to what was essentially a prison, even though he was innocent.

RJ had done it to protect Ben. No wonder no one had ever come after him, no one had pulled him out of formation and arrested him for manslaughter.

Because RJ'd taken the fall, and he'd never admitted the truth—that Ben was guilty, not him. But why?

That night of the wreck, Ben had been so drunk he'd been heaving his guts out while RJ tried to help the little kid. He remembered that much, but for almost twenty years, he'd tried to forget asking RJ to take the blame and tell the cops he'd been driving. Ben had been so god-damned jealous of RJ, of his fame, the fact he was their parents' favorite, that he didn't care what happened. He'd rationalized, told RJ that since he was just sixteen and Ben was an adult and too drunk to get behind the wheel, he could go to prison for a damned long time. As much as he hated himself for doing it, he remembered asking his brother to lie, but he didn't remember much else after the mother and her child died that night.

He remembered getting arrested. Impossible to forget that. They'd both gotten out when their father had come and posted bail and taken them home, but only RJ had been charged. Ben had enlisted while RJ's case was still in court. He'd never contacted his parents to find out how it all ended. Over the years, he'd just figured RJ'd gotten off. He was a kid. He hadn't been drinking. Hell, he was a damned Olympian, a media star. Girls asked for his auto-graph. He had an agent, for fuck's sake.

All those years, he'd imagined his brother living the highlife, while he slogged away in war zones around the world. They'd never send RJ to prison.

Except they did.

His mother said she was sure he'd gotten out a long time ago, but no, they hadn't kept in touch. Didn't know where he was, what he was doing. Didn't care.

In their eyes he had thrown away a career they'd given him. It was a slap in the face to two parents who'd sacri-ficed everything for an ungrateful child who hadn't cared how much his actions humiliated and embarrassed them. They didn't care that two people were dead. No, they'd been upset because he'd made them look like terrible par-ents, to have raised such a flawed and thankless son.

No mention of the grueling hours of training RJ had

gone through, the lost childhood while he'd spent every free moment with a harsh coach, swimming, perfecting his style, building strength and endurance.

His parents said RJ had failed them.

Even Ben knew their parents had failed their sons. They never should have been parents, but he didn't tell them that. He didn't say anything. He'd merely turned away and walked out the front door.

Now, sitting here in the rental car, parked at the cemetery where a mother and her son would rest forever, he realized there was only one thing he could do. He had to find RJ. Find out what happened. Find out if he was okay.

He would find a way to make things right.

He gazed across the shadowy expanse of green, of wilted flowers at a few plots, and knew exactly where the young woman and her child were buried. But just like that other night when he'd come here, he didn't have the courage to walk across the grass. He was a fucking coward, afraid to stand over her grave and apologize for the terrible thing he'd done.

He'd start with RJ. Once he cleared things with his brother, maybe then he'd be able to somehow beg forgiveness of that poor woman.

Ben had his laptop, but he hadn't expected this to be so hard. It was after seven, the day just about shot, when he picked up a newspaper and stopped at a cafe in the Tenderloin for something to eat. No sign of RJ. He'd tried searching under Richard Lowell and RJ Cameron, but found only a small amount of info about his Olympic wins and brief career, a short article about his time at the California Youth Authority for involuntary manslaughter, but no recent word of his brother, not when he got out or anything about him after the trial ended.

As a juvenile, the records had been sealed.

He tried to remember if RJ had any friends, but the only one he recalled was some nerdy twerp named Marc. Marc something. Started with an *R* . . .

The waitress brought him a cup of coffee and took his order. He finished the first section of the paper and opened the next, the one with more local news. A photo of a sharp looking, dark-haired man at some sort of premiere caught his attention. He looked vaguely familiar. Ben glanced at the caption: *Marcus Reed.* Could this be a grown-up version of Marc? He was introducing some kind of fancy new jewelry business, but it had to be the same guy.

Maybe he'd know how to find RJ. Now, if Ben could just find Marcus Reed. He pulled out a twenty and caught the waitress's attention. "I have to leave. This should cover the burger. Give it to someone who can use a free meal." Handing her the money, he went in search of Marc.

It was after nine when Ben pulled up in front of what looked like a converted row house on Twenty-third Avenue a few blocks south of Golden Gate Park. Actually, the whole street was lined with the houses—in all shapes, sizes and colors—creating a colorful row of seemingly attached yet distinctly separate homes with the garages beneath, living quarters above.

The streetlight was out, which made it feel even darker in the neighborhood than it already was. It was late—too late to be knocking on a stranger's door, and he knew he should wait until tomorrow, but now that he was so damned close to finding RJ, he couldn't stop. Not after finally talking Marc into giving him the address, even though this wasn't RJ's.

Marc Reed had been a shock. Ben remembered him as a shy, skinny kid, and he'd never really figured out the friendship between him and RJ, but according to Marc they were still close. Composed, quietly self-confident, and obviously successful, Marc had been surprised to see Ben, but hadn't said much, and wouldn't say anything at all about RJ. He was still quiet, but he'd remembered Ben, oddly enough without any overt animosity.

Had RJ kept the secret from Marc as well? It was hard to tell, but he obviously wasn't real comfortable giving out RJ's information. Not until Ben said he'd come looking for his brother to right some very old wrongs. Marc had studied him for a moment without any comment, nodded, and then he'd written down this address.

Not RJ's house and not RJ's phone number. No, Marc had sent Ben to the girlfriend's house. His girlfriend's place where her two roommates also lived. He'd said the girlfriend had some sort of trouble up in the wine country, and RJ might still be there with her. Marc wasn't sure what was going on, but the roommates would know.

And no, he wouldn't give up RJ's phone number. The last thing his friend needed at this point in his life was a cold call from the brother who'd walked out when RJ needed him. He had enough on his plate.

But he wouldn't tell Ben what that might be. And he hadn't tried to disguise his obvious disapproval of Ben. It was only fair.

Ben glanced toward the door at the top of the stairs, got out of the car and locked it with his duffel and laptop inside. It was late for a strange man to be knocking on their door, especially since the porch light wasn't on, but bright lights glowed through the curtains.

With luck they'd let him in, or at least answer his questions.

No matter. He had to find RJ. Had to somehow fix what he'd screwed up so long ago.